THE
SUN
DWELLERS

Book Three of The

Dwellers Saga

David Estes

This book is dedicated to my parents,
David and Nancy Estes,
for being my biggest fans.

Prologue

Subchapter 14 of the Moon Realm
Two years ago

Despite her nondescript gray tunic, the woman sticks out like a sparkling diamond in a coal mine, her shiny blond hair peeking out from beneath her dark hood. But it's not her hair, or her face—which is remarkably beautiful beneath the dark shadows—that identifies her as a foreigner in the Moon Realm. Instead, it's her gait, the way she carries herself: straight-backed and graceful and regal. Next to her the passing moon dwellers look hunched, their backs question marks and their faces turned to the dust.

She knows it's the middle of the day—thus ensuring the girl will be at school—but the amount of light afforded by the overhead cavern lights is appallingly minimal, the near-equivalent of a Sun Realm dawn, or perhaps twilight.

Although she clearly doesn't belong amongst the rundown and crumbling gray stone shacks, she doesn't hesitate as she strides down the street, ignoring the stares she attracts. Unable to hold back her nerves any longer, she pauses—just a barely noticeable stutter step—as she nears her target: a tiny stone box, no larger than a medium-sized shed. She wonders how the two most powerful Resistance leaders could possibly be tucked in such an unremarkable corner of the Moon Realm. The front yard is barren rock, full of crisscrossing cracks and stone chips that roll and slide underfoot as she approaches the thin doorframe.

Before she knocks, her eyes are drawn to her feet, where she stands on the only unmarred stone square. Within the block is a single word—*friend*—elegantly cut with the skill of a professional stone worker. A hint of a smile crosses the woman's face before she looks up. Despite all her doubts and fears and indecisiveness while making the decision that's led her to this place, that one word chiseled at the entrance gives her hope that there's a better life out there for her eldest son—that maybe things can improve for him and for the Tri-Realms as a whole.

Her life is forfeit—stomped out by a loveless sham of a marriage, to the President no less—but her son's...well, her son's life could change everything.

After a single deep breath, she gathers her courage in a raised fist. When her knuckles collide with the door, the sound is final and hollow in her ears, but in reality is only a thud.

Tilting an ear, she listens for footsteps, but is rewarded with only cluttered silence. The clutter: her mind, which trips and stumbles over a thousand questions. *Is anyone home? Will the door be slammed in my face? Have I made a grievous mistake? Have I failed him? Have I failed my son? Have I failed myself?*

Unexpectedly and without fanfare, the door swings open; a dark-haired woman wearing a plain brown, knee-length tunic fills the gap, her eyebrows raised in surprise. If not for the foreigner's information, which she received from a very reliable source, she wouldn't believe this woman to be a revolutionary. Except for her eyes, that is. There's a fire in her pupils that she's only seen once or twice in her life. It's the same fire she sees in her eldest son.

When the woman with the jet-black hair doesn't speak, the intruder realizes her eyebrows are an unspoken question: *Yes? Why have you wandered onto my doorstep?*

Before answering the silent question, she pulls back her hood, releasing her golden locks and forcing away the identity-protecting shadows on her face. A spark of recognition flashes on the woman's face, but fades just as quickly. Finally she speaks. "First Lady Nailin—why are you here?"

"Mrs. Rose—I have a proposition for you. May I come in?"

One

Adele

Present day

The light gleams off the barrel of the gun with a brightness that blinds me if I look directly at it. My hands are sweaty as I clutch the weapon that once upon a time was so foreign, but now seems so familiar. The gun's every detail is burned into my memory, from the temperature of the cold steel against my palm, to its weight tugging on my wrist, to the strong yet delicate scent of burning gunpowder.

When I turn the corner and enter the room, it's all happening again. My dad is bound and lying prostrate on the rough stone floor, the executioner's gun to his head. A half dozen other sun dwellers bar my way forward. There's more than the last time, but it doesn't matter. A million of them couldn't stop me. Not this time.

I raise the gun and start shooting. Six booms later my foes are all dead, red and warm and blank-eyed. In the heat of the moment, I continue shooting, this time at the executioner, but the *click click click* announces that I'm out of bullets.

I toss the gun aside and charge forward, kicking his bland face with my heel. He slumps to the side, his own weapon discarded by his weakened fingers. I've done it this time. Saved him—saved my father. But I know something's not right as I realize my sister isn't by his side like she should be. The glitter of light reflecting off something hanging from my neck distracts me. I reach up, close my hands around an emerald necklace, the one my mother gave me *after* my father died. The necklace my father gave my mother. This isn't right—none of this is right.

As I lean over the face of the man who I immediately know is not my father, the Devil's eyes flash open, the gateway to a black and soulless human shell.

"Didn't you know?" the President says. "Your father's already dead. And you're next."

My heart is in my throat as the demon lifts his hand, which is now holding a long glinting sword with a diamond-encrusted hilt, which I either didn't notice before or which has magically appeared.

As his white-knuckled hand darts forward, I scream. Although I don't close my eyes, blackness surrounds.

* * *

9

I'm still screaming and seeing darkness when a pair of strong arms cradles my head. "Shh," a voice says.

I quiet but I'm still breathing hard, panting like I've just run a long way, my chest heaving. An instant later there's a soft glow as a lantern is lit, casting dancing shadows on the rough, brown tunnel walls. Tristan's arm is still behind my head, and when he sees me looking at him, he retracts it quickly, his face flush with embarrassment. "You were dreaming," he says. "I heard you cry out."

I close my eyes, try to will the frantic pace of my heart to slow, as I remember where I am. In a tunnel on the way to the Sun Realm. On a mission for my mother, General Rose. As Tristan's father pointed out in my nightmare, my father's still dead—nothing can change that. No amount of fresh killing or revenge or trigger pulls will make one bit of difference. And yet the furnace of revenge burns hotly in the pit of my stomach. Kill his father. Kill the President. That is our mission.

I open my eyes and, despite my vengeful thoughts, say, "I'm tired of all the death." I realize my hand is clutching my necklace, just like in my dream. Slowly, I release the emerald, watch it swing gently back and forth, wishing I'd never had to leave my mother.

Tristan's face worries its way to a tight smile. "Only one more person has to die, right?" The ever-present buzz whenever Tristan is near me hums along my scalp and down my spine. The urge to get as close to him as possible tugs at my arms, but I hide it well, not even flinching.

Even after the disturbing nightmare, I can't help but grin when I'm talking to him. "Yeah, just your dad—hope you don't mind."

He laughs. "He's no one's father."

"Not even Killen's?"

"Especially not Killen's," he says. "We were only ever puppets to him, used to do his dirty work, nothing more."

It saddens me to hear Tristan talk like that, but I know it's true. I'd rather have a dead father than a living one like his. I sigh, wishing I had the same boldness now as when I kissed him back in the Moon Realm.

"What was your dream about?" he asks.

I tell him, watching as his hands tighten into fists, curling and uncurling with each sentence. When I finish, I say, "I don't know if I'll be able to do it when the time comes."

"You're strong, Adele. I've seen it time and time again," he says, his dark blue eyes never leaving mine.

"Does it take strength to kill?" I ask, almost to myself. "Is that what makes your father strong?"

His hands relax and he folds them in his lap. "It takes strength to defeat evil," he says wisely. "In any case, I won't mind being the one to do it when the time comes."

Despite his more relaxed posture, there's a thirst for blood in his eyes that I've never seen before, which both scares and comforts me. Changing the subject, I say, "So what's with you and Ram?" I've been itching to ask Tristan about his strange relationship with the dark-skinned gargantuan who's part of our merry little death squad.

"What do you mean?" Tristan says, his eyes giving away his hidden laugh.

"Umm, I don't know…maybe the fact that he threatened to kill you at the council meeting, and you seemed to find it funny. Does that ring a bell?"

Tristan's laugh finally presents itself, lighting up his face. I bask in it for a moment as I wait for him to respond. "Let's just say our friendship has had its ups and downs. Right now we're on an up."

"C'mon, tell me," I push. "What were the downs?"

"He hated me," Tristan says bluntly. "He didn't trust me, tried to beat me up a few times, tried to block me from trying to help."

I guess it makes sense that he'd have opposition—even within the Resistance. Still, a smile plays on my lips. "He *tried* to beat you up? The guy's a behemoth."

Tristan looks away, cringing slightly, but then turns back, his lips turned up once more. "Okay, okay, he *did* beat me up, but it's not like I tried to fight back—I didn't want to upset anyone by getting into fights while trying to convince people to trust me."

"Sure, tough guy," I say.

We're both quiet for a few minutes, but it's not awkward, which is one of the things I like about Tristan. Just being near him feels right. It's been that way since I met him. It's like all the nerves and nodes and synapses in our bodies thrive on our nearness. At least that's how it is for me, and how I hope it is for Tristan.

He must be thinking the same thing because he says, "Isn't it weird that we're here together?" He laughs and I'm silent, but I know exactly what he means. We saw each other across barren rock, through a barbed-wire, electrified fence, past hordes of his screaming, undergarment-throwing, adoring fans—me in freaking prison and him the prized attraction in a parade—and yet here we are, together; like *together* together. Weird is the perfect word for it.

"Have you ever thought that maybe it's more than just coincidence?" he says, his eyebrows question marks.

"Like fate?" I say, trying to hide my surprise at his question. I haven't told him what my mom said to me before we left the Moon Realm:

It's no accident that you and Tristan met.

"Maybe. I dunno. Something like that."

My thoughts come fast, careening around in my head like fish in a cave pond. In my world, the only fate is illness or death. We don't have much else. However, from the time I laid eyes on Tristan in the flesh, I *have* felt an indescribable pull toward him, like someone wants us to be together. But despite my mom's declaration that it wasn't an accident that we met, there's no logical explanation for any of it, which doesn't work for my pragmatic mind. I shake my head. "I don't think so. It's just plain random chance."

It's no accident that you and Tristan met.

Tristan frowns. "There's something I have to tell you."

I stop breathing. Here it comes. For a while now I've felt there was something he was holding back, something big— maybe life-changing.

"Did I ever tell you that I fainted once thinking about you?"

Huh? I'm guessing that's not what he's been keeping from me. What does that even mean? I sigh. "Umm…" Well. Hmm. No?

"I did. Roc and I were training, fighting with wooden swords. This was shortly after I saw you for the first time, mind you. The fight was over and your face popped into my head…" He ducks his head sheepishly and sort of cringes, like he's wondering why he decided to tell me this, but knows he can't go back now. "And, well, I passed out right then. In the time between fainting and Roc waking me up, I dreamt that my father murdered you right in front of me. It was creepy."

My head spins. Why is he telling me this? So I made him faint? I don't know what to say, but he's not done yet.

"Then I nearly passed out again when I saw you the second time, when you were trying to break out of the Pen."

I can't help but laugh now. "Are you sure it wasn't the fumes from the bombs blowing up all over the place?"

His face is dead serious. "No, it was you. I had a physical reaction to seeing you, almost like my body couldn't handle it."

This is definitely not the direction I thought the conversation was going. "I didn't take many baths while in the Pen so normally I would guess it was my body odor that caused it, but I had just showered that day, so that can't be it," I joke.

"Perhaps it was your remarkable beauty," Tristan says, sending warmth into my cheeks.

"Knock it off, charmer, I thought you were being serious."

"I *was* being serious," he says, which doesn't help stem my flush.

"Look, you probably just hadn't eaten in a while, or were dehydrated," I say, trying to steer the conversation away from what he thinks of my looks.

He tilts his head to the side, his eyes wandering to the tunnel ceiling. "That's possible…" he says, but I know he doesn't really think so.

When he looks back at me, there's resolution in his eyes. Although we're already sitting close to each other, he slides closer, right next to me. The normal strength of my pull toward him is super-charged, and the only desire I have is to hold him, to be held by him. He must feel the same way, because his arm curls around the back of my neck, drags my head to his chest. His warm breath caresses the back of my neck, electricity shooting off his skin as he gently presses his arm against mine.

"This is the good part of life," he says, and I sigh, although I shouldn't. Not when my dad is dead, my sister maimed. Cole. No, I don't deserve this, I think. Not now. Not until the President is dead. Maybe never.

Going against every instinct, I unwind my body from Tristan's grasp, stand up, and walk away with the lantern in tow, wishing I didn't have to.

"I've got to get rid of this gun," I say over my shoulder, plucking the gun my mom gave me—*the gun I failed to save my father with*—out from beneath my tunic.

Two
Tristan

"Wait!" I say, wishing I hadn't been so bold. I seem to have scared her away.

Jumping to my feet, I jog after the bouncing glow of the light. By the time I catch up to her, she's marched past the sleeping lumps that are Trevor and Ram, and is approaching Roc and Tawni, who agreed to share tonight's first watch. Backlit by another lantern, their silhouettes are sitting cross-legged, facing each other, their knees nearly touching. The slap of cards on rock gives away their method of passing the time.

I grab Adele's arm, feeling a zing of energy. "I'm sorry, I didn't mean to—"

She stops, glances down at my hand on her elbow, her lips curled into a tenuous smile that evaporates immediately. "No, Tristan, it's not you," she says, gently prying herself loose. "This is just something I have to do. It can't wait any longer."

"What's going on?" Roc says beyond us. "Are you guys lost? Because if you're looking for the nearest hotel, it's back the way you came. Not that I'd recommend it."

We both turn to find the shadows turned toward us, watching. Adele lifts the lantern, illuminating our friends' faces. Roc's wearing a black tunic that makes his brown skin look ghostly pale in comparison. He's also wearing a smirk. Tawni's delicate features are framed by her milk-white hair, above her silver tunic. Together they're the yin and the yang; I can't decide who is which.

"Tawni, I have a favor to ask," Adele says.

Cocking her head to the side, Tawni purses her lips. "Yes?"

"Hang onto this for me," Adele says, holding the gun out handle-first.

Tawni freezes, her pale face managing to whiten even further. "But why? I mean, I can't…I don't even know how—"

"I'm not asking you to use it—just to keep it safe for me."

Wrinkling her nose, Tawni reaches out a bony hand and slips a single finger into the metal trigger loop, allowing the gun to dangle like a dirty sock. "Where should I put it?"

Adele reaches under her tunic and works her fingers for a few seconds before pulling out a waist holster. "This fits in the small of your back," she says, handing the gun carrier to her friend. "You won't even know it's there." If the gun is a dirty sock then the holster's its matched pair, and although she takes it with her other hand, Tawni clearly doesn't want it. "Please," Adele adds, her previously firm voice pleading now.

"Sure," Tawni says with a sigh, placing the items in a pile on the tunnel floor.

Roc stares at me curiously, his lips opening slightly, a question on his tongue. "What are you guys doing up anyway? Your shift isn't for two hours."

Adele's green eyes flick to mine. *Don't tell them I had a nightmare*, they plead. "My stomach was growling so loud it woke us both up," I say, my eyes lingering on Adele's for a moment before facing Roc.

"I'd give you some of my ration," Roc says, "but I already ate it." He rubs his stomach, grinning. Tawni laughs.

I lunge at him, tackle my friend, pin him down. "Tomorrow I get both our rations," I say. "Don't I?"

"Not unless hell freez—" But Roc doesn't have a chance to finish his thought, as a huge, black shape enters our field of vision from the side, a blur of speed and muscle. I fling myself to the side, trying to avoid the impact, but I'm too late. The beast rams its shoulder into my chest and I'm thrown backward, my spine shuddering as it glances off the rock wall.

Ignoring the pain, I'm on my feet, ready to fight, ready to defend myself and Adele and my friends. The black shadow looms over me, a head taller and...and laughing. Deep, throaty, *Ram*. The same Ram that Adele was just asking me about. What she doesn't know is that before being added to our team, he was my biggest enemy within the Resistance. He was always watching me, calling me a liar, convinced I was a spy for my father. And now he's my friend, I think? Maybe? Sort of?

My body relaxes and instantly a bolt of pain shoots down my spine. I cringe. Roc moves between us with a flashlight and

Ram's massive grinning face looms over him. "Everyone all right?" Roc asks. "And by *everyone* I mean Tristan." He laughs, claps a hand on my shoulder. "Serves you right, buddy. Me and Ram, well, let's just say we've come to an agreement. Isn't that right, bud—I mean, Ram?"

Ram's dark eyes are violent and yet full of humor. "That's right. No more picking on your weakling friend," he growls.

"Right," Roc says. "Except for the weakling part."

Great, I think. Even Roc's tighter with Ram than I am. This might be a long trip.

"I think I'll join Team Ram, too," another voice says, approaching from the tunnel behind us. Trevor. Trevor with the curly chestnut hair. Trevor who was Adele's mom's right-hand man. Trevor who saved Adele from Brody in the Star Realm. Although his tousled hair and blinking eyes are still full of sleep, he wears an easy smile, one that looks like it could stay on his lips all day.

It's only the first night of our mission and already none of us can manage a proper night's sleep. Yeah, it really is going to be a long trip.

* * *

Since we're all awake, we decide to just keep moving, to save sleep for another time, maybe once the war is over.

At first Adele walks with Tawni, speaking in hushed tones. I wonder if she's telling her about her nightmare, about my arm around her, about my questions. I can just make out the bump on Tawni's lower back where Adele's gun is.

Ram's bulky arm is around my shoulder, as if he's my best mate, when really he's just trying to intimidate me. I shrug it off.

"Ooh, the tough prince exerting his strength," Ram taunts.

I laugh. "If you weren't three hundred pounds I'd do more than that," I say.

"Pity. I'd like to see that," Roc says from my other side.

"I reckon I could take all three of you," Trevor says from behind us.

I glance back at my newest acquaintance. He's got a big mouth, but for all I know he might be able to back it up. His forearms are cut like stone and I can just make out the start of a toned bicep before it hides beneath the sleeve of his green tunic. I doubt Adele's mom would have included him on the mission if he couldn't fight.

Ram grunts.

Roc chuckles. "I'm out. You three can settle this on your own."

"We might just do that," I murmur, always one for a challenge.

Ahead, Tawni drifts back from Adele's side, zeroing in on Roc. I take advantage of the opportunity to stride ahead, nonchalantly pulling up next to Adele. "Hey," I say.

"Hey yourself," she replies, glancing at me.

"You okay?" I ask.

Staring straight ahead, she says, "What did my mom whisper to you before we left?"

She answers my question with a question of her own, but I don't mind. I'm just happy to be talking to her after the abrupt end to our previous conversation. "She said that it probably made sense for her to ask me to take care of her daughter, but in your case she knew it wasn't necessary."

Adele glances at me again, and this time holds my gaze for a moment. Pride covers her face like a mask. The urge to intertwine my fingers with hers strikes me, but I ignore it, afraid I'll scare her away again. She's so unlike the girls in the Sun Realm. The girls up there are weak and wouldn't last ten minutes in the Moon Realm, and yet they approach guys with a confidence bordering on arrogance. *You know you want me, but the question is: Do I want you?* Whereas, Adele's as hard as diamond, and yet, other than when she kissed me, she's timid when it comes to being close to me.

As if she can read my thoughts, Adele's face falls. "I can take care of myself, but not my friends and family," she says.

I try to swallow but a lump congeals in my throat. I have to tell her what I think. "I think my father targeted Ben to get to me."

"That makes no sense," Adele says right away. She's determined to take the blame.

"He's trying to get to me, to do anything he can to take the fight out of me, so I'll either turn myself in, kill myself, or do something stupid."

"Turning yourself in or killing yourself would be something stupid," Adele replies, not missing a step. "But regardless, attacking my dad and sister has nothing to do with you."

"It does if he thought…I cared…about your father," I say, my words sticking to my tongue like underground river leeches on a swimmer's legs.

"Did you? Care about my father?" There's an edge to Adele's voice, which is full of steel and glass.

21

"You know I did." My brain struggles to formulate the right words. To make her understand the depth of my admiration for Ben Rose. "I didn't know him for long, but he treated me like a son—"

"Which would make me your sister," Adele says, her gritty words replaced with her usual sarcasm once more.

I laugh. "It doesn't bother me if it doesn't bother you," I say.

I'm happy when she smiles. "Sooo, my dad was like a second father to you?"

I shake my head. "No, more than that. For me, a father is just the one whose genes you share. Ben—your dad—was like a mentor to me. He believed in me. Counseled me. Gave me confidence in myself." Suddenly I remember something important. Something that will matter to Adele. "Can I show you something?"

Adele shrugs. "Sure."

Without breaking stride, I swing my pack around to access it. Tucked beneath two tunics and a canteen is a book, leather-worn and brittle, its pages yellowed and thinned by time and history. Not a book—a diary.

"Your father gave this to me," I say, handing it to Adele. "Well, lent it to me, really, but then…" I start to say the wrong thing, but manage to stop myself just in time. Adele doesn't seem to notice.

"What is it?" she says, holding a flashlight to the cover.

"The diary of a young girl named Anna, from Year Zero. She got picked in the Lottery, was taken below, given a new family, the whole deal. I think your father gave me her diary to help give me some perspective, you know, remember what it is we're fighting for. You can have it."

Her eyes are wide open now, as she flips to the first page. For the next hour she walks and reads in silence, holding her flashlight over the pages, not even noticing when I put a nervous arm behind her so she doesn't walk into the wall.

* * *

It's a well-constructed tunnel, plenty high and wide enough for us to walk at a brisk pace. According to Adele's mom (another Anna), the Resistance constructed it during the first Uprising, in case they ever had the need to sneak a small group into the Sun Realm. We walk for what feels like hours, when we should be sleeping. Sleep walking.

Adele reads the diary for a while, and then tries to hand it back to me. "You keep it," I say. She tucks it in her pack without saying anything, and then takes my hand, sending shivers up my forearm. My hand's sweaty and I desperately try to think cooling thoughts, but it doesn't help. Adele, seemingly lost in her own thoughts, doesn't recoil, so I guess she doesn't notice. She's remembering her father, I think.

Although I remained silent while Adele was reading, there were muffled conversations and occasional laughs from the rest of the group behind us. Roc seemed to be doing most of the talking, telling stories and jokes and otherwise making friends with everyone, which is just the kind of thing that he does. It's fine with me because I'm with Adele.

But eventually everyone goes silent, from exhaustion and fatigue and because the damn tunnel keeps going up and up, getting steeper each time we round a bend. The tunnel gods try to make up for it by cooling the tunnel air as we get closer to the Sun Realm, but it's not enough to combat the rise in our body temperatures from the heavy exercise. We are made of sweat and blood and bone and muscle. But mostly sweat.

The light long-haul tunic I was outfitted with before we left is sticking to my skin, held tight against me by the multiple weapons I'm toting. Against my left calf is a short dagger, sharp and deadly but the least of my weapons. Against the other calf is a shiny new handgun, afforded to me by the star dwellers, who were in turn supplied by my father as part of his ridiculous plan to pit the Lower Realms against each other. My sword is in its scabbard and hangs loosely at my side, occasionally bumping my knee. Tight on my back is a tightly strung bow and a satchel of arrows, hand carved and feathered. The moon dweller weapons maker named Hans who constructed them promised me they'd fly straight and true.

The rest of our group is outfitted similarly, and although I've seen the tough side of Adele many times before, there's something about her getup that I find quite sexy. Her black tunic is a shadow, tight against her curves, serving to enhance her beauty rather than emasculate her. She wears a thick, tight belt, ornamented with various short daggers, as well as a thin, long blade. Like me, she has a bow, but hers hangs from a strap over her shoulder. The hilt of a partly hidden knife protrudes from the bottom of her long tunic, lashed to her calf.

Finally we stop. Someone suggests it, but I'm not sure who, because I'm so tired and my mind is squishier than a bowl of mushy, oversaturated rice. Heck, it might have been me, I'll never know.

We should have a lookout schedule, but this time there are no volunteers and I don't think anyone could keep their eyes open anyway, so we take the risk. This *is* a secret tunnel after all.

There's no rhyme or reason to the sleeping arrangements—we just lie where we fall. Which happens to put me next to Adele. It reminds me of back in the Moon Realm, shortly after I first met her, when I was bruised and cut and bleeding from my brother and his thugs. I took a risk then and it was wonderful. We held hands all night, our first physical experience together, innocent and beautiful.

Despite my exhaustion, I'm determined to make tonight (or is it the day now?) our second.

At first we lie on our backs, using our packs to prop up our heads, but then she turns away, curling up like a ball. I don't know where the boldness comes from, but I put my arm around her and she stiffens. But then she relaxes, drops her arm over mine, pulls it into her chest. We are so close together it's as if we are one being, separated by only the thin fabric of our tunics.

We sleep.

Three

Adele

I feel better waking up without the gun near me. My subconscious agrees because I have no memory of a nightmare. I feel bad about giving the cold steel weapon to Tawni, but at least I know she won't use it. The only good kind of gun is one that hasn't been fired. I hope I never have to again.

The other good thing about waking up is finding Tristan's arm on me. I vaguely remember him draping it over me the night before, pulling it around me, the warmth that came with it, but overnight it moved and is now resting lightly on my side, his fingertips barely grazing my hip. His breathing is rhythmic and deep.

Ever so carefully, I use my fingers like pincers and pluck his wrist from my side, lifting his arm high enough to slide out from underneath. Freed, I watch him for a moment. Although he's the biggest celebrity in all the Tri-Realms, sleeping he's just a guy, almost childlike, his wavy blond hair messed and over his forehead, his magnetic blue eyes hidden beneath closed lids, his athleticism and poise all but invisible.

Less gracefully than I'd like, I clamber to my feet and pick up the long-burning lantern we use as a nightlight. As I scan the other sleeping forms, I notice I'm not the only one who enjoyed the sleeping arrangements. Roc's and Tawni's legs are tangled up together, whether by design or overnight movements.

Past them, snoring lips buzz through the dark. The offender: Ram. Strangely, he's curled up the most of anyone, almost in the fetal position. It's odd seeing such a large man in that position. I almost laugh.

Trevor's the only one missing, his thin blanket in a ball nearby. There's the almost imperceptible soft glow of a light down the tunnel a ways. I make for the light.

He's sitting shirtless with his back to the wall, a flashlight in one hand and a book in the other. It's an old, small square and reminds me of the diary Tristan gave me, which my dad gave him. It was an unexpected but appreciated gift.

"Good morning," Trevor says without looking up from the page he's on.

"How long have you been up?" I ask.

"A half-hour I reckon. Although time doesn't seem to pass in this tunnel, so it's hard to tell."

"Did it pass better in the Star Realm?"

He laughs. "Not really."

It's weird to be having a relatively normal conversation with Trevor, especially given the particularly rocky start to our relationship. Without anything better to do, I sit down next to him.

"Whatcha reading?" I ask, catching a glimpse of a handwritten page over his shoulder.

He snaps the cover shut, making me jump slightly, which makes him grin. "Just my journal, nosy. I like to reflect on the past sometimes. It helps me avoid making the same mistakes twice."

A surprisingly intelligent remark. I get the feeling there's a lot about Trevor that will surprise me. "How'd you meet my mother?" I ask. The unspoken question: And why does she trust you so much?

"I'd do anything for her," he says. "She saved my life."

My head jerks to the side, locks on his wistful gaze. He's remembering something. He answered the unspoken question first—and it's not the answer I expected. Although I have half a dozen follow-up questions, I'm silent. I don't want to be called nosy again.

He sighs. "Do you want to know the whole story?"

I nod hopefully.

He starts with a question. "Do you remember what I told you about my family?"

How could I forget? At the time I still had a dad, so although I was truly sorry about what had happened to Trevor's father, I didn't really understand. But now...now we have that in common. "He worked at the lava flow. He...he stole something," I say.

"A bed. For my brother and I to share."

I nod. "He went to work and never came back."

"That wasn't entirely true."

"It wasn't?" I say, suddenly back on my heels.

Trevor faces forward, speaking in a monotone voice, apparently oblivious to my trepidation. "He showed up at our doorstep a week later, badly beaten. Ribs crushed, arm broken, teeth chipped. I don't think he'd eaten or drank since he left. He was so skinny, broken, his lips cracked and bleeding, along with his spirit. But the worst was when he turned around, pointed at the back of his head."

I squeeze my eyes shut, try to think of something—anything—to get the visions out of my head. It's like Cole's story all over again, and that one didn't end well.

"His skull was cracked open and gushing blood," Trevor continues evenly. "It was a fresh wound. The Enforcers had abused him for a week and then brought him home, only to inflict the final wound just before dumping him on our doorstep."

"A message," I whisper, opening my eyes to blurred vision.

"Yeah, don't steal from the Sun Realm." He pauses, but I know that, just like Cole's story, this one's not over yet. All this is somehow leading up to my mom. "We struggled on for a while, my mom procuring flour by trading our meager possessions, which she used to bake bread. Every day she rolled her bread cart into town, traded loaves for basic necessities and more flour. We ate the leftovers.

"But eventually the trade in our subchapter dried up. She couldn't get enough flour to make her bread, and even if she could, there was no one to trade with."

"What did she do?" I ask.

"There was nothing to do. The only ones getting by were the miners, so she applied for a job in the mines. Yeah, she and a few hundred other star dwellers, all men, with experience to boot. She was laughed off the site.

"By then I was sixteen. Not quite old enough for the mines, but old enough to help. A friend of mine told me about a way to get food. Not legal, mind you, but we were desperate."

I glance at him, understanding flashing in my eyes. He doesn't have to justify his actions to me.

"The Enforcers were put up in the nicest accommodations in town, supported by the President's 'Safety and Security' budget. Of course they were well fed too. My buddy learned where the food shipments came in, at what times, and how many men would be unloading them. Twice he'd managed to slip into the truck and steal whole cases of canned food. He almost got caught the second time, but he figured with a partner it would be easier to avoid detection."

"But you got caught?" I guess.

"Actually, no. Evidently we were natural thieves, because we got away with it for weeks. The first time I brought home my share of the takings, my mom wept. She never asked me where I got it from; instead, she chose to thank God for the food in our nightly prayers."

"So…" I say, unsure where all of this is going.

"Sorry, this is all linked—I swear," Trevor says. "So one night I went out with my friend for our usual thieving, but someone else had beaten us to it. We were biding our time, being patient, waiting for the perfect moment to make our move, when one of the truck guys came out of the building and entered the truck via a ramp. We heard him say, 'What the hell—you filthy rat!' His feet stomped back down the ramp. He was carrying this scrawny, dirt-smeared kid, whose hands were clenched around a couple of bags of rice as big as his head. The trucker shouted something to someone inside, and a moment later an Enforcer the size of a house was on the loading dock, grinning like he'd just been given a gift."

Even with my eyes open, I picture the events unfolding, like a crumpled-up paper being gradually smoothed out. Trevor puts his journal flat on the ground next to him, settles the flashlight in his lap so it's facing up, casting an eerie spotlight on his face, and then starts punching his fist into his hand.

"My friend said, 'Let's get the hell outta here,' and then took off, not waiting to see if I'd follow. Perhaps I should have. But something about the kid reminded me of myself. Hungry. Alone. Willing to do anything for a couple of bags of rice. I ran out of my hiding spot behind the truck's tire and bashed into the trucker's knees. It was just the distraction the scrawny kid needed. The guy dropped him and he was running before he even hit the ground. The Enforcer grabbed at him, missed, but managed to get a hand on the collar of my tunic as I tried to scramble away." I know how the rest of the story goes. He went to a juvenile facility—like me—and then turned eighteen and ended up in the Max—just like I would have if I hadn't escaped. But wait—

"You didn't even touch the Enforcer," I say. "Surely your sentence in juvie wasn't more than a year or two."

Trevor smirks. "You know the system all too well. I got fifteen months, assuming good behavior, which you shouldn't assume."

"What did you do?"

"Once inside, I started fighting. I was determined not to let any of the weaker kids get bullied. I don't know what it was—something to bring me back to life, I suppose. A reason for living you could say."

"There are some bad dudes in juvie," I say, speaking from experience.

"And I wasn't a good fighter," he admits. "But that didn't stop me. I learned the hard way. I had four broken noses, many a cracked rib, always bruised knuckles, and more black eyes than I can count. But I managed to not die, and with each fight I got tougher and more capable. Some of the tough kids even started to respect me because I never ran away from a fight. The weaker ones who I protected were thankful, and I watched with joy as their sentences expired and they were able to leave juvie unharmed."

"Meanwhile, your sentence grew with every fight."

Trevor grimaces. "Exactly."

"But didn't you want to get out so you could see your family?"

"Of course. But I wanted to do it on my terms. I couldn't just sit by in an oblivious haze while the helpless kids got the poo kicked out of them." Inside, I'm ashamed, although I know that's not Trevor's intention. What he's just described is exactly how I spent my time in the Pen. *An oblivious haze.*

"Okay," I say. "So you turned eighteen?"

"Six months ago," he says. "They moved me to the Max straight away. I almost got killed my first day." His tone is light but his words are serious.

"You tried to fight just like you did in juvie," I say.

"Yep. Just like in kid prison, the Max had the weak and the strong and everything in between. The only problem was that the strong were a lot freakin' stronger. So I'm in the yard scoping things out my first day. I'm all alone, you know, because I don't know anyone. A bunch of tall, ripped dudes are playing hoops, some other monsters are throwing up dumbbells and doing pull-ups and stuff, and I'm just watching, trying to learn the ropes. A small stone in a big mine."

My mind grabs hold of each piece of new information and sucks it in, looking at it from every angle, and putting it on a new shelf for safekeeping. It could have been me in the Max, experiencing the same things Trevor did.

"As I'm scanning the yard, there was an accidental bump as one of the bigger guys passed a tall, scrawny punk who looked like he didn't belong. It all happened so fast, I don't even know how…" His calm narrative hitches for a second and I can almost feel his heart beating faster as a rush of adrenaline pours into his system from just the memory.

It was a major event in his life.

"Before the big dude takes a swat at the skinny guy, I'm already on my feet moving, thinking I'm back in juvie. I dunno, it just became an instinct for me. Just as the heavyweight landed the knockout punch on the guy's nose, I came up behind him, ready to land my own finishing blow." He pauses, rubs his jaw for a second, as if feeling an old bruise that's never fully healed.

"I reckon this dude had at least ten times the experience in fighting that I did, along with more grit, more raw firepower, and better overall instincts. While I thought I was going to hit him with a surprise attack the size of a small train, he felt me coming the whole way, probably because he'd been in dozens of street brawls where he had to have eyes in the back of his head to avoid getting a rock or bottle smashed over his skull from behind.

"His elbow flew back at the exact moment I was gonna hit him, cracked me in the jaw, broke it in four places. I don't remember this part, but I was told afterwards that my head slammed off the ground. But the guy wasn't done yet. Evidently he didn't appreciate me coming at him from behind, because he moved in for the kill, to snap my neck or stomp my brains out or something. That's where your mom comes in."

"My mom?" I stare at him incredulously.

"According to what I heard later, she flew in like a bat—no one seemed to know exactly where she came from—jumping between the gargantuan and my half-destroyed body. Although the dude had her by about half a foot and a hundred pounds, she was way quicker and had ability to boot. Ten kicks later—my best guess is there were two to the groin, three to the head, two to the stomach, two to the knees, and one to the throat—and the guy was out cold. She saved my life that day, so now I'll do anything for her, which includes doing whatever it takes to protect you on this mission."

I'm speechless. Even though I've seen my mom act all tough general while in the Star Realm, I've never seen her fight. If Trevor's to be believed, she's incredible. I find my voice. "Wow, so that's it? That's why you trust each other?"

"After that I sought her out, thanked her, and we sort of became friends. She taught me to fight and I pledged myself to her."

"So you can actually fight now?" I ask.

"Hold on a minute, I could fight before, I just wasn't—"

"Chill. I'm just messing with you," I say, cracking a smile.

Trevor's face goes slightly red, but he manages an awkward smile. "Right, I knew that." It's good to see him on the defensive for once.

"So why were you such a jerk to me when we first met?" I ask.

Trevor really laughs now. "You weren't exactly a peach," he says.

I screw up my face. It's true. "I know, but I didn't know you, and—"

"And what? I didn't know you either."

"*And*...you knew my mom, so I would have thought you'd have trusted me," I say, feeling good about my argument.

"Hey, I pledged myself to your mom, not to you. And considering all the rumors going around about you and Tristan hooking up..."

"There was no *hooking up*," I say.

"Whatever you want to call it," he says. "Chasing each other around or whatever. If you were with him, then I thought for sure something was wrong with you."

"But Tristan's on our side," I argue.

"Yeah, but from where I was coming from that was pretty farfetched."

"And now?" I ask, sticking my chin out.

"Now what?"

"Now that you know Tristan's one of the good guys, do you still think something's wrong with me?"

"Jury's still out," he says, straight-faced.

"Ha. Ha. Right back at ya."

"Did I hear my name?" Tristan says, surprising me from the side. I'm surprised because I didn't feel him coming. I know it sounds weird, but usually I can sort of sense when he's near, and when he gets closer the pull toward him gets stronger. But this time I feel nothing. Come to think of it, the buzz in my scalp and the tingles along my spine are gone too. I've gotten so used to them whenever Tristan is near that it's almost stranger *not* feeling them.

"I was just telling Trevor how he can only trust you as far as he can throw you," I joke, trying to cover up our missing magnetism. Does he still feel it?

"She's right," he says, playing along. "I'm a real scoundrel at heart."

"When we have a bit of a training session later today, you might be surprised just how far I *can* throw you," Trevor says.

"We'll see about that," Tristan retorts.

Guys, I think, always flexing their muscles, whether with words or fists. "Anyway," I say, "considering I'll probably beat you both later, let's get some breakfast and save the talking for the strategizing."

"Hand-to-hand combat is no place for a girl," Trevor says with a sneer. He sounds more like the old Trevor now.

"Then you haven't seen her fight," Tristan says, pride in his voice. My cheeks and neck warm when he says it.

"Actually, I have," Trevor replies. "And I wasn't that impressed."

"So you *were* impressed," I say, catching him in his words.

"Mildly," he says, "but I'm not sure I'd be comfortable hitting a girl anyway."

"Then I guess that'll make it easier for me to hit you," I say.

* * *

Breakfast is quick and bland. We won't train until later, choosing to travel when we're energized.

Our upward climb continues for three, four, five, six hours, who knows? I stop paying attention to time at some point. There's very little talking as that takes energy—energy we can't afford to waste. We only stop twice to pee and rehydrate.

Eventually the tunnel levels out and a few hundred feet later we find words scraped into the rock wall: *Welcome to the Sun Realm*. I silently thank the Resistance tunneler for the casual signpost.

We've done it! Well, the easy part that is—just getting here. The hard part is still to come. The funny thing is that it doesn't feel any different than the Moon Realm—at least not yet. It's still just a dark, gray, monotonous tunnel. A Sun Realm tunnel technically, but a tunnel just the same.

Another mile or so down the track we find a set of stairs leading up to the right. My mom warned us about this: that there would be a number of tunnel exits, before a sudden end. This is the first we've seen and therefore, the tunnel continues further on, so we have a choice to make. Onwards or upwards. Unfortunately there's no map for this tunnel, because it's never been used. Before we left, Mom told us that because the passage was constructed so haphazardly and the rebellion was snuffed out so quickly, there wasn't even a chance to map it. Originally the plan was for the secret tunnel to loop underneath each and every sun dweller subchapter, to be used in the event of an invasion by the Lower Realms, but there was only time to make it a few subchapters deep. They just haven't had the time or the manpower to continue the project in earnest.

"What do you think?" I say to Tristan. "Any idea where we are?"

"Well, we left from Moon Realm subchapter one and headed due east. My guess would be somewhere between subchapters eighteen and twenty-one in the Sun Realm. What do you think, Roc?"

Roc strokes his now-stubbly chin. "Sounds about right. But it's possible we haven't even gone that far yet. We could still be in the subchapter fifteen to seventeen loop somewhere."

"So where does that leave us?" Ram says, his voice a deep rumble.

"If we're trying to get to subchapter one…" Roc says.

"We are," Tristan confirms.

Roc nods. "Then we'll need to either catch a train from subchapter seventeen or twenty-one, or cut across the Realm starting with subchapter eighteen."

"If we decide to go on foot, it'll be a three-day march at top speed," Tristan adds.

"Why don't we just scope it out first and then decide," I suggest.

"The fewer people the better," Trevor says. "I'd say two at the most."

"I'll go," I say immediately.

"Me, too," Tristan says. I'm glad. It might give me a chance to ask him about whether anything's changed for him, like it did for me.

* * *

We start up the steps, me in front, Tristan close behind. I shine the flashlight up and up and up—at least fifty steps—but I can't see the end of the staircase.

When we're out of earshot from the others, who remain behind in the tunnel, I stop for a second, looking down at Tristan, who's just two steps behind me. He stops, too, looking up at me curiously.

"Have you noticed any *changes* this morning?" I say.

"What do you mea—" he starts to say, but then stops. He raises an eyebrow and squints an eye and generally looks confused—but then there's a spark of recognition. He flinches and a look of something—pain?—crosses his face. "It's…it's gone," he says dazedly. "The pull—it's gone."

So he's felt it too. Or, more like *un*felt it. I sigh. "I was hoping maybe I was just having an off day." I feel a surge of something…relief or concern, or maybe both…through my bones.

"But how?" he asks. "Why?"

I turn and continue climbing the steps; the taps of his footfalls follow shortly after. "I don't know," I say. "It's like we lost our electric charge."

"But I…I still *like* you."

I laugh. "I still *like* you, too," I say, mimicking his emphasis. "We're still the same people, have the same personalities, have the same attractions. But whatever drew us together in the first place is gone. I don't know how else to describe it."

"Are you saying it was something supernatural?" There's a smile in his tone.

I've got no freaking clue. The whole thing makes no sense. I mean, I thought I was just attracted to Tristan because he's hot and a celebrity and a really, really nice guy, caring and generous and loyal, and everything else a girl could want in a guy—and I *am* attracted to him for all of those reasons—but now I get the feeling that there's more to the story, although I can't even begin to explain it, especially not after what my mom said to me. *It's no accident that you and Tristan met.*

"Not necessarily supernatural," I finally say, "just something beyond us." My explanation makes no sense, but it's all I've got.

Tristan is silent for a few minutes, his presence given away only by the soft scrape of his boots on the stone.

The steps continue to rise before us, rough and jagged and almost haphazard, like they were built in a hurry, on a whim. Although my calves are burning slightly, it feels good, and helps to take my mind off of the *change*.

Tristan eventually breaks the silence. "Does this change anything?" he asks, a hint of concern in his voice.

I laugh again. "No. At least not for me. It's just strange, that's all."

"Okay."

Silence ensues, as awkwardness palpably churns through the air, which is unusual for Tristan and me. I guess something *has* changed.

Thankfully, the top of the climb isn't far off, the steps peaking at a small landing. I wave the light around to take in my surroundings. Curved rock walls rise maybe fifteen feet to a bare ceiling. The space is empty save for a thin gray ladder attached to one of the walls. At the top of the ladder: a circular metal porthole.

"Up and out?" I say, when Tristan steps beside me.

He grins and moves to the ladder, taking the lead. When he's a few rungs up, I grab the third or fourth hold and begin to climb. Twelve steps later, we're at the top and Tristan is running his hands along the underside of the portal. "I don't see a latch," he whispers.

"Just push on it," I hiss.

Placing his hands palm side up in the center of the circle of metal, Tristan tries to force it upwards. It doesn't budge.

"Maybe if we both push," I say. "Move over."

Obediently, Tristan shifts to one side, keeping one foot on the top rung while the other dangles precariously off the side. Pushing off with my legs, I squeeze myself beside him. I'm as close to him as I've ever been, as close as we were when Cole tackled us, saving us from death by arrow, as close as we were last night when he held me to sleep, so close that his breath tickles my neck. My scalp might not be buzzing, the tingles notably absent from my spine, but there definitely *are* feelings—and lots of them. No, nothing has changed. At least not as far as I'm concerned.

The look on Tristan's face—blue eyes shining under the soft glow of the flashlight, lips parted slightly, eyebrows raised—tells me he's feeling the same way. Here we are, on the Sun Realm's doorstep, and maybe death's too, and I've got the urge to kiss him.

I force back the impulse and say, "Ready?"

He blinks hard, as if snapping out of a daze, and notices my hands on the portal. He raises his arms and places his palms next to mine. "On three," he says. "One, two…"

Right on three, I shove upwards with all my might, Tristan doing the same beside me, his arm muscles bulging as he strains against the barrier. The portal gives way, but doesn't fly up, as I expected; rather, it pops up an inch and then meets a strange resistance that offers weak, but adequate defense against our entrance. "To the right, to the right," Tristan says, grunting.

We shift our direction of force to the side and the disc skims along the floor, settling with the hole half-uncovered. Or half-covered, depending on who you ask.

But we still can't see anything, because something is covering the hole. I reach up and touch it, finding the object to be fuzzy and soft. A carpet or—

"A rug," I say.

Together we push on what is clearly a rug, and then fold it over the portal, revealing only gray darkness beyond. Poking my head up, I take in my surroundings, ready to clamber down the ladder at the first sign of trouble. Even without a flashlight, I have no problem seeing. It's dark—clearly nighttime—but not like it gets in the Moon Realm. Night there is not so much darkness as it is the *absence of light.*

"I don't see anyone," I whisper to Tristan.

"Okay, let's go in, but be careful," he says. I nod. Square my jaw. Instinctively clutch my mother's necklace. Ready myself.

When I pull myself into the room there's a burst of glow filtered through a clear, glass window. I approach the window in awe, eating up the light with my eyes. It's like no artificial light I've ever seen before—so real, so complete, so...

"Moon," I murmur, no louder than a breath.

In the night sky—could it really be the sky?—so dark and blue-black and endless, there's an orb of light, a perfect circle, casting light upon all under its watchful gaze. It's perfect. Too perfect.

The pictures of the real moon I'd seen in old books at school made it appear friendly, full of winks and dimples and smirks and nods, but this version of the moon is sterile, staring, man-made. But I still love it.

"Pretty cool, huh?" Tristan says quietly.

My head jerks to the side where Tristan is now standing. "Amazing," I say. "Have you always had a moon?"

"My father's scientists developed the first artificial moonlight twenty-five years ago and hung it on the roof of subchapter one before we were born. But for a decade and a half every Sun Realm subchapter has had their own moon."

And this remarkable technology hasn't been shared with the other Realms? Of course not. I turn away from the selfish moon, my eyes searching the rest of the room. A table and chairs crowd the corner. The flat surface is made of something brown and knotted with circles and thin fibers. "Is that...wood?"

"Yes," Tristan says. Another revelation. Since the moment I was born, my world's been dominated by stone. Buying something made of wood costs a small fortune. A whole table? Impossible.

The flare of light comes just before the demanding voice:

"What the hell are you doing in here?!" the voice yells.

Four

Tristan

I'm momentarily blinded by the bright ceiling light. The effect is worsened due to the fact that I've been in the darkness of the Moon Realm for so long.

I blink the spots away and glance at Adele, who is opening and shutting her eyes and waving a hand in front of them. She's probably never seen a light this bright, so adjusting will take her longer.

In front of me is a young guy, perhaps my age, perhaps a year younger or older depending on whether he looks his age. He's wearing the seal of a sun dweller guardsman on his red sleeping tunic. His hair is disheveled and his face weary with sleep. His eyes are darting from me to Adele and back again. Over and over. "But that's impossible. You're…you're…"

"Supposed to be in bed recovering from temporary insanity?" I finish for him. "Yeah, that was a lie my father told."

"But she's…"

"A wanted criminal. I know, but look, it's not what you think," I add, taking a step toward him, my hands extended peacefully.

"Tristan, I can't see," Adele says from behind me.

Still facing the young guard, I say, "Keep them closed and open them a little more every few seconds. What subchapter are we in?" I ask the guard.

He's caught off guard by the simple question—because who wouldn't know what subchapter they're in?—and therefore, like most people, his natural inclination is to answer it. "Eighteen, but why…" This guy can't seem to finish a sentence.

I take another step and suddenly he's on the defensive, the tiredness in his eyes replaced with alertness; I can almost see the big red flashing lights going off in his brain. None of this makes sense to him, as it shouldn't, and his instincts and training are about to kick in. Which makes him dangerous. And deadly. Despite his young age, I know how well trained my father's guardsmen are.

He takes a step back toward the exit.

"We're lost," I lie. "I'm trying to bring my prisoner in, but I seem to have made a wrong turn. Do you know where the nearest Enforcer station is?"

Another step back. "I'll just call my supervisor," he says warily. I consider going for the gun lashed to my calf but think better of it; a gunshot would surely alert others to our presence. I mirror his step, like we're performing a ballroom dance together. "That's not necessary. If you can just direct us to the Enforcers, we'll be on our way. I'd hate to have to report your lack of assistance to my father," I add in a last-ditch effort to force his cooperation.

His eyes widen and I think I've finally gotten through to him, but just as quickly they narrow and I know no amount of talking will save us now. My father's probably told his guardsmen that I'm not thinking clearly, or some rubbish like that, and if they see me to apprehend me immediately.

Not today.

I spring into action, closing the gap between us in one second flat, ram my forearm into his cheekbone, and there's a satisfying crunch of small shattered bones. But as I knew he would be, the guy is a professional, taking the blow like a champ and spinning away, rushing for the door. Strength in numbers is the guardsmen motto, and he knows if he raises the alarm, they'll have us cornered.

Surging forward, I dive at his legs, tackle him to the floor, and he grunts as the breath rushes out of his lungs. His fingernails scrape the stone floor, his feet kick at my face, and he generally does everything in his power to get away from me, but I hold on fast, pulling him back to where I can silence him.

In an unexpected change in strategy, he thrusts his body back at me and deadly steel glints in the light—he's pulled a knife from somewhere, his butt for all I know.

I release his legs and grab his wrist, stopping the knifepoint less than a foot from my throat. I'm the son of the President and yet he's striking to kill. Is my father's order to *kill me* on sight? As I stare at the razor-sharp tip of the knife, my mind whirls with anger. How dare he? I'm his son for God's sake! But then I remember: My order is to kill him too. Maybe the world is in alignment after all. A father/son grudge match. Brought to you by the politics of the Tri-Realms.

I let the warm flow of anger course through my muscles, strengthening me beyond my own power. I twist his arm hard and he cries out, dropping the knife as his wrist snaps. He's howling in pain but no one comes to help him. Either they're impressively deep sleepers or he's manning this guard station alone.

The fierce hot fury toward my father, toward this young (stupid!) guard, toward my heritage—the Sun Realm—swarms all over me like a horde of angry bees, looking for something—anything!—to sting, to prick, to ravage. To kill. KILL!

I have an out-of-body experience.

My soul rises above my clenched body, as if I'm trying to remove myself from the muck of human violence, and I watch, watch—

—as, in one swift motion, I snatch up the knife and jam it into the guardsman's chest with the force of a wild beast, my eyes bulging, my teeth snapping, my grip like iron on the handle. He's not crying out anymore, just wheezing with sharp gasps, sucking at the air as if it's some magic potion that can save him from the death wound my body has already inflicted. And it is my body, acting of its own volition, that's done it, that's killed this boy—for that's what he is: just a teenager.

At least that's what I'm telling myself, as I hover above the blood that's creating a crimson pool on the floor. *It wasn't me!*

Not really, I reason with myself. I'm up here and *he's* down there.

My argument is crushed to rock dust as my mind, my soul, my heart swoop down and back into my heaving body, so close to the boy's blood I taste it on my tongue. Horrified, I push with the bottom of my feet, scrabble backwards, doing everything in my power to distance myself from the smell of death.

"Tristan," Adele says, and I jerk my head back, my lips mangled and creased. I duck my head, not wanting her to see me like this, the animal I've become.

"I heard noises. What happened?" she asks and I really look at her for the first time. She's squinting, her green pupils a thin line through her slitted eyes and long, feathery eyelashes.

And with that one question, I'm back. The level-headed, instinct-driven Tristan who doesn't make mistakes. "We have to go," I say. "There's not a minute to spare."

I don't want her to see the guy, to see the truth of what I've done—although somewhere in the back of my mind I know she'll understand—so I guide her to the hole in the floor without turning on the light.

"Are your feet on the ladder?" I ask.

"Yes, but Tristan, please, what's going on? What happened?" she asks.

"I killed him," I blurt out.

Adele's face is unreadable as she squints up at me. Silence. She hates me. She thinks I'm a monster. I've lost her. "You did what you had to do," she says. "He would have raised the alarm."

I know she's right. "Go," I say. "Get the others. We're entering subchapter eighteen." I begin to move back into the room, but Adele grabs my arm.

"I won't tell them," she says.

I nod. "Thanks," I reply, and then she's gone, clambering down the ladder three times as fast as we climbed them. Her feet slap the rock steps, each footfall more distant than the one before it.

There's no time to lose. Trying not to look at the guy's eyes, which remain open in an eternal stare, I drag him by his feet to the corner, use an old military tarp to cover his bloodstained form. There's an iron-gray sink and a brown towel against one of the walls, which I use to mop up most of the bloodstains before they set too deep into the valleys between the stone floor tiles.

I stuff the soiled towel beneath the tarp before turning off the light.

In darkness once more, I wait with my thoughts and regret.

The red-hot fire is gone.

I am stricken with sorrow. I clench my hands together to stop them from shaking. He was going to kill me. He was going to raise the alarm. All my friends would have been killed. Adele would have been killed. Like Adele said, I did what I had to do.

Thankfully, the others arrive quickly, saving me from myself. The flashlight beam comes first, and then the flashlight, gripped by Adele's pale fingers. By the time her head pops up, I've shaken off my dark thoughts and I'm all business. As the others climb through the gap, heads bobbing around the room, I say, "The moon's bright enough that we won't need our flashlights, and they'll only draw attention to us anyway." Like

Adele, Tawni and Trevor gaze out the window at the false moon, like they're seeing the real thing for the first time. Now that would be something worth getting excited over—the real thing.

Roc, who has seen many artificial moons in his day, moves to my side. "What are we doing? What is this place?"

"A royal guardhouse," I say, my eyes darting to Adele, who's watching Tawni and Trevor.

"What?" Roc says, his face as flat as cardboard.

"I don't think anyone's here though," I say. Not anymore, I think, my eyes naturally resting on the rumpled tarp with the human-sized bump in the corner.

Ram's by the door, beckoning to the rest of us with his eyes, his impatience thinly veiled. "This is no sightseeing mission," he growls.

"Let's go," I agree.

The guard station is really a small tower, only large enough for a couple of guards, even during the day—and apparently one guard at night. We're on the first floor, so exiting is as easy as leaving the room, locating an outer door in a semicircle hallway, and pushing into the cool air.

Unlike the stagnant air in the Lower Realms, a gentle breeze wafts through the subchapter; another one of the luxuries developed by my father's engineers and reserved solely for the use of the Sun Realm. Although the taste of privilege became bitter to my mouth long ago, I prefer it to the coppery tang of death that sits on the back of my tongue like a frog on a stone.

The city is sleeping and I wonder why. Typically sun dweller cities are alive late into the night, as the citizens try to get the most enjoyment out of each and every day. "It's quiet," I murmur.

Roc's frowning. "Doesn't make sense," he says. "Maybe because of the war?"

I shake my head. "I doubt a little thing like a war would stop these people. They probably think the whole thing will be fought in the Moon Realm." And they're probably right, I think darkly.

"Wait—what day is it?" Roc says.

"I have no clue. Why?"

Roc's counting with his fingers, trying to figure out the damn day of the month. For what purpose? I wait to find out.

"Oh, God," Roc says finally, his eyebrows narrowed. "It's the eve of the Sun Festival."

What? "But that's not for weeks," I say.

"Yeah, when we left the Sun Realm weeks ago it was," Roc says. "Now, it's tomorrow."

"Surely it'll be cancelled," Adele says. "They do know a war's on, right?"

"No way," I say. "Maybe some other year, but not this one. This is the big one."

"Celebrating five hundred years since Year One," Roc agrees.

"My father will use the day to reinforce how lucky we all are, try to garner support for ending the war peacefully."

"Yeah, he'll be talking peace while bombing the bejesus out of the Moon Realm," Ram adds.

"Probably," I say.

"So that's why everyone's inside? Because of the Festival?" Tawni asks.

"Absolutely," I say. "This is *the* event of the year for these people. You've seen it on the telebox before, right?"

Adele and Tawni nod. "Sure," Adele says. "Everyone watches it."

"Well, what you don't see is how everyone goes to bed early the night before, so they are well-rested for the forty-eight-hour party that starts the next morning."

"So the Sun Realm's going to be swarming with people for the next two days," Roc adds. "Our timing couldn't be worse. It's the calm before the cave-in."

"Shit," Ram says. I look at the faces around me, their lips pursed, their expressions grim.

"Why wouldn't my mom have told us?" Adele asks, practically pulling the question right out of my mouth.

Trevor sighs. "She did. She told me."

Adele's head snaps to face Trevor. "What?" A flash of pink appears on her cheeks and her fists tighten at her sides.

"She told me," he repeats. "She thought the Festival would likely be cancelled, but she told me just in case it wasn't—so we'd have a contingency plan."

"Why didn't she just tell all of us?" I ask, still not understanding all the secrecy.

"She didn't want to worry everyone about something that probably wouldn't matter," Trevor explains.

No one speaks for a moment as we ponder his statement. Finally, I ask, "What's the contingency plan?"

"To blend in," Trevor says. "Rather than sneaking around, we might actually be able to pass for a group of sun dwellers enjoying the Festival. There will be lots of people, right?"

"More than you can imagine," Roc says.

I glance at Adele. Her cheeks are pale again, her hands open. "He's right," she says. "I think this is a good thing. The more chaos there is up here, the better chance we have of blending in. My mom would have known that."

"I agree," I say. Perhaps it is a good thing. The sun dwellers will be too busy getting drunk and celebrating to notice the traitors in their midst. At least I hope.

While the others chew on Adele's words, I take in our surroundings, and I understand why this guard tower is so undermanned. It rises above the subchapter, in the center of the city, like a single finger held in the air. In a time of war, like now, most personnel will have been dispatched to the subchapter borders, leaving the least experienced guard—the boy—to hold down this well-protected tower. Whether the Resistance purposely chose their secret entrance into subchapter 18 to be in a guard tower, or whether the tower was built later on, I do not know.

I notice that, like me, Adele's scanning the city. Under the moonlit night her face is a luminescent pale, her mouth slightly open as she gawks at a world that is like another planet to her. Wide, rich, brown cobblestone streets intersect the city, marching in every direction like dominoes. Red-bricked buildings and apartments rise all around us, grand and regal and *wealthy*, with large spotless glass windows and marble balconies hanging off the sides.

The windows remind me that we're far too exposed.

Ram's thinking the same thing. "We gotta move," he rumbles.

I look at Roc. "We can't use the main intra-Realm tunnel," I say.

"I think there's an old shipping tunnel that's not used much anymore," Roc says.

"Lead the way."

We move out, jammed against the buildings, single file. Everyone's on the balls of their feet, reducing the footfalls to no more than whispers in the dark. Even Ram manages to jog noiselessly, which impresses me considering his size. We stick to the shadows, in case some insomniac sun dweller decides to peek out their window just as we pass by. The Enforcers aren't a concern because the Sun Realm has the lowest number of Enforcers of all the Realms—our crime rate is close to nil.

We pass a circular courtyard, hugging the curved edges, gazing at the massive statue of the first Nailin president, Wilfred Nailin, in the center. The one who started it all.

It's an eerie feeling, zigzagging through the sun dweller city at night, the breeze ruffling my hair and clothes. It almost feels…nice. It takes my mind off what I did in the tower, what I might have to do in the next couple days. I draw the line at saying it's peaceful, but that's how it feels. Far too peaceful.

Dark gray rock walls loom over us as we exit the bounds of the city, crossing a wide plain of rock, far from the edge of the city. At ground level is the black mouth of a tunnel. We don't break stride as we race toward it, seeking the safety of darkness. As its jaws close around us, I let out a sigh of relief.

We play our flashlights around the space, which is empty aside for a cluster of large rocks at one side.

"Where does this lead?" I ask Roc in the dark.

"It leads to—" Roc doesn't have a chance to finish before the spotlight bursts in his face, darting around the side of the rock cluster.

As he throws his hands over his eyes, a voice says, "It leads to hell."

Five

Adele

Not again, I think. Blinded by the light, I'm blinking, blinking, trying to see the sun dweller guardsman, waiting for the sickening sounds of death as Tristan kills another one.

He had no choice.

Heavy boots thud all around us.

My vision clears much faster this time, and when the world reappears it's much worse than before. We're surrounded by a dozen red-uniformed men in various stages of alertness and dressing. Based on their half-clothed attire—some are bare-chested, wearing only thick red pants, others have their red tunics through one arm but not the other—we've stumbled upon a sleeping sun dweller platoon. They were behind the big rocks on the edge of the cave, well-hidden from our prying eyes. Some quick-witted and wide awake night watchman must have alerted them just before we snuck into their camp.

Just our luck.

None of them move, just stare at us with angry eyes and half-snarls. Each bears a weapon, some swords, some bows with arrows cocked, most black guns. My favorite. Instinctively I try to sense the weight of the gun strapped beneath my tunic in the small of my back. But then I remember: it's not there; Tawni's got it. Stupid, stupid, stupid. I do have a small knife strapped to my leg, which I mostly use for small jobs, like cutting ropes. Not for killing. Never for killing.

Now what?

"Get on your knees!" one of the sun dwellers shouts. He's naked from the waist up, with dark curly hair all over his chest, like he might have an ape for a father and a human mother—he spits on the ground—no, make that an ape for a mom, too.

None of us move.

"NOW!" the ape yells, his voice booming through the naturally acoustic cave. *NOW, Now, now...* His voice fades in the distance, down the "safe" and "unused" tunnel we're supposed to be heading down.

Still no one moves.

The guy cocks his double-handled gun, probably an automatic or semi-automatic.

"We have no choice. Do what he says," Tristan commands. Although on the face his words sound compliant, there's a hint of resistance in his tone, as if he has other plans.

Roc and Tawni are on their knees even before Tristan can obey his own order; I suspect they were halfway there before he spoke. Trevor and I slide down next. Sharp needles of rock pierce and prick my clothes. Ram's the last to join us, his big nostrils flaring like a bull, his eyes wide and wild, and for a second I think he might attack them all on his own. But eventually he drops to one knee, his other boulder-sized kneecap angled forward as if in a stretch.

"Both knees!" the ape yells, taking three big steps forward. I expect him to beat his chest any second. Instead, he snaps a sharp kick at Ram, who tries to duck, but doesn't have time. Evidently these soldiers sleep in their boots, because they're all wearing heavy footwear, their apish leader included. Ram is the unfortunate recipient of the likely steel-toed footgear, his head snapping back at an unnatural angle.

I cringe, and Tawni cries out, but to everyone's—none more so than the sun dwellers'—surprise, Ram doesn't fall to his side. His head rebounds forward, revealing a wicked inch-long gash on his temple.

First blood has been drawn.

If the rest of us comply from this point on, perhaps it will also be last blood.

The only problem: most of our group, me included, aren't too good at compliance.

And Ram's laughing—of all things, laughing!—a deep grumble of delight, like a foot to the head is just what he needed to make today the perfect day. Still chuckling, he shifts his right-angle knee so it's also flush with the rough ground. Six ducks, all in a row. At least four of us are thinking of the best way to hurt these guys.

"Secure their weapons," the ape says to his men. "Bind them." The men move forward from all sides, as if they're a single organism, an extension of the ape himself. I do the math.

Twelve enemies. Six of us. Assume Tawni stays put. Assume Roc can take one of them. That leaves two for most of the rest of us. I've seen worse odds.

There's a surge of warmth as blood pumps to my extremities in anticipation.

My fingers tingle with nervous energy.

We'll go down fighting, one way or the other.

Ram's the first one up, exploding from his haunches like a missile, his shoulder a battering ram, shattering the sternum of the unlucky soldier who was about to use a small snatch of rope to secure him. Tristan, Trevor, and I snap to our feet simultaneously, each attacking the closest soldier. Mine is tall and broad and holding a sword in front of him like he knows how to use it. But even he's surprised by the swiftness and ferocity of my attack, probably because I'm a girl, and not particularly big. My father's face appears in my mind a split-second before I hit the guy. His words: *Even the big ones will fall if you hit them in the right places.*

He swings high with his sword, a head-lopping attempt, but I duck under and thrust my leg straight up toward his crotch. *The right place.* He's in agony the moment I connect, dropping the sword and clutching himself. I fling my knee as hard and as high in the air as I can, audibly hearing the crunch of his jawbone as I catch him under the chin, his teeth chattering from top to bottom. The worst hit: the back of his head off the unforgiving stone when he collapses to the cave floor.

One down. I'm due another. Gunshots explode through the night.

I whirl around, searching for my next victim, anticipating the need to dodge a bullet or an arrow—or maybe another blade. Or—

None of the above.

As it turns out, I was deemed a lesser threat. Tristan and Trevor are each finishing off their own victims—Trevor bashing a bulky dark-skinned guy in the head with the butt of his own gun and Tristan straddling a sturdy white soldier, clobbering him repeatedly in the face—but it's Ram who's in the thick of things. And that's where the bullets are flying, both toward him and from him. He's managed to steal a gun from one of the soldiers and is firing at six or seven sun dwellers, each of whom are firing back at him. His tunic is blotted in at least three places with growing circles of darkness. His face is scarred with the trickling river from his initial head wound. And yet, he's still fighting, trying to take out as many of the soldiers as he can before they take him out, for our sakes, not for his.

"No!" Tristan shouts as he charges toward the line of enemies. Trevor and I follow in his wake, both yelling at the top of our lungs, as if the loudness of our yells will determine the strength of our attacks. I pass Tawni, who's splayed on the ground, clutching a bloody knee, Roc hovering near her, a downed sun dweller soldier nearby. Roc got his man and I'm glad.

More gunfire: a soldier drops, then another. To my right: Ram's fallen to two knees again, his chest covered in swarming darkness, a death plague eating away at him. Still shooting. Another enemy down.

Tristan smashes into one of the last four from the side, knocking him into another. The third and fourth men turn toward Tristan, trying to find their aim. I'm too far away. Trevor is closer, but not close enough.

Boom, boom!

The last two upright soldiers, one of whom is the ape man himself, slump to the ground, their eyes rolling around like marbles. The thump of Ram's body follows a second later, his final act completed.

My head is on a swivel, trying to take in the carnage before me: Ram's crumpled mass; Tristan kicking away the guns of the two soldiers he tackled, a strange guttural groan rising from his throat and out his mouth, moving toward Ram; Trevor rushing forward and kicking the final two men in the head, knocking them unconscious; Tawni sobbing somewhere behind me, Roc muttering soothing and utterly unbelievable words; red sun dweller soldiers strewn across the cave like boulders, some dead, some out cold. And me in the midst of it all, dazed and energized and sad.

I walk numbly to where Tristan is huddled over Ram, his head bowed, his hands folded reverently in front of him, as if in prayer. Tristan's words about Ram echo in my head: *Let's just say our friendship has had its ups and downs. Right now we're on an up.*

The up has crashed to a lower down. The lowest.

I place a hesitant hand on Tristan's shoulder. He jerks slightly as he tilts his head back to look at me. His eyes are rimmed with red and filled with moisture, but his cheeks are dry. I don't expect he'll shed tears today, not while in the Sun Realm with all of us one mistake, one wrong tunnel away from death.

"I'm sorry," I say, and although I don't know Ram that well, I avoid looking at the dead man's face.

"Me, too," Tristan says, standing up. "We have to make this look like a one-man job." There's coldness in his voice—his attempt at pushing aside the loss of a friend.

"Okay," I say. "What do we do?"

Trevor's picked up on the vibe and pitches in right away. "All the bodies have to be in the same general area, so it's believable that Ram could have inflicted all the damage on his own." He practically did anyway, I think.

"But they're not all dead," Roc chimes in. "One of them will just tell them the truth."

"None of these guys will wake up anytime soon," Tristan says, giving one of them a harsh kick to the head as if to illustrate his point, or possibly as a final act of revenge for what they did to Ram. "By the time they do, we'll be long gone."

"But they'll know we're coming," Roc persists.

"That's unavoidable," Tristan says.

"Not if we take the rest of them out," Trevor says. I bite my lip.

Tristan stares at Trevor. I know they're both thinking it's not only the smart thing but the just thing. My lip starts to bleed.

"We can't kill them—they're unarmed and unconscious," Tawni says, the only voice for humanity in our group.

"It's no different than what they did to Ram," Tristan says flatly. "It's what they deserve."

Tawni looks at me, her eyes wide and white, all color sucked from them under the glare of the spotlight, which continues to cast a beam of light through the center of the cave. "Adele, tell them they can't do this."

I've endured so much death in just the last few weeks that I feel as if there's a hole in my heart, because although I know I should be on Tawni's side, I'm not. I understand what Tristan is feeling; it's the same thing I felt when I killed my father's executioner, when I killed Rivet after Cole's murder. Although they were still conscious and dangerous when I killed them, had they not been, I would have done the same thing. Stabbed Rivet. Pumped hot steel into my dad's murderer. If I could have killed them twice I would have.

I don't say anything.

"Adele!" Tawni exclaims, horror creasing her tear-stained face. "Don't let them do this."

I don't say anything, look away from my friend, a pathetic act of avoidance.

I look at Tristan. "She's right," he says, to my surprise.

"She is?" I say.

"I am?" Tawni says.

"No, Tristan, we don't have a choi—" Trevor starts to say.

"There's always a choice," Tristan interrupts. "We can fight them, but we can't become them. And we can thank Tawni for reminding us of that. C'mon, we don't have time to sit around and talk about it."

No one argues and everyone pitches in, dragging dead and unconscious bodies in a circle around Ram's fallen form, like a final monument to his character, like he defended us from all of them. It's not far from the truth.

Finished, we stand and pay our final respects to a man who was a mystery to me, maybe a mystery to all of us. The only words spoken are by Tristan: "You've more than paid your debt, new friend," he says, and I wonder what his words mean, but don't ask. It's not the right time, nor can we linger much longer. We flick on our flashlights and extinguish the spotlight, thrusting us back into a shaky-red form of existence.

From there we run, shouldering our packs and weapons, heads down, flashlights aimed just far enough in front of us that we don't ram ourselves into a boulder or sprain an ankle in a rut. The shipping tunnel is wide and tall, perfect for trucks hauling goods and supplies to be distributed within the Sun Realm. But not anymore, according to Roc. There are bigger and better shipping tunnels now, leaving this one available for us. Which is probably why the soldiers were camped there, biding their time until their orders came in, to be dispatched to the front lines of the attack on some vulnerable moon dweller subchapter. At least until we came along. Now they're headed for the infirmary if they're lucky—or the morgue if they're not.

An hour later we're still running, sweating tears of salt from exertion and for Ram, who even in death might buy us some time, help us accomplish our mission. More than six miles already separate us from our foes, but it's not enough. We need to be a few subchapters over before they learn the truth of what's happened, and even then it won't be far enough.

Another hour passes with sweat blinding and stinging our eyes.

Twelve, thirteen, fourteen miles, maybe more. An endless tunnel. We drink as we run, spilling the precious liquid down the tops of our tunics; I relish the coolness on my skin as rivulets of water meander down my chest, my torso, my legs. But my thirst never seems to be quenched; it's as if the water spills from my pores the moment I swallow it, leaving me wanting. My feet are sore from the never-ending slap, slap, slap of my boots on the pebbly tunnel floor. Every muscle burns, even ones I didn't think I really used while running—my abs, for example. It's farther than I've ever run and yet I don't think to stop. Might never stop.

But then I have to pee.

At first it's just a minor urge, but within a few minutes it escalates into a major problem. "I've got to stop or I'm going to explode," I say, slowing my strides.

"We need to find a safe place to camp," Tristan says, encouraging me forward with a hand on my back.

"No, you don't understand, I'm literally about to wet myself," I say, stopping.

"Me, too," Tawni adds, pulling up beside me, her face sheened with sweat.

"I'm shocked you made it this far. Usually girls have to go constantly," Trevor says in such a way that makes it sound like something we should be ashamed of.

"I've got to go, too," Roc admits sheepishly, bent over.

"Okay," Tristan says, "we'll all take a bathroom break except for Trevor, who will prove his manhood by holding it until we camp."

A joke. It's like a key part of our survival—our ability to laugh. As important as food or water or sleep. The thing we've all needed since we watched Ram die protecting us.

I laugh because if I don't I might cry.

The others do, too, including Trevor, who says, "I didn't say I didn't have to go."

Girls head one way—just Tawni and I—boys the other. We meet back in the middle.

My muscles protest, cramping and aching and burning, as they anticipate the start of the next phase. I'm not sure I can—

"I don't think I can run another step," Tawni says.

"Me either," Roc says. "I'm spent."

"Well, we can't stay here," Tristan points out.

"You all start walking as fast as you can," Trevor says, "and I'll run on ahead and scope things out." I don't like the idea of any of us separating, but I'm too tired to argue, and Trevor looks so keen—I have no clue where he gets the energy from, but I'm impressed.

Moments later, Trevor's out of sight and we're on the move again, but thankfully at a much slower pace. It's probably good that we walk anyway, to warm down our bodies before we sleep, otherwise we won't be able to move tomorrow.

Tristan and Roc lead the way, while I drop into stride with Tawni, matching her long strides with extra-long strides of my own. An awkward silence squirms its way between us. We've come so far together, and yet neither of us seems able to find the words. I know it's up to me. It's my fault things are awkward.

"I'm sorry I didn't back you up earlier," I say.

She glances at me, her mouth a thin line. This time it will take more than a simple apology to earn her forgiveness. "I'm *really* sorry?" I say.

"Is that a question?" Tawni asks dryly.

"Look, I—I thought those guys deserved what was coming to them, and if it helped keep us alive, all the better. It's not like I *wanted* to kill them. Even now the thought of it makes me sick."

"Yeah, but they were just lying there completely defenseless!" Her voice is rising and I know this is another of her principles.

"I'm not as strong as you, Tawni, I don't have the right answer for every situation. I see gray sometimes."

Pouting her bottom lip out, she blows air up past her nose, pushing a few loose strands of her white-blond hair off her forehead. "You're the strongest person I know," she says, compassion in her voice, and just like that, we're fine again.

I hold up an arm and tighten my bicep, and we both laugh. "I really am sorry," I say. "I've got your back from here on out."

"I know you do," Tawni says.

We walk in silence for another ten minutes. With time to think, my mind can hardly make sense of reality. We're in the Sun Realm, a place I've never been, a place I never thought I would go, on an insane mission to assassinate the President of the Tri-Realms. Based on the opposition we've faced in only the first subchapter we've entered, this isn't an *insane* mission, it's an *impossible* one. No, not even that's right. It's suicidal. That's the only word for it. My stomach churns.

Finally, I speak, needing a second opinion. "Is this a suicide mission?" I ask Tawni.

Although I glance at her, her gaze remains forward. "It always was," she says wistfully.

She always knew this and yet *she came*. To me the mission was two thick bands, one for the good of the Tri-Realms and one to avenge my father's death, braided together into a tight rope. A rope to form the noose to hang President Nailin with. But for Tawni it was a suicide mission, and yet—

She came.

Those two simple words speak volumes to her character. She's willing to face death on a mission that she's not even expected to contribute much to, other than occasionally being the conscience of the group. But she's here, by my side, a true friend, still trying to make amends for the sins of her parents against my family, or some such rubbish that she had nothing to do with in the first place.

"Thanks for coming with me," I say.

"I wouldn't have it any other way," Tawni says with a slight grin.

So it's a suicide mission. I don't know why gaining an understanding of the true nature of our mission has such a profound effect on me; I guess because I always expected to walk away from it alive. But now that I know, it gets me thinking: Did my mother know there's a close to zero chance I'd survive?

"Tawni, do you think my mom—"

"She knows, Adele," Tawni says tiredly.

She knows? But then how could she send me on such a mission? Doesn't she want me to live? Her words from before: *This is not a time for fearful mothers to hide away their capable daughters. It's a time to be bold, to take risks. Your father trusted in your strength, in your abilities, and now it's time for me to do the same. God knows I don't want to. I've lost a husband already and my other daughter is in bad condition, but I cannot hold you back because I'm scared of losing you. You are a fantastically capable woman and I'm so proud of you, Adele.*

She thought I was the one who could do it—that's why she sent me, even knowing I would probably die. She thought I had the best chance to accomplish the mission before being killed.

That's when I realize:

My mother sending me on this mission was the bravest act in the world, by the bravest woman in the world.

Six

Tristan

"Are you okay?" Roc asks me.

"I should be asking you the same thing," I say. "Those soldiers were tough."

Glancing at me, Roc says, "I don't mean about the soldiers. I mean about Ram."

I try to cover a twitch with a laugh. "We didn't even like each other," I say.

"I know that's not entirely true," Roc says. "Give me some credit."

And I should. Roc's perceptiveness is uncanny sometimes. Maybe he knows me better than I know myself.

Sighing, I say, "It's just, I think we were becoming friends. Maybe even good friends, eventually."

Roc nods. "He did what he felt was right. It was his sacrifice to make. A sacrifice that we all…" His voice trails away down the empty and endless tunnel.

He doesn't have to finish the statement. *That we all might have to make.* The image of Ram's shattered and bloody body pops unbidden into my mind, a hero in life, a hero in death. My friend? I suck in a breath and try to force away the ache in my chest. Another person I'll never see again. Another person I owe my life to.

A bad feeling fills my gut. We can't waste Ram's sacrifice. Nor Ben's. We can't linger in this death tunnel, sure to be trapped and killed by the sun dwellers. We need to get out. I'm about to stop and relay my paranoid opinions to the others when sharp footfalls sound from the passage beyond us.

I extract my sword with a metallic screech, instinctively pushing Roc behind me, my flashlight beam disappearing around the shadowy bend in the tunnel.

I ready myself for violence.

A blade flashes before me, reflecting the light back in my eyes, momentarily blinding me.

Clang!

My opponent swipes my sword aside and my stomach drops when a leg sweeps behind my knees. I grunt when I contact the stone floor, but am already twisting to escape my enemy. But he's quicker, barring my movements with a firm knee on my chest and a forearm on my throat.

Through my star-filled vision, a face begins to emerge. Roc's laughter fills the silence.

My vision returns, and Trevor's atop me, grinning from ear to ear, his face glistening with sweat. "Some protector you are," he says smugly. "Good thing no real baddies attacked while I was away."

"Get off me," I growl.

"No problem," he says, rolling off and to his feet.

Angry, both at myself for my weakness and at Trevor for making me look bad, I push myself up, cutting off Roc's continued laughter with a sharp glare. I notice Adele stopped nearby, watching the scene with something between interest and amusement, her right eyebrow raised. Heat rises in my head and I have to bite back a thousand angry words at Trevor.

I settle on pretending like nothing happened. Classic denial. "Did you find out what's ahead?" I ask through clenched teeth.

"Of course," Trevor says. "While you were all merrily strolling through the tunnel, I was reconnoitering a few miles ahead." He pauses, clearly enjoying the attention.

"And?" I say impatiently.

"And I've got good news. Just a couple miles down the road is the next subchapter."

"Which one?" Roc asks. "Eight?"

"Sorry, I failed Sun Realm geography," Trevor says. "You tell me."

Roc looks at me as he answers. "I don't know this tunnel that well, but I do know it angles northeast in the direction of the lower-numbered subchapters. There are two clusters, one that includes subchapters five through eight, and another for one through four. We've likely reached the edge of the first cluster, and therefore, subchapter eight. Does that sound right?"

He knows I don't have his sense of direction, but with all eyes on me, I say, "Uh, yeah. Makes perfect sense to me."

"But shouldn't we continue on so we can get to the second cluster? We're trying to get to subchapter one, right?" Adele asks. She's looking at me, her expression thoughtful.

"We can get there on a train from subchapter eight," I say, glancing at Roc for confirmation.

"We can," he says. "Plus, if I remember correctly, this shipping tunnel curls back to the west and in the direction of the upper subchapters, so we don't really have a choice."

"Do you really think we can just hop on a train without anyone noticing?" Tawni asks.

"It won't be easy," I say, "but the celebrations tomorrow will only help us blend in."

"Not tomorrow," Trevor says.

I look at him strangely.

"Today," he explains. "It's well after midnight. Today is the Sun Festival."

"We need to sleep," Adele says. "There's no way we can do this without sleep."

I know she's right, but the tunnel is too dangerous and—

"There's a partially hidden alcove up ahead," Trevor says. "I think we'll be safe there."

After the way he made me look bad in front of everyone, I'd rather not take his advice, but I don't have a better option. "Okay," I say. "Let's go."

Without discussing it, we all start running again, knowing every extra second of sleep could make a difference today. My muscles and bones protest with each stride, burning through my nerve endings like a lit fuse, but I ignore them as I have so many times before, like when I used to train in the presidential courtyards.

Pain is nothing. Words my father once spoke to me just after whipping a backhand across my cheek. It was the first time he ever hit me. I was only eight, but remember it as vividly as if it was yesterday. The sting of the blow brought tears to my eyes.

Pain is nothing, he repeated. *Tears are weakness.*

I blinked away the tears that day and rose to my feet, hatred for my father in my eyes. When my mother asked me how my mentor session was with my father, I wanted to tell her, wanted to ask her why my father would hit me, but instead I answered only *Good.*

He hit me eight other times in my life, each harder than the last. Until I turned fifteen, I didn't know that he hit my mother, too, either because I didn't want to know, or because I was too dumb or naïve to consider the dark truth.

Pain is nothing.

For me, his words are true, and soon the burning in my calves and thighs is nothing more than background noise against the slap of our shoes on the tunnel floor.

Trevor leads, and thirty minutes later he slows to a walk, running his hand along the high wall. "We're close," he murmurs. "Yes, here it is."

To his credit, he was right about the alcove. It is well hidden, just a thin crack in the impenetrable stone tube, barely wide enough for us to squeeze through sideways.

I let the others push through first, Trevor, then Roc, then Tawni, and finally Adele, who reaches out and grabs my hand for just a moment before releasing it. I'm so used to the crackle of electricity that her touch—or even her presence—normally releases down my spine, that I almost don't notice a few

73

different feelings that arise. Warmth, like the heat from the artificial sun, spreads up my arm and into the rest of my body; flittering excitement bounces around my stomach and in my chest; there's a numbness in my toes, almost as if I'm floating, or like my feet have disappeared. It's as though when our connection or magnetism or whatever it was that we had before was severed, it opened my body up to a whole rash of new and wonderful feelings, ones that perhaps were previously overwhelmed by the tingling in my scalp and spine.

Just before Adele slides into the crevice, she smiles back at me, as if she knows what I'm feeling. Grinning, I follow after her, barely noticing the scrape of the textured rock walls on my skin.

The alcove is much larger than I expected, long and rectangular, its ceiling double my height. An old unused fire pit sits ringed by small, white stones and solid stone benches. Above the pit is an opening in the roof, a conduit for the smoke to escape to some unpopulated cavern.

"A shipping rest stop," Roc says.

"Whatever it is, I'm glad it's here," Trevor says. "I'm about to be dead to the world for a long time. Wake me up when something exciting happens."

We unpack our bedrolls and lay them in a circle around the barren fire pit. Roc, always a gentleman, settles in close to Tawni, but not too close. Trevor collapses a bit further away, his breaths deepening almost immediately. I place my bedding a respectful distance from where Adele is standing, holding her own pack. To my surprise, however, she drops her pad in a heap next to mine, lowering to her knees to smooth it out, avoiding my gaze.

74

As I lie down facing away from her, she nestles in close to me, tracing my legs with her own. The gentle beat of her heart taps lightly against my back, sending slight vibrations along my skin. The feelings from before reappear: warmth, flittering excitement, floating.

My strength sapped, I close my eyes and feel wakefulness start to slip away.

"My mom said it's no accident that we met," Adele whispers in my ear.

"Mmm," I murmur, unsure of whether I'm awake or in a dream.

Seven

Adele

Despite the warmth in my heart and body as I lie next to Tristan, sleep doesn't come easy. For a while I can't turn off my brain, as I think about the conversation I'll need to have with Tristan now that I've told him what my mom said to me. In my mind it goes something like this:

Tristan: So if it's not an accident that we met, then who caused it?

Me: I dunno.

Tristan: Did you ask your mom?

Me: Nope.

Tristan: So what does this mean for us?

Me: I've got no clue.

Yeah, not very productive. I vow to pretend like I never told him.

Eventually, however, I do slip into something of a half-sleep, my mind alternating between awake and asleep. At one point when I open my eyes, a dark figure looms over me, holding something long and sharp. I try to scream as the blade hovers over me like a guillotine, dripping something wet and sticky on my face. I place a hand on my cheek to wipe away the moisture, and when I pull it away, it's red with blood. In the split-second before the blade slashes downward, my brain sizes up the situation. The intruder, the blood, the blade: at least one other of my friends is dead, maybe all of them.

With the long knife arcing toward my chest, I have no time for grief, no time to grasp the reality of my horror-filled life, no time to be *human*. Instinctively, my body reacts to the attack, rolling to the side and narrowly avoiding the death blow as it rips into my bedding, tearing straight to the rock floor and shattering into shards of metal that tinkle like broken glass as they scatter around me and my attempted murderer.

Pushing hard to my feet, I take a few quick steps back to buy time while I size up my enemy, but it's unnecessary, because the looming shadow doesn't advance, just stares at me with invisible eyes.

"You killed my friends," I state, my words like splinters of metal. My body is empty, like there's nothing left inside me; no heart, no blood, no tears—I'm just a hollow shell of flesh and bone. I know in that moment I will kill this man, and then I will kill the President.

Silence fills the dark gap between me and the swordsman. "Answer me!" I roar, my face and hands clenched and full of rage.

Instead of responding, the shadow laughs, heavy and arrogant and *evil*. He takes a step forward but I remain firm, revenge my only motive; there's death on my fingertips, making them twitch and jerk.

Another step takes him into a beam of light from an unseen source, perhaps a hastily discarded lantern.

I gasp when I see his face.

The attacker is President Nailin.

This is it. This is my moment. The culmination of our mission in a strange fated meeting. My friends dead; me soon to be. But not before him.

Screaming out senseless words, I charge, wrenching my knife from its ankle holster in the same motion. The President keeps laughing even as I approach him, and I hesitate for a moment, wondering why he would let me kill him so easily. And where are his guards? His soldiers?

In the moment of hesitation, I leave myself open. With a speed that seems inhuman, he pulls another sword from behind his back, where I couldn't see it, and thrusts it forward like a javelin, piercing my gut just above my bellybutton.

I know the pain has to be intense, but I don't feel it. I feel nothing. No pressure, no agony, nothing.

Leaving the sword—which is bouncing up and down slightly—embedded in me, President Nailin moves forward, leaning his sweaty, red face close to mine, so close I taste his hot, foul-smelling breath on my tongue. "I will kill you," he breathes.

I don't understand why he would say that, because he's already got me on a skewer like a stuck pig; threats aren't necessary. I look around us and I realize: it's not real. The cave is gone and we're surrounded by white pillars, sparkling with diamonds. Huge wooden chairs surround us, each occupied by lavishly adorned men and women, wearing jeweled necklaces and bracelets, brightly colored silk tunics, and gaudy fur hats. Spectators.

I shut my eyes so tight I feel like I might squash them in their sockets, will myself to awake from this nightmare, to return to a place where I'm warm and safe in Tristan's arms, a place where my friends are alive.

Wake up, wake up, wake up!

WAKE UP!

My eyes flash open to murky darkness, broken only by the flickering glow of soft candlelight—our night light. I'm breathing heavily, almost panting, my heart racing unnaturally in my chest. As I deepen my breaths, Tristan's long, slow exhalations whisper next to me. We're no longer tangled together, but I'm still warmed by the waves of heat radiating off his body.

Warm and safe.

For now.

Although I'm pretty sure I've only slept for a couple of hours—if I'm lucky—I'm wide awake now. My eyes feel like they're being held open by matchsticks, unable to close even if I want them to.

I sit up and Tristan stirs, his eyes fluttering for a moment as he rolls onto his side, away from, but he remains sleeping. The others are asleep, too, Tawni the closest, on her stomach, her arms along her side. My heart rate's back to

79

normal, but with my normalized breathing comes an empty feeling inside my gut. It's not hunger, I realize, but loneliness, a loneliness I haven't felt since before I met Tawni and Cole in the Pen. I know it doesn't make sense because I'm surrounded by my friends, but it's there, like a creature of evil inside me, eating away at my soul.

My father's face flashes into my mind and tears well up before I can even consider holding them back. The loneliness is because I know I'll never see him again, never hear his words of wisdom, his heavy laugh.

Grief's a funny thing. You think you've got it under control, and then it's right there again, creeping up on you when you least expect it. It seems like no one really knows how to grieve, or even if there is a good way to do it. Me, I stayed in bed for a long time, but when I got up, I wrongly assumed I'd left the grief in the bed. Really it followed me like a shadow, waiting for a moment of weakness to pounce.

I wipe away the tears, thinking of how to best distract myself. I consider waking Tawni so I have someone to talk to, but she needs her sleep. My hand absently fumbles through my pack, extracting items and returning them. Then my fingers close on an unfamiliar item: a book. The diary my father gave Tristan, which he gave to me. I'd read maybe twenty pages of it since, and was shocked by the truth of Year One, of what the girl, Anna, had to go through. It's just the distraction I need now.

I flip to the earmarked page and begin from the top of the entry. It reads:

Today the President assigns me to my new family. I don't see the President, but that's what the big soldiers say when they come for me. They say my last name is Nickerbocker now—except I like my old last name just fine. I don't say that though, because no one argues with the soldiers.

The Nickerbockers are all right, I guess. They don't say much, just stare at me and at each other. They explain everything when I move into our new "house," which is made of stone and barely big enough for us all to sleep in. Mr. Nickerbocker—"Call me Dad"—isn't exactly married to Mrs. Nickerbocker. He was assigned to her after we moved underground. His real wife and three kids were left aboveground, so they're probably dead, just like my family. Mrs. Nickerbocker—"Call me Miss Fiona"—wasn't married when she got selected in the Lottery. Neither of them smile much, but then again, neither do I.

I cry today when I think about my real family and how they were left above. My last memory: their faces, cold, harsh, and devoid of emotion. I know they did it to help me be strong, but it only makes it hurt more. Their smiling, happy faces are lost to me. When the tears start falling, my new dad tries to calm me, by telling me stories and singing to me. Miss Fiona tells us both to shut up, which makes me glad I don't have to call her Mom.

Later the Nickerbockers let me go out to play. The streets are crowded, full of kids and adults milling about with zombie faces. Under the dim light of the candles and flashlights everything is an awful, bland shade of gray. A few kids try to get a game of tag going, but no one seems too interested. Me, I can barely will one foot in front of the other. Before I left, my mom told me that time would make the pain go away, but I'm not so sure.

I go back inside without looking at my new parents, who are ignoring each other across the room, staring into space. I huddle under the tiny blanket on my thin bed pad, willing myself to another place, to another time, when bedtime meant a story from my real dad and a tuck-in from my real mom.

My new world vanishes beneath my eyelids and for just a moment before I fall asleep, I smile, the first time all day.

I finish reading Anna's passage and close the book. *Anna.* My mom's name. I still have my mom, my sister. Although the pain of losing my dad continues to ache in my chest, the empty pit of loneliness in my stomach disappears. Anna lost everything: her entire family, all her friends, her way of life. Everyone has struggles, and although mine might be more than most, there are those who have worse things happen to them. Now is not a time to languish in grief while a power-hungry madman destroys our way of life. Now is a time to act.

It's strange to think about how things work out sometimes. Despite all the terrible experiences I've had since leaving the Pen, I'm still alive, still fighting, against some pretty slanted odds. I mean, if Tawni hadn't spoken to me that day, I might still be in the Pen, Cole might still be alive, Tristan might still be just a celebrity in some faraway land…

But instead I'm in that faraway land, fighting for something worth fighting for. Doing my part. Trying to—

"Couldn't sleep?" a voice says from behind me.

I glance back and spot Roc's brown skin, which is even darker with the candlelight as the backdrop. He's grinning slightly, the way he seems to be a lot of the time. He's a good-looking guy—with full, dark hair, serious eyebrows, and three days of black stubble. Tawni could have done much worse, that's for sure.

"No. You?"

Roc shakes his head. "Too many things for this active brain of mine to think about. I can't seem to shut it off."

I laugh. "I know exactly what you mean. Although I think mine's broken sometimes."

It's Roc's turn to laugh. "Hey, do you want to get something to eat?"

"Sure," I say, relieved I'm not the only one awake anymore. Perhaps Roc can save me from my own thoughts.

We shuffle over to the unused fire pit, where a single candle provides a bobbing halo of light, and sit on a right angle to each other. Roc digs through his pack and eventually pulls out a small bundle of paper. I eye the parcel curiously as he unwraps it delicately, like it might shatter into a thousand pieces. Once the paper is peeled away, I get my first look at what's inside.

"What is that?" I ask.

Roc grins. "Dried fruit," he says. "I've been saving the last of it since we left the Sun Realm. I guess now that we're back I don't need to save it anymore, as we can get more of it quite easily now."

I've never had fruit. Occasionally, a shipment of it would come into our subchapter, and all the kids would gather around and watch as those who were able to spare a few Nailins would buy brightly colored fruit they called apples, red and yellow and green. I never asked my father whether we could have any because I already knew the answer.

When I asked Dad how they made fruit in the Sun Realm, he told me they grew it, from trees and bushes and such.

Trees? Like in the books grandma reads me?

Sort of like that, Adele, but these are underground trees. They have technology in the Sun Realm that allows them to grow things underground.

Daddy?

Yes?

I wish we could grow things down here.

Me, too, honey. Me, too.

"Uh, do you want one?" Roc says, snapping me out of the memory. He's staring at me strangely, holding out a piece of dried fruit. I wonder how long he's been holding it like that.

"Yes, of course, thank you," I say, hastily grabbing the crispy morsel from his hand.

"It's not the same as fresh fruit, but it's still delicious," he says, crunching on a piece.

I don't care if it's been dried, kicked around the yard, soaked in water, and then stepped on. I'm barely able to stop from shoving it into my mouth like a half-starved madwoman. Instead, I turn the coin-sized piece of fruit over in my hand, examining it, committing it to memory, for that's all it will be in a moment.

I pop it in my mouth and just hold it there for a moment, allowing the flavor to reach my taste buds. It's sweet, but not overly, with a taste that I can't compare to anything I've ever tasted before. It's…it's…

"Delicious," I say around the hunk of fruit in my mouth, copying Roc's word from earlier. "What kind of fruit is it?"

"You mean you…"

"Nope. Never had it before."

"But don't you get sick? Fruit has all kinds of important vitamins in it," Roc says.

I laugh. "Vitamins? What are those? There's a lot of disease in the Lower Realms, but over time I guess we've just adapted to a diet without fruit. Every household also receives a vitamin ration every six months. It's supposed to be this big benefit for paying taxes, but everyone knows it's just so the men are strong enough to work in the mines."

Roc smiles wryly. "Well, that changes everything. The one you just ate is banana, but I've got apple, apricots, and mango, too. You should have all of it." He pushes the dried fruit toward me, but I put out my hands to stop him.

"No, Roc. We'll share it. Please."

"You don't have to tell me twice," he says, animatedly crunching another piece of what I now know is dried banana.

I laugh. "But save me some," I say.

"Here, try this one. It's different. It's soft. We call it mango."

Eagerly, I snatch the new piece of fruit from Roc, feeling the difference in texture with my fingertips. Whereas the other piece—the banana—was hard and crisp and yellow-brown, this is squishy, sort of gummy, and orange. Mango.

I take a bite. "Mmmm," I murmur when the flavor registers. It's incredible and weird at the same time. The taste is incredibly delicious, but it's also so different than the banana, which is weird. I mean, they're both fruit, right?

"You like that, huh?" Roc says.

"Mm-huh," I say, smacking my lips as I chew the mango.

"Here, have the rest of that one. I prefer the others anyway." This time, I accept the offer, resting the fruit on my crossed legs. For a few minutes we sit in silence, eating dried fruit by candlelight.

Then Roc says, "Isn't it crazy that we're here?"

"What do you mean?" I ask, right away thinking of my thoughts from earlier. It's like Roc read my mind.

He runs a hand through his black hair. "Well, there are so many variables at play, from the timing of events, to the political climate, to what time we wake up each day. It just seems crazy that it all happened the way it did, that we're here, you and Tristan, me and Tawni…"

"Trevor?" I say.

"Sure. Yeah. Him, too. Do you believe in fate?"

His brown eyes are studying me carefully, as if everything hinges on my response to this question. I never realized how serious a guy Roc is. I always thought he was just a jokester, quick-witted and clever with his words. This is a new side to him.

"I don't know," I reply honestly. "I sort of did, but then my mom told me something that made me question everything that has happened."

Cocking his head to the side, Roc says, "What did she tell you?"

Although I had originally planned to keep my mom's revelation to myself, I've now told Tristan, who may or may not remember it, and I'm about to tell his best friend. But everything about Roc feels trustworthy, like he's a guy you could share your darkest secrets with and never lose sleep over it.

"She told me it was no accident that Tristan and I met." My words come out louder than I'd planned, echoing twice off the walls before fading into the night.

"I knew it!" Roc hisses, keeping his voice down.

Huh? It's not the reaction I expected. "What are you talking about? Knew what?" I whisper, leaning my head in.

Returning the remaining dried fruit to his pack, Roc clasps his hands together, his grin wider than ever. He leans toward me, mimicking my movements. "From the beginning I knew something was off," he starts. "Tristan was acting so unlike himself."

"How so?"

"After that first day he saw you, was *near* you, he was so fixated on finding you again, on testing the feelings he felt for you. There was no arguing with him, which is unusual. Normally, he listens to me, listens to reason. Yeah, he hates the Sun Realm, but to pack up and leave it all for some girl—no offense, but it's just not like him."

I frown. So much of what Roc's saying makes sense. I'd had similar thoughts myself. Everything about the way we met—how he left the Sun Realm, how he tracked me down, how he protected me from Rivet—seemed so surreal that I could barely comprehend it. But with no other explanation available, I'd just chalked it up to our powerful connection and coincidence. But maybe I was wrong.

"But what did my mom mean by 'no accident'?" My mind is racing. Did someone force us together somehow? Were we hypnotized or given some strange elixir that altered our judgment? Everything just seems so farfetched.

"Has he told you about the fainting?" Roc asks.

"Yes, but…what does that have to do with anything? Any number of things could have caused him to faint. Hunger, thirst, lack of slee—

"But none of those things caused it. *You* caused it."

It's like I'm incapable of comprehending anything Roc says to me. Each new piece of information is like a shard of glass from a broken window, except no matter how many combinations you try, the splinters refuse to fit back together again.

"But I didn't *do* anything. I wasn't even sure Tristan saw me. And I certainly didn't know he was chasing me—at least not until he defended me from Rivet at the edge of the Lonely

Caverns." And yet...yet something about what Roc is saying makes sense, because it lines up perfectly with my mother's words. There's something else, too.

"The scars," I say. My mind conjures up an image so vivid that it's almost like I'm experiencing it for a second time: Tristan's naked back as we dressed his wounds after the fight with Rivet, his muscles toned and beautiful, his skin spotted with scars; the exhilaration I felt as my fingertips brushed his skin, working to clean him up; the one scar that looked so different than the others, midway up his back, on his spine, unnaturally crescent-shaped. At the time I was curious about the scar, but I chickened out and didn't ask him. Then, when Tawni told me about a scar on my back that I didn't know about—also crescent-shaped and in a similar location—I wished I had.

"What scars?" Roc asks his eyebrows arched.

"Tristan has a scar on his back."

"He has a lot of scars."

"But this one is different. And I think I have the same scar in the same spot," I say.

Roc is silent as he stares at me, processing the information.

Everything is lining up too nicely to just be a coincidence. "It just can't..." I start to say, trailing off.

Roc's watching me carefully. "Can't what?"

"Can't be true," I say lamely, a sinking feeling settling into my gut.

"Because if it *is* true, then that means your feelings for Tristan, and his feelings for you...aren't natural? Is that what you're worried about?"

Roc's perceptiveness once more takes me by surprise. I really didn't know him at all. He's got me figured exactly. Mine and Tristan's "relationship," although slow moving and separated by hundreds of miles of bare rock and tunnels and subchapters at times, has intensified as of late. But if we were brought together by some unnatural force, then we're living a lie. Our relationship is a sham. He's just another guy.

"Yes," I admit.

"You can't think like that," Roc says, and I jerk my chin up from where it's fallen to my chest. "Think of it this way. Different people are brought together in all different ways. It's what you feel once you're brought together that matters, regardless of how you got together in the first place. Does that make sense?"

It does, but our situation is different. "Yes, but what if what we felt for each other once we were together wasn't natural either? What if something was causing those feelings? Then they wouldn't be real, would they?"

Roc opens his mouth to answer. "I don't know," he says, and my head falls once more, because deep down I'd hoped he'd have a better answer, that he'd contradict my line of thinking, come up with some wise alternative.

"What are you guys doing up?" Tristan's voice asks from the side, and a shred of anger at having been interrupted creases my temple, which is totally unfair to Tristan, who's done nothing wrong. But the thought of not being able to finish my conversation with Roc, and having to carry on a normal conversation with Tristan, makes me angry for some reason.

Before I say something I might regret Roc comes to the rescue. "We couldn't sleep," he says.

Rising from his bedroll, Tristan approaches, glancing from my face to Roc's, and then back to mine, his dark blue eyes piercing my soul, and for a second I'm worried my doubts are exposed, running down my face and arms like sweat. But then every fear—every doubt—is replaced by a warm sensation radiating out from my heart and reaching every part of my body. It's the feeling I'd felt earlier when touching Tristan, except this time I'm feeling it just being in his presence. It's not the tingly spine and buzzing scalp—no, those feelings are long gone—but in a way it's better.

"Everything all right?" Tristan asks.

"Yes," I say, my reply a lie and the truth, all at the same time.

Eight
Tristan

Her expression is unreadable, but I feel like I'm intruding on something private.

"What did you say to her?" I say to Roc, an accusation in my tone.

"What? Why do you always think I've done something wrong?" Roc says, throwing up his hands.

"Maybe because you usually have," I say.

"That's an obvious exaggeration," Roc says, smirking.

"What about the time when you stole Killen's boots and blamed it on me?"

"I had forgotten about that. It was pretty clever, wasn't it?" Roc says.

"Or the time you overslept and didn't complete any of your chores so I had to do them all to cover for you?"

"Never happened as far as I'm concerned," Roc says, his eyebrows rising innocently.

"That's because you were sleeping," I say, unable to stop a laugh.

Roc laughs, too, his eyes sparkling in the light. "There are two sides to every story," he says.

I glance at Adele, and I'm surprised that she's not laughing, too, her gaze averted from us, as if she'd rather look anywhere else. Something really is wrong.

"Can't you all keep quiet for a few more hours? I need my beauty sleep," says Trevor, propping himself up on his elbows to look at us.

"You can say that again," Roc says.

"I need my beauty sleep," Trevor mimes. "Didn't you hear me the first time? What time is it anyway?"

"Time to get a watch," Roc says.

"Ha ha. Sorry, we weren't privileged to own such luxuries in the Star Realm," Trevor retorts.

"Good point," I say, glancing at my watch. "It's five in the morning."

"We should try to get a little more sleep," Adele says suddenly. My eyes flick to hers. She's wearing a strange expression. Looking away, she says, "I mean, we can't leave now, right? It's too early."

"She's right," Roc says. "The festivities won't start until at least eight. We'd stick out way too much wandering the streets now."

"Now that I'm up, I don't think I can go back to sleep," Trevor says.

"Me either," I say.

"Want to play a game or something?" Roc jokes.

"Or we could train," Trevor says, narrowing his eyes at me. "If you're game, that is," he adds.

"Sure, why not," I say. "Roc could use a little training."

"After what Trevor did to you earlier, you could, too," Roc says.

"Oh, it's on!" I say. "Adele—you in?"

"Is this really the time for training?" she asks.

"It's *exactly* the time," Trevor says. "If we don't stay loose our muscles will tighten up. Think of it as a bit of stretching."

For the first time since I woke up, the usual gleam returns to her big, green eyes. "Okay. I'm in," she says.

"I'm out," Tawni says, rubbing her eyes as she approaches.

"Good morning," Roc says cheerfully. "It wouldn't be a bad idea for you to learn a few things, Tawni. You need to be able to protect yourself, in case anything happens."

"And you're going to teach her?" I ask.

"That's right," Roc says. "While you three are beating the gravel out of each other, trying to prove your manhood, or whatever it is you're trying to prove, we'll be getting ready for battle."

"I'm most certainly not trying to prove my manhood," Adele says, finally letting a short laugh slip out.

"I should hope not," I say. "Okay. Roc, you give Tawni the basics on this side of the fire pit"—I motion to the right half of the cavern—"and we'll train on the other side."

"Good luck," he says, glancing between me and Trevor, "but honestly, my money's on Adele."

"Thank you, Roc," Adele says, and once more I get the feeling that there's some private *thing* between them that I don't know about. I really hope Roc hasn't told her anything he shouldn't have, like what my father showed me on my fifteenth birthday. How there is a whole city miles above us, on the Earth's surface. I know I need to tell her, need to tell everyone, but not yet. The time just doesn't feel right.

The others are already moving to retrieve their swords, and I watch as Adele picks her thin blade from the ground beside her makeshift bed, leaving the sharp blade covered by her sword guard. She slashes it one way, and then the other, the weapon elegant and controlled in her grasp. The way she moves is mesmerizing and I find myself staring as she parries an invisible attacker and then stabs forward. I hope it's not me she's imagining impaling.

She looks up and frowns when she sees me looking at her. "You ready or what?" she says, no friendliness in her voice. I've never seen her this angry at me. Roc must've said something to her. I'll have to find out later.

"Uh, yeah," I say, grabbing my own sword. I raise it to head level, hold it out from me, close an eye, and gaze down the sword guard. It's not the same as looking down the perfectly flat steel, but I can still tell that the weapon is straight, and without the sword guard would be lethal in the hands of someone who knows how to use it. Like Adele, I take a few practice swings, my arms adjusting to the heavier weight of the protected sword, using the right amount of force to perform each motion.

Off to the side, Roc's showing Tawni how to stand, how to hold the sword. He stands close behind her, gently repositioning her hips and arms with his hands. Although he probably really does want her to learn how to protect herself, clearly he has ulterior motives, too.

"C'mon girls," Trevor says, twirling his sword rapidly above his head. "Come take your medicine."

I ignore the verbal jab and stride into the open area opposite Trevor. Adele follows me, creating the final point of our human triangle. Her eyes never leave mine, and I recognize the look: determination. Like I've seen each time she's headed into a fight. *As long as I beat Trevor*, I think.

I hold my sword in front of me, my eyes darting from Trevor to Adele, and then back to Adele. Always back to Adele. In her dark body-hugging fighting tunic, she's a vision, as beautiful as she is dangerous. With a practiced flick of her hand, she pushes her long, black hair away from her face and behind her head. Then she moves toward me, her strides graceful but strong.

She swings her sword and I move to block, bracing myself for the blow, but it never comes. Instead, she stops mid-swing and whirls on Trevor, closing the distance between them in two springing steps, slashing hard at his right shoulder, her sword leaving an arc of black long after it passes through the air.

Although the attack was swift and surprising, Trevor is up to the challenge, managing to parry and then go on the counter-offensive, pushing Adele back toward me, their swords making dull thuds as they connect with each other. Her back is to me. I've got her.

A surge of adrenaline races through my blood.

Launching off the balls of my feet, I leap toward her, planning to tackle her from behind. Just when we're about to collide, she drops hard to the ground, air rushing against my body as I fly past her. I barge into Trevor, slipping past his outstretched blade and ramming into his stomach. He grunts and stumbles back, taking my full weight on his chest.

I'm no stranger to unusual fighting positions. My mind cycles through the situation in an instant, determining the best course of action: Trevor beneath me, unprotected; Adele nearby, unguarded and within striking distance; me, vulnerable to an attack from my girlfriend, who, for some unknown reason, seems to want nothing more than to beat me senseless with the broad side of her sword. Only one option: get the hell as far away from the kill zone as possible, as fast as possible.

Using the momentum from our fall, I push off hard from Trevor's chest, feeling him squirming beneath me, and duck my head, rolling forward in a somersault. My sword is flailing about, but I manage to tuck it at my side, keeping it from impaling me or my opponents. There's a bone-jarring *thud* as my back slams off the rock floor, sending shivers through my already sore muscles.

Ignoring the pain, I come out of the roll, twisting around to face whoever might be charging. The scene before me is frozen in time, motionless and expressionless. Trevor's on the ground, struggling to get his breath. Adele's standing over him, the dull tip of her protected sword at his neck. It reminds me of an old statue in the National Museum depicting the Sun Realm's crushing defeat of the Lower Realms during the Uprising. The statue shows a sun dweller soldier in a spotless red uniform standing over a gray-coated moon dweller revolutionary, a foot on his chest and a sword through his throat. It even came complete with a gushing stream of crimson blood pooling around them. My father told me that he requisitioned completion of the statue by the finest sun dweller sculptor just after the end of the Uprising, as a reminder of what happens to those who rebel. The blood was his idea, and if he'd had it his way, it would have been real moon dweller blood, but the sculptor informed him that due to the congelation that occurs with air-exposed blood, water with red food coloring would have to suffice. The President grudgingly agreed. According to him, the field trip to the museum was all part of my training. I hated that trip.

For a moment I think time might really be frozen, as Adele stares at me unblinking, but then she smiles. "One down," she says. "You're next."

I grin back, feeling a slight flutter in my chest at the prospect of a one-on-one *anything* with her, even if it's a fight. "Bring it," I reply.

Her smile drops away, replaced by an animalistic snarl. The snarl is directed at me, either for something I've done, or something Roc's told her. I wish I knew what it was.

Stepping off of Trevor, who's still gulping at the air, Adele moves to my left, her steps slow and methodical. Stalking her prey. Me. Although I shouldn't be intimidated because I've been in plenty of fights, I am. Because she's a girl. Because she's my girlfriend.

Faking a confident smile, I follow her movements, striding to the left, as we circle each other. My stomach swirls with a mix of trepidation and elation. Trepidation because I've seen her fight before. Elation because she looks so damn hot when she's like this.

We circle once, twice, then a third time, both of us content to wait patiently for an opening. I playfully stick the tip of my sword out toward her and she slaps it away with her own blade, the sound thumping dully through the cavern. I sense movement to my right: Trevor drags himself away, toward the fire pit, where Roc and Tawni have stopped their own sword practice to watch the fight. No pressure, right?

I stick my sword out again and she smacks it away, twice as hard this time. Her anger radiates from her in waves. What have I done? I consider stopping the fight now, but I know both Trevor and Roc will never let me live it down. Although we all might die anyway, so maybe that's not the worst thing.

To my surprise, Adele sticks her own sword out, grinning slightly. Was the whole angry girlfriend thing all an act? My muscles relax as I relish the thought. Lazily, I swing my sword to knock hers away, an act of humor, but at the last second, she pulls her blade back and whips it two handed at mine, connecting solidly and fiercely, shooting splinters of pain through my fingertips.

Trying to fight off the numbness in my hand, I sling my sword back to the left, barely blocking Adele's next slash attempt. She moves in close, the only thing separating us a bit of air and our locked swords, a gleaming X between us. Adele's piercing green eyes bore into mine, and I feel like dropping my sword and hugging her. She licks her lips as she redoubles her efforts, pushing with all her strength against me. It just makes me want to toss my sword aside and kiss her.

I ignore the urge, and instead, shove her back as hard as I can. Her eyes widen as my larger frame wins the short-term battle, lifting her off her feet slightly as she's thrown back. Lithely, she lands on her feet, almost like the way the palace cats used to jump noiselessly from the china cabinet to the table to the floor.

She moves forward again, waving her sword back and forth in a fury-filled attack. I block to the left, to the right, and back to the left again. She attempts a jab but I swat her sword downward, ringing it off the ground. I try a new strategy: distraction. "Nice moves," I say.

Ignoring my comment, she slashes again but I knock it away. "I can do this all day," I say.

"So can I," she replies. "But I'd rather end it now."

"Good luck with that."

She swings high, forcing me to raise my sword to repel her blade, but before our swords connect, she ducks in low, simultaneously swinging a roundhouse kick at my exposed hand. Shards of pain sweep through my hand and wrist as her thick-soled boot slams into the point where my limb meets the hilt of my weapon. Reflexively, my fingers open up, dropping my sword with a clatter.

Her own weapon in an awkward position, she flings another kick, this one aimed at my head, but I duck and am able to grab her foot with my uninjured hand as it flies by. She bucks her leg, trying to dislodge it, but I know just what to do in this situation.

I throw her leg upward, as hard as I can. The momentum pushes her entire body back and up, her head snapping backward, her leg rotating high over her head. Trying to maintain control, she releases her own sword, using her arms to keep her balance as she performs a perfect back layout, once more landing on her feet. But this time, she's weaponless. We're back to even.

Sweat drips from my forehead to my nose to my chin. A disgusting trail of liquid meanders beneath my tunic, too, flowing down my spine. Suddenly I feel confined and trapped beneath my shirt. I pull it over my head, wipe my face, and toss it aside, immediately relishing the feeling of the air against my sweat-sheened skin.

"Trying to distract me?" Adele says, her lips curling into a smile that sends warmth all the way to my toes.

I laugh. "You could do the same thing and I can guarantee it would work," I say flirtatiously.

"In your dreams," she says, her smile vanishing.

She attacks.

As usual, she leads with a kick, aimed low, somewhere in the vicinity of my knee. Dodging to the side, I whip my own kick at her hip, but it misses when she jumps back.

"Want to just call it a draw and have a reconciliatory hug?" I joke.

"You'd like that, wouldn't you," she retorts, faking a high kick from the left and then sweeping her other leg along the ground from the right.

Jumping her tripping attempt, I lean forward, grabbing her from the front in a bear hug. Using my strength-advantage, I pick her up and force her to the ground, settling my own body firmly on top of hers. A light, airy feeling floods my chest, moves into my throat, and there's a flush of heat in my head. Our bodies have never been closer. She's breathing hard, and I am, too, our warm breath mixing as our lips drift closer, me tilting my head downward and her raising her head slightly. The tingly-warm-airy surge of pre-kiss exhilaration flutters through me just before our lips meet. I close my eyes.

Just as my pouting lips meet hers, she knees me in the abdomen and twists hard to the side. Our faces are still jammed together, but her lips are no longer open to receive mine. Instead, they're a tight determined line, still full and beautiful, but somewhat scary, too. Shoving a forearm against my jaw, she says, "Concede."

I don't care about the victory anymore. I just want to know why she's so angry at me, why she wants to hurt me. What I've done to wrong her. "Not until you kiss me," I say.

"Forget it," she growls. "It wouldn't mean anything anyway."

"Why not?" I say, struggling to breathe as she adds pressure to my windpipe.

"Don't you remember what I said to you before you zonked out just a few hours ago?"

I think hard. We lay down. I felt warm and loved. My vision started to blur as sleep took me. Adele said something, but I thought I was dreaming. What was it?

"I can't remember. I thought it was a dream."

"It wasn't."

"Then tell me," I plead, choking the words out. "I can't read your mind! All I know is I woke up, you were talking to Roc, and now you seem to hate me and I don't know why."

There are wrinkles and pain on her face, and moisture in her eyes. "I told *you* that my mom told *me* that it was *no accident* that we met. Don't you get it? Someone wanted us to find each other. Someone *did something* to make us want each other. Everything's been a lie from the very beginning."

What? No, I don't get it. How could I? None of this makes any sense. But before I can ask her anything, she pushes off me and stalks away, leaving both my body and mind in pieces on the ground.

Nine
Adele

I glance at Roc as I pass. His wise brown eyes are unreadable, his lips a thin line. I don't look at Tawni or Trevor. Yeah, training could have gone better, but seriously, how was I supposed to train with what I have on my mind? It's like asking a miner to dig a hole with a loose boulder hanging above his head. Kind of hard to concentrate.

The bad thing about caves: there's nowhere to go when you want to get away. I stomp to the other side of the cave, slip through the thin crack in the wall, and march into the shipping tunnel. Probably not the wisest thing to do given what we did to a bunch of sun dweller soldiers at the other end of the tunnel, but I need to cool off, and I can't do that with my friends watching me.

Argh! I silently scream. How could I be so stupid? Did I really think that the son of the President of the Tri-Realms would be interested in me? His veins were probably full of some kind of love potion, mixed up by a mad scientist with an agenda and a proficiency for creating potent elixirs. But the thing is: I fell for Tristan, too, which was so unlike me. So maybe I'd been slipped a bit of the potion, forcing us together in the unlikeliest of pairings. The buzzing in my scalp and spine every time I was near Tristan was just a side effect of the drug, a neurological response to a catalyst. Nothing more. Not a connection, that's for sure. When the buzzing and tingling stopped, perhaps the drug had worn off. We kidded ourselves into thinking that we still had feelings for each other, but really it was over the moment we peed or sweated or spat the last of the toxins from our bodies.

Could it really be a drug? My mind doesn't even believe my own reasoning. It seems too farfetched, too sci-fi, too *ridiculous*.

Something my father once said to me pops into my head:

Sometimes the hardest things to believe are the ones that are the most true.

But sometimes they aren't, too. Right?

Behind me there's a scrape of cloth on rock and the scuffle of feet on hard ground. I didn't even realize I stopped, but now I'm acutely aware that I only made it ten or so feet from the entrance to our hideaway before pulling up to puzzle over things in my head.

I stride in the other direction, hearing Tristan say, "Adele, wait!" behind me. Breaking into a run, I wish with all my heart that he'll just let me be, leave me alone for however long it takes me to come to terms with what's slowly dawning on me: we're not meant to be together.

He doesn't.

Instead, he races after me, his heavier, louder footfalls drowning out my own. I know he'll catch me because he's faster, but I don't stop until his hand grabs my shoulder from behind.

I whirl on him, fire in my chest and eyes. "What!?" I scream, much louder than I should, given where we are.

"Please, Adele. We need to talk," Tristan says, his face a mixture of white concern and red exertion. He's still bare-chested, his muscles tight from our fight. I try not to stare at them. "Please," he repeats.

Looking at his pitiful face, I can't hold onto my anger, although I definitely try. He's just so damn handsome, his wavy blond hair an inch from his evening-blue eyes, his lips red and full and a perfect match for his right-sized nose and strong jaw. And his voice is so full of longing that my mind draws a blank when I try to come up with a sarcastic comment.

With my ebbing anger, my shoulders sag and my knees weaken. The adrenaline from our harried sprint catches up with me, and it's all I can do to lower myself slowly to the ground, lean back against the wall and hug my knees.

"I really don't want to talk right now," I say honestly.

Tristan dips down next to me, looks at me even though I refuse to look at him. Puts an arm around my shoulders, and although I feel like I should, I don't shake it off. Swarms of bats flap unbridled through my stomach. Right away, I feel bad about all the things I've said to him. It's not his fault we got played, like life-size pawns in some real chess match. He's been nothing but good to me, even if he wasn't entirely in control of his actions.

"Adele, I—I..."

I'm scared of his next words, scared they'll make everything even worse, even harder.

"I just want to understand," he says, and I let out a grateful breath. He deserves to understand. "Did Roc tell you something that you might have misunderstood? If he told you about what happened when I was fifteen, I swear I was going to tell you—"

"No. He didn't say anything about that. What happened when you were fifteen? That was the year your mom disappeared, right?"

Tristan sighs, pulls my head into his chest, which I allow because I have no fight left in me. And because it's pretty awesome to be close to him again, to his heart, which is beating against my cheek. "Yes, that was when my mom left us. I just don't think it's the right time to talk about it."

I pull back from him, anger surging through me once more. "When will be the right time?" I say, raising my voice. "Because you always seem like you want to tell me something important, something that might bring us closer, but then you never do."

Tristan hangs his head and I feel bad again. He's been so calm and patient with me, and I'm throwing a tantrum. "Look, I—I just want to know you better," I say.

He shoots me a troubled stare. "That's kind of hard to do when you're acting like you don't want to be with me anymore."

Good point. "It's not that I don't want to be with you, it's just that something brought us together, and I don't know how much of it was real and how much wasn't. Every time I think that someone's been messing with my life, I get so angry."

"*Our* lives," Tristan says, and I tilt my head to the side in confusion. "You said 'my life,' but it's both of our lives that are being messed with," he explains.

"I know, Tristan, it's not your fault, but when I fell for you so hard—I mean, you're the first person I've really ever liked like this—I really wasn't prepared for it." My voice is shaking as my emotions spiral out of control, and I worry the tears might start falling soon. I pause, take a deep breath, try to get control, wait for Tristan to reply.

"What did Roc think?" Tristan asks, making me glance up at him.

"Roc?"

"Yeah, you talked to him about it, didn't you? That's why you were so weird when I interrupted your conversation. Roc's usually right about things. I don't know how and sometimes I hate to admit it, but he has really good instincts. I trust his opinion."

"Well, after discussing all the facts, he thinks it's possible our relationship is a sham," I say bluntly.

"He said that, did he?" Tristan says, his lips curling into a one-dimpled smile that takes my breath away. "'Sham' just isn't a word I would expect him to use."

I find myself smiling back, taking yet another strange twist on the endless emotional miner's cart ride I seem to always find myself on. "Okay, maybe not *sham*, but definitely *fraud*."

"Mm-huh," Tristan murmurs, not trying to hide his disbelief.

"Okay, okay. Technically he didn't say that either. He just said 'I don't know.'"

Tristan grins again. "That alone is enough to scare me," he says. "Roc usually always has an opinion."

"So now you're worried too?" I raise an eyebrow.

"Nope. Because I trust my feelings for you. They're as strong as they've ever been. When I'm near you, when I touch you, when I just think about you, I just feel good. That's enough truth for me." Tristan's cheeky grin is gone, replaced by big earnest eyes and a serious mouth.

The desire to kiss him wells up like hot lava bubbling from a crevasse, and I can't stop from leaning into him and doing just that, crushing my lips to his. His hand burrows into the hair on the back of my head, running through it to my scalp. He leans back, pulling me on top of him as we move our lips back and forth and up and down hungrily. My want—my need!—to be close to him is so strong that I'm losing control of myself, running my hands along his bare chest and sides, feeling his hard muscles tighten and contract as we enjoy each other. Our tongues find each other's, moving across and around. Before Tristan, I'd never kissed a guy. And before now, I'd never kissed Tristan *like this*. It feels amazing and I want it to go on forever, but then Tristan laughs mid-kiss.

"What?" I say, frowning and staring down at him, while he continues laughing to himself, as if at some inside joke. "Am I doing it wrong?" I ask, suddenly concerned that in my zealousness I've made some grievous kissing mistake due to my naivety.

"No, no, sorry," Tristan says, still cracking up. "Trust me, you're doing *everything* right."

My concern dissipates and I look at him curiously. "Then why the laughter?"

"Because as we were making out I had a funny thought."

"You mean you weren't thinking solely of me while we kissed?" I joke, punching him lightly in the stomach.

"Oh, I most certainly was. The funny thought was about you," he says, laughing again.

Oh great, so I'm some big joke. "Would you mind sharing with the group?" I say, wanting to know what it is about me that's so freakin' funny.

"I was just thinking that a few minutes ago you seemed ready to kill me—literally—and now you're all over me. It just made me laugh."

My face flushes because he's right. I've been acting ridiculous, like I'm made up of nothing but mind-controlling emotions and crazy hormones. Not my usual, logical self, willing to discuss the facts, and figure out a solution to a problem. "I'm sorry," I say.

"You already said that," Tristan says. "But please tell me that we're okay."

Like Roc, I really don't know. "I can't," I say. "Look, Tristan, I still have feelings for you, but how do I know that it's not just someone controlling me?"

"Your mom said it was no accident that we met, right?" I nod. "That could mean anything. And she might not even have all the facts straight."

"But there are other signs," I argue. "You yourself said that you noticed a change when we were near each other. You didn't feel the same pull that you did before."

"No, that's not right. I *still* feel a pull toward you, an attraction. It's just different, more natural. Are you saying you're not attracted to me anymore?" His lips are so close to mine I could reach them just by inching forward a little.

"Obviously, I am," I say, kissing the dimple in his cheek. "What about your fainting?" I say, raising a finger in the air.

"In the past," he says, shaking his head. "I haven't felt that way in a long time, plus it has no bearing on how I feel right now."

"And how is that?" I ask, flirtatiously running a finger from his shoulder to his chest.

"Like I'm in lust with you," he says, cracking up again.

"Jerk," I say, slapping him playfully on the cheek.

"You asked."

An image of Tristan's scar pops into my head. I have to tell him. "You have a scar," I say.

"Umm...what?"

"You have a scar on your back—I saw it when we bandaged your wounds after the fight with Rivet."

"I have lots of scars, so what?"

"But this one is different. It's crescent-shaped, but that's not the interesting thing..." My heart is pounding as I know this is the truth we've been missing, a clue to how a moon dweller girl and a sun dweller guy happened to be brought together at the most critical of times for the Tri-Realms.

"What, Adele?" Tristan says, rubbing my back softly.

"I have the same scar, in the same place."

I expect Tristan to say I'm acting crazy again, that he has a lot of scars from years of training, that any resemblance between our scars is merely coincidence. But he doesn't say any of that. "Show me," he says.

Ten

Tristan

She turns away from me, sliding in between my legs. As she lifts the back of her shirt, I feel a certain lightness, a thrill, as if I'm discovering something new about Adele. Which I am, I suppose. Her pale skin is marked by circles of dark bruising, fresh, likely from when I tackled her to the hard ground during our fight. Despite the imperfections, her back is smooth and beautiful to me. When she gets partway up, she can't lift the fabric any further herself, so I take over, gently tugging the thick battle tunic up toward her neck.

A little past halfway I see it. A small scar, slightly raised, crescent-shaped. As the tips of my fingers graze over it, Adele shivers beneath me. "Where'd you get this?" I ask.

"I don't know," she says. "I wasn't even aware of it until Tawni noticed it. She thought it resembled a scar on your back, but we both sort of forgot about it. Where exactly is it positioned?"

I run my hand along her vertebrae. "It's on your spine. Maybe…three quarters of the way up."

"That sounds like exactly where yours is," she says. "Let me see."

Dropping her tunic so it drifts back over her skin, I scoot back and rotate around to face away from her. Her knees are at either side of my hips as she kneels behind me. When her fingers graze my skin, sparks practically fly off of them. I could do this all day.

"Do you feel where my fingers are?" she asks.

"Umm, yeah. I feel them," I say, holding back the extent of what I'm feeling.

"That's where your scar is. It's a curved sliver, a raised bump, just like you described mine."

"It feels like it's in almost the exact same place as yours is," I note.

"It is."

We sit in silence for a moment, her finger drifting back and forth across my spine. I don't want to ruin the moment, but I know I have to. "What do you think it means?" I ask.

"Someone did something to us," Adele says angrily. "Injected a drug, messed with our spines, something. Somehow what they did linked us together, like as soon as we were near each other, we were inexplicably drawn to each other. That's what the weird scalp-buzzing and spine-tingling was."

Not this again. "I don't care," I say. "I'm glad I found you, no matter how it happened. And now the effect seems to have worn off and I *still* want to be with you, regardless of who wants us to be together."

Adele's sigh tickles the tiny hairs on the back of my neck. "It might not be that simple, Tristan. I want to be with you, but what if it's your father who wants us to be together, to give him a reason to crush you? Maybe he sensed your rebelliousness and knew you'd cause him problems in the future. A scandalous moon dweller girlfriend would do just the trick. I mean, that's possible, isn't it?"

I think about it for a minute. "Anything's possible with my father," I say. "And I didn't exactly hide my rebellious side, so it's likely he thinks Killen should succeed him as president, as he would carry on the Nailin family tradition of rule by an iron fist."

"And the only way to do that…" Adele says, letting me finish her sentence.

"Is to either kill me or throw me in jail. But you don't know my father the way I do. He murdered Roc's mother in cold blood, Adele. He didn't need an excuse to hurt me. He could've just had one of his men "accidentally" kill me in training, or even kill me in my sleep and then make up a story about how it happened later. But mess with our neurological systems, draw me to a moon dweller girl just to create a scandal? It's just not my father's style—too complex and risky."

"But it's possible," Adele says, hugging me from behind.

I shake my head. "No, I don't think so. I mean, he could have easily done something to me, but how would he have gotten to you?"

"I was trapped in juvie," she says. "He could have had one of the guards put something in my food, in my drink, something…"

"But your mom seems to know something about it," I argue. "Otherwise why would she have said that to you—about it being no accident we met?"

Her head slumps and I realize she was hoping for any other explanation other than her mother being involved directly.

I capture her hands across my chest. "Don't worry, we'll figure it out," I say. Feeling her body against my back, her arms around me, I close my eyes and let the cares of the world fall away beneath her gentle touch. "Do you still want to be with me?" I ask.

A pause. I hold my breath, wait for the hammer to drop, crushing my heart into gravel. "Yes," she says, and I let out my breath slowly, trying to hide the fact that I was holding it at all. "But I also don't want to cost you the presidency."

"It's already lost," I say, knowing it's the truth. "All that's left is vengeance."

"We should go back," Adele says, abruptly releasing me and standing. "It's too dangerous out here and the others will wonder where we've run off to."

I clamber to my feet and then face her, sweeping my eyes across every inch of her majestic form. She watches me suspiciously. "What," she says when my eyes return to hers.

"You're beautiful," I say.

"And you're such a guy," she retorts. "C'mon." She grabs my hand and pulls me back down the tunnel. For me, despite

113

scars and conspiracies and vengeance, the world is right again. If I die today, at least I'll die with Adele by my side.

But I don't plan to die.

* * *

Every few minutes I feel Roc's eyes on me, but I studiously avoid them, pretending to organize my pack or clean my weapons. I know he wants to talk, to ask me a million questions, but I'd rather not. It'll only dampen my relatively good mood.

Trevor continues to annoy, however, shooting comments like, "Ooh, the two lovebirds are back together?" or "You two make such a cute couple—when you're not trying to kill each other." Adele finally gives him a death stare and he backs off, his hands in the air, palms out. "Easy, wild woman," he says, "I'm just kidding." Since then, I've just had to deal with Roc's silent stares.

"We're going to pee," Tawni says, grabbing Adele's hand and pulling her away.

"But I don't have—" Adele starts to say.

"Yes you do," Tawni says. Adele glances back at me, a shrug in her eyes, if not on her shoulders.

I'm alone and unprotected. Roc saunters over. "What's going on?" he asks, and I see Trevor stop rolling his bedding to watch our exchange.

"Nothing," I say. "All good."

"It wasn't *all good* when Adele beat you up and yelled at you in front of everyone," he says.

"She did not beat me u—"

"Yes she did," Trevor comments from across the fire pit.

114

"Like you did any better," I retort. The nice, peaceful feeling from making up with Adele is gone, and there's a fire in my belly once more.

"We're talking about you," Trevor says.

"Shut up, Trevor," Roc says. And then: "Talk to me, T, I'm worried about you."

"I'm fine, I promise," I say. "We're fine."

"But what about—"

"We've worked it out, Roc. We're moving on—you should too." My eyes challenge him to say another word, which usually doesn't even come close to working, but this time it does. Roc clams up, fires a final glare at me, and then goes back to packing for our trek across the Sun Realm.

Adele and Tawni take a long time "using the bathroom." Trevor occupies himself by swinging his sword around like he's fighting hordes of angry sun dwellers, while Roc sits facing the wall, just staring. He's mad at me because I'm keeping things from him. He'll get over it. I unpack and repack my bag a half-dozen times before the sound of approaching footsteps echoes through the cavern.

They appear through the murk, walking side by side, Tawni wearing a slight grin and Adele sporting a wry smile. From the look Adele shoots me I know: Tawni is completely up to date on the situation.

Roc turns, looks at Tawni, and realizes the same thing. He directs another glare at me, one that says, "See, Adele told Tawni. Why won't you tell me? You're supposed to be my best friend."

"Sorry, buddy," I try to relay to him telepathically, "There's nothing to tell." Clearly he doesn't get the message as his eyes narrow further, until they're thin slits of annoyance.

"Are we *finally* ready to go?" Trevor says, slipping his sword back into its loop. "I think there's been enough drama for one morning."

"Yeah," I say, agreeing on both counts, "let's go."

We shoulder our packs and file out of the hidden cavern, me in front, then Roc, Trevor, Tawni, and Adele. I pause at the narrow entrance to the shipping tunnel, being far more cautious than the last time I barreled from under cover. I don't hear anything from either direction, so I step out, flicking my flashlight around me. Only gray, barren rock stares back at me. When I shine the beam on the ceiling, a dozen gray bats gaze back through closed eyelids, sleeping upside down in the dark.

"Either they haven't figured us out, or they haven't caught up yet," I note as the others step into the clear.

"Or they're setting a trap for us," Roc says skeptically.

"We'll be careful," I say, avoiding Roc's eyes.

Flush with the wall, I move onwards, pausing every twenty steps, counting each one as if our lives depend on it. After three such segments, I turn and say, "Trevor, how far did you say it was?"

"We just started, man. I don't know, a couple miles. Take off your women's underwear and set a decent pace."

Biting back a comeback, I turn and set off faster, still stopping occasionally, but much less frequently. Each time I do, I hear the soft tread of the others as they catch up, and then only silence when they stop. A mile passes without event.

Five minutes into the second mile, there's an unexpected sound. I freeze in mid-step and then am bucked forward when Roc crashes into the back of me. "Oh, sorry," he says.

"Shhhh!" I hiss back, cupping a hand around my ear.

Roc tilts his head—and we both hear it: *Thump, thump, thump!*

The beat of a drum, or the rumbling tire treads of a tank; it could feasibly be either one.

Trevor and the girls catch up, and Tawni says, "What is that?"

"Sounds like a cannon," Trevor notes.

"No," Roc says, "it's a bass drum. The party has started."

Nodding, I say, "I agree. Have you ever heard sun dweller music?"

"Of course. We're not aliens," Trevor says.

"Yes," Adele says, directing a frown at Trevor, "it's the only kind of music to listen to. It's usually loud and fast."

"Have you ever heard it live?" I ask.

"How could we, sun boy?" Trevor says. "It's not like sun dweller bands go on tour through the Lower Realms. We're lucky if we get it on the radio."

I ignore him. "Well, you're about to get a heavy dose."

For the next few minutes there's only the *thump, thump, thump* of the bass as it echoes through the tunnel like a war gong. Soon, however, there are other sounds: the high-pitched squeal of an electric guitar, the metallic clangs of someone bashing a full drum set, a shrieking voice belting out lyrics to some manic song.

"The Sun Rockers," Roc says from behind me. "Four number one hits and a dozen other top ten songs. Been around for maybe five years."

"Thank you, Professor Trivia," Trevor says. "I've heard of them."

I can't help the smile that sneaks across my lips. Although Trevor can be a royal star dweller pain in the arse sometimes, he's also quite funny. Somehow I like him a lot more now that he got beat up by Adele. Not that I'm surprised. If we'd been able to finish our training fight, I might have been in the same position as Trevor—defeated.

"Are you sure we should be heading toward the sound?" Tawni asks.

Glancing back, I start to reply, but Adele beats me to it. "Our only chance is to try to blend into the Sun Realm, become a part of the festivities, just five more faces in the crowd."

"Oh," Tawni says, looking unconvinced.

As we continue forward, the music reaches a fever pitch, shrieking through the tunnel and into our eardrums. Then, suddenly, it stops. I raise a hand, drawing our group to a halt.

"That's the end of the song," Roc says. Glancing at Trevor, he says, "And for the trivia buffs out there, The Sun Rockers are known for fast starts and stops to their songs."

Trevor grins at the joke. Perhaps he's starting to like us a bit more, too.

As Roc predicted, the music roars to life once more, as the band goes from silence to teeth-chattering noise in about two seconds flat. It's right on top of us, like we're part of the band. We must be very close. Ahead of us the tunnel curves to the left, so I tiptoe across the path, positioning my back against the opposite wall, and then shimmy around the bend. I don't look to see if the others are following, just keep my eyes forward, my wits on high alert, and my senses trained on the direction of the sound.

When I reach the final section of the bend, I peek around the bulge of rock, feeling more than hearing the rush of the music smash into me, sending vibrations through my bones and naturally speeding up my heart.

Game time.

Before me stands a large break in the tunnel wall, as it curves back to the right, large enough for a full sized truck to drive through with room to spare on either side. Beyond the break: chaos.

Lights are flashing, bodies are moving, people are screaming and cheering, and, of course, music is blaring. I can't see the band—just the press of bodies, as reveling sun dwellers try to push closer to the action.

When I swivel back the others are looking at me, question marks in their eyes. "Well?" Trevor says.

"We're here," I reply.

"What's the plan?" Adele says, and I realize how stupid it is that we haven't really talked about what to do once we reached the next Sun Realm subchapter. I guess we were too busy talking about other things.

"Stay close to Roc and me. Keep your weapons tucked beneath your tunics. Act like the other sun dwellers. There will be a lot of people wearing strange things, so we probably won't stick out too much, except for Adele and I, whose faces have been plastered all over the place for weeks. We should all keep our heads down as much as possible just in case. However, if someone does try to stop us, or raises an alarm, follow me and run like hell. Our only hope will be to get the crowd between us and our pursuers. Any questions?"

"How do other sun dwellers act?" Tawni asks, and I realize just how strange this place is for the others. Probably similar to how strange the Moon and Star Realms are for me.

Roc answers. "Like crazy people, basically. Full of energy, dancing, hollering, carrying on. You'll catch on quick enough. Just remember, the crazier you act, the *less* you'll stand out. It's essentially the opposite of what you're used to."

"Great," Adele says sarcastically. "We'll just unlearn everything we've been taught and we'll be good to go."

"Exactly," I say. "Anything else?" Adele is smirking, Tawni's wide-eyed, Trevor's practically dancing already, and Roc's expressionless. "Okay then, let's do it."

I turn.

The moment I step out from behind the bend, a group of sun dwellers stumble into the tunnel, their eyes locking on me before I can duck back into hiding.

Eleven
Adele

We come around the bend to find Tristan frozen in place, just staring forward. *What the hell?* I follow his gaze to the next curve in the tunnel, where six silhouettes are highlighted against a bright and churning backdrop into a sun dweller city. The silhouettes are moving, sort of chaotically, holding each other up as they stagger toward us.

As they approach, my fists reflexively clench at my sides, preparing for physical confrontation. My heart rate picks up just a notch.

"Heyyy! Who goesh there?" one of them slurs, as they move into the light from our flashlights. A guy, young, perhaps twenty, clearly drunk. His hair's unnaturally black and spiky, speckled with something that glitters like diamonds in the light. He's flanked by two girls and two guys, each with their arms around each other. One of the girls is blond, her hair long enough to reach her waist and streaked with locks of blue and pink and green, some braided, some not. Dark mascara rims her eyes, running slightly from her alcohol-affected blue eyes. The other female is a brunette with a buzz cut, although most of her head is hidden beneath a wildly tall black top hat, stuck with at least ten multi-colored feathers. They're both wearing tight mini-tunics that show off their toned and tan legs, which seem to go on for a mile before reaching their strange shoes with a thin spike in the back, which they wear without socks. Scooping U-necks show the entire world just how mature they are. They're beautiful women by any standards, but their clothes just make them look desperate, trashy. The other two guys are as pretty as the women, with high cheekbones and tan faces. They're tall and muscular, their biceps and shoulders exposed in their tank-tunics. Right away, one of them eyes Tawni, looking her up and down, while the other traces my curves with his stare.

It makes me want to kick them where the artificial Sun Realm sun don't shine.

"Heyyy," the center guy says again, raising a blue bottle. I notice they are all holding bottles, the girls' pink, the guys' blue. Then, speaking slowly, he says, "What are you all doingsh here?"

I wait for Tristan or Roc to reply. After all, this is their world. Instead, they're silent. I glance from Tristan to Roc, and can almost feel the angry heat coming off of them. Evidently the way the guys were looking at Tawni and me pissed them off. I'm glad, but this isn't the time for chivalry. Our position is precarious to say the least.

"We heard the best party is in this subchapter," Trevor says, surprising us all.

The guys laugh and the girls titter, as if Trevor just made the funniest joke in the world. "Yoush got that right," the spokesman says. "We were jusht about to havsh our own party. Wanna come?"

If the party involves slapping the drunken smiles off their faces, I'm in.

"Thanks anyway, man," Tristan says, finally snapping out of his temper-induced haze. "We want to hear the band."

"Are you sure, honey?" the blonde says to him. "We can make our own music." Her flirting tone makes me dig my nails into my hands. Now I know how Tristan felt when the guy was undressing me with his eyes.

"Yes, but thank you all for the very kind offer," Tristan says, using his most diplomatic voice.

"Hey, where'd yoush get those digs, anyway?" the guy asks, sweeping a hand across us, motioning to our battle outfits.

"It's a new style coming out of subchapter one," Roc says, lying easily. "I heard they'll be selling them in every subchapter soon."

"I gotsh to getsh me some of those."

"You should," Tristan says. "Well, we'll see you all later. Have fun." His voice is awkward and stiff, but the partygoers don't seem to notice.

As we pass by them the blonde touches Tristan's arm. "You look just as handsome as Tristan Nailin," she says. "What'd you say your name was?"

Tristan goes beet red, but I know it's not from the compliment. I've noticed he always seems uncomfortable with lying. I hold my breath, hoping he can overcome it now.

"I, uh, my name is..." Not looking good.

"Trevor," he says finally, his face returning to its natural color as a smile crosses his face.

"All right, Trevor. I most certainly hope we see *you* later," she sings. Ugh. If we weren't about to get past them without a fight, I would relish knocking the bleach out of her hair and the fake tan off her skin. If only.

As if by some unspoken agreement, the five of us walk with our heads forward, forcing ourselves not to look back, which might appear suspicious. Just when we're approaching the entrance to the subchapter and I think we're home free, the guy yells behind us. "Hey!" We freeze, turn slowly, look at him. The alcohol has worn off, I think. He's going to realize we don't belong, recognize Tristan or one of us from the news, sound the alarm, give chase.

"I highly recommend the crowd-surfing," he says instead. I smile, an easy smile that comes from a narrow, heart-pounding escape. I speak for the first time. "Thanks for the tip. We'll do that," I say.

My head's spinning before we even slip through the entrance to the city. Our close encounter with the partiers, the pulse of the music slamming around in my head, the thrill of being thrust into the midst of the biggest celebration in the Tri-Realms: it all adds up to a muddled brain.

When we trot into the subchapter, all battle-clad and full of adrenaline, my jaw drops to the floor. A brilliant, yellow orb hangs high above the city, shooting shockingly bright light across everything beneath it. I try to look at the ball of light, but am instantly blinded, forcing me to use a hand as a visor. *An artificial sun.* Nothing could have prepared me for it. Compared to the dim, overhead lights of the Moon Realm, this subchapter is lighted as if by a thousand fires, and yet all that brightness comes from one big ball hanging from the cavern roof. After a few seconds the spots and stars clouding my vision dissipate, and I take in the rest of the scene before me, continuing to use a hand to shield my eyes from the artificial sunlight.

Although the other sun dweller city we passed through was beautiful and incredible—far surpassing anything I'd ever seen—it was empty of humans, the population getting a good night's sleep before a day of fun and celebration. But this…this is just plain nuts.

The streets are wide and long and straight, jammed with thousands of people wearing the most colorful outfits I've ever seen. They're moving their bodies in what I assume is meant to be dancing, but is more like convulsing, their hips gyrating to the beat while their arms flow over each other like waves. On top of the crowds are dozens of people doing what I'm pretty sure the drunk guy was referring to before: crowd-surfing. Hundreds of hands pass the bodies across the crowds, roaring with delight.

Everyone seems to have a drink of some sort in their hands. Some of them are blue and pink bottles like we saw before, while others hold crystalline mugs and conical glasses full of liquid of varying colors. Somehow most of them manage not to spill their drinks while they move like maniacs. I assume it must come from lots of practice.

The band, The Sun Rockers, is dead ahead, on a raised stage in the middle of the road. They're wearing bright red, plastickylooking outfits with pointed shoulders and knees. The lead singer's black hair is sculpted into a red-tipped Mohawk. He's clutching the microphone like a rope, using both hands, while he wails a melody about how he's "gonna hit the party hard."

"C'mon!" Tristan hisses, and I realize I've stopped and am just staring out at the crowd, while the others are moving down a ramp and into the fray.

"Act like the other sun dwellers," I mumble to myself, recalling Tristan's advice.

Jogging slightly, I catch up to the others, pushing in close to them as we form a little pod which we can hopefully use to push through the crowds. Tristan leads the way, slipping between the bodies, unafraid to bump and jostle his way through. I cling to Tawni's back, while she clings to Roc, instantly feeling claustrophobic. Despite living underground my entire life, and having endured many tight crawlspaces and tunnels, this is far worse. Sweaty, churning bodies. Hands all over the place, unabashedly groping at me in all the wrong places. Cheering and screaming so loud I'm starting to worry I might lose a portion of my long-term hearing. I wasn't prepared for this at all.

Hang on to Tawni. Just hang on. You'll get through this just like everything else.

I can tell Tawni's feeling the same way, unable to mask her horror as a tall, muscly, shirtless guy smacks her on the butt as she passes by.

"Just go to another place, Tawni," I say, squeezing one of her shoulders. She glances back, manages a nod.

At first we're able to make steady progress through the herds of sun dwellers. There are a lot of strange and interesting people. A girl with pink hair tied into tight little braids. A guy wearing just his undergarments, both on his head and in the more normal pelvic area. Three guys who look identical, wearing more makeup on their faces than many of the highly makeupped women. The men really are as pretty as the women. Many of the men have long hair, lustrous and silky and full of glitter and colorful hair ties. Most of their ears are pierced, adorned with diamond studs or shiny, gold hoops. Some of them wear dark eyeliner and lipstick.

Definitely not like the Moon Realm.

Tristan's head bobs and bounces as he fights through the crowd, hopefully taking us in the right direction to eventually give us some breathing room. He's heading straight for the raised stage, and as we get closer the way forward gets more difficult, as the bodies mash even closer together, almost no space between anybody. With our movements slower, it gives me the chance to watch the reactions of people as we pass by. Right away I realize that Tristan is our biggest problem. He seems to know it, keeping his head tilted down and a raised hand over his face, but it still doesn't stop some people from recognizing him, just like his tramp-admirer in the caves thought he looked like the son of the President. Heads turn as guys and girls alike stare after him, not sure if they were mistaken at having just seen the heir to the presidency. A few of them even say things like, "Whoa! Wasn't that Tristan Nailin?" or "Dude, did you just see who I did?"

Not good.

Eventually someone will act on what they see and chase after him, trying to get an autograph, a touch, a kiss, or maybe all three. I decide to take a chance. The only good thing is that they're less likely to recognize me with him marching along in front.

Just as we push past a row of dancing bodies with their backs to us, I grab one of their hats right off their head. The reveler, too busy grinding up against other nearby bodies, doesn't even notice. The hat's got a huge brim that can cover a whole face, is littered with metallic stars and hearts and other bobbles, and has a bright blue bow around the dome top. Other than clearly being made for a woman, it's perfect. Tristan will just have to deal with it.

I pass it forward to Tawni. "Pass this up to Tristan," I say.

She gives me a look that says, "You're crazy," far better than any words could, but sends it forward to Roc anyway, relaying the message. Roc hands it to Trevor, who hands it to Tristan. He looks at it like it's a rare disease, holding it away from him, and for a minute I'm scared he'll just toss it away, but then he sort of shrugs and plops it on his head, using a hand to pull the wide brim over his face. *Yes!* I think.

Our progress, which has been like walking through mud, abruptly grinds to a halt. We're about twenty feet from the stage, and I can clearly see the band now. The lead singer is running around now, not even bothering to sing, like he's on drugs. "I can't go any further!" Tristan yells back. "We'll have to go another way."

I cringe. The thought of going around or back or any way that keeps us in the press of the crowd any longer is too unbearable. I look past Tristan, my eyes naturally zeroing in on the maniac singer, who suddenly throws his microphone to the stage and leaps off, landing on a bed of hands, which draws even more screams from the audience. That's when it hits me.

Why go through when we can go over?

Little did I know at the time, but the drunk guy had given us the best suggestion of all. The singer is passed around, moving rapidly across the sea of helpers. It's certainly a far faster way to travel than our current method.

"Tristan, up!" I yell above the noise, letting go of Tawni's shoulders with both hands for the first time, so I can motion up.

"Too risky," he yells, which draws a few strange stares from nearby frolickers.

"Not more than it already is," I say. "Quick and fast. We can run at the end if we have to."

We're getting more and more looks, but it's not because of our exchange. It's because my hands are still in the air, raised to the roof. Apparently it's the universal sign for crowd-surfing.

"Need help up?" a big guy says, lowering his hands to the ground, like a step.

"Thanks," I say, not waiting for approval from Tristan. They're just going to have to follow my lead this time. I step into the guy's cupped hands, and then the world spins as I'm thrown into the air.

I'm off balance and out of control, but when I come back down, I land much more softly than I expected. The feeling is new and weird and kind of cool at the same time, as hundreds of tiny little fingers and palms touch me all along my legs, arms and back. It's almost like floating while getting a newfangled type of massage at the same time. I check that my assortment of weapons is still tucked safely beneath my clothes and in their sheaths. They are, although even if they weren't, the intoxicated partiers would probably just think they were fakes and part of our costumes—just another sun dweller fashion statement. The only thing I didn't think about:

How to steer.

I'm already heading in the wrong direction, away from the stage, back toward the entrance to the shipping tunnel. Where are the brakes on this thing?

Not sure what to do, I yell as loud as I can, "To the stage!"

To my complete and utter shock, the people beneath me shriek with delight, instantly changing my direction. Although I'm heading right for the band now, which is where Tristan wanted to go for some reason—I have no idea why.

I look around me, trying to find one of my friends' faces, but there are only strangers with funny hats, strange piercings, and dyed hair. Then I spy it: the hat I stole for Tristan, its blue-bowed dome top rising above the crowd. I'm going to drift right past it.

At that moment, Tawni is flung up and above the crowd, her white hair magnificent under the artificial sun, the blue streak down one side almost making her fit in with the rest of the sun dwellers. The look on her face is somewhere between giddy and frightened, a half-smile that never quite makes it to her eyes.

As I coast up next to her, I say, "Headed my way?"

Her head jerks in my direction and a full smile finally crosses her face. "How do you control this thing?"

"To the stage!" I yell again, and like before, the crowd cheers, pushing us both toward the front, just a couple of seasoned crowd-surfers.

Tawni's high, melodic laugh rings out as we skim along unknown hands. "Fun, eh?" I say.

"Yes! Why haven't we ever done this before?"

"Have you ever seen a crowd like this?" I counter.

"Good point. What are we going to do about the others?"

"They'll catch up," I say, craning back to find Roc, Trevor, and Tristan lying flat above the masses, moving in all different directions. Trevor's just going in circles—clearly he hasn't worked things out quite yet.

We zero in on the stage, which is now occupied by just the band members minus their lead singer, who's been carried off elsewhere. A jolt runs up my legs as my foot bangs off the foot of the platform. "What now?" I shout above a hammering drum solo.

"Maybe he wanted to get behind it!" Tawni cries.

"Okay! Left! Left!" I yell, hoping the drunken, crazed fans below me can remember their right from left.

At least one person does, as we're pushed hard across the width of the stage. I'm so close to the rockers that the sweat glistens on their skin as they strum, drum, and scream out the loudest music I've ever heard.

Then an amazing thing happens.

We round the edge of the stage and the hands disappear.

Twelve

Tristan

Just when Trevor, Roc, and I get the hang of crowd-surfing and are headed in the direction of Adele and Tawni, they drop out of sight. "What happened?" I say toward Trevor, who's between Roc and me.

The question's intended for Roc, but Trevor answers instead. "I think they got dropped."

My heart skips a beat. Getting dropped in the middle of the mosh pit we're riding on is a dangerous thing. Not only could you break a bone from the fall, but you might get trampled by the hundreds of sightless, stamping feet that can't tell the difference between a human body and an inanimate object that's in their way.

"Or they just reached the edge of the crowd!" Roc yells over Trevor.

"That still means they got dropped," I return.

"But they'll be safe," Roc says. I know he's just guessing, but it still manages to give me hope that they're okay.

I will the hands below us to push us forwards faster, to get me to Adele, but our pace, albeit reasonably fast, remains consistent. A minute or two later we reach the left edge of the stage and by straining my neck and lifting my head, I realize Roc was right. The press of sun dwellers is thinning, the hands are disappearing, and I get the strange sensation that we're about to go over a waterfall.

Adele and Tawni are nowhere to be seen.

I squeeze my muscles tight, preparing for the drop. With a final firm push by some wandering hand directly on my butt, I'm thrown forward, out of the reach of the sea of partiers. There's a quick pull of air in my gut, my stomach dropping as I fall. Curling my legs beneath me, I manage to land on my feet, but in an awkward, crouched position, my ankle turning and crumbling beneath my weight and the hidden weight of my steel weapons. The ground is hard and unforgiving, hammering my knees and scraping my shoulder as I'm pitched forward.

I come to a stop just outside of a broad shadow cast by a gigantic speaker set next to the stage. Being this close to the speaker makes it feel like the *pump, pump, pump* of the music is actually inside my head, making it hard to think.

There's a voice that sounds like it's miles away, a mere whisper by the time it reaches my ears. "Nice landing, ace," Adele says.

I glance around, seeking her, but all I see are Trevor and Roc careening off the edge of the crowd simultaneously, Roc bouncing off the rock on his butt, and Trevor hitting flush on his side, his head jerking in a cringe-worthy manner. "Dude, you okay?" I say to Trevor, who seemed to get the worst of the fall.

"I'm good," Roc answers. "I've got lots of padding down here," he adds, rubbing his butt.

"I meant Trevor, butt wad," I say, motioning to the last member of our group, who's still lying face first motionless on the ground.

"Oh," Roc says. "Trevor, you good?"

"Uhhhh," Trevor says, flopping over onto his back. He takes a deep breath, raises a hand to his head, holding it gingerly. A trickle of blood squeezes through his fingertips.

"You're bleeding, man," I say.

"You think?" Trevor retorts. "I know I've got a hard head, but that was a nasty blow."

"Can you walk?" I ask, knowing we need to get away from the edge of the crowd, which is ebbing and flowing like a living organism. Any second it might move in our direction, trampling us into the dust.

"I'll do my best," he says.

Roc pushes to his feet, still massaging his well-endowed behind, while I stand up and limp over to our fallen comrade. My ankle and knees are throbbing and there's a burning sensation in my shoulder, but it's nothing I can't handle right now, while the adrenaline is still flowing. Later—I don't know. Bones and muscles and tendons might tighten up, walking might be difficult. But I'll cross that inter-Realm bridge when I get to it.

Together, Roc and I haul Trevor to his feet, his head bobbing around like last year's heavyweight champ's skull after taking an unprotected uppercut by the contender, a gargantuan by the name of Moe Bradley. (Yes, Moe is now the new heavyweight champ.)

We manage to hold him up, however, one arm draped over each of our shoulders. His feet are like rubber, stumbling and flopping like a baby's legs during their first attempt at walking. We've got him up, so the next concern is finding Adele and Tawni. Did I imagine her voice mocking me when I fell? Perhaps I hit my head too.

"Over here," Adele hisses, an invisible voice from the shadows behind the speaker.

Roc and I glance at each other, shrug, and then assist Trevor to the side of the stage. With each step, his legs seem to recover, requiring less and less of our help to walk. By the time we reach the shadows, he's practically walking on his own, a good sign.

We step into the dark, blinking away the drastic change in lighting. It's incredible how dark it is once you're out of the watchful gaze of the artificial sun. After spending so much time in the gloomy Lower Realms, I've almost forgotten how different the world I grew up in is. We expect things to be bright because that's the way it is.

"Is he okay?" Adele's voice says right next to my ear. I half-jump out of my skin, cursing under my breath.

"Holy—" I spout. "You scared the stuffing out of me."

"You've got stuffing?" Roc asks smartly.

"Sorry," Adele says. "Can't you see us?"

"Not yet. We're flying blind at the moment."

"I can see them," Trevor mumbles.

"Yeah, well my night vision isn't as fine-tuned as yours," I retort, sounding unnecessarily harsh, even to my own ears.

"That sucks," Trevor says, laughing.

A hand touches my shoulder. "I'm right here," Adele says. "Tawni's here, too. Is he okay?" she asks again.

"I think he might have a concussion," I explain, as Trevor continues to giggle beside me. "He took a pretty hard knock to the head. We need to find a place to rest and get fixed up. We also need to find a place to switch clothes."

"What?" Trevor screeches beside me. "I'm wearing the hottest new trend to come out of subchapter one in fifty years! I'm not switching clothes!"

Ugh. He's getting worse. "Why do we need different clothes?" Tawni asks.

"Although we're able to blend in here, in a less crowded place we *will* stick out," I explain. "That line about our clothes being trendy in another subchapter will only work on drunkards and morons."

"So most of the sun dweller population," Roc chimes in.

"You lied to me!" Trevor wails. "I thought this outfit was in."

Ignoring both stupid comments, I say, "The sooner we look like everyone else, the better."

"You're halfway there with that lovely hat already," Adele says.

"Yeah, thanks for that," I say, finally seeing Adele's outline in the dark. "Roc, any thoughts on where we can hide out for a while?"

"Everything will be closed today, so if we're willing to smash a window or pick a lock…"

"We're willing," I say.

"I'm good at smashing stuff," Trevor says.

"Okay, then we should hit the first clothing store we come to. I think there's a Paradise Sun around here somewhere. Or maybe we can find an In Crowd. Both of those stores will have everything we need to disguise ourselves appropriately."

* * *

We end up at In Crowd, which is only two blocks down and one across. Although we pass several late festival attendees, they're so focused on getting to the concert that they barely even notice us.

As Roc predicted, a red "Closed" sign hangs on the door of the multi-level store. After a quick glance down either end of the deserted street, we lean Trevor up against the wall. He hasn't spoken in a while, for which I'm grateful, but he is humming to himself, his eyes closing for periods ranging between five and ten seconds, much longer than a normal blink, even a particularly slow one. So much for him being the one to break the glass.

"There's no alarm system," Roc notes. "We don't have much crime up here. Other than the occasional drunken brawl, that is."

"But breaking the glass might draw attention," I point out. "Plus anyone passing by will definitely notice a shattered window."

"I can pick the lock," Tawni says.

"What? Really? That's awesome," Roc says, gazing admiringly at her.

"How'd you learn that?" Adele asks.

137

"When I ran away, before I was caught, I learned all kinds of interesting things, not all of them legal," she says.

"Go for it," I say, stepping aside.

"Anyone got a thin knife?" she says.

"I think I've got something that might work," Roc mumbles, rummaging through his pack. "Here!" he exclaims, handing Tawni a tiny paring knife.

"What do you use that for?" I ask.

"If you have to know, cutting my toenails," he says.

"Gross."

Tawni's already got the knife jammed in the lock, twisting and turning it at various angles, trying to get the mechanism to line up in the right way. A minute passes with us just watching her and Trevor mumbling something that sounds like a poem under his breath.

Another minute passes and then, "Got it!" she cries, as the lock clicks and the door pushes open. *We're in.*

Tawni and Adele go in first, while Roc and I help Trevor. "I don't want to go to school today, Mommy," he murmurs, his head lolling lazily to the side.

"Don't worry, little Trev-Trev, we're going to put you right to sleep," Roc coos, making me crack up.

When we get inside, the girls are already roaming the aisles, relying on the dimmer security lights to check out the merchandise. Their eyes are wide and their mouths slightly open. "What do you do in here?" Adele asks when we approach.

"Uh, shop," Roc says.

"Shop?" Tawni says.

"Yeah, you know, like pick out clothes and try them on. If they fit well, you buy them at the register."

"Register?" Adele says.

"Um, don't worry about it," Roc says. "We won't be doing it that way anyway."

"We should move upstairs," I say. "Anyone passing by the front window will be able to see us."

The escalator is turned off, so Adele and Tawni run up the steps, while Roc and I haul Trevor, who now appears to be sleeping, his breaths slow and deep, after them, one step at a time. When we get to the top, I say, "Let's dump him somewhere to sleep it off."

"Good plan," Roc agrees, smirking.

We find a cozy corner, and while I hold Trevor up, Roc piles up long, brightly colored dresses to use as a bed. We lie him down, rolling up one of the coats—a turquoise one—for a pillow.

"Now what?" Roc says.

"Now we shop."

We find the girls standing in front of a rack of shoes, just staring. "What are these?" Adele says, picking up a pair of red, ultra-high heels.

"Shoes," I say.

"No way!" Adele says. "How could anyone walk in these?" She sits down on a nearby bench and starts taking off her boots.

"They can and they do," Roc says. "Most of the girls here wear them. It seems the heels get higher every year. Being tall is in."

"But they're not really tall," Tawni says.

I chuckle. "True, but that's not what matters. It's all about image. Most of what you'll find in the Sun Realm is artificial— just like the sun."

"But why do people care?" Adele says, standing up unsteadily, now wearing the red heels. "A shoe's a shoe," she adds, trying a cautious step forward.

"Not to these people. They want their clothes to make them stand out," I explain.

"But they don't," Tawni says. "They still all look the same, just different than moon and star dwellers. If they really want to stand out, they should visit the Lower Realms wearing those." She points to Adele's heels.

Adele, clutching a rack of shirts as she moves forward another step, says, "I can't even walk in these, much less run or kick."

I laugh again. "Sun dweller women don't do much running or kicking. They mostly just go tanning, go to the salon, go shopping, that sort of thing."

"But how do they...*live?*" Tawni asks. This is all clearly blowing both girls' minds.

"Usually they have rich boyfriends or husbands who deal in shipping or own mines in the Lower Realms," I say. "There's a lot of old money up here that's been passed down for generations."

"So while we're all working like dogs for our next meal..." Adele starts, taking off the heels.

"The sun dwellers are up here attending parties, killing time, and generally enjoying their lives," I say coldly. "Can you see now why I left?"

"Not really," Tawni says. "Wouldn't that be a good reason *not* to leave?"

Roc surprises me by saying, "Tristan's got too good of a heart for that. He doesn't like to see people suffer while others take advantage of them."

"Thanks," I say.

"We shall never speak of this compliment again," Roc says, smirking.

"I'll remind you every day," I joke.

"That's the last time I say something nice about you."

"We don't have to wear these—what do you call them?— *high shoes*, to blend in do we?" Adele asks, her face scrunched with concern. "Because I don't think I can walk more than a few blocks without killing myself."

I take the shoes from her. "High *heels*," I correct. "You can if you want, but I think we can find something much more sensible, but still fashionable."

"Sounds good. Where do we start?"

"You and Tawni should pick out some tunics that you like. Pretty much anything in this store is in style right now, so it's hard to go wrong. Roc and I will get ourselves and Trevor outfitted and then help you with your shoes and accessories."

"Accessories?" Adele and Tawni say at the same time.

"We'll show you later," I promise. "Try and have fun with it."

"Yeah, girls are supposed to like shopping," Roc adds.

Adele and Tawni look at each other like we're completely out of our minds, but then move off into one of the aisles full of the new Beau Gabore line of flaring-bottom tunics.

"This should be interesting," Roc says.

"Thanks for the compliment," I say again, trying to keep a straight face.

"Don't make me regret it."

"I'm not sure I can do that," I laugh.

* * *

An hour later we've made good progress. I've torn strips from a dark training tunic to bandage my scraped shoulder. Roc found a chest of ice to apply to his bruised tush. Trevor's still out, and we had the unfortunate experience of undressing him, pulling a brand new black Rizzo tunic—very stylish and modern—over his head, and getting him into a matching pair of what are known as "chairman's pants," high-waisted and straight-cut all the way to the brown Montgomery boots we found in his size. The pants were the trickiest, and required Roc and me to both take a leg, while we cringed, desperately avoiding touching anywhere near anything we wouldn't want touched ourselves.

Once finished with Trevor, we split up and decked ourselves out. Roc found a whiter-than-white ribbed tank-tunic that contrasts nicely with his brown skin, thick bright orange marching pants (sun dwellers tend to like parades), and fake leather white moccasins, which are all the rage right now. I was able to complement my light blue nylon tunic with a navy blue leather jacket, complete with turquoise buttons and arm studs. My pants are blue camouflage, which has just come back after a decade of being out of style. Due to my well-known appearance, I decide to continue wearing a hat, but replace the woman's hat Adele nicked for me with a silver fedora with blue trim that casts a decent shadow across the upper part of my face when worn sufficiently low over my eyes. Unwilling to stoop to the level of moccasins, I find a pair of rugged brown boots that are only in fashion because they have a decent-sized heel that I normally wouldn't be caught dead in. But they definitely beat the thin-soled slippers that Roc's wearing.

Finished with the men's section, we leave Trevor to his comfy pile of dresses—"Sleep well, Sleeping Beauty," Roc says before we go, drawing a strange look from me. "You know, like the story your mother told us when we were little?"

I raise an eyebrow.

"You're hopeless. She must have told it to us a dozen times. It was about a princess who is cursed and falls asleep for eternity or until her one true love kisses her."

"Are you going to be the one to kiss him and wake him up?" I say, smirking.

Roc ignores me and heads for the women's department to find the girls.

We find them in the changing rooms behind thinly curtained cubicles. A pile of discarded clothes is growing in the center of the waiting area.

"This stuff is crazy," Adele says, hidden save for a dark shadow of her profile.

"I kind of like some of it," Tawni admits.

"Any luck?" I say.

"I think I'm all set," Tawni says, pushing her curtain aside with a flourish.

"Oh. My…" Roc says.

"Is it okay? I had no clue with the makeup and hairstyle, so I just tried to copy some of the sun dweller models from the fashion magazines they had lying around."

Tawni's got on a long, no-sleeved silvery blue dress that rises all the way to her neck. It's tight at the top and hugs her hips, leaving nothing of her figure to imagination, before flaring out at the bottom. Blue and silver crystals sparkle wildly even in the dim security lighting. Her long, white hair is up in a bun on the top of her head, held together by blue and silver butterfly pins. Several turquoise-inlaid rings adorn her slender white fingers, while dark blue heels add an extra three inches to her already above-average height. Her face shimmers with some kind of luminescent makeup, accenting her ultra-feminine features.

Roc's making weird gasping noises next to me.

"I think he likes it," I say. "But is it practical? Can you even walk in it?"

"She can walk in it," Roc says hopefully. "Can't you?"

"I've been practicing," Tawni says. "It's not so hard once you get the hang of it. I just take small steps and place every foot carefully."

"Yeah, it's easy," Adele says sarcastically from the change rooms. "I'd break my neck in those things."

"What if we have to run?" I say.

"I'll just kick them off," Tawni says matter-of-factly.

I hate to delay longer to find something else for her to wear, plus she seems perfectly happy in her new outfit…

"Okay. We'll go with it."

"Yay!" Tawni says, looking genuinely happy. It's almost like she's forgotten that we're here on a mission to kill the President. But if that helps her feel comfortable, it's fine by me. We'll all need to blend in for the next day or so.

Tawni walks carefully over to Roc, rubs a hand gently on the shoulder of his new shirt. "My, my, aren't you gentlemen dashing."

"Oh. Uh, thanks," Roc says, his face turning a darker shade of brown.

"Almost done in there, Adele?" I ask.

"Umm…"

"Do you need any help?" I say, grinning.

144

"You wish," she retorts. "I think I've got it. There. Finished." There's a zip, and then a deep breath. "Yeah. I think these will work just fine."

Unlike Tawni's, her curtain moves slowly across the top, revealing the new Adele inch by inch. I don't gasp like Roc, but I do stare, my mouth falling open slightly. I think my tongue even hangs out, like a happy dog.

"It's *awful*, isn't it? I knew I should have had Tawni do the makeup," Adele says, placing a hand on the curtain as if she wants to thrust it back over herself.

"No—no, that's definitely not the word for it," I sputter, still shocked at the transformation. "I was thinking more like *amazing*, or *incredible*. Adele, you look…"

"Hot!" Roc exclaims, earning him a slap on the arm from Tawni. "I mean, you look very nice, Adele," he corrects.

Adele's face reddens. "I look what?" she asks me, one hand on her hip.

I drink her in with my eyes. She's wearing tight, black pants that, when combined with her form-fitting emerald-green leather silver-studded tunic, show off her gorgeous, hour-glass figure in a tough, rugged kind of way. The pants are tucked into high, black boots with a wide, modest heel that even I could walk on. She has on a half-dozen gleaming steel rings that match the studs on her shirt. Her long black hair is braided down the back and wrapped with silver, shimmering ties. Although she doesn't need it, her eyelashes are lengthened and thickened with dark mascara, giving her green eyes a definite feline look. Her lips have just a touch of pink, leaving them glossy and intoxicating.

145

She tucks her emerald pendant into her tunic, and I realize the outfit is an outward expression of the jewel that hangs from her necklace. A memory of her father.

"Hellooo," Adele says. "Am I that hideous that you don't even have a word to describe it?"

"N—no," I stutter, trying to gain my composure. "Roc got it right the first time. You look *hot*," I say, nodding vehemently.

A flush heats up Adele's face once more. "I look ridiculous," she says, looking down at her getup.

"Again, not the word I would choose," I say. Changing the angle of the subject, I ask, "Can you move okay? I mean, if you had to fight or run or whatever, could you?"

Before I know it's coming, her shiny boot flashes upward, stopping less than an inch from my face, making me flinch. She holds the kick for a second, and then returns her foot to the floor, a half-step in front of her other one. Her arms are in a boxer's stance, her fists knotted.

"I guess you can fight," I say breathlessly.

"I guess so," she smirks.

Thirteen
Adele

I'm happy with my new clothes. Although they're not really me—too tight and revealing—at least I can fight in them. And hopefully they'll help me fit into this crazy world.

Honestly, at first I was somewhat mesmerized by the artificial sun, the beautiful people, the interesting clothing, but now I'm just sickened by it. Not necessarily because it's not cool, or fun, but because they don't share it. While the star dwellers live in squalor and filth and *darkness*, and the moon dwellers are impoverished, hungry, and hopeless, the sun dwellers enjoy the high life, basking in their beautiful sunlight, surrounded by elegant buildings, pristine city streets, and everything money can buy. I always knew the Sun Realm was privileged, but I never knew how much.

As we pass one last time through the racks of vibrant and well-made clothes, I wonder whether people are just born a certain way and that's it, or whether they can be changed. The sun dwellers are born in this place where clothes are used for *fashion*, rather than utility. It's all they've ever known, it's all they've ever seen. So is that it? Is it really their fault that they don't see the reality of the inequality at play in the world? Are they a product of their inherent natures, or their environment? Or is it a mixture of both?

I think of myself. Although I've never been mean-spirited, I'm clearly a result of my parents' upbringing, but I've also been changed significantly from my experiences. I guess it all comes down to how one reacts to the things they see, the things that happen to them. Like I can take everything I've been through—my father's and Cole's death, my sister's maiming, mine and my parents' imprisonment, the people I've killed— and wallow in self-pity, hate myself for not being strong enough, give up on everything...*or* I can rise above it, seek the good in the Tri-Realms, fight for those I've lost and those I still have. I can be better. It's up to me. It's a choice that only I can make.

The sun dwellers have a choice: to be blind and ignorant and uninterested in the stark difference in living conditions between the Upper and Lower Realms, or see this travesty for what it is—evil and hate. No, these people do *not* get a free pass just because they've never known any other life. If they took one minute away from their own skewed self-images, greed, and slothfulness, they would see what I can see as clear as the spray of water from an underground waterfall: they're not human anymore. No, not even close. They're robots, programmed only to care about themselves and enjoying their own lives, not the pitiful lives of those born beneath them.

I'm done with my rambling thoughts; it's time for action. I'm not perfect, nor do I pretend to be. I've killed. I've said and done things I'm not proud of. But I'm better than these people. If these robots refuse to see the truth, we'll show it to them—the hard way if we have to.

On the way out we pass a rotating display of tinted glasses. I remember seeing many of the partiers wearing similar glasses as we crowd-surfed past them.

"It's bright out there," Tristan says. "These will come in handy, both to protect our eyes and our identities."

"What are they?" Tawni asks, picking up a pair of thick, blue ones and holding them up to her eyes.

"Sunglasses," Roc says. "We use them to make our vision darker, due to the brightness of the sun."

"Artificial sun," I correct, snatching a pair of black ones from the rack. I put them on, watching how my vision dims into near-blackness. "I can't even see with these on."

"That's because the lighting in here is dim already. Wait until we get outside," Tristan advises.

I shrug and tilt the sunglasses onto the top of my head, the way Tristan and Roc are wearing their own pairs.

Tristan is just about to open the store's front door, when Roc says, "What about Sleeping Beauty?"

"Huh?" I say, frowning.

"He means Trevor," Tristan explains. "He was still sleeping off his head injury when we left him."

"We could just leave him there," Roc suggests. "He'd probably be safer."

Raising an eyebrow, Tristan says, "Yeah, until the Sun Festival ends, at which time the stores will open, he'll be found, arrested for theft and breaking and entering. Then when they determine he's a star dweller invading the Sun Realm during a time of war they'll connect him to the soldiers we killed or injured in the shipping tunnel, and he'll be put to death. He'd be safe, all right."

Roc shrugs. "Well, if you put it that way, maybe we should bring him along. But I don't want to have to lug him around everywhere."

As we march back through the store, I avoid looking at any of the stuff that just makes me angry. We reach a corner that's filled with piled up clothing, almost like a bed.

"Crap," Tristan says.

"Where?" Roc says, checking his shoes. "Hey, where's Trevor?"

"You mean you lost him?" I ask incredulously.

"Uh, no, of course not," Tristan says. "We just misplaced him."

"Is there a difference?" Tawni asks.

"Not really," Roc says. "It just sounds better saying it that way."

Ducking back into one of the aisles, Tristan says, "He can't have gone far—I'm sure we'll find him around here somewhere. Trevor!"

We follow his lead, branching out into the store like a human net, each of us calling our lost friend's name. I reach the end of the men's section and, with nowhere else to go, proceed into the women's section. Considering the extent of Trevor's head injury, it's entirely possible he's trying on women's undergarments at this very moment.

Sure enough, when I approach the women's change rooms, someone's talking. I can tell right away that it's Trevor.

"...lookin' good, my friend," he says. "Sick shirt, awesome pants, nice shoes..."

"Trevor?" I say softly, not wanting to scare our concussed friend away.

"In here!" he calls.

When I peek around the corner, I find him standing in front of the mirror, posing, flexing his muscles and grinning at himself. "What do you think?" he asks, turning to show off his new clothes.

"They're okay," I say, downplaying the fact that he actually does look pretty good in his new digs. He's not a bad-looking guy. Nor is he a bad guy—he can just be a bit trying sometimes.

"Okay? They're awesome!"

"I found him!" I yell to the others. And then to Trevor: "Are you okay?"

"Never felt better," he says. "Other than the hammer smashing against my head every second, I'm perfectly fine," he laughs. "How'd we get here anyway?"

"You mean you don't remember?"

"I don't remember a thing after falling from the crowd, feeling my head crack the stone, and then making a smartass comment about how hard my head is," he says.

"That's probably a good thing," Tristan says, walking in. "You weren't really yourself."

"I don't know," Roc says, entering next, chuckling to himself, "I think he was exactly himself."

"I don't know what you goobers are talking about, but what I want to know is how I got out of my old clothes and into these?"

I hadn't thought of that. There's only one way…

"You dressed him?" I say, glancing between Roc and Tristan, who are looking down, scuffing their feet against the floor.

"Aww, how sweet is it how the guys take care of each other," Tawni says, arriving last.

"Uh, yeah, sweet," Roc says. "I washed my hands three times afterwards."

"You owe us, dude," is all that Tristan says.

"If it wasn't so creepy, I'd thank you," Trevor says, grinning. "At least you've got good taste."

"Thanks—I think," Roc says. "Now, can we ditch this popsicle stand?"

"What's a popsic—" Tawni starts to say.

"I'll explain another time," Roc says. "Are you sure you're okay, Trevor?"

"I think so."

"Good. Let's move," Tristan says. "Make sure your weapons are out of sight."

Once more, we retrace our steps to the front door. Keeping low, we peek out the windows, watching for potential witnesses to our crime. The beat of the music continues to thump from a few blocks away. A good sign. The crowds won't have dispersed as long as there's entertainment.

A gaggle of four or five young girls in tight dresses and high heels wobble past. Even through the glass I can hear them chattering away, all at the same time, not bothering to listen to what each other has to say. They're speaking so fast it's almost like a foreign language. One of them stumbles as her heel bites into a crack in the stone. She nearly falls, but manages to regain her balance and pull the heel out and resume walking like one of her legs is longer than the other.

"They look ridiculous," I scoff. "Tawni, are you sure you don't want to change shoes?"

"I'll put them to shame," Tawni says. "Besides, those heels are at least twice as high as mine."

She's right, but I still worry that when the time comes to run—which it inevitably will—we'll be waiting for her to unclasp her shoes with bullets flying all around us. As I picture the scene in my head, it's almost comedic.

The girls turn the corner, leaving the street deserted once again. "Game time," Tristan says, pulling the door open.

We file into the street in a line, the same way we're used to marching through the tunnels. I squint as the artificial sunlight peeks over the top of one of the buildings, blinding me. Tristan stops, chews on his lip, eyes the group. "We look way too stiff," he says, sliding his sunglasses over his eyes. "We're just a group of sun dwellers out to have a good time. Sunglasses down."

I obey, marveling as the tinted glasses filter out just enough of the light to be tolerable, without making it hard to see.

"Better," Tristan says. "Now act looser, more relaxed. We're not out looking for a fight—we're looking to have fun. You know, eat, drink, and be merry."

"Never heard of that before," Trevor grumbles.

"Well, now you have. This is life or death, guys. The fate of the Tri-Realms may depend on your ability to act like sun dwellers."

"Thanks for the pep talk, chief," Trevor says.

"The Tri-Realms might be screwed," Roc adds.

"Oh, come on. It's just like dress-up when you were kids," Tawni says, her eyes lighting up. "Didn't you ever play dress-up?"

"Dress up?" Trevor says. "Is that like wearing dresses or something? I try to be open-minded, but even I'd draw the line at wearing a dress."

"Grrr, you guys are so frustrating sometimes," Tawni says. Then, looking to me for backup, she says, "Adele, you know what I mean, don't you?"

"Elsey used to play dress-up. She'd pin blankets to look like a dress. She always said she was a princess waiting for her knight in shining armor. So maybe it does mean wearing a dress?" I say cautiously, fearing Tawni's wrath.

"You all are hopeless," she says. "All I mean is that we need to pretend, to be in character. Honestly, use your imaginations. We've got the clothes, but now we have to have the sun dweller mindset. I think that's what Tristan means."

"Exactly," he says.

"I think I can do that," Trevor says. "I'll just act like an idiot."

"Shouldn't be too difficult for you," Roc mumbles under his breath.

"Or you," Trevor retorts.

"Guys, not the time," Tristan says sternly. "We have to move on, find the train station."

Trying to think like sun dwellers, we set off down the road in a staggered group, less *stiff*—as Tristan put it—than before. Tawni really gets into it, walking in her short, high-heeled steps, one arm around me, the other around Roc. Every once in a while she laughs, although nobody says anything funny. Tristan and I have our arms around each other, too.

At first the whole thing is awkward, but after we make it down the block, turn right, and make it another block without seeing anyone, I loosen up a little, start to enjoy being so close to Tristan. His usual warmth pulsates through me as we pretend-stagger along. I kiss him on the cheek, making it extra sloppy for effect and to get a laugh out of him. He returns the favor, wetting my cheek, just next to my lips. It's funny, we're pretending to be drunk, to be falling all over each other, having a good time—but we're also not faking it. It feels amazing doing this with Tristan. We're relaxed and carefree for the first time in our relationship, and I feel like I could do anything with him. If we weren't on this freaking mission, I'd pull him away to a dark corner, and—

My frivolous thoughts are interrupted when a group of sun dwellers pass, going in the other direction. My heart races, my knees tighten, and I'm glad I'm wearing the sunglasses, because my eyes narrow under the weight of my frown.

"Stay in character," Tristan whispers, slapping Trevor on the back and laughing merrily.

As we pass the locals, four girls and three guys who are dressed like girls, all of whom are strutting down the center like they own the road, one of the girls says, "Party's this way, boys," throwing Trevor a perfectly white smile on a perfectly fake face. A lock of bleached hair tumbles across her cheek.

"We gotta get some more booze," Tristan replies, planting another kiss on my cheek and not missing a step.

"You can share ours," the girl says, holding up a thick green bottle with gold lettering on the side.

"Maybe next time," Tristan says.

"Your loss," she calls over her shoulder, ushering her group forward.

When they're out of earshot, I finally breathe again, as Trevor says, "Told you I look good in these new clothes. Did you see the way she looked at me?"

"We saw," I say, "but I wouldn't be too proud of it, she didn't look too picky."

"Jealousy doesn't suit you," Trevor retorts, leaving me huffing.

Block after block of exquisite apartments pass as we shuffle along, just a happy group of sun dwellers looking for action. Roc steers us down a road to the left, sending us diagonally through the city. Up ahead, a pile of what appears to be rubbish spills out of a gaping hole into a dark, gray building with massive steel roll-up doors on one side.

"I didn't know sun dwellers were slobs, too," I comment, catching a whiff of putrid rotting garbage as we approach. "What's with all the garbage?"

"Now that's interesting," Tristan says.

"What is?" Tawni asks.

"Sun dwellers are typically very clean. That hole leads to giant Dumpsters that, when full, are shipped to the Star Realm for destruction in the lava flow."

"But that's a lot of garbage," I say. "My subchapter wouldn't create that much garbage in a month."

"People are very wasteful here," Roc says. "That's probably a day's worth."

I cough, choking on breath. "A day! That's ridiculous," I say.

Roc shrugs. "It's a different world up here. But still, whether it's a day's worth, or a month's, it shouldn't be piling up on the street—it should be shipped away."

"It seems that's not happening anymore," I note.

"Seems not. Given the war, all inter-Realm shipping would be cancelled indefinitely. I guess there's not a backup plan for managing the trash."

"Funny," I say. "Perhaps the Sun Realm is more dependent on the Lower Realms than anyone realizes."

"You don't know the half of it," Tristan says. I glance at the shining steel doors on the building. "Trash, taxes, building supplies, gemstones, iron ore: it all comes from the Lower Realms. The Sun Realm wouldn't exist without it."

"Which is exactly why your father is moving so fast to knock us back into line," I add, immediately thinking of my mom and sister. With the strength and resources of the Sun Realm, their hope of survival is minimal if we don't succeed in our mission. Instead of fear rising, it's determination that wells up, heating my chest. Failure is not an option—never was.

Before Tristan can respond, the raucous grinding of gears sounds to the right. A dark crack appears below the roll-up doors, growing thicker as the twin risers are pulled inside. Then: the rumble of an engine joins the cacophony of noise.

"Quick, away from the doors!" Tristan says. "Make like we're just hanging out."

We rush to the side of the opening, against the wall, sort of facing each other, as if we're just having a conversation. In my peripheral vision a monstrous truck emerges from the garage like a troll from its cave. With a roar, the closed-bedded truck hangs a hard right and blows past us, sending a mixed rush of hot air, exhaust, and old garbage over us.

"Whew! That stinks like the Star Realm," Trevor says. "I thought you said the garbage service would be shut down."

"It should be," Tristan says. "There's no way that truck's headed below." He motions to the ground.

We stare at the ground in silence, each puzzling over the mystery.

"It could be going to subchapter four," Roc says.

"Why four?" I ask.

"There's an incinerator there. It's mostly used for easily disposed of waste that doesn't require the lava flow, but they're desperate, so maybe they'll try to destroy whatever they can there."

"Good call, Roc. That's the only place they could be taking it," Tristan says.

"Doesn't matter," Trevor says. "All we care about is reaching subchapter one. Where's the train?"

"Dammit," Roc says, as if just remembering something. "It's the Sun Festival. Even trains won't be running today."

"Are you sure?" I ask, dreading having to hike another dozen or more miles through an intra-Realm tunnel which is probably full of sun dweller soldiers looking for revenge for their fallen comrades.

"Pretty sure," he says.

"Why not?" Tawni asks. "Wouldn't people want to be able to get to the best parties?"

Roc's expression is thoughtful. "You'd think so. But there's a lot of pride in one's subchapter up here. There are buses to transport people within the city, but no intra-Realm travel is permitted on Festival Day."

"We have to check anyway," Tristan says. "Do you remember how much further?"

"Maybe six blocks."

"Move out."

We walk faster this time, presumably because we all want to know whether our plans have indeed been foiled by a silly holiday in the middle of a war. Even Tawni picks up the pace, performing admirably in her heels. Two more clusters of sun dwellers pass us, but both are too busy laughing and carrying on that they don't say a word to us, which is fine by me.

When we reach the train station, the truth stares us in the face:

Linked metal chains seal the doors.

Fourteen
Tristan

Stupid, stupid, stupid. I should have remembered. Everything was going so well I got complacent, assumed we'd be able to just coast into my hometown on a golden train. Not today.

"We can hide out somewhere," Roc suggests. "Wait until morning and then hop the early train while all the sun dwellers are sleeping off the festival."

On the face of it, it seems like a good suggestion. We seem to be relatively safe here in our disguises, and soon no one will be in any condition to identify us. We haven't seen a single Enforcer, as most of them have probably been sent to join the army. Deep in the Sun Realm, it's unlikely that any of them are stationed here. However, there's one problem:

"The Moon Realm might be defeated by morning," Adele says. "If not already."

The truth of her words ring in all our ears. Although the world seems like a happy, peaceful place in subchapter eight, in reality it's a war-ravaged battleground. I know my father will be pushing hard to finish the siege quickly, perhaps desiring to make a victory announcement the day after the biggest celebration of the year.

"I agree. We can't wait. We have to get there no later than tonight," I say. "Any other suggestions?"

Silence.

"How far is the walk?" Trevor asks.

I cringe, dreading the thought of running all the way to subchapter one; for running is the only way we'd make it by the end of the day on foot. "Far," I say.

Roc cranes his neck and stares at the cavern roof high above. "I think there's a twenty-eight-mile-long tunnel that would get us to subchapter four. At least then we'd be in the right cluster. Then we could just take the Nailin Tunnel to the capital. That's only a little over a mile."

"So twenty-nine miles, not including the time and distance to get to the right tunnel. Even at a manic pace it will take us at least three hours," I say, "and we'll be in no position to fight anyone when we arrive."

"Subchapter four..." Adele murmurs, almost to herself. Then, turning to Roc, she says, "Isn't that where you said the garbage trucks might be headed?"

"Yeah, so?" Roc says.

I know where she's going with this. "No, absolutely not," I say. "It's too dangerous."

"No more dangerous than everything we've had to do this entire mission, and a hell of a lot less dangerous than what we still have to do," she says hotly, giving me a look.

"Am I missing something?" Tawni asks, to no one in particular.

"She wants to ride in the garbage trucks," I explain.

"I don't *want* to. But it may be our only choice. You said it yourself—getting there on foot will be long and tiring."

"But a garbage truck?" I say.

"Suck it up, sun boy," Trevor says, "I've waded through some pretty nasty sh—"

"Fine. If everyone agrees, I'll do it," I say flatly, hoping someone else will disagree.

"What if there aren't any more trucks today?" Roc asks.

"Did you see the amount of garbage piling up outside the chute?" Adele says. "They have no choice—they have to take it somewhere."

"But we'll destroy our new clothes," Tawni says, looking down at her expensive dress, a look of horror on her face.

"I forgot about that," Trevor says, brushing a bit of gray dust off his black Rizzo tunic. "Maybe there's another way."

"Now who should suck it up?" I say mockingly.

"I retract my previous insult," Trevor says seriously.

Adele looks at us like we're crazy. "We can just steal more stuff in subchapter four if we have to." It seems she's got an answer for everything.

"I don't know if I'm comfortable with all this stealing," Tawni says, reverting to her role as the moral conscience of the group.

"You *are* the one who picked the lock," Roc points out.

Tawni blushes, her sparkly makeup looking even shinier over the red of her cheeks. "Okay," she says. "I'm in."

This time I lead the way through the streets, easily remembering the zigzagging path back to the garbage chute. As we near the chute, it's clear that the shipping door is still open, either because more trucks have recently come through or because more are about to come through. I'm hoping it's the latter.

Creeping along the building's wall, I risk a glance around the corner, into the garage. Two men wearing thick black gloves are hauling bags of trash from a conveyer belt to a truck, tossing them into the back one by one. The truck bed is already half full.

"There's one about to leave," I whisper back to the others.

"That's our ride," Adele says, her green eyes fierce and sharp, even more so because of the black makeup.

"Move when I do, as close behind me as possible," I say. "Tawni, you'd better carry your shoes."

She nods and begins unclasping them, her hands deftly slipping them off. "Ready," she says a moment later.

I sneak another peek into the garage. The truck is nearly full now, and the men are engaged in a conversation near the cab door, which is open. Their backs are to us.

Without checking that the others are paying attention, I steal into the garage, tiptoeing to prevent an errant footstep from betraying our presence. I hear nothing behind me, which either means they're not following me or they're being equally careful with their footing. My heart is pounding; if one of the guys turns, there's nowhere to hide. But they don't turn, and I manage to safely reach the still-open cargo hold, indulging in a quick glance back.

The others are right on top of me, their faces white and focused. I turn back to the truck, clamber inside, and screw up my face when the rotten stench of garbage hits my nostrils. Trying to breathe out of only my mouth, I reach back and help Tawni inside. Adele, Trevor, and Roc pull themselves up unassisted. We're all in, but we're far from safe. One of the guys will be back any minute to shut the gate.

"We've got to get behind the garbage," Roc hisses.

Fun.

Luckily, the trash is in big canvas bags, but it still makes for an unsteady and constantly shifting climb to the top of the pile. A few of the bags have rips and tears in them, spilling some of their contents onto the heap. Half-eaten food, like rotten apples, mystery meat, and spoiled unidentifiable gelatinous ooze, squishes under my treads, making me glad I have thick-soled shoes, unlike Roc. Tawni's the worst off, forced to plow through the muck in her bare feet. The price of fashion, I think wryly.

Just as I reach the top of the heap, the front door of the truck slams. I look back, ushering Tawni, Adele, Roc, and Trevor past me and behind the mountainous pile. The engine rumbles to life. Just before following, I glance back once more to find one of the guys hooking around the back of the truck. Without thinking, I dive down the smelly hill, tumbling head over heels, knocking into someone, bouncing off, and then knocking into another someone.

Arms and legs are tangled in a mess of limbs. There's a head in my armpit, and my face is near someone's feet—Trevor's, I think, by the look of them. We're all frozen in place, none of us crying out or complaining or so much as breathing while we silently pray the man didn't see or hear us.

There's a *thud*, presumably when the guy mounts the truck bed, and then a click and a clatter, as he rolls the door down, casting us into darkness.

"Good to go!" he yells, and then the truck lurches back, the bags of garbage shifting slightly from the rear acceleration. I finally risk a breath, but still don't speak, expecting the truck to slam to a halt, the door to fly open, the men to come at us with big guns. We do stop, but only because the truck has reversed out, and is now ready to move forward. With a harsh roar, the truck shoots forward, and we're thrown back into the trash pile.

"Get your armpit outta my head!" Roc hisses.

"Your head's in my armpit," I retort.

"Someone's foot is in my face," Adele whispers.

"Sorry!" Tawni says.

"This is foul," Roc says.

With the truck door closed, we're locked in a steel box, the air thickening with each passing second. The stench is so strong it's almost like I'm eating it with each breath. Every few breaths I gag, wishing I could throw up, but knowing the others would never let me live it down.

"Are we there yet?" Trevor asks after a few minutes.

"I truly hope you're not going to ask that every five minutes," Roc says.

"Maybe every ten," Trevor says, his smile obvious, even in the dark.

We're probably talking too much, but it's comforting to hear my friends' voices in the dark, and the drone of the engine is more than sufficient to drown out any sound we make before it reaches the driver's ears.

"I feel unclean," Roc says after a few minutes of silence.

"Join the club," I agree.

"Are we there—" Trevor starts.

"No!" the four of us say collectively.

"Okay, no need to get so testy. I was just checking."

"What's the plan when we get there?" Adele says, thinking ahead, as usual.

"Not get killed?" Roc suggests.

"That's a good start," I say dryly. "Look, when the truck stops I'd say it's highly unlikely we'll be able to get out without being seen…"

"So we'll have to fight our way out," Adele says.

"Exactly."

"You children can stay in the back while I take care of it," Trevor says.

"Just like you took care of things with your crowd-surfing dismount?" Roc says.

"That wasn't my fault!" Trevor says.

Although the banter between Roc and Trevor should put a smile on my face, it doesn't. Instead, a lump forms in my throat. I swallow a few times, but it refuses to be dislodged. A dark cloud settles over me—not one of stinky garbage, although that's there too, but of untold truths and sadness. The silent truth: one that Roc and I have held onto since I was fifteen, since right before my mother disappeared. The sadness: that I haven't told Adele, or Trevor and Tawni for that matter. They deserve to know, not only because they volunteered for the dangerous mission we're on, but because they're good people. Eventually, the world needs to know, but first they should.

"I've got something I have to tell you," I say, my voice shaky. My skin is tingly and hot, and my heart races as I prepare to unleash the burden that's been weighing on me for over two years now.

"This isn't the right time," Adele says, to my surprise.

"But you don't even know—"

"It doesn't matter what it is, I know now is not the right time."

"Then when?" I say, still shocked that Adele wants me to wait even longer to give her information she knows I've been keeping from her since we met.

"After this is over."

"What you are guys talking about?" Trevor asks.

Ignoring him, I say, "That's too long. I have to do it before we get to the President. It will help you all to know what you're fighting against and what you're fighting for."

"We already know that," Adele says. "We're fighting against evil, against injustice, against all that's wrong in the world we live in. We're fighting for each other, for our friends, for our families."

"But there's more to it," I say.

"Now that we've got a ride, we're ahead of schedule," Roc points out. "There are places we can stop between the subchapters to rest, plan, and *talk*." Roc to the rescue. He's the only other one in our party who knows the truth—the importance of getting it out.

"Okay. Can you wait until then, Tristan?" Adele asks, her voice comforting in the dark.

"I can do that," I say.

"Damn. I was hoping for story time in the hot, stinky pile of garbage," Trevor says. "Whatever you're keeping from us, it had better be good after all this talk about it."

"Trust me," I say, "it's good."

Fifteen

Adele

When the door opens we're ready, Tristan on one side, me on the other, and Trevor, who volunteered for the job, right in the middle. Drums beat and cymbals clang in the distance. Curious, I think.

"What the—" we hear a deep voice say when light floods the inside of the garbage truck.

Trevor's voice is innocent, the usual confidence and smartness stripped from it. "I must've gotten on the wrong bus," he says. "Is this the Laguna Club?"

What "the Laguna Club" is, or whether it even exists, I don't know. What I do know: Tristan's giving me the signal, one finger up, meaning it's time for action.

I swing out from my hiding spot behind the edge of the truck, whipping my boot around like a club, changing my direction slightly when I see the exact position of the big-eyed, wide-mouthed guy. Tristan's moving, too, lunging like a battering ram headfirst, his body a blur. My foot hits the guy's jaw about the same time Tristan's plows into his chest. Close enough anyway.

I follow through, landing on two feet and one balancing palm, swiveling my head to scan the area around us, which is full of trucks but empty of humans. There's a punching sound, because, well, Tristan's punching the guy in the head, either knocking him senseless, or knocking some sense into him, I'm not sure which. When he gets to his feet the guy's not moving.

A door slams, echoing through the aluminum garage, vibrating off the steel support girders and piping that run along the ceiling. "The driver," I whisper, as I hear the approaching clop of feet on concrete.

Trevor hops off the truck bed, his lips curled into a grin. "I'm not letting you have all the fun," he says, accelerating around the corner. As I start to chase him, a man says, "Who the he—" and then the hollow ring of flesh meeting the thin metal side of the truck.

By the time I catch up, the guy's flat on his back, his head lolled to the side, his tongue bleeding and hanging partway from his mouth. "I think he bit his tongue when he accidentally ran face first into the truck," Trevor says.

"Nice work," I say.

"Why thank you."

"Is there anyone else here?" Tristan asks, striding up.

"They'd be all over us if there was," I say. "Trevor's method of subduing this guy wasn't exactly discreet."

"Everyone's a critic," Trevor says.

"We should do some quick reconnaissance anyway," Tristan says. "Roc, Tawni—c'mon out."

Roc hops down and offers Tawni a hand, which she takes, stepping gracefully from the truck. "I think my feet squished in goo," she says.

"Roc—there's something on your tunic," Tristan says, pointing.

"Blech," Roc says, prying a strip of something black from his shirt. "I don't know what that is, but its presence in that truck alone means I desperately need a shower."

"Can you wait like two, three hours until we get to subchapter one and kill our father?" Tristan says. "Then we can all use the nice palace showers."

"Ooh, hot water," Roc says, his face lighting up.

"You've got hot water?" I say, unable to hide the look of disgust from ambushing my expression.

"Uh, yeah," Tristan says, chewing on the side of his lip.

I shake my head. The wonders of the Sun Realm never cease to amaze and anger me.

Changing the subject, Tristan says, "Let's split up and check the rest of the garage. Trevor and I will dispose of the bodies."

"We will?" Trevor says.

"Yes."

"Are they…dead?" Tawni asks.

"No, but I want to tie them up and hide them away so they won't be found for at least a day. Hopefully by then this will all be over."

Translation: the President dead. Us maybe dead, too. Hopefully all resulting in a ceasefire, which might just give the Resistance enough time to get their legs under them.

The garage is small, but is still able to fit almost ten trucks, each of which is sealed up and standing idle against one edge. Like the prongs of a fork, me, Tawni, and Roc branch out, each of us walking between a different set of trucks. Seeing nothing, we meet on the other side and then walk back by different routes, thus ensuring we hit every nook and cranny where a sun dweller trucker might be hiding. We even look underneath the trucks. Nothing.

We finish by hauling each of the truck tailgates up to look inside. Every truck, except for ours, is empty, the garbage having already been hauled off to wherever the incinerator is. Like the garbage, the truck drivers are gone, too.

"Where do you think they went?" Tawni asks.

"They're probably done for the day and have joined in the festivities," Roc says. "Subchapter four has one of the biggest Sun Festival parades."

That explains the drums and cymbals. A parade. Which means: lots of people. Here we go again.

When we return to our truck, Tristan and Trevor are finished with the two unconscious guys. They've used small swatches of rope to tie their hands and feet together, and used strips of cloth cut from the guys' tunics to blindfold and gag them.

"We should put them in one of the empty trucks," I say.

"They'll find them too easily," Tristan says.

"No, they won't find them until the truck returns to one of the other subchapters to get more garbage. They have no reason to open the ones that are already unloaded. They'll probably just think the other workers didn't finish with the last truck so they could join the parade early."

"Brilliant," Roc says. "By the time they realize what's happened, it will likely be tomorrow."

"Good call," Tristan says, his blue eyes bright.

While Tawni closes the gates on all of the trucks except two, Roc and Trevor haul the driver's body into the back of one of the remaining vehicles, and Tristan and I lug the other one. When we slam the final gate it clicks and latches into place with a final ring that sounds eerie in the mostly empty garage.

"You should put your heels on," Tristan says to Tawni when we're finished.

"Ugh. I'll ruin them," she says.

"People don't walk barefoot here very often."

Her nose curls up, as she slips her filthy feet into her shoes, clasping them. "Satisfied?" she says, one hand on her hip.

"Now you look like a sun dweller," Roc says. "But we all really need to get cleaned up before we move on. We'll turn heads for all the wrong reasons looking like this."

Luckily, there's a wash basin for the truckers, full of soapy water, which we use to get most of the grime off our skin and clothes.

Finished, I say, "Let's go," feeling the light thrill of anticipation in my stomach. We're almost to our destination, a place that seemed impossibly distant when we first began our trek through the Sun Realm. Despite the shortness of our journey in terms of hours, it feels like we've been seeking our quarry for weeks, if not months. I suddenly feel the strain of the miles and the violence in my bones, my muscles, my very *being*, as if it's all become a part of me, just caked on and patted down like a lump of clay, weighing me down.

I shake my arms and legs as we walk toward the lone door that exits the garage.

"What?" Tristan says, looking at me strangely.

"I'm just cramping up from the truck ride," I say.

Nodding, Tristan raises a hand to a push bar halfway up the door. "Remember?" he says, raising his eyebrows.

"Blend in," I chime. "We got it."

His eyes meet mine for a too-short moment before he pushes outward, striding through the door as if it's the most natural thing in the world.

The parade is in full swing, but, thankfully, not on our block. As Tristan and Roc lead us toward it, I look up at the subchapter roof, my eyes widening as I take it in. Another artificial sun, this one hot white, fills the city with light. Even wearing my sunglasses, I can't look directly at it. Covering the dark ceiling roof are speckles of light, shimmering like diamonds, reflecting the rays of the sun in a thousand different directions.

"Tawni, look," I breathe, my eyes lost above.

"Wow," she says when she looks up. "What are those?"

"Diamonds," Roc says.

So not shimmering *like diamonds*, shimmering *because they're diamonds*.

"Where did they all come from?" I ask, finally looking away from the spectacle to meet Roc's eyes.

"Where do you think?" he says, his voice lowering into an angry tone.

No, can't be. All the blood and sweat I saw on his face and clothes when he came home from the mines. The worrying when there was a cave-in—that maybe this time I'd be the one to lose their father, not the girl down the street, or the boy two

174

blocks over. The two Nailins a day wages, barely enough to buy half a bag of rice to eat with our week-old bread and well water. All for what? To supply the Sun Realm with a million diamonds to plaster their subchapter roof with so they have something pretty to look at every day when they wake up?

My lip turns up into a snarl. "My father mined them," I growl.

"Some of them for sure. Subchapter fourteen was the biggest diamond mine in all the Tri-Realms. Eighty percent of the diamonds above us are from the mine your father worked in."

He survived the harsh working conditions: the stifling and disease-causing air, the claustrophobic tunnels, the filth and the grime, the crumbling support beams, the unstable mining dynamite and razor-sharp pickaxes. All to get him to a single moment—one that haunts me still—where one man crushed *everything* in my world.

I slam a fist into my palm, generating a loud *slap* that makes Tristan turn toward me, his eyebrows raised, his mouth opening to ask a question.

"I'm fine," I say, cutting off his unspoken inquiry.

Another reason I like Tristan: he usually knows when to let things go. He nods and continues on, leaving me to work things out on my own. Just his simple act alone helps to calm me. Come to think of it, the only time he's ever really pushed me when I wanted to be left alone was after our fight. At the time I thought I wanted to be alone, but really, I needed him more than ever. If he hadn't chased after me, who knows where we'd be in our relationship right now? Even when my father died and I fell into a deep, dark depression, he knew not to force my feelings out; instead, he was just there for me, by my side, every chance he had, despite the fact that he had lost a friend too.

My father trusted Tristan. Even when many others didn't.

And so shall I.

As we approach the first cross street, I cast my thoughts aside as the parade passes. Although there are hordes of sun dwellers, just like in the last subchapter we were in, I can see the action pretty clearly, as those in the parade are raised on high platforms, which are being pushed by muscular, shirtless men of all different colors, black, brown, white, their heads down, their muscles toned and flexing.

"Are those…?" I say, trailing off.

"Slaves?" Roc says. "Is that what you were going to say?"

Honestly, I'm not sure what I was about to say, which is probably why I didn't finish the question. As far as I know, there's no such thing as slavery. At least not anymore. We didn't learn much about the old ways in history class at school, but we did learn that people used to use slaves to do things they didn't want to do, but that it was abolished long before Year Zero.

"I'm not sure," I say. "Do they volunteer for that?"

"They're not slaves," Roc says. "Well, not technically. They're servants, like I am…I mean, like I *was*. But they might as well be slaves. They don't get paid, just fed and sheltered and clothed."

"Why don't they just leave?" Tawni asks, lowering her voice as we get closer to the back row of the crowd.

"It's called a breach of contract under the law, punishable by being sent to the Lower Realms or by imprisonment—usually both. Wealthy sun dwellers travel to the Lower Realms to find servants. They promise them an extravagant lifestyle, easy jobs with lots of time off, gourmet food, things we could only ever dream about."

"You mean, you were a moon dweller?" I ask.

Roc laughs. "My father's father was a *star* dweller." His laugh fades and he screws up his face, wincing slightly, as if he's just been slapped. "I guess he's not my father anymore," he murmurs, staring off into space.

"So the man who raised you—his father was a star dweller?" I ask, trying to distract him from his dark thoughts.

"Exactly," he says. "He was recruited by President Dervin Nailin to come and work as a servant for him."

"Mine and Roc's grandfather," Tristan adds without turning around. Apparently he's been listening to every word.

Tristan plows into the cheering crowd, jostling his way through. I dive after him, heavier things on my mind than bumping into a bunch of sun dwellers. As I swim through the sea of parade watchers, I notice something. These people seem different than the ones in subchapter eight. They're less…*horrible.* At least that's my initial impression. There are kids, for one, riding on their parents' shoulders and laughing and craning their necks to see the next float coming down the street. And the adults seem more civilized and fully sober, cheering and making noise, yes, but in a much more respectful manner than the young partiers we came across in the last sun dweller city.

A different crowd.

Even their clothes are different, albeit still strange and unusual to me. The women wear long, elegant gowns in silvers and purples and greens, some sparkling, some shining, all beautiful. The men are in gray or white suits, the kind I've only seen people wearing on the telebox. In my subchapter you'd look ridiculous wearing a suit like that. But here it just seems normal. The kids are dressed like their mothers and fathers, their faces bright and cheerful as they dance with delight at the parade passing by. I wonder whether the people here are really bad, or just ignorant. On the face they don't look bad, which gives me hope.

The throng parts momentarily and I have a good view of the parade. Girls wearing flowery dresses dance and wave flags over their heads and around them, fully synchronized. Behind them are men dressed in sun dweller red, riding horses, carrying rifles and wearing black hats.

My first thought is: *Horses!* And then: *Soldiers!* Instinctively, I duck, trying to get out of their sight.

But then Tristan's by my side, holding my hand. "They're not real," he says, his lips practically touching my ear. "It's just for show."

My heart slows and my face goes warm. *Duh.* Of course all the real soldiers would be fighting in the war.

I gaze at the horses, having never seen the majestic animals in person before. They're much bigger than they look on the telebox, their majestic heads held high above the heads of the people. Magnificent. That's the only word to describe them. With lustrous black, brown, and white coats, they prance along, bucking their heads from side to side at the people lining either side of the street. Growing up, I always wanted to see the horses, especially after my grandmother read me a story about a girl and her horse, and the adventures they went on together. Why there are no horses in the Moon Realm, I do not know.

Tristan pulls me away from the parade just as a squad of smallish acrobats dressed in bright gypsy outfits appears, leaping and somersaulting and springing through the air.

Watching the parade and the horses, I've almost forgotten why we're here. There's no time for fun when death awaits.

Due to the much thinner and more well-mannered crowd, we manage to make good time getting to the end of one of the longest streets I've ever seen. Three quarters of the way, the line of people ends, wrapping around a bend and onto another street, where the parade continues along. It's weird walking along with just the five of us again, our voices naked in the hushed silence where the only sounds are distant and almost surreal. The road ends at a T. To the left is a sign that reads: To Nailin Tunnel, Spoke 3.

"We're heading that way, right?" I say to Tristan.

"Yes. Once we get in the tunnel, it's only a little over a mile to subchapter one."

Roc adds, "This is called the Capital Cluster. It's four subchapters—one through four—number one being in the center and the other three surrounding it. Subchapter one is connected to each of them by a separate tunnel, like the spokes of a wheel. The spokes have numbers, always one less than the subchapter they lead to."

"Which is why we're heading into Spoke 3 when we're in subchapter four," I say to confirm my understanding.

"Exactly," Roc says.

"So if the trains aren't running today the only way to get out of subchapter one will be…" I say.

"Through the tunnels," Tristan says.

My heart sinks. In other words: once the alarms sound, the tunnels will be blocked and we'll be trapped.

Sixteen

Tristan

I hate seeing the look on Adele's face when she realizes we don't have an escape plan, when and if we complete our mission. But it only lasts a second before being replaced by narrow eyes and tight lips and a proud incline to her chin. I have the urge to kiss her right here, but the others are watching and now's not really the time.

She understands the situation, so I don't say anything more. Instead, I start down the road that leads to the tunnels, seeing no one. The entire subchapter is at the parade, enjoying the festivities like the rest of the sun dwellers, while the other two-thirds of the Tri-Realms fight for their lives. It disgusts me, although this is one of my favorite Sun Realm cities. The people here are kinder, less radical, a slightly older crowd, more family-oriented—but they're still spoiled, just like everyone else up here.

The road runs right up to the cavern wall, which rises hundreds of feet above us, all the way to the diamond-studded roof. Cut into the rock is a massive tunnel, arched at the top and rectangular at the bottom, wide enough for a hundred men to walk side by side, and tall enough for a dozen people or more to stand on each other's shoulders, if they were into that sort of thing.

As we enter the gaping tunnel mouth, Adele cranes her neck, as if she wants to watch herself being swallowed whole by the earth. "Will we run into any sun dwellers in here?" she asks to the tunnel roof.

"If we do we can just *blend in* anyway," Trevor says. "In these digs I fit right in."

"It's unlikely we'll see anyone," I say. "As Roc said earlier, most people will stay in their own city for the Sun Festival. It's kind of a tradition, like people are proud of the celebration their subchapter comes up with. They're always trying to outdo each other."

Nodding, Roc motions to the wide expanse of the tunnel. "On any other day, the tunnel would be pretty much full from side to side, end to end. People in the Capital Cluster frequently travel to the Capital and back again, either for work, shopping, or entertainment," he says.

"I'm glad it's not any other day," Adele says. "I've had about enough of large crowds for my entire life."

"I don't know," Tawni says. "I kind of enjoyed it."

"Me, too," Trevor says. "Although I had the urge to smack most of 'em around."

I laugh, my voice echoing through the empty tunnel. "I know the feeling."

We walk in silence for a few minutes, the orange tunnel lights pulling our shadows forward, back, and then forward again. It's a wonder this group ever runs out of things to say, especially with Trevor around.

"Where should we stop?" Roc says.

"Stop?" I echo.

"To tell your BIG *secret*," Trevor says, over-exaggerating his words. "Or have you chickened out?"

Ugh. Yes. I might feel more comfortable if I had any clue how they would react. Especially Adele—her reaction worries me the most. I mean, what will she say when I tell her that Dwellers have been living aboveground for years now? It doesn't help that I've kept it from her this long. I swallow a thick gulp of spittle, which only adds to my nervousness.

"Uh, yeah. I mean no. I mean I'm going to tell you. I have to."

"Where?" Roc repeats, glancing to the side as we pass the doors to a rest stop meant for the oldies, who can't make it the whole way through the tunnel without stopping to use the bathroom or rest their legs.

"Maybe at the next stop," I say, trying to delay as long as possible.

"I think there's only one left," Roc says.

"That'll do," I say, my mind whirling through what I want to say, how I want to say it. It's like all the information is there, but is broken into a million pieces, none of which I can make sense of, or which fit together. As I desperately try to connect the facts, they disappear, as if my memory's been wiped. My palms start to sweat. My lips are dry. My mind's a black hole, empty of logical thought. I'd rather face my father in a fight to the death a hundred times over than tell the truth I've hidden to those I know it will hurt the most.

"Last rest stop is just ahead," Roc says, and my head jerks to the side, my eyes locking in on the doors I dread opening, the doors that might change my relationship with Adele forever. Where did the last few minutes go? It's like I blinked and we were a quarter mile further along the track, some trick of time and distance. My face is hot and my chest tight, my breathing short and shallow. What is wrong with me? Step up and be a man. I've faced much graver dangers than this—dangers that threatened my life and the lives of those I care about—and yet I'm much more scared now.

"I'm ready," I say, not to them, but to myself, trying to convince myself that I am.

We reach the doors and I stop, just stare at them. They're the exact opposite of how I'm feeling: bright pink and blue striped with ornate carvings of a city—the Capital, the presidential buildings, a statue of the first Nailin president. A happy and light scene leading the way to a tale of darkness and the unfairness of the world my father controls.

"Are we...going in?" Trevor says from behind, a verbal kick in the butt.

I want to move aside, to let Roc or Adele or anyone else open the door, but I know I have to do this myself; by opening these doors I'm metaphorically opening the door to what Roc and I know. The door to the truth.

I take a deep breath. Take a step forward. Place a hand on the door.

Then I'm in, having pushed the door open without even really realizing it, holding it for the others behind me.

Once everyone's inside, I let the door swing shut behind me. We're in a sanctuary of sorts. A sanctuary from the sun dwellers, from the tunnel that leads to our destiny, from my father. The room has brown wooden floors and crimson matted walls. Table lamps light a plush seating area with a half dozen couches and chairs. A second door leads off to an area marked as a bathroom.

"This is the nicest room I've ever seen," Trevor announces, which doesn't help me at all. Just another example of inequality in the world we live in.

"You should all sit down for this," I say, motioning to the couches. I wonder how the seating positions will end up. Naturally, Roc and Tawni sit together on a black two-seater, Trevor grabs a solo lounge chair, immediately resting his feet on a cushioned ottoman, and Adele snags the end of a large couch, clearly inviting me to join her.

I sit down next to her, but keep a space between us, leaving it up to her whether to eventually fill the gap. I take in the four faces watching mine. Tawni looks interested, Roc serious, Trevor amused, and Adele uncertain, her expression neutral, with clear eyes, her brows raised slightly, her lips as straight as a sword.

"Do you want me to participate?" Roc asks, a kind offer, one I know I must reject.

"Thanks, but no. All your information is secondhand, whereas I've experienced it." Roc nods, as if he already knew what my answer would be and agrees: it has to be me.

"We shouldn't linger too long," Adele says softly, pushing me to get started. She slides her hand into the space between us, palm up. An offer.

I meet her eyes, thankful for the gesture, and then place my hand atop hers, embarrassed by the moisture on my skin. I take another deep breath but it catches as a lump forms in my throat. My body's rebelling against me, I think.

"Where do I start?" I say under my breath, trying to gather up all the crap in my mind and turn it into a coherent thought.

"From the beginning," Adele suggests, raising an eyebrow.

Yes. The beginning…which is where exactly?

My fifteenth birthday. My father's gift. Not a new sword or a trip to the Sandy Oasis or a new dress tunic, but a revelation.

"The day I turned fifteen," I start, "was one of the worst days of my life." I look around, checking for reactions. The faces are like stone, frozen on me, not giving away anything. Even Trevor's managed to suspend his amusement for the moment.

"I woke up ready for a day of presents and cakes and a party, but instead, my father was waiting by my bedside. 'Today I have something to show the entire family,' he said. 'Something you'll all one day be a part of.' By that point in my life my father and I had already grown miles apart, but I didn't hate him. Not yet. Not until later that day."

I pause, breathe in, breathe out, choose my next words carefully.

"None of us knew what to expect—not even my mom. Killen was excited, only thirteen at that time, I was curious but wary, and my mom was very quiet, like she knew something bad was coming. My father was himself: stern, gregarious, intimidating. 'After this you become a Nailin,' he said to me as we left the presidential buildings, slapping me on the back. He didn't ask if I wanted to be a Nailin.

"A black car took us through the city, past the statue of the first Nailin President, past the shopping district, past the train station, until we reached an ordinary black stone building in a corner of the capital that I'd never seen before. The security was the tightest I'd ever been subjected to. Even with my father in the car, they searched it, checked all of our identification, as if we were somehow Nailin family look-a-likes. It was crazy. It's the type of thing that would normally set my father off, but he was calm and patient through the entire thing. He even said that all the procedures were to be strictly enforced, no matter what, under his orders."

"Why all the rigmarole?" Trevor asks.

"There was something hidden inside that no one could ever know about—not even the security guards. Even my father's family didn't know about that place, at least not until that day. Only my father's most trusted advisors and top scientists knew about it. Oh, and those sun dwellers, moon dwellers, and star dwellers who were recruited to participate in the project."

"Project?" Adele says, her hand tightening on mine. "What project?"

"And since when was your father interested in input from moon or star dwellers in anything he did?" Trevor asks.

I put a hand up. "Please. I'll get to all that in time."

Adele murmurs, "Sorry," while Trevor leans back and motions for me to continue.

"Where was I? Oh, yes, security. We weren't done yet. After parking the vehicle in a covered lot full of black cars, we went through a physical pat down by a guard each, a metal detector, and then a chemical identifier. And that was before even entering the building.

"Once inside, we filed down a hall, and then rode a lift to the eighteenth floor, which was marked as RESTRICTED on the panel—my father had to use a key to access it.

"The eighteenth floor was like nothing I'd ever seen, full of men and women in white coats running around doing who knows what."

A few eyebrows go up, but I rush on, not wanting any questions just yet. "One of them—a bald guy with a nametag that identified him as Dr. Markus Kane—recognized my father and came to greet us. He introduced himself, welcomed us to the Nailin Center, and then led us through a maze of desks and expensive-looking lab equipment.

"A door at the other end of the floor provided access to this crazy bridge. It was glass on all sides, including the floor and ceiling, and shot out of the building, high above the edge of the city, and disappeared into the side of the cavern. I was so shocked at the feeling of flying as we walked through the glass passage, I didn't notice what was at the other end until we were right on top of it."

"Let me guess, another bald white-coated scientist?" Trevor says, curling a lip.

"Close. A vault, complete with a card reading device and a little black panel that read fingerprints. Like I said before, this place spared no expense on security, and we were apparently headed for the most secure area of all."

"And you say the vault led into the side of the cavern, as in out of the city?" Adele asks.

"That's right," I say.

"So basically a hidden cave on the outskirts of the city."

"That's correct. The only way in or out of this cave was through the black building and the glass walkway. Anyway, the scientist inserted his ID card in a slot, stuck a finger on the reader, and then turned a huge wheel, which opened the door.

"The cave was completely different to the eighteenth floor. The walls were rough, the lighting dim, and only three people manned the station, each of whom snapped to attention as soon as we entered.

"Although Dr. Kane introduced them to us, I can't remember their names anymore. But I can remember what they did. They controlled access to the Cylinder."

"The Cylinder? What is that—like a big tube?" Trevor asks.

"Pretty much," I say. "But a big freaking tube, made from concrete. It rose from the floor all the way to the ceiling. There was a hatch cut into the side of the tube."

"So they had three people just to control access to this tube thingy?" Adele asks.

"That's right. I'm sure they did other things, too, but if anyone was scheduled to use the Cylinder, I guess these people would be there. Before we entered the tube, we were each given metal bracelets to wear on our arms. They snapped on our wrists, clasped so tight we couldn't move them at all. The only way to get them off was with an electronic device that controlled the locking mechanism."

"What were they for?" Adele asks.

"They told us two things: First—to track us. Second—as a symbol of our authorization to enter the next secure area."

"Another secure area?" Trevor says. "This all seems just a little over the top. Even for sun dwellers."

"It was pretty nuts to me too," I admit.

Tawni asks her first question: "Why would they need to track you?"

"Everything was just very controlled. They wanted to know where everyone was at any given time. In case anything happened, I guess."

I look around, glad everyone—except Roc, who's just watching, his lips pursed—is engaged and participating. Somehow hearing other people's voices is helping with my nerves. I'm in a rhythm now, the words flowing freely, my mouth on autopilot. My heart rate has even slowed to a seemingly normal pace. But as soon as I realize I'm closing in on the moment of truth, my blood starts pumping again, and my chest vibrates to the *thud, thud...thud, thud...thud, thud...*of my beating heart knocking against my bones.

I continue slowly, trying to delay. "We went into the hatch and the door closed behind us. My mother had been silent for most of the trip, until now. 'Where the *hell* are you taking us?' she said. It was the first time I'd ever heard her curse, and I could feel a surge of anger, or maybe fear, coming off of her."

"And she never got angry," Roc adds, finally breaking his silent streak.

"Which scared me," I say. "My father wouldn't answer her, just kept saying, 'You'll see. Just wait.' He wasn't smiling exactly, but he did wear his typical arrogance like a cloak that day. As usual, he knew he had all the power, and we were forced to cooperate with his every whim.

"The pod started moving. It was very hard to tell which direction it was moving—sometimes it felt like we were dropping, other times rising, and sometimes moving to either side, maybe even diagonally. It's very possible we were moving in all different directions. There was nowhere to sit, so we were all stuck standing for about thirty minutes, until we finally felt the pod start to slow.

"My mother demanded to know where we were, even going so far as to grab my father's shirt. I'd seen her argue with my father before, but never raise a hand to him. He slammed her against the side of the pod—you should have seen his face, all red, veins popping from his forehead. 'Don't ruin this, woman!' he yelled, and then slung her to the floor."

I realize Adele is rubbing my hand with one of her fingers. There's a tear in my eye but I don't care. It's for my mother and she can have it.

"I should have gone to her, comforted her, but I was too scared of my father, too scared of what he might do to me. I'll never forgive myself for just standing there, watching my mom huddled on the floor."

"You were just a kid," Adele says.

"It was two years ago," I say.

"You've changed a lot in two years," she says, and despite having not known me when I was fifteen, she's right. I squeeze her hand.

"Just finish, Tristan," Roc encourages lightly.

"When the door opened it was dark and there were men in orange plastic suits with big clear bubbles over their heads. They had black guns and black boots. The way they charged into the hatch I thought they might shoot us, but they didn't. First they checked our bracelets, scanned them with a handheld device. Then they escorted us from the pod into an alcove, using flashlights to guide us. We entered a monster tunnel. The tunnel kept getting brighter and brighter as we moved forward. By the end I was squinting.

"The passage led into a holding area, which we entered without the orange men, who closed a hydraulic air-lock door behind us, locking us into a glassed-in section of tunnel with showerheads all over the walls. 'Prepare for detoxification,' a voice droned, before the showerheads burst into life, spraying us with hot water that smelled a bit chemically. We still had all our clothes on and soon our tunics were sticking to our skin. When the water stopped, the door on the other side of the airlock opened, and men wearing black and gray uniforms entered, scanned our bracelets once more, and escorted us by the elbows to a room with two doors, one for women and one for men. My brother, father, and I took the right door, while my mom was forced to enter the left door alone."

I pause, realizing my mouth is dry from speaking uninterrupted for so long. I hope someone has a question to break up my monologue, but no one does. They're all just staring at me with eyes that want me to continue. Thankfully, Roc hands me a canteen and I'm able to swish some water around to moisten my tongue and lips.

"There were dry clothes in the changing rooms. We put them on and then met my mom back outside. She had new clothes on too.

"We went down another tunnel to where the men in uniforms were waiting, none of them having spoken a word to us since our arrival. Finally, one of them spoke, an older bearded guy. 'Do you want to tell them anything before we head through?' he asked my father. 'No,' was all my father said. 'All right,' the man said, handing us each a pair of sunglasses. 'You'll need these.' Then he opened the door."

The breath leaves my lungs. There's tension in the room, as if all the air's been sucked out, as everyone leans in closer.

Adele's fingers are no longer stroking my hand, but are frozen, waiting for me to speak. I take a final deep breath, feeling sudden and unexpected emotion well up in my eyes.

"We stepped onto Earth and the sun blinded us," I say.

Seventeen
Adele

His words have no meaning to me. They're just words. Either he's not being very clear or I've been dumbstruck.

…*stepped onto Earth?*

…*the sun blinded us?*

"You've got to be kidding me," Trevor says, ironically all joking filtered from his tone.

"Do I look like I'm kidding?" Tristan says, his expression more serious than I've ever seen before.

"You walked 'onto Earth'?" Tawni says. Evidently she's having trouble with the wording too.

"Yes," Tristan says, confirming the meaningless words.

"Like a pile of rocks or what?" I say.

"No, like *the* surface of the earth. You know, up above."

A shiver runs up my spine. My head spins. I feel faint. *What?* I'm missing something. A punch line or a piece of information—like maybe I dozed off and didn't catch a detail or two. But I know that's not true; I was wide awake, riveted the whole time.

"That's the biggest load of bat turds I've ever heard," Trevor scoffs.

"It can't be," Tawni says heavily.

But Tristan's ignoring them, his eyes boring into mine, his face clouded with concern, his eyes thick with emotion. He's worried about my reaction. I realize I've pulled my hand back from his, a reflexive sign of separation.

"You're saying you went above? To the surface of the earth?" I ask again, because I'm still not sure what I'm hearing.

Tristan nods.

Which means...

"Earth is safe again?" Tawni asks.

Still watching me, Tristan says, "Not exactly."

"You should tell them everything your father told you," Roc suggests.

My head is getting hot. Tristan is still staring at me and it's starting to annoy me. Like what he's telling us only affects me. My hands tighten and I tuck them at my sides.

"Tristan?" Roc says again when Tristan doesn't respond.

"Why didn't you tell us before?" I growl. "And don't give me any of that crap about it not being the right time."

"I was scared of how you would react," Tristan says, his face a blank piece of paper.

"We deserved to know before we went on this mission."

194

"I know," he says. "The longer I waited the harder it got. It's the best-kept secret in the Tri-Realms. It's why my father tried to capture or kill me back in the Moon Realm—when we first met. I think he knew I would tell someone eventually."

"This is ridiculous," I spout, my anger growing.

"Would it have changed anything?" Tristan says, his voice rising. "If I told you just before the mission, or the moment we met, or anytime along the way. Would it have changed your mind about coming, or changed the Resistance strategy, or had any impact at all?" His own hands are fisted now, too, his jaw a tight line.

I fill my lungs once, twice, three times. Try to get control of my emotions. Think logically. If he had told us there were people on the surface of the earth before we left on the mission, how would I have reacted? My shoulders slump.

"No," I say. "It would have just fueled our desire to overthrow your father. Knowing he's kept such a truth from the very people he's meant to be leading…"

"Unforgivable," Tawni finishes for me.

"That was my reaction when he told me," Roc says. "It took him a few weeks to tell me, too. Give him a break, this is a big deal. It's not something you tell someone in normal conversation. Can you all just back off and let him tell the rest of the story? It's important."

Tristan's eyes flit to Roc's, soften somewhat, and then return to mine, seeking approval. "Okay. I'm sorry," I say, not sure if I mean it yet.

"Are you guys really buying this?" Trevor says.

"Shut it," I say, warning him off with my eyes.

"Thanks," Tristan says. "And I'm sorry for not telling you sooner. We literally walked outside onto the surface of the

195

earth," he starts again, trying to hammer home the crazy truth that I'm still trying to come to terms with. "Even with the sunglasses I couldn't see for ten minutes, forced to cover my eyes with my hands, letting through a little more light minute by minute. My mother and Killen were the same, but my father adjusted quickly, because it wasn't his first time above."

My heart leaps suddenly as a thought hits me. "Were there clouds?" I ask, my voice a little too squeaky for my liking.

Tristan smiles for the first time in a while. "You should have seen it. The sky was dark red, spotted with bits of grainy clouds, which moved across the heavens faster than you would believe. The sun was nothing like our artificial suns. Compared to it, they are but a single hair on a person's head, whereas it is the entire head of hair. Bright enough to light a thousand earths, it turned my skin red in only fifteen minutes."

"It burned you?" Tawni asks.

"Yes, my gosh, how it burned. My skin ached for days and then became paper thin and peeled off as if I was a snake shedding my skin. There were trees and plants everywhere, but only in the Bubble."

"The Bubble?" I say, curiosity getting the better of me.

"Sorry," Tristan says. "I'm not explaining things right. I mean, there's just so much to tell it's hard to decide where to begin."

"Tell them about the city," Roc prompts.

"There's a city?" I ask, my brain buzzing with too many questions to ask them all.

"Yes. That's where we were. The only city left on Earth, at least as far as anyone knows. It's called the New City, although informally people just call it the Bubble, because there's a huge glass dome surrounding it, which looks like you could pop it by sticking a sword in the side. In reality though, it's three feet thick and nearly unbreakable."

"Who built it?" Tawni asks.

"Aha. Good question," Tristan says, looking more and more comfortable with the subject now that we're asking questions and not giving him a hard time about not telling us sooner. "Everything I'm about to tell you my father told us, so I'm assuming it's true as he had no reason to lie or volunteer the information. Two hundred years ago, well before my father was born, my great-grandfather had his engineers build unmanned probes to send to the earth's surface. When they returned, the rock and air samples they brought back were very encouraging. After weeks of analysis, fact checking, and experimentation, the scientists determined there was a greater than fifty percent likelihood that Earth could be safely inhabited once more."

"But you just said it's not exactly safe on the earth's surface," Tawni says, her eyebrows raised.

"It's not *exactly*, but I'll get to that. My great-grandfather had a grand vision of building what he called the New City, the first city on earth since Year Zero. But he wasn't about to go up there, not without some pretty strong evidence that it was safe. Nor was he willing to put sun dwellers in danger. So he personally recruited a collection of moon and star dwellers to be the guinea pigs."

Trevor grunts. "Look, man, I'm trying to believe this—I really am—but do you really think your grandfather—"

"*Great*-grandfather."

"Whatever. Do you really think he could've kept it quiet? Once he started involving people from all the Realms, surely someone would have gotten the word out."

"I asked my father the same thing. Keeping it hidden all these years is what he was most proud of. It was easy, really. When the moon and star dwellers were recruited, they simply acted like they'd won some kind of a lottery, a chance to move to the Sun Realm, live the high life. But really, they sent them to the earth's surface. No one was any the wiser."

"What happened to them?" I ask. Everyone's so worried about all the damn details, but what matters—what really matters—is what's happened to all these so-called recruits.

"They died," Tristan says, looking down.

"All of them?" Tawni asks.

"Yes." Tristan says the word into his lap, slightly muffled.

"That's horrible," Tawni says.

We all agree, which is why no one speaks for a few minutes. I stare at Tristan, who refuses to look at me. Tawni plays with her fingers. Roc taps a toe. Trevor, well, even he's quiet, although I can tell the silence is getting to him, because he keeps sighing and looking around at everyone, as if he wishes someone would speak but doesn't want to be the one.

"How did they die?" I ask finally. Now I'm interested in the gruesome details for some reason.

"Exposure to semi-toxic air," Tristan says, raising his head slowly to meet my eyes.

"*Semi*-toxic?" Trevor says, almost bursting to join the conversation. "If they all died it sounds fully toxic to me."

"Only to us," Tristan explains. "They weren't used to the air above."

"But it's the same air we breathe down here," I argue. "We get it from the earth's surface."

"Yeah, but ours is highly filtered, going through multiple air locks where potentially harmful dust and bacteria are removed from the air. Our lungs aren't used to the real air up there. Maybe we never will be. The initial earth dwellers only lasted a little over a month before contracting various types of irreversible cancers."

"Let me guess, they got more moon and star dwellers for round two," I say, feeling slightly ill.

"Yes. This time they equipped them with heavy-duty protective clothing, an earlier generation of the orange hazmat suits the guys were wearing when we first arrived on the surface. Even wearing the suits around the clock, they only lasted six months before their bodies gave out. But they had made a significant start on building a city—a city that was uninhabitable, at least if you wanted to live to see your next birthday. My great-grandfather was getting old at that point, so he passed the torch to my father's father, who realized that even if he continued to use dwellers from the Lower Realms to build the city, replacing them as they died, he would still be stuck with a city that no one could live in."

The story is coming together, feeling more and more real with each added detail. "So he built the Bubble?" I ask.

"Not him, of course, but yes, more 'recruits' built it, an airtight globe that protects the New City both from the dangerous rays of the sun and the noxious air on the earth's surface. It filters and recycles the air using a system very similar to what we have in the Tri-Realms. A hundred thousand people now live in the New City," Tristan says.

A big question remains. The biggest, really. "Why didn't your grandfather tell the rest of the Tri-Realms once the city was livable?" I ask.

Deep lines appear in Tristan's creased forehead. "Because he's a Nailin," he says. "Look, he and my father are cut from the same marble block. They're cold, hard-hearted, and think they're better than everyone else. My grandfather had a good thing going. President of the Tri-Realms, a good life, everything he ever wanted. A drastic change like Earth being inhabitable again? That might have destroyed everything he worked so hard to build. The hundred thousand people up there aren't allowed to come back down, which is fine by most of them. Ninety percent of the earth dwellers used to be sun dwellers, and were selected over time to populate the surface of the earth."

"And the other ten percent?" Tawni asks.

"Moon and star dwellers. Up there only to do the jobs that the sun dwellers don't want to do, like garbage disposal, cleaning, cooking, all the same stuff they do in the Sun Realm."

"Slave labor," I say. The messed-up world we live in has just become even more messed up.

"Pretty much," Tristan says.

"And your father wanted to maintain the status quo, too?" I ask, already knowing he'll answer in the affirmative.

Tristan nods. "He knows telling the people will just encourage them to rebel. They'll demand to go above, to see what they've been deprived of their entire lives."

"Then we have to tell them," I say firmly, clasping my hands together, daring him to contradict me.

"I agree," Tristan says.

Roc, who's been relatively quiet for a while, says, "Tell them about your mom, Tristan."

Tristan's eyes immediately go glassy. He closes his eyes, opens them when he starts speaking. "My father took us on a tour through the New City, told us the whole story along the way, bit by unbelievable bit. He didn't hold anything back, probably because he didn't realize how negatively my mom and I would take it. I'm not making excuses for Killen, but he was younger, more in awe of what my father had accomplished than anything else.

"Well, my mother just took it all in, not visibly reacting, just listening to every word, capturing every sight with her eyes. I took my cues from her, staying mostly silent and trying not to miss anything. When the tour finished, and it was time to go back into the pod and down to the Sun Realm, my mother refused. She said she wasn't done taking mental notes so she could accurately share what she'd seen with the world."

"She was a strong woman," I say, immediately thinking of the risks and sacrifices my own mother has made.

"She was. But not strong enough. My father was livid. What he did to her on the way up in the pod was nothing to what he did now. He punched her in the face, breaking her nose and blackening her eye. When she fell to her knees, he kicked her in the ribs repeatedly, until she collapsed from pain and exhaustion. I tried to stop it, but he was stronger than ten men, such was the intensity of his rage, and he threw me across the room like a jewelry box. I broke my wrist and couldn't walk for a week. My mom couldn't get out of bed for a month."

"He's the Devil," Tawni says, her voice a whisper, almost reverent.

"Not far from it," Tristan says, his eyes dark and brooding. So much of the pain he's hidden from me is in this story, it takes me by surprise. Because I'm a moon dweller and he's a sun dweller, I've taken for granted that my life is harder than his, that, if anything, he owes me. In reality, however, neither of us owes each other anything. We've both had it bad. We've both felt pain and loss. We've both lived in a world where nothing felt right.

But something's still missing.

"What else about your mother?" I ask, knowing this story is far from over.

Before I'm half-finished with the question, Tristan's nostrils are flaring as he sucks in a breath. "She recovered, of course, eventually. When she did, she came to me. I'll never forget what she said. 'Tristan, your father is a bad man,' she said. 'We need to tell everyone about what he showed us. We're in this together—you and me. You understand?' I did understand and I told her. I promised her I would do whatever I could to tell the world the truth. 'Not yet,' she said. 'Wait for what feels like the right time.'

"Then she got all misty-eyed, hugged me, and said, 'I might not always be around, Tristan, but know I'm always with you, in here.' She patted my chest, a tear dripping from her chin. 'I'm so sorry I haven't been able to protect you the way I should have.' I was crying, too, and I didn't know why at the time. I mean, yeah, I loved my mom, but it's not like she was going anywhere. I didn't realize until she disappeared three days later that she was saying goodbye." There's moisture on Tristan's face but he either doesn't notice or isn't bothered by it. My heart wells up for him, a dull ache in my chest that doesn't sufficiently encompass the emotion of losing a mother. I give him my hand again, which I've so selfishly denied him as he's told the hardest story he's ever had to tell. When he grasps my fingers I shiver, because his hand is as cold as ice, almost blue.

Sad like him and sad like me.

202

Eighteen
Tristan

Adele doesn't hate me for keeping the truth from her. Or at least she's decided to support me until a time when I'm not a mess anymore, perhaps for the good of the mission. Even Trevor's backed off with his smartass remarks, although I suspect it will be a short reprieve.

I know they all have a zillion more questions, at least half of which I won't be able to answer, but we all seem to realize that they aren't really important right now, not when we have a president to kill. So we leave the tunnel rest stop to begin the last stage of our journey, a brief and uninterrupted walk into the capital.

Although my heart is heavy because of the dark truths, both about my father and about my mom, that I've dropped like a dead weight on my friends, my mind is lightened, like a ball and a chain (and maybe a wall or two) have been removed from my skull, opening my mind to a whole new world, one without secrets and lies and inequality. We're not there yet, but I feel like we're making progress, without even having accomplished anything yet.

I sense a renewed determination in all of us. Perhaps it was just resting for a few minutes, or the group understanding that we all now have. Or maybe it's just because we're all sick and tired of being held under the foot of a tyrant. Whatever the case, we all want the same thing, and we'll do whatever it takes to get there.

When we enter the capital, subchapter one of the Sun Realm, a place I called home for most of my life, a strange thrill zips through the very marrow of my bones. If nothing else, the city is beautiful, a notch or two above even the finest sun dweller cities. The simulated sunset is nearly complete, and the artificial sun is glowing red, a fiery ball above the buildings and parks. The automatic streetlights are blinking on, one by one, preventing any semblance of gloom from ever infiltrating my father's kingdom.

Without talking about it, we stop as a unit to watch the red sun darken, until, a few minutes later, it goes dark completely, disappearing on the roof of the cavern. Instantly, the rocky firmament springs back to life, as hundreds of blinking stars and a glowing moon appear, casting nighttime light across the subchapter.

I glance at Adele, whose head is craned toward the ceiling, her green eyes sparkling like emeralds under the shine of the artificial stars. Her lips are parted slightly, an air of wonder in her expression, her skin porcelain, her hair a silk curtain. She's looking at a beautiful sight and I'm looking at her—another beautiful sight.

"It's wonderful," she says softly and almost mournfully, which surprises me until her next words. "But I bet it's nothing compared to the real moon and stars."

As I cock my head to gaze at the artificial moon I grew up with, I realize that in that simple statement is an important truth: no matter what we try to recreate down here, none of it will ever be as good as what's up there, on Earth. And that's crucial to understanding the magnitude of the responsibility on our shoulders. Not only must we *remove* my father from his position of power, but we must take the Tri-Realms on a journey, both in their way of thinking and also in where they live, to give them back their humanity. This is our solemn duty.

"Am I right?" Adele says, turning her head toward me.

"About what?" I ask, not remembering her having asked me a question.

"About the moon. The real one is better, right?"

"Oh. That. I honestly don't know. When we left it was still sunny. But considering how much better the real sun was, I'd guess you're probably right—the real moon is way better."

"I want to see it," she says. "Tawni and I are moon dwellers and we've never even seen the moon. It's weird." This is a side to Adele I've never really seen. She's almost reflective, the way she's looking at me with those intelligent eyes, like there's a poem on her lips and a song in her heart. It's another part of her I want to understand better.

"Might be sooner than you think," I say, wishing I could promise her what only my father has the power to authorize.

"You think?" she says, smirking, not buying the lie.

Night fully upon us, I lead the way into the city, feeling at home and like an outsider all at the same time. I keep my hat and sunglasses on, as I'm more likely to be recognized in this place than any other. The people here love my father and anything that belongs to him, which, from their point of view, includes me. Both my father and the people are in for a surprise.

The streets are crowded, the day's Sun Festival events concluded, the night's festivities yet to begin. This in-between period is the perfect time for us to make our move, when people are buzzing with excitement and the effects of whatever liquids they've consumed during the day. It will also mean my father has finished with his normal Sun Festival duties and is back at the palace getting ready for the typical presidential party that he throws on this day every year. Except this year is different, because he's also trying to fight a war, so he'll be with his advisors, getting the latest news, making decisions on what moon dweller subchapters to bomb, which innocent civilians to murder in cold blood.

I can't think of a better time for us to go say hello.

We melt into the flow of traffic, just another group of sun dwellers out for a night of fun, oblivious to the death being dealt by my father's troops below. Up here, death is something that happens to old people, after living a long and enjoyable life, not something in the present, in the here and now.

After ten minutes we're still on the outskirts of the massive capital city, moving shoulder to shoulder with the other citizens, who are taking their time, clapping and singing and moving lazily forward like they have all night to get from one block to the next. Which, of course, they do. But we're on a much tighter schedule, one that can't wait for anything or anyone.

Leading the way, I hang a right, from busy street to busier street, in the hopes of finding a deserted alley we can use to cut across the city. Unfortunately it's just another sea of people, brightly dressed, moving in all different directions as if they all want to get to a different place at the same exact time. *Crap.*

"Turn around," I say to Adele, who's right on my tail.

"To where?" she says, looking at me like I'm crazy, which I probably am.

"I don't know. Back, I guess."

"Tristan, there's nowhere to go. This place is a madhouse."

I know she's right, but we can't exactly stand where we are and hope my father dies of a heart attack from having too much fun at the party. Although I do remember hoping for something very similar at last year's Sun Festival party when, in my mother's absence, my father was dancing with two of his bleach-blond personal aides.

"Need some help?" Roc says, bobbing up next to Adele at just the right time, as usual. How does he do that?

"We need to get some breathing space," I say.

"Follow me," he says, turning directly into the bulk of the crowd.

"Follow you wher—"

"Urgent message for the President!" Roc shouts, his voice booming even over the dull roar of the masses. Dozens of heads turn toward us and I look at the ground, trying to keep the brim of my hat over the majority of my face. And then Roc's moving forward, a path opening miraculously before him, like a zipper being unzipped.

Luckily, I have enough sense to stay with him as he moves through the temporary gateway, because the crowd continues to press all around me, as if it cannot possibly leave such a gap open for more than a few seconds. Every five or six steps Roc repeats his message, sometimes prefacing it with "Make way, make way! On order from the president!" He really is amazing sometimes.

On Roc's efforts alone, we swiftly travel another block and across the street, where Roc ducks into a dark alley between the buildings. At most, a shred of light from the streetlamps manages to penetrate the narrow passage, but it's just as well considering our need for stealth and privacy. There won't be anyone walking in a place where it's dark. Not in this, the city of everlasting light.

In the alley, we pass a shadowy Dumpster overflowing with trash. Evidently the garbage overload is affecting even the capital. I gawk at the garbage because it seems so out of place here, in a city that's always been perfect and pristine, because my father wouldn't have it any other way. It's almost like a chink in a seemingly impenetrable suit of armor—the first sign that maybe, just maybe, the dark knight within isn't so invincible after all.

As I'm taking hope from the thought, the garbage seems to rise up, levitating in the air, forming arms and legs and a head, like it's becoming a trash man or woman, just to prove that even rubbish in the Sun Realm is powerful beyond the waste in the Lower Realms. The garbage creature speaks: "Tristan Nailin," it says.

We're already on high alert, so when the voice shatters the eerie silence in the alleyway, we all visibly jump, instinctively drawing our weapons from where they're hidden beneath our sun-dweller-worthy clothing. I don't know if a being constructed of trash can be destroyed by a sword alone, or whether it will simply laugh from the mouth of a tin can as it reconstructs itself with old broom handles, food cartons, and rusty bike frames, but I'm sure as hell going to try.

"Whoa! Hold on there. No need for those," the thing says. "We're on your side."

As if by magic, another two garbage creatures form up on either side of the original.

"What the hell is going on?" Trevor says. "I've never been to the Sun Realm, so maybe this is a normal, everyday occurrence, but come on!"

"It's not normal," Roc says.

"Who are you?" I say, squinting through the gloom.

"Oh, right, the disguises," the voice says. A garbage-soiled arm lifts a smelly hand to a waste-covered head, and then lifts the scalp of the *thing*, as if it's removing its skin from the top. Like a cloak, the garbage peels away, revealing a young man of perhaps twenty with dark hair, dark skin, and even darker eyes standing before us.

"My name is Bren," the guy says. "My companions are Linus and Sinew." The two garbage people on either side of Bren do a similar trash-cloak-removing trick to show who they truly are: a girl of no more than sixteen with a light-brown complexion and hair so dark it blends in with the night, barely visible in a bob knotted tightly on the top of her smallish head; and an even younger boy, perhaps twelve or thirteen, with wide light-brown eyes that stand out against his darker skin.

"Bren?" Roc says. I glance at my friend, who wears an expression I've rarely seen on his face: one of surprise, of

209

shock, an incredulous expression that shows he both knows these people and knows them well.

"Roc—is that you?" Bren says, using the overflowing garbage as a ramp to step off of the Dumpster.

"Yeah, it's me. What are you doing in a Dumpster?"

"Why are you wearing the garb of a sun dweller?" Bren asks. "I thought you joined the Resistance."

The two guys stand in front of each other, just staring for a long second, before grabbing each other in a firm, back-slapping embrace.

"How are you, man?" Roc says.

"Been better. Never thought I'd see you again. You remember my brother Linus and sister Sinew, right?" The two no-longer-garbage people raise a hand in greeting, but don't move from their roost on the edge of the Dumpster.

"Of course," Roc says. "Good to see the whole family is spending quality time together playing in the garbage."

Bren laughs. "It's a disguise."

"Who are you hiding from?" Adele says, bringing everyone's eyes to her.

"This is Adele," Roc says. "And my girlfr—I mean, her friend Tawni." He's suddenly very interested in something on his shoe.

"I know who they are," Bren says. "We've followed their journey quite closely, although always with a grain of salt—you know how much propaganda is on the news these days."

"And I'm Trevor," Trevor says, interjecting himself into the conversation. "This is all interesting, but we don't really have time for chitchat. Can we cut to the chase here?"

Bren laughs again. "Your other friend is right, Roc. We mustn't tarry; too much is at stake on this night of frivolity. Let me explain as succinctly as possible. I am also a servant, like Roc once was, working for a key sun dweller vice president who I will not name. My brother and sister also work in the same household, as aides to the master's children."

I raise my eyebrows, a question on my lips.

"I met Bren at a party many years ago hosted by your father," Roc says to me, reading my mind, as usual. He doesn't mention that my father is his father, too. "There's a sort of society of sun dweller servants. We meet in secret when we're running errands for our masters, share news and information, that sort of thing. You could say we're linked by time and circumstance."

"What you did not know, Roc," Bren says, his eyes narrowing, "is that I was part of a faction within the servant society, one with a singular goal of helping to overthrow the government and bringing balance back to the Tri-Realms." There's a tremor in his voice as he speaks, not one of fear, but of pride, as if his passion for the cause is trying to get out in any way it can. The coldness of gooseflesh rises up on my arms.

"But why…?" Roc says, a question in his tone and in his eyes. He doesn't finish the question, but Bren seems to discern the rest.

"I didn't know to whom your or Tristan's loyalties were," Bren says. "You were on a shortlist of potential new inductees into our group, but then you ran away from the Sun Realm. That's when we knew for sure you were one of us."

"So you're hiding in the trash as part of your work for this clandestine radical group?" Adele guesses.

"Oh no, we are not radicals," Bren says. "We are revolutionaries. But yes, we seek to escape this place to join the Resistance below. If others are fighting, then we too shall fight.

This Dumpster is a meeting place. The others shall join us soon. Then we make our way to the Moon Realm."

Bren has a funny way of speaking, almost proper-sounding, not like Adele's sister, Elsey, who tends to overdramatize things, but very formal and serious, as if the fate of the world depends on his diction and word choice. But regardless of the manner in which he conveys his message, his words are pure. This is a guy who wants to do the right thing. He's one of us.

"Can you help us?" I ask, not really realizing the trust I'm putting in the servant until the words escape my lips.

"We cannot linger here much longer, as even now I fear the war is slipping away below us. But we will do what we can."

"All we need is safe passage to the palace—I mean, the presidential complex. Can you show us the best way?"

"Ah, now that is truly a simple request. We'll have you there within the hour. But then we must be off to join the forces below, for we will not sit idly by while the fate of the world rests on a knife's edge."

What Bren doesn't know is that we're the ones holding the knife.

Nineteen
Adele

I'm glad to be off the streets again.

Meeting Bren will either be the greatest stroke of luck to grace our mission thus far, or the coincidence that leads to our demise. Being a servant, he is one I'd certainly trust over anyone else up here. In any case, we've decided to follow him through the underground sewer system below the city, a dark, dank, and somber place that reminds me more of home than anything I've seen in the Sun Realm thus far.

We walk along the edge of the cylindrical concrete shaft that we find ourselves in, avoiding getting our feet wet sloshing through the thin stream of water that runs down the center.

Tawni's heels are off again, this time for good. Before discarding them in the water, I overheard her say, "I'll miss you, pretty shoes," which I don't understand at all, and probably never will.

Bren has a flashlight, which saves us from using ours. As he walks abreast with his still-silent brother and sister, he explains the situation as he knows it. "I have information from a reliable source that the sun dwellers launched a coordinated attack last night on every major moon dweller border. They started with heavy bombing, which was then followed by large contingents of soldiers moving in to take control of each subchapter. The moon dwellers had little chance of stopping them."

I can't breathe, the thick oxygen sticking in my throat like glue. I stop, wheezing, my elbows dropping to my knees.

"Adele, what's the matter?" Tristan says. His hand gently touches my back.

"What subchapters?" I choke out.

"I do not know," Bren says. "But I do know subchapter one was hit the hardest."

My legs start shaking and my vision blurs. Unable to hold up my weight any longer, I roll to the side, my shoulder thudding off the unforgiving concrete. My cheek scrapes against the rough surface, but I don't care. No mark on my face could be as bad as what I've just heard. "We're too late," I moan. "It's over."

Tristan's face appears through my tears as he kneels over me. "There's still hope," he says. "If she survived there will be a trial. She'll be sentenced to death, but we might be able to rescue her before that happens."

"And if she didn't survive?" I say, images of my mom's battered face cycling through my mind in black and white.

"She did," Tristan asserts, "but if she didn't, you still have your sister to take care of. If we can finish our mission, it could still make a difference for anyone still alive, especially for the non-military."

Elsey's face appears, replacing my dead mother. She's smiling as usual, despite the war and my dad dying and my mom maybe dying and me being on a potential suicide mission. Just seeing her face for a moment, even if only in my mind, lifts my spirits long enough for me to blink away the tears and allow Tristan to help me to my feet.

"I'm sorry," I mumble, unwilling to look any of my comrades in the face after my mini-meltdown. "I'm okay now."

"Screw 'em," Trevor says. "As long as we're alive, they've got a fight on their hands."

When I look up my friends are staring at me. Tristan's brow is furrowed and worried. Tawni looks ready to throw her arms around me. Roc is, well, he's Roc, solid and steady and reliable, his hand half-extended, as if ready to catch me if my legs fail again. And Trevor: his face is a scowl, an expression that represents the righteous anger inside him, an anger that will only help us finish this mission together. His face, more than any of the others, steels me the most. My knuckles tighten at my sides as a surge of fire runs through me.

"Let's end this," I say.

We continue our march through the sewer, and my legs feel the lightest they've felt since leaving the Moon Realm. I can almost feel my friends, my sister, my mother, even my father, holding me up, becoming a part of me, supporting me. We're in this together, still alive, still whole, still hopeful.

What was a steely determination to kill the man who ordered the death of my father, the maiming of my baby sister, has turned into a fierce and burning desire for revenge. Not just for those who I know that have been harmed by the cruel dictator who sits on his throne deep in the capital, but for *everyone* whose lives have been negatively impacted by his evil ways. We can't get to him fast enough for me. Every muscle and ligament and bone in my body is firing perfectly, working efficiently as a team, and I know that when we do meet him I'll be unstoppable, the most powerful and deadly force that he's ever seen.

And then I'll kill him.

Unfortunately, another hour of tromping, head stooped, through the sewers, takes just a bit of the fight out of me. Mostly we've been silent, although every once and a while Trevor will say something to try to fire us up, but even he's been quiet for the last ten minutes.

"How big is this city?" I finally ask, in frustration.

"Big," Tristan says. "Bigger than you can possibly imagine. Think the biggest moon dweller city and then multiple that by a hundred."

His explanation makes it even harder for me to imagine. How can one fathom the fathomless? Anyway, we're not trying to get all the way across it, just to the center, so it can't be that far, right?

Wrong.

Neck aching, legs burning, mouth dry, spirit shattered, I stop an hour later when Bren pulls up in front of us.

"We've got to be close," Tristan says, making my head perk up a little. He knows the size of the city better than me.

"We are," Bren says. "And this is where we must part ways. For our path takes us below, while I suspect yours takes you straight to your father."

"Good to luck to you, Bren," Tristan says, clasping the servant's hand. "We are forever in your debt."

"Succeed in whatever your mission is, and all debts shall be forgiven," Bren returns. Then, turning to Roc, he says, "Brother, forgive me for not trusting in the purity of your heart sooner. I very much would have liked to stand beside you in this fight."

"And you, my friend," Roc says, once more embracing him. "Linus, Sinew—listen to your brother. He has good instincts."

The silent siblings nod solemnly, before the threesome head in the other direction, beginning the long walk back to where they started, and then on a dangerous journey to the Moon Realm, or what's left of it. Just before the head of Bren's flashlight disappears in the dark, Tristan calls out, "Where do we go?"

"A hundred yards more and you'll reach a ladder. That'll get you close," Bren shouts, his echoes fading into the distance along with him.

"When we get to the ladder we can rest and make plans," Tristan says. No one can argue with that idea.

I'm still feeling the effects of our bent-over jaunt through the sewers, but somehow it doesn't hurt so much now that I know the end is near. Evidently my companions feel the same way, as our pace is redoubled and we reach a dead end only a minute later.

"I'm ready for a nap," Trevor says, sprawling out along the curving edge of the tube.

"You do that…while we kill the president," Roc says.

It's strange hearing Roc say something like that, especially when he now knows the President is his father.

"Ooh, I don't want to miss that," Trevor says. "I guess I can sleep later, maybe when I'm dead."

"You're not going to die," I say, sitting down. "None of us are." It's the biggest lie I've told in my entire life, and, selfishly, I think I told it to comfort my own fears rather than anyone else's.

"So what's the plan?" Tawni asks, hugging her knees next to me.

"Bust in, kill anything that moves, shoot Tristan and Roc's dad in the head," Trevor says bluntly.

"Our *father*," Tristan corrects.

"Yeah, him, too," Trevor says.

"I think we might want to try a slightly stealthier approach," I say. "That is, if we do want to live through this. And I do—I've got a sister to look after." I glance at Tristan, who gives me a slight nod, which I return in thanks for the not-so-subtle reminder he gave me earlier. No matter how bad things get, there's always someone who needs me as much as I need them.

"She's right," he says. "We need to split up."

"No!" I say right away. "We said we would stick together. Apart we'll be hanging bats. Dead meat."

"Hear me out," Tristan says. "Roc and I know the palace better than anyone, my father included. When we were kids we explored every nook and cranny. We know the best ways in, the fastest routes from point to point, and the safest ways out. If we each lead a team in a different direction with the goal of

218

eventually reaching the same destination—in this case my father's throne room—it doubles our chance of success."

"If one group is captured, the other might still make it," Roc adds. Evidently they've already discussed this without us, although I have no idea when. "If we're caught together, it's all over."

I shut my eyes. *Argh!* I'm mad, but not because of their plan, or that they came up with it without us, but because they're right. It's the best, and most logical, way to improve our chances for success.

"Who goes with who?" I say, giving up the argument without a fight.

"We wanted to leave that up to the group," Tristan says.

"At least you left *something* up to the group," I grumble under my breath.

"I want Tawni with me," Roc says right away.

"Bad idea," Trevor says. "We can't let personal feelings get in the way of the mission as a whole."

"I agree," I say. "Tristan and I will split up, and so should Tawni and Roc."

"Wait a minute. I'm not sure that makes the most sense," Tristan says, frowning. "Strategically it might make the most sense to have you and me together."

"It doesn't," I say, wanting more than anything to relent, to go with him, to seal our fates together with this decision. But I can't. Trevor's right, for once.

"Trevor and Adele are right," Tawni says, glancing at Roc. "I'm sorry, I want to go with you, but…"

Roc chews on his lip, turns to Tristan, who's doing much the same thing. "Three against two," I say. "Couples must be separated." Again. It's the third time I'll be separated from

Tristan since first seeing him. If history repeats itself, we'll both face great dangers before we ever see each other again.

"I don't agree," Tristan says, "but I'll go along with the group's decision."

"Don't make me beg," Roc says to Tawni.

"Roc, I'm sorry."

"Rrrr, fine. Okay. I'll go with whoever we decide."

"Me and Tawni," I suggest, reverting naturally to the combo that's gotten me this far.

"No way," Tristan says. "Tawni's not a fighter. You need at least two fighters."

"She'll fight if she has to," I argue, which draws a smile from Tawni. "She even practiced with Roc, remember?" I add.

"That's not helping your argument," Tristan says. "Roc's got spirit but he's not exactly a professional warrior."

"Hey! I've saved your skin more than once already," Roc complains.

"I'm not contending that. I'm just saying that one training session with you won't put Tawni on even ground with a palace guard."

"But she'll have me," I say. "No one will touch her on my watch."

"Unless you get killed," Tristan says grimly. "You're tough as hell, Adele, but you're not invincible." And that, my friends, is the problem. No matter how much righteous anger and lust for revenge courses through my veins, I can't guarantee anything. "Just take Trevor with you. Please."

And there it is. The compromise. If Tristan can't be there to protect me (as if *I* need protecting), he wants the next best fighter to be with me. Which leaves him with Roc, who, although determined and loyal to a fault, is no warrior, as Tristan already pointed out. But wait a minute…

"I thought you said you and Roc have to be separated, so each squad has someone to help navigate through the palace," I say.

"That's correct," Tristan confirms. Then that means…

"You're going with Tawni?"

"That's what I'm suggesting."

I shake my head in wonder at the nerve of my boyfriend. If he thinks he can get away with the exact same thing that I just tried to get away with, he's got another thing coming. "Not a chance. If that's the way you want to play it, I'm going with Roc. You take Trevor and Tawni."

"Perfect. Done," Trevor says, clapping his hands together. "I'm ready."

"Wait a sec," Tristan says. "I disag—"

"All in favor," I say, cutting him off.

"Aye," Tawni and Trevor say in unison.

Roc shrugs. "Sorry, buddy, that's three votes already. It's probably for the best anyway."

Tristan's shaking his head, his eyes closed. I can tell his teeth are clamped tightly together beneath his pursed lips. He's worried about me, which I feel bad about, but I know we've made the right decision. He and Tawni will be safe with Trevor, and Roc and I can look after each other. I know I was a bit cold to him, but *that* I can make up for.

I move in close, hug him around the chest, rest my cheek on his shoulder. "We'll be fine," I whisper.

He opens his fathomless blue eyes. Says, "I don't want to lose you." I lean into his honest lips, kissing him longer and deeper than I ever have before.

"You won't," I murmur when we pull away.

Twenty
Tristan

That didn't go the way I planned. I thought I could convince Adele to go with me, or at least to go with Trevor. Instead she's the only real fighter in her group, while I've got Trevor, who's more than capable.

We've worked out the details of our plan—approximately how long it will take for each team to reach the throne room (twenty minutes), what to do if something goes wrong (keep going), whether to wait for the other team upon arrival at the throne room (wait five minutes, and then go in)—and I watch Adele climb the ladder first, her lithe form almost catlike in her sun dweller clothes. Everything about her is an enigma to me.

The way she can be so tough and yet so gentle. The beauty she wears like a mask on her determined face. Her humble upbringing seeding a life destined to do such great things.

And now we're parting without saying goodbye, with only a kiss to keep us going, because that's the way she wants it. It's probably better that way. Saying goodbye is like assuming failure, like we won't see each other again. "Until we meet again!" I say instead. Adele fires a strange look down the ladder and keeps climbing.

"We'll go through the gardens and around the government buildings," Roc says.

I look at him. "Too dangerous. We'll go that way and you take the *safer* route through the family quarters."

"She'll want to see the gardens," Roc says.

"This isn't a sightseeing trip, Roc. This is not debatable."

"We'll go through the gardens," Adele cries from above.

I grit my teeth. It's like the entire world has teamed up against me. Or maybe it's just the four people I'm supposed to be teamed up with. With Adele three quarters of the way up the ladder, there's no time to argue. "Fine," I growl. "Don't do anything stupid."

"So don't do anything you would do then?" Roc says with a smirk.

"Just go," I say, unwilling to take the bait.

Trevor's shadow boxing the wall, while Tawni's waiting for me patiently. Roc gives her a soft kiss on the cheek before following Adele.

"Shall we?" Tawni says, turning her head to hide the pink on her face.

"Let's give them a minute to start their move. The fewer of us together to draw attention the better," I say.

I sit down, close my eyes, take a few deep breaths. My mouth is dry, like it's been coated in a layer of rock dust, my tongue as limp as a wet rag. Although I'm at rest, my heart beats faster than it should.

Tawni slides in beside me. "You're worried about her," she says.

"Is it that obvious?"

"Your foot's moving a mile a minute," she says, pointing to my leg. I didn't even realize, but she's right. My knee's twitching up and down rapidly, my foot tapping out a wild beat on the concrete.

I put a hand on my leg, calming it. Even my body is out of my control. "Urrrr!" I growl, just as there's the clink of the manhole cover being replaced above us. "I just didn't picture our attack on the capital like this," I say.

Trevor stands over me. "How did you picture it? You and Adele, holding hands, skipping through the palace gardens? Fighting hordes of guards—still holding hands, mind you—storming the throne room, each plunging a sword through your father's chest in perfect synchronization?"

I glance up, frown at Trevor. "No, of course not. I just thought we'd fight together."

"Ignore him," Tawni says, bringing my gaze to hers. "You *will* fight together. And then you can skip through the gardens all you want." Even in the sewer, her pale blue eyes are mirthful and wise. I can see why Adele is so close with her. I find myself smiling. "Did you really want to go with her to fight with her, or was it perhaps so you could keep an eye on her?"

"Yes—I mean, no—I mean, I don't know, maybe. I just feel more comfortable when she's near so I can help if she needs it." My head is a muddle of thoughts, worries, and memories. All I know is she's up there, and I'm down here.

"News flash. She doesn't need your help. She doesn't need anyone's help. She's the strongest person I've ever met." Tawni's expression is so serious I can tell she means what she says. But she's wrong.

"She told me she needed your help. She told me she never would have escaped the Pen, never would have rescued her sister, never would have done any of the incredible things she's done without you."

"What? She said that?"

"Yes, Tawni. She thinks the world of you, and believe it or not, she needs you as much as you need her. We all need each other. Together is the only way we're going to get through this. Together."

Tawni's eyebrows are raised and she's staring off into space. "I never knew," she says.

"Well now you do. You have a part to play in this as much as anyone else." I don't know if that's right exactly, but the words feel right on my tongue, coming off my lips. In any case, Tawni will have to fight, just like the rest of us, before this is all over. That's a certainty.

"I'll do what I can," she says, standing, her dress swirling around her legs and looking incredibly out of place amongst the sewer water and time-darkened concrete.

"Ugh. If this love fest is over, can we go?" Trevor says, stepping on my foot.

"Ladies first," I say, motioning for him to climb the ladder in front.

As it turns out, the sewer ended just inside the palace gardens, directly below a flower patch. At first I wonder who the idiot engineer is who designed it that way, but then I realize it was probably my father's idea. He always liked building secret passages, hidden rooms, and alternate escape routes from the palace. This is probably meant to be one of those, not that he ever intended to need it. Little did he know it would be used against him.

After replacing the flower-spotted manhole cover and patting the dirt around it to hide our presence, we slide along the inside of the wall, me in front with Tawni close behind. Trevor guards the rear. The few times I glance back, Tawni's mouth is opened wide like an O, her eyes nearly as round, and her expression one of barely contained delight. Evidently she likes the gardens, and seeing her enjoying her first time in them makes me wish I could've seen Adele's reaction. I know, I know, in my own words, *This isn't a sightseeing trip,* but still, it would've been nice to see.

Decades-old trees spring up to our left, the artificial stars winking between the crisscross of their muddled boughs; brilliantly colored flower arrangements dance in the artificial moonlight, an optical illusion provided by the shadows and night sky; skillfully cut statues of men on horses—past Nailin presidents—and men with swords—again, past Nailin presidents—dot the landscape. Unfortunately for Tawni, we're only looping around the edge of the gardens to reach the residential wing, whereas the others are going right through it.

When we reach a corner of the high, white palace walls, we turn north, making our way along the final third of the gardens. Abruptly the shade of the trees ends, and we're thrust back into the fullness of the world my father has created. The deep blue night sky, an effect of specially designed panel lights on the cavern roof, looms over us, big and magical and beautiful, even to me, who's seen it a thousand times.

"Is it like this every night?" Tawni whispers.

"My father wouldn't have it any other way," I say, watching my companions take it all in. Even Trevor looks impressed by it all.

"Well, at least he did something right," Trevor says.

I never thought about it like that. I guess I've only seen the President's power be used for evil, so I've never really considered all the good that could be done if the power was given to someone who wanted it for the right reasons.

Shaking off the thought, I lead the way across a wide expanse of grass that covers the area from the wall to the house that I grew up in. It's not really a house, just an extension on the massive, mansion-like presidential buildings, what I like to refer to as *the palace*. A warm, soft haze of orange light spills from the three stories of living space windows, and if the building wasn't so big, it would almost look inviting and homey. The spires of the main buildings rise above us like white spikes, casting away any doubt that this is an ordinary place to live.

"Where are all the guards?" Tawni asks, her eyes following the purely architectural spires to the cavern roof.

"They'll be focused on the entrance to the party, more toward the government side." Our eyes meet and she frowns, her expression saying what I left unsaid: *where the others are going.* "But we still have to be careful. There will be guards here, too, and they'll be roaming the house randomly. Keep alert."

This is happening. This is real. Those two thoughts hit me as we edge along the side of the place I grew up, a place of laughter and fear, where one half of my upbringing gave me hope and love, and the other half gave me bruises and twisted ideals. I'm about to see my father again, and then I have to kill him.

This is happening. This is real.

Well, that gets the adrenaline pumping. It's like I've just taken a shot of caffeine, my senses on high alert, my muscles energetic, my eyes seeing everything.

We reach a corner. I know that one of the back entrances cuts through the wall perpendicular to us. Our first real danger. The door might be guarded, or might not. My father likes to mix things up with his security, more for his amusement than anything else. I poke an eye to the side, catch a glimpse of a red-garbed guard, duck back. In the split second of vision, his black double-holstered belt stares at me like two black demon eyes.

But we have weapons, too. And the guard will be bored, wishing he was going to be attending the upcoming party inside, giving us the invaluable element of surprise.

"There's a guard," I hiss at the others.

"Want me to take him out?" Trevor says, making me think it *is* better that he's with me and not Adele.

"No. Thanks. All guards are instructed to first raise the alarm if they spot an intruder. Apprehending the intruder is secondary. We have to ensure he doesn't have a chance to do that. Any ideas?" I ask.

"I'll scale the building, and while you rush him from the side, I'll drop on him from above," Trevor says. "Simple and clean."

"Simple? Sounds like a disaster."

"You got a better idea?" Trevor says.

"I've got about ten better ideas. Like I could toss something out onto the lawn and when he goes to check it out, we jump him. Or I could make a little noise to draw him over and then we club him in the head."

"There's still a good chance he'll alert other guards before he goes to check," Tawni says, tapping her teeth with her fingers. "What about this? I provide the distraction."

"With what?" Trevor asks.

"With me," she says.

"Bad idea," I say, right away thinking about what Adele would say if she knew we were using Tawni as bait. *What were you thinking, Tristan?!*

"You were the one who said I have a role to play in all this," Tawni points out. Why do I always open my big mouth?

"You do, but not like this."

"She's got a point," Trevor says. "She's the only one who might just look like a normal sun dweller partygoer. If they see you, they'll freak out, because you're supposed to be locked in your room with a mild case of mental trauma. I look as much like a sun dweller as a hunk of coal looks like a diamond. That leaves Tawni."

"I'm doing it," Tawni says, sounding more like Adele than herself.

With a toss of her head she throws back her long, white locks, bats her eyes, and then strides from behind the corner. I fight off the urge to spring from our hiding spot and charge the guard when she says, "Oh my gosh, I'm so glad I found you."

"Ma'am, you're not authorized to be here," the guard says professionally.

"Don't I know it," Tawni replies. "You see, I seem to have gotten turned around somewhere. I was on my way to the party and then I made a left. Or was it a right? I can't remember. In

230

any case, I'm hopelessly lost. Can you by any chance direct me?"

"I'm assuming you have an invitation?"

"Of course, silly, how do you think I got through the front gate. It's right he—well, that's funny, I had it right here in my hands. I must've dropped it somewhere on the lawn. Can I trouble you to help me find it?" Flawless. That's the only word for it. Who knew Tawni was an actress? Her tone of voice, the light way in which she requests help, and I'm sure her body language, too: it's all so disarming that even the most well-trained guard wouldn't feel threatened by her approach.

"Well, uh, I shouldn't really leave my post…"

The fish starts to swim away.

"Oh, please, sir. They won't let me in without it and I would be devastated if I missed out on the best party of the year. I might just give you a little reward for being my hero, too," she says flirtatiously.

She wiggles the bait one more time.

"Well—I—uh—I suppose I could help for a few minutes, but then I have to get back. Now where did you say you lost it?"

Hooked!

My muscles tense in preparation for violence. "I got this," Trevor whispers in my ear.

"No!" I shoot back. All we need is to fight over who takes out the guard that Tawni has practically gift-wrapped for us.

"Just around this corner, somewhere on the lawn, I expect," Tawni's voice rings out.

When she rounds the corner, her feet tangle together and she tumbles to the grass, crying out as she falls. "Ma'am, are you okay?" the guard says before coming into view. He passes us, not noticing our forms hidden in the shadows. His entire attention is on Tawni. A damsel in distress and a potential reward. "And where are your shoes?"

As he bends over to help Tawni up, I rush him, molding my fists together like a club, which I bring down on the back of his head. "Oof!" he says, but then collapses face first on Tawni.

"I get the next one," Trevor says, striding up.

"Get him off me," Tawni squeals.

"Gladly," I say, pushing him off with the toe of my boot. "You did awesome, by the way."

"I did?" Tawni says, accepting a hand from Trevor.

"Not bad at all," Trevor adds, pulling her up.

"I was scared to death," she admits. "But it was kind of thrilling at the same time." She tucks a wayward piece of hair behind her ear.

"Time to take this operation inside," I say.

After dragging the guard into the shadows cast by the building, we tiptoe across the lawn to the now-unprotected entrance. I open the windowless iron door, silently praying there's no guard just on the other side coming to relieve the now unconscious doorman. The red-carpeted hallway inside is empty, save for the familiar ornamental wall sconces positioned every few feet.

I move inside, holding the door for Tawni, who holds it for Trevor. "We're east of the throne room," I say quietly. "Follow me and I'll try not to get us all killed."

"Thanks for that," Trevor says.

Due to the sheer size of the place, there are a number of paths that can be taken between any two points, so I've got some choices to make. We could cut through the kitchen and risk a meeting with a stressed and angry knife-wielding chef, where it's likely that a broken plate or clattering pot will alert half the subchapter to our presence. Or we could take the long route through my brother's and my adjoining bedrooms where we might bump into a maid or steward who decides to scream upon seeing us. Or we could take the fastest and most direct route down the main hallway, through the grand foyer, and into the government wing, where we will likely butt heads with at least a dozen guards, have to dodge an army of servants, and possibly face my greatest arch nemesis, Mrs. Templeton, the palace housekeeper, more loyal to my father than even his most trusted advisors. Not someone I hope to see tonight. I opt for a more creative route.

Halfway down the hall I cut to the right, past a set of double doors, behind which is a lounge room with large flat-screen teleboxes on all the walls, and dozens of plush lounge chairs around the edges. It's where my brother and I used to spend our evenings sometimes, watching the best entertainment the Sun Realm has to offer. Those days are long past.

Although I think the route I've chosen is the safest path, we're completely exposed now, with nowhere to hide if a servant or guard happens to turn the corner at one of the many cross hallways that intersect the long hall we're making our way down. Or they could suddenly exit one of the many carved-oak doors that flash by on either side. As luck would have it, we make it to the end unseen, having worked our way to the northernmost point of the east wing. And it's here where I do the unexpected.

I take the stairs to the second floor.

"Dude, is the throne room on the next level?" Trevor asks, taking the steps two at a time to catch me from behind.

"No," I say.

"Then what are we—"

"I grew up here," I say, cutting him off. "Just trust me, it's the safest route."

I can tell he wants to say something, but he doesn't, falling back to cover the rear again. When I reach the top, I freeze, right away wishing I could take back the words I said to Trevor. For striding toward me are two of the biggest palace guards I've ever seen.

Twenty-One
Adele

The palace gardens feel so unreal that it's weird when we emerge from them to find the largest collection of buildings I've ever seen. I half-expected the palace to be a really giant tree, complete with windows and doors cut into the sides of the trunk, balconies propped delicately on the branches.

Instead the palace is a series of interconnected buildings, grandly designed with large, intricately cut granite blocks along the base and wide sheets of shiny, dark marble that rise ten stories up and hundreds of yards in every other direction. Dozens of sharp, white, knife-like spires shoot above it all, nearly scratching the tip of the cavern roof. Three-dimensional, multi-faceted windows protrude at equidistant intervals along each wing, each glowing with a different color from within: green, or blue, or red. Unlike many of the windows in the Lower Realms, no bars protect the glass portals.

In front of us is a grandly overstated entrance, framed by a half-dozen black pillars, cut from what appears to be marble, shiny and lustrous under the shine of the brightest yellow evening lamps I've ever seen. Although the lights seek to illuminate anything and everything within their bounds, for us, who remain outside of their perimeter, they have the opposite effect, shrouding us under a healthy cloak of shadow.

The entranceway is a buzz of activity, as party invitees arrive in cars of shiny pink, purple, yellow, and every other bright color imaginable. Each car pulls up, the occupants exit the vehicle wearing the gaudiest clothing I've ever seen, and then a white-, or dark-, or brown-skinned servant gets into the driver's seat and whisks the car away to some hidden storage lot. At least they don't discriminate here. To be a servant the only requirement is being poor.

We watch for a while, me because I'm in awe of the strange world I find myself in, and Roc because he's probably scoping things out to decide the best way to infiltrate the palace. Although my attention should be sufficiently held by the extravagance of the sun dwellers—there goes a woman wearing a hot-pink dress that resembles a wagging tongue, a curved flap rising high above her head and casting a soft gray shadow across her face; her shoes are blood red and have four-inch heels—I find myself thinking about Tristan's revelation from earlier. People inhabiting the surface? A huge cover-up by the Nailin family, sans Tristan and his mother, who have vowed to tell the world? A giant-bubble-covered city where sun dwellers live and moon and star dwellers serve? If Tristan hadn't looked so serious and scared the whole time he was telling us, I might've thought it was all a lot of exaggeration or even an outright lie. But I believe him, and now that the thought is in my head—e*arth dwellers* for goodness' sake!—I can't seem to eradicate it.

"We'll head west through a servants' entrance in the side," Roc says, interrupting my thoughts.

"I'm right behind you," I say, gawking at a man with a blue-capped, yellow-brimmed hat so tall it's nearly knocked off by the ten-foot-high door frame.

Following Roc's lead, I creep along the edge of the gardens, resisting the urge to stop to touch, smell, and feel the beautiful flowers and bushes that slip past with nearly every step. Another time, perhaps. We're soon out of sight of the crowded entrance, as both the gardens and the buildings curve to the right.

"We have to cross the driveway to get over to the buildings," Roc points out, "but it should be easy—there are always large gaps between the cars."

So we wait for our opportunity. A gorgeous white car with gold trim slips past, rounds the bend, and disappears from view, its red and yellow rear lights the last to fade away. Our chance. We run, knees bent, shoulders hunched, arms flapping unnaturally at our sides. Across the lawn between the gardens and the drive, and onto the cobblestone road, which turns out to be at least twice as wide as it appeared to be from our shadowy vantage point.

When we're almost halfway across, headlights hit us like a spotlight. There's nowhere to hide; there's no time to hide. For some odd reason I feel the instinct to freeze but know that makes no sense whatsoever. Stopping in the middle of the road—particularly when a two-ton vehicle is bearing down upon you—rarely makes sense. I charge ahead, get out of the light and off the road, turn to find Roc.

He's standing in the middle of the road, his arm out, palm facing forward. *Halt!* his body language urges the car. I start to run back, prepare myself to tackle him out of the way before the car flattens him into human goo on the road, but then pull up when the car slows, slows, slows, and finally stops mere inches from Roc's determined form.

"What are you doing?" I hiss.

Roc's head turns slowly, almost lazily, as if he's in a daze. I guess watching a car roar toward you, wondering if it will stop will do that to a person. "We've already been seen. We have no choice. He'll sound the alarm if we don't stop him."

By *him* he means the guy behind the wheel, one of the many servants responsible for parking the guests' cars. Through the glass windshield is a perplexed man, with wrinkles on his forehead that are curled in much the same manner as his thin mustache. His hands are frozen on the steering wheel, his eyes focused on Roc for a moment, then me, then back to Roc. He's confused, doesn't know what's happening, but will soon recognize one, or maybe even both of us—Roc from working in the same household with him and me from the telebox—and then he'll run Roc over while simultaneously raising the alarm. Time to act.

I stride over to the passenger door, trying not to look threatening, open it. The whites of the guy's eyes are huge and shiny against the dark interior of the car. "Who are you?" he says.

"A friend of the President's," I say. "We need to borrow your car."

Without waiting for his response, I grab the top of the car and swing in feet first, slamming both heels into his jaw, rocking him back against the inside of his door, hearing a sickening crunch when his head hits the window. He slumps forward and for a frightening second or two, his forehead lays on the horn, blaring the loudest, most obnoxious sound across the palace grounds. I'm sprawled out awkwardly on the seat, my head and arms hanging out the door. But then Roc opens the other door and pulls him away from the wheel, stopping the ruckus.

"We were meant to take control of the vehicle quietly," Roc says, pulling the guy out and muscling him into the back seat.

I pull myself into the seat, shutting the door behind me. "I didn't think you were going to hijack one of the guest's cars," I fire back. "Do you even know how to drive one of these things?"

"Sure. We all had to learn so we could run errands around the city." Easing the backdoor closed, he hops in beside me, the car lurching forward before his door is fully shut. "Don't you have cars in the Moon Realm? I think I've seen them there."

"Few people have them."

We curl around the bend, across a wooden bridge, and onto a large cement slab. "Get down!" Roc cries.

I'm already ducking when he says it, having seen the danger up ahead. Dozens of servants, having parked cars, are walking across the lot, working their way back to the entrance to collect more cars. From my low position, I see Roc wave casually as he passes a few of them.

"Will they recognize you?" I whisper.

"It's too dark in here. I probably just look like one of them," he says.

"We can't park it here. Someone will see the guy in the back."

"We're not parking here," Roc says.

"Oh. Is it safe to get up yet?"

"Not yet," he says. One beat, two. "Okay, you're fine now."

I pop my head up, glance back as the last of the servants walk away, far behind us. We've passed the parked cars, too, which look funny all next to each other, brightly colored and gleaming under the moonlight.

"I've never seen this many cars in my life," I murmur. "Are they gas-powered or electric?" Where I'm from they're all gas-powered, which creates a heavy layer of smog and grime over everything. We have a removal and filtration system for all the fumes, but it's not very effective. Many people believe the low life expectancies in the Moon Realm are directly related to the high level of pollution.

"Hybrid," Roc replies, glancing at me. "Part electric, part gas-powered."

I frown. "Then why isn't there any pollution in the city? Even with hybrids there should be pollution—both from the cars and from all the plants generating the electricity to charge the batteries. You have at least ten times the number of cars that we have."

"The air in the city is completely sucked out and refreshed every half hour using filtered air from above," Roc says matter-of-factly. "Also, our electricity mostly comes from solar panels—technology that harnesses the power of the sun—on the earth's surface. It's all part of the agreement with the earth dwellers."

I don't say anything because I'm afraid of what I might say. Silently I fume. It's another example of the blatant disregard for equality by the people meant to protect us. There's so much energy at our fingertips, and yet, the Lower Realms are kept in the dark. I take deep breaths, get control of myself. After all, inequality is the reason we're on this mission.

Ahead of us the parking lot ends, but there's another road shooting out the drive.

"This'll take us to the loading docks," Roc explains. "All deliveries would have been completed yesterday, leaving today free for celebration. We'll be able to sneak in that way."

I'm completely at the mercy of Roc's best judgment on how to get in the palace, which I don't necessarily mind—he hasn't steered me wrong yet, and he has spent his entire life here.

The new road curves to the right sharply, but Roc takes it like a driving pro, without breaking speed. As we approach a medium-sized building with a large horizontally slatted gray rolling door, he says, "Can't get too close to it," and then stops well short of the structure, turns off the engine, and kills the headlights.

"Why not?"

"Automatic door. If we pull up close to it, it'll open, which makes a noise that plenty of people will hear. They'll be all over us like sun dweller skanks on Tristan when he's shirtless." When he sees my expression, he clamps a hand over his mouth, says something through his fingers that sounds like, "By Idn't bean dat."

"Oh, you meant it all right," I say. "Did he *like* having girls always trying to get to him?" I ask.

241

Roc uses his other hand to peel his fingers off his lips. "He hated it. Was always complaining about it. Called them sun sluts."

"Good," I say. "Let's go."

We exit our stolen vehicle, transfer the guy in the back to the trunk, lock the car, and throw the keys in the bushes for good measure. I want to go touch the leaves on the bushes, but there's no time. I follow Roc to the side of the loading garage, where there's a steel door with no keyhole and a combination lock beneath the handle. The code: 0475.

"The year of the Uprising?" I say.

"No. The year the Uprising was squashed," Roc says, pulling open the door.

"Same thing."

"Not to the President."

The garage is pitch-black so Roc flicks on a flashlight. The inside is an empty shell, clearly built for utility rather than beauty. At one end is the automatic door and the other end a large platform with four sets of smaller steel doors, presumably for bringing deliveries into the palace. To the far right is an even smaller door, used for entering and exiting. Roc heads straight for the smallest door.

Standing in front of it, Roc says, "This is it. This door will take us inside the government side of the palace. Tristan, Trevor, and Tawni should be working their way from the opposite end. We'll meet in the approximate center, where the president's meeting room is located."

"The throne room?"

"That's what we like to call it. There will undoubtedly be guards in this area tonight, it's only a question of how many and where we'll run into them, so be alert."

"Be careful," I say unnecessarily.

Roc nods and pushes open the door.

Twenty-Two
Tristan

The guards—giant men, with heads that, standing upright, would nearly touch the ceiling—are hunched over, looking down, reading something. A memo, or orders, or something else urgent; whatever it is, it has their undivided attention, so they don't see us yet, which gives us half a chance. But only if we act quickly.

I risk a quick glance back to get Trevor, but he's already aware of the danger, already by my side, with Tawni ushered behind him. Slowly, we slip our swords from their scabbards, pressing our backs against the walls on either side of the upstairs hallway. I notice Trevor's movements are very similar to mine—fluid, designed to blend in and not attract the attention of the distracted guards. It's good to have a partner as well-trained as he is.

The guards continue toward us, lost in whatever message is on the paper. When they're less than three feet from us, the one on Trevor's side glances up, probably sensing the staircase is near, but looks straight between us, flinches, perhaps realizing something is wrong in his peripheral vision.

Trevor and I move as if we're arms controlled by the same creature, simultaneously and with force.

But these aren't inexperienced or helpless guardsmen. These are professional warriors, men I probably have scars from training with in my youth. And did I mention they're big? Like the size of some of the smaller trees in the palace gardens.

The men transition from reading to fighting in an instant, dropping the papers and raising their swords before my blade has arced halfway toward them.

Clang! Our swords meet theirs in unison, and we're both thrown back by the sheer power behind their blocks. I hazard a glance at Trevor, our eyes meeting for a second as we both realize: we're overmatched. Don't take that as me being pessimistic, just realistic, and that doesn't mean I think we're going to lose, because I don't. It just means we're going to have to be a little more creative with our approach to the fight, especially if we want to end it quickly, which we do, for fear that more guards will arrive.

When I charge, I count on the fact that Trevor is an experienced fighter, that he'll read my mind, that his brain has calculated the odds of various strategies and come up with the same idea as mine.

Not exactly.

Just before my slashing sword connects with the guard's sword on my side, I cut to the right, planning on switching enemies, hoping Trevor does the same. I collide with Trevor, who's thrown his sword and launched himself like a torpedo at his original opponent. Crunching him into the wall, I feel a tremor as my bones rattle from the impact. As we land, his elbow accidentally (at least I think it's accidental) cracks me in the chin, snapping my top and bottom teeth against each other.

Luckily, both of our minds continue to work overtime, still plotting and planning and trying to predict our opponent's next move. In this case, it's obvious. I mean, what would I do if the two people I was fighting crashed into each other and fell to the ground? Attack hard and fast while they're in a weak position.

Before we've come to a complete stop I raise my sword above us. Just in time, too, because my original enemy is slashing down with his sword. *Clang!* The blow is so powerful that it sends shivers through my hand and wrist and I almost drop my sword. But somehow I manage to hang on, barely keeping the guard's blade from piercing my chest.

Trevor, now sword-less, is not idle. As soon as I block the attempted kill stroke, he uses my shoulder as a wedge to launch himself off of, catapulting himself onto the back of the behemoth guardsman. Using every ounce of my strength, I push back with my sword, forcing my attacker away from me. It works, and the guy stumbles back, tripping on the fallen form of his comrade, who has Trevor's sword sticking out of his chest. Perhaps Trevor's plan was better than mine after all.

I leap to my feet in one swift kicking motion, move in on the final enemy, who's on his back, bucking and writhing as if trying to escape some invisible enemy. Where's Trevor? Other than the two downed guards—one dead, the other twitching as if in mortal pain—the hallway is empty.

Then I see them: two hands wrapped around the guard's neck from behind, splotched red and white, squeezing. The guard is still squirming, his hands pulling at the fingers, but less forcefully now. His white face is tinged with blue, his eyes bugging out.

I'm half in awe, half disgusted by the scene, as the guy flops two or three more times before going still. I stand frozen, expecting the dead body to rear up, possessed supernaturally for a final battle, but it remains as motionless as one of the Nailin statues in the gardens.

"Get 'im offa me," Trevor grunts beneath two hundred and fifty pounds of muscle and flesh.

I'm tempted to leave him underneath, but he did just singlehandedly take out two impressively large men in a most creative fashion, so I bend down and push the body off him, as requested.

He's smiling, an unusual—and if I'm being honest, sort of freaky—reaction to having just killed. "Oh, hi," he says. "I didn't realize you were still here. It felt like I had to do all the work myself. And it was almost as if I was fighting three people." Maybe having Trevor on my team isn't so good after all.

"He would have taken both our heads when we were on the ground if I didn't block his sword," I say.

"He was your responsibility. And we wouldn't have been on the ground if you hadn't decided to tackle me." Trevor's still smiling.

"Never mind," I mutter, determined not to let him get under my skin. "Good work," I add grudgingly.

247

"What do we do with them?" Tawni asks, rejoining us.

"Leave 'em," Trevor says. "We don't have time to be hiding bodies."

"Bad idea," I say. "We don't know how long finding my father will take. If the alarm is raised we're screwed."

"Fine," Trevor grunts, grabbing one of the guy's feet, the one with half a sword sticking out of his chest, and starts dragging him down the hall. "You get the other one."

I clutch the choked guard's legs and start pulling. *Ugh.* It's like pulling a truck full of raw iron ore. Tawni brings the discarded swords and follows us through the first door we come to—one of the hundred or so visitor apartments that are used for important guests. Luckily, it's unlocked, but I'm pretty sure Trevor wouldn't have hesitated to kick it in if required.

It's also recently been occupied, probably one of the many guests attending tonight's party, with clothes strewn haphazardly on the bed—here a shimmering green gown, there a tiny black dress; a handful of white lacy things that I can only guess as to the purpose. The aftermath of a very picky woman trying to decide what to wear to the ball.

We dump the bodies at the foot of the bed, hide their swords in the bathtub behind the curtain: a big surprise for the woman when she comes back to her room. Tawni's reading the guards' papers when we ready ourselves to leave. She's frowning.

"What is it?" I ask.

"It's a trap," she says, her face awash with terror. "He knows we're coming."

Adele

The long employees' corridor in front of us is empty. As Roc expected, no one is using the loading dock tonight. We're more likely to run into action as we approach the throne room.

For just a moment I wonder about how Tristan and Tawni and Trevor are doing—there's a twinge of fear in my stomach—but then I shake it off, refocus on the task at hand.

We pass through a set of double doors, moving out of the sterile white of the maintenance hallway and into the plush luxury of the government offices. The floor is shiny, black marble, likely recently hand-polished by one of the many servants. The walls are stone, but not like the stone walls I'm used to. Into these walls are chiseled ornate designs, almost mystical. There's a ball of fire—the real sun maybe?—raining down chariots of fire on the earth below. The chariots are driven by men with horns, wielding multi-pronged whips. Clearly it's a war scene, but a war against whom? On the earth, directly in the path of the falling chariots, are people with spears and knives, looking wholly inadequate to face off against the fire chariots and whip-wielding, horned invaders. In fact, many of the people are fleeing, their weapons dropped during their hasty retreat.

The entire scene is a blur as we stride past, and I'm left wondering as to the significance and purpose—if any—of the artist's stonework.

We also pass a number of beautiful, dark brown wooden doors. Behind some of them there are voices, heavy discussions that likely involve power, money, and the pursuit of both. As we rush on my heart beats faster and faster in my chest as my expectation of being discovered rises with each step.

When we turn the next corner, I gasp, as the hall appears to go on forever, cut straight and true—there's no way we'll make it to the end of this corridor unseen. Yet Roc starts down it, seemingly unconcerned, and I have no choice but to follow my guide. As it turns out, the hall is so long it cannot be isolated to only one building. No, this passageway connects five or six buildings. At each intersection, the ceiling of the hall rises to a glassed-in atrium with a one-hundred-eighty-degree unobstructed view of the man-made night sky.

After going through the first atrium, I assume we'll take this corridor all the way to the throne room, but Roc has other plans. Upon reaching the second glassy connection point, he pushes through a door and into an outside patio, which is surrounded on all sides by buildings, each with similar glassed-in alcoves. We skirt around a lone statue of the current President Nailin—his foot is propped up arrogantly on a large stone, as if he's just conquered it (another inanimate object defeated, yeah!)—and then into another door that leads into one of the adjacent buildings. Given the maze-like quality of the place, I'm hoping Roc doesn't faint from exhaustion or dehydration. Without him, I may not reach my twentieth birthday before I locate the throne room.

Into another luxurious hallway, turn right, turn left, down a half flight of white marble stairs, up a half flight of the same type of stairs, out and across another patio, and into another building: we cut a seemingly random path through the collection of buildings that I can only assume is the safest—if not fastest—route.

The entire way, we don't see a single soul.

I'm still trying to decide whether that's a good or a bad thing, when I hear familiar voices.

Tristan

"What do you mean, 'a trap'?" I ask, grabbing the paper and skimming through the text.

Tawni waits patiently for me to find the spot. When I do, I read it aloud, my heart skipping a beat or two before I finish: "I fully expect a convoy of five or six intruders, including my son, to attempt to assault me before, during, or after the Sun Festival event. Your orders are to draw them to me, allow them safe passage—I want them all, especially my son, taken alive." My heart is in my chest. He knows. He's waiting.

"So we weren't as stealthy as we thought," Trevor says. "The right move is to pull out, try again when he least expects an attack."

"We can't," I say, closing my eyes.

"Why not?"

"Because Adele and Roc don't know," I say. "We have to get to them first, try to warn them so we can all escape together."

Trevor's eyes narrow. "But the only place we'll be sure to meet up with them is…"

"Yeah, that's where we're going," I say. "The throne room."

Trevor opens his mouth to say something, but then stops himself. We all know what he was going to say: *that's suicide.* He's right, of course, but he stopped because he knows, like me, that we have no choice. None of us will abandon Adele and Roc, nor would they leave us if the roles were reversed.

"But if they were supposed to let us through, why did those guys try to kill you?" Tawni asks.

"You couldn't see very well because you were behind us, but the guys were reading the paper as they approached," I explain. "They were probably given their orders late, were trying to catch up to the situation, perhaps hadn't read far enough yet, or maybe were just so surprised to see us that they overreacted."

"Unlucky for them," Trevor says, resting a foot on one of the dead guards.

"Can you not do that?" Tawni says, motioning toward his foot, her nose crinkled with disgust.

Grinning, Trevor moves his foot from the guard.

I say, "Adele and Roc might already be closing in on the throne room. We've got to go."

"Hopefully all the other guards got the memo and they just let us through," Trevor says.

"Don't count on it," I say.

Although we now know that the guards have been ordered to let us make it all the way through to my father, I still check both ends of the hall before slipping out of the room. You never know who might not be in the loop, like the two dead behemoths we just left in our wake. I go left, determined to make up as much time as possible, running soft-footed down the corridor. Reaching the end, I go left again, followed by a right at the end of the next line of guest rooms. Three quarters of the way to the end of the next hall is the opening to a wide staircase that descends directly beside my father's favorite room in all of the buildings: the throne room.

I gaze over the balcony, try to see past the curving edge of the spiral staircase, listen intently. I don't see or hear anything. In fact, it's so quiet you could hear a pebble drop from the treads of one's boot. *A trap*. It would have felt like one even if we didn't have the paper to prove it.

Could Adele and Roc already have fallen into my father's well-laid web? The plan is for the first team to arrive at the throne room to wait only five minutes and then go in, in case the other team has already been captured. But maybe they arrived only a few minutes earlier and are still hiding below, waiting for us before breaching the final obstacle on our quest to change the future history of the Tri-Realms. If so, will we be able to sneak back into the night and save the conclusion of our mission for another day?

A lot of questions. A lot of doubt. I descend the stairs quietly.

One curve, two; the third—and last—curve. The foyer outside the throne room is empty. Waiting for Trevor and Tawni to catch up, I quickly check behind the base of the staircase, hoping against hope that they're waiting for us there. Empty. I stare at the splinters of light radiating out from the seven-layered crystal chandelier above me, welcoming the spark of head pain that results from looking directly into the bright light.

"Either they're not here yet, or they've gone in," I say.

"Do you want to wait?" Trevor says, surprising me. Typically he's more of the shoot-now-consider-alternatives-later type of person. His cautiousness shows his different-but-equal concern for our friends.

"But what if they're already in there?" Tawni says. "They'll need backup."

Both pairs of eyes are on me, leaving me to make the decision. If they're in there, my father may kill them immediately, either to enrage me or simply because he has no use for them. Waiting could mean their deaths. Too risky.

"We're going in," I say, breaking the wait-five-minutes plan, and potentially making the biggest mistake of my life.

Trevor says, "We're with you." Tawni just nods, biting her bottom lip.

I open the door, which doesn't lead straight into the throne room; no, that would be way too ordinary for my father. Instead, it opens to an outer ring that surrounds my father's sanctuary. Every twenty or so feet there's a break in the raw-cut stone wall, giving multiple entrances (and multiple exits) to the place my father spends much of his time.

Voices echo through the chamber. My father's voice: loud and firm and relentless.

"Kill them all," he barks.

"Sir, if we do that there will be no one left to pay your taxes and support our way of life." One of his advisors. By the sound of his screechy voice it's a guy who I've only ever known as Sanders.

"To hell with taxes!" the President roars. "I want the blood of all those who oppose me!"

"This time we'll get all the rebels," Sanders promises. "We'll round everyone up, interrogate them, pit them against each other by threatening their friends and family, make them talk. Anyone who is even remotely a threat to you will be shot."

"Hmm, I like the way you think, Sanders. That must be why I keep you around. It's certainly not because of the timbre of your voice." My father's laugh is gruff and out of place. Continuing to listen, I lead Trevor and Tawni along the wall to the first entranceway.

"I suppose we can do it your way, so long as we kill enough of the *lesser* dwellers to ensure their future cooperation."

We reach the gap and I peek around the corner. A single light is illuminated, highlighting my father's plush oak chair in the center of the room. Near him stands Sanders, a pitifully skinny man with a heart that's equally shriveled. He gestures with his hands, like he's giving a speech to an audience much larger than one.

"Yes, yes, of course. We'll send a message in the strongest of terms that treachery will not be tolerated in the Tri-Realms."

My father leans back in his chair, rubs his hands thoughtfully against the red velvet armrests. Sighs. "Yes, that should do just fine. Give the orders to carry out the plan as you suggested."

"Thank you, my President," Sanders says reverently, his voice grating my eardrum like cheese. He turns to go, making directly for our gap.

"Send in the generals on your way out," my father orders behind him.

He stops for just a moment to say, "As you wish," before continuing his path toward us. I frantically scan the space outside of the lighted area, looking and listening for any signs that this truly is a trap. Hidden guards, unable to stay still for long periods of time, perhaps scraping a toe on the floor, breathing heavily, letting a cough slip from the back of the throat. I see nothing. I hear nothing.

Surrounding the heart of the throne room are black pillars, not required to hold up the ceiling, but instead intended to give the room a solid beauty. Naturally, my father's idea. The pillars also make great places to hide. Sanders passes between the pillars on his way to the gap, looking more at his feet than up, probably still reliving and relishing my father's acceptance of his plan.

I pull back behind the wall, wait for the moment Sanders rounds the bend, his skeleton-like face diminishing further as it falls under shadow. I grab him by the throat, crush his voice box so he can't make a sound, hiss in his ear, "One noise and you die, understand?"

His already buggy eyes protrude even further from his head, and he nods. His silence saves his life, but not his consciousness. I release him, punch him so hard in the head he'll feel it for days, catch him lightly in my arms, and then set him down in the outer passage. At least he won't be inviting the generals in anytime soon.

To Tawni, I say, "We'll enter first. You come in behind us and duck behind one of the pillars. Stay there." She nods vigorously.

To Trevor, I raise a fist. He raises his own and bumps it firmly against mine. Game time. Adele and Roc don't appear to be here, but they may have been captured and taken away already. Either way, I have to find out, question my father. And if it turns out not to be a trap, hopefully kill him, too.

I enter the throne room, not trying to hide my presence, striding toward my father as if I belong there, as if I never left, as if he's expecting me, which he might be. Trevor's with me every step of the way and I sense when Tawni moves in behind us, ducks off to one side.

My father, who's looking at his lap, suddenly looks up, as if sensing our presence. His face lights up with a smile that's as big as it is fake. "Ahh, Tristan, you made it after all!" he booms.

I eye him warily. "How did you know?"

He laughs. "Are you really so arrogant to think you could enter *my* kingdom without me knowing? When you killed some of my soldiers you should have killed all of them."

The men who killed Ram. The ones knocked out but not dead. Although it's cost us the element of surprise, I know we did the right thing letting them live.

"I was beginning to think you wouldn't have the guts to show," my father says.

"It was never guts that I lacked," I say, trying to control my sudden desire to launch myself at the man who created me, jam my sword into his heart; that is, assuming the space within his left breast contains an organ and isn't just a black and empty cavity.

"Mmm, really?" he says, running a hand through his short blond hair. The last time I saw him there were salt-and-pepper flecks of gray on his scalp, and deep lines on his face. I took it as a sign that even the most powerful man in the Tri-Realms can't fight against time. But now the gray is gone and his face is as smooth as a twenty-year-old's, tan and chiseled. Hair coloring, wrinkle treatments, tanning beds: my father can even thwart the signs of time. "Last I checked, you would run and hide when I put your mother in her place."

I immediately feel my blood pressure rise, my head go hot, not from embarrassment but from pure anger, rising to a boil. Through my teeth, I say, "Don't speak of my mother. She is everything you're not. Good, pure, gentle, caring. You were never worthy of her."

"Ha ha ha ha!" my father bellows. "You are so much like her it's scary. But you misspoke. You said 'She *is* everything you're not.' I believe you meant *was*."

I freeze, my anger falling away like a warm coat, leaving me naked and cold. I shiver. There's a pit in my stomach. "What the hell do you mean?"

"Surely you noticed your mother's not around anymore," my father mocks. A sudden awareness floods through me, causing my muscles to ache, my bones to feel bruised. It's as if I've swallowed shards of glass, which are now cutting me apart from the inside.

"What did you do to her?!" I roar, the anger returning, white-hot and hungry. I take a step toward him.

"Temper, temper, Tristan. What did I teach you about controlling your anger?" He readjusts his sitting position, leans back more casually, one leg crossed over the other. "Where were we? Ah, yes, your mother. She did something very naughty, so I had to punish her—that's all there is to it."

I stand there seething, unable to move, my body wracked with a blind fury the likes of which I've never experienced before. My father takes my silence and stillness for weakness.

"Cat got your tongue?" he says. "Let me spell it out for you. I killed her with my bare hands! And I loved watching the life drain out of her face; loved kissing her lips as I held her down and she took her last breath; loved feeling her body go cold as we lay in bed together one last time." He's almost licking his lips with delight.

A profound sadness wraps around my anger, but I thrust it off. There will be time for grief later. For now, all I desire is revenge.

Adele

Tristan's voice! We did it! We've both arrived at the throne room at the same time, so there's no need to wait. I'm shaking with excitement as I run the last few feet to where a door stands wide open. *Is this it?* I mouth to Roc.

Yes, he silently communicates.

We creep into a rounded corridor, hearing the voices loud and clear now. Not just Tristan; someone else, too. Another familiar voice, but one that I've mostly heard in my nightmares: President Nailin. The Devil. My father's executioner. My target.

"What did you do to her?!" Tristan screams, his voice echoing off the walls in the outer hallway. Whatever's happening, he's losing his cool. We need to be there for him. I creep another few steps.

"Temper, temper, Tristan. What did I teach you about controlling your anger?" Nailin says, as Roc and I close in on a gap in the wall, off to our left. "Where were we? Ah, yes, your mother. She did something very naughty, so I had to punish her—that's all there is to it." Even out of sight, his words are as cold as darts of ice—aimed at Tristan's heart.

I move closer to the gap, waiting for Tristan's response, but silence rules. Something clips my foot and I trip, nearly fall, barely manage to catch myself with a hand on the floor.

"You okay?" Roc whispers in my ear.

"I'm fine. I just tripped on something." I feel around beside me, the tips of my fingers finding a soft lump wrapped in some kind of cloth. I work my way up it, trying to locate something that will identify the object. More cloth, sort of bumpy, and then—

—human flesh. I pull back sharply, barely able to clamp a hand over my mouth before letting out a high-pitched squeal which only makes it as far as the inside of my mouth. "It's a body," I say, dreading looking at the face of another dead friend, Trevor or Tawni this time.

Roc flicks on a light, careful to keep the beam focused toward the wall.

A stranger, mousy and thin. "An advisor," Roc whispers. "Tristan probably knocked him out. His chest is moving, still breathing." He extinguishes the light.

We hear: "Cat got your tongue?" The president's voice, full of sarcasm. "Let me spell it out for you. I killed her with my bare hands! And I loved watching the life drain out of her face; loved kissing her lips as I held her down and she took her last breath; loved feeling her body go cold as we lay in bed together one last time."

Although neither Tristan nor his father have mentioned the name of the woman they speak of, I know who it is. His mother, a woman he loves. Once I promised to help him look for her after this was all over. Now I know that won't be possible.

Something bad is about to happen—I can feel it. The President wouldn't be egging his son on if he wasn't well-protected. And Tristan won't back off now that he knows the truth. We need to move.

I jog the last few steps to the gap, peek around the corner, see the back of Tristan—Trevor next to him. Tristan's just standing there, his knuckles curled at his side, his shoulders rising and falling with heavy breaths. Between them I can just make out the relaxed figure of the President, sitting on his throne, not a care in the world.

Something bad is about to happen.

My mother's necklace is heavy around my neck, as if the spirit of my father has entered it upon reaching the location of his murderer.

Tristan charges, ripping his sword from his side, holding it high above his head and letting out a fury-induced cry that would surely raise the dead. Trevor rushes after him, pulling his gun from its holster, and I'm about to spring from our hiding spot when I sense movement from above. Glancing up, I see them:

Dozens of red-clothed guardsmen leap from their perches on platforms near the top of the pillars spread evenly throughout the room. One lands directly in front of Tristan, blocking his path to the President. Another lands behind him, raises his sword...

I start running, already knowing I'm too late. Too late *again*. Just like with my father. There's a familiar voice behind me—not Roc, more high-pitched—but I don't stop—can't stop—my eyes fixed on the gleaming metal that will kill the only person I've ever really—

A flash bursts from the muzzle of Trevor's gun, accompanied simultaneously by an ear-shattering *BOOM!* Before his sword falls on Tristan, the guardsman cries out in pain, arches his back, slumps to the floor. As I enter the circle of light, there is red everywhere, more foes than I've ever faced, but if I can just get to Tristan and Trevor, maybe...

Three guardsmen pounce on Trevor, slash his gun with their swords, sending it clattering to the marble floor. He's barely able to rip his sword from his scabbard and sweep aside their probing weapons. Tristan's got his hands full with three others, probably unaware that he would be dead if not for Trevor. He goes for the gun at his calf but his opponents are attacking too fast and he has to remain standing to fight them off. I'm flanked by two men who finally notice my entrance into the battle. They're smiling slightly, as if they foresee getting some twisted pleasure out of fighting a girl.

My bow is out before they have the chance to even think about taking a step toward me. I notch an arrow, send one through the first guy's heart, and, fitting a second, let it fly into his partner's gut, who collapses on top of him, blood dribbling from his mouth. Time to help Tristan and Trevor.

I shift my attention to Trevor, who's the closer of the two. One of his opponents is writhing on the marble floor, a shadow of blood spreading under him. The other two are still putting up a fight, but are clearly losing, as Trevor's superior sword skill starts to overwhelm them. Then I see it: a red form rise up, on its knees, blade held high. The guy who tried to kill Tristan from behind earlier, cut down by Trevor, injured but not dead. I level an arrow at the would-be killer, trying to get a bead on him, but Trevor's body keeps moving in the way as he tries to fight off his opponents.

"No!" I yell, sprinting toward my friend and one-time savior.

He sees me coming, parries his two frontward opponent's swords, slashing downward to cut off one of their hands, drawing a cry of anguish. Still running, I shoot the other one through the heart, hoping to free Trevor up to get away.

"Watch out!" I cry, drawing a confused expression from Trevor. But still he doesn't move, just stares at me.

His attacker's sword is in position. I'm three steps away but running through mud, my strides in slow motion. In fact, everything's in slow motion, seconds feeling like minutes, minutes like hours, hours like years and years.

Beyond Trevor, Tristan turns, perhaps upon hearing my voice, sees the danger, slashes his sword across to disarm Trevor's attempted murderer. Too late. Like me, he's too late.

With a roar, the dying guardsman lunges forward, plunges the sharp point of his blade into the soft part of Trevor's lower back. "No!" I scream again, seeing Trevor's eyes widen, his mouth open. The blade comes all the way through, sticking from his stomach gruesomely. My tears are already falling, but I don't stop, can't stop, can't let such an atrocity go unpunished.

Scattering my bow and arrows like a bundle of sticks, I draw my thin sword and slash it hard across the back of one of Trevor's opponents. When he drops, I jam it into him again, ensuring his demise. When I pull my blade from him it's slick with the blood of revenge, but it's not enough. I jab it at his other opponent, the one who's now missing a hand. He's just staring at his severed wrist, babbling something, when my blade enters his gut. His eyes jerk to mine, as if surprised, but then he falls, dead before hitting the floor.

Behind Trevor, Tristan swings his sword once more, this time connecting with the murderer, a brutal killing stroke.

Trevor drops to his knees, his eyes glassy and fixed on mine. I cough, a choking sob that hurts my throat and head and soul, raise a hand to my chest, mouth *Thank you*, as tears run over my lips and tongue.

His lips curling into an unexpected, beautiful and heart-wrenching smile, Trevor says, "Finish this," and then collapses to the floor. I know there's no saving him and yet I rush to him, try to pull the sword from his back. I'm crying and groaning and straining with all my might to extract the damn sword—why won't it budge?—which is compacted in bone and muscle and Trevor. *Oh God, why another friend, why not me? Why do I live while others die?*

On the edges of my vision I see Tristan whirling and spinning and fighting to keep the guards off of me. While I'm mourning my dead friend, the fight goes on. There's no time for mourning.

I pull myself away from my dead friend, who saved me *and* Tristan, who always helped to keep the mood light when everything was so dark, who my mom trusted with her life, who was willing to die for what he believed in.

I'll never forget you, Trevor, I silently promise. I stand and rejoin the fight, the hot coals of revenge burning in my heart.

Twenty-Three
Tristan

He's dead. Despite all our differences and his sometimes annoying, sometimes funny jokes, the weight of his death rests on my shoulders like a coil of thick, metal chains. I feel like I should take the blame, assume the responsibility as the leader of my group, but I know that's more self-loathing than I deserve. For the blame lies not with me, but with my father, the black-eyed snake. Through the net of guardsmen that surround us, I can still see him. He hasn't moved from his perch. His legs are still crossed lazily, as if the turmoil, the violence, the *death* around him is just part of normal, daily life. When he yawns, I snap.

I charge the line, intent on breaking through or dying in the attempt. Instead of fighting back, the guards merely block my strikes with their swords, wary of me but not afraid. Not willing to harm me, which is probably my father's orders. He wants to break me before he kills me.

I back off, bump into someone, whirl around, and find that it's Adele, her face tearstained but not defeated. There's an intensity in her green eyes that makes her appear dangerous. A huntress. With a single nod she tells me she's ready to fight. And so am I.

But before we're able to attack, a garbled yell shoots from the back of the room. I whip my head in the direction of the sound. One of the guards has collapsed, having been stabbed in the back by an unexpected foe.

Roc.

Sword gleaming silver and red, he stands behind where the guard fell. He makes eye contact with me just as one of the men turns toward him. *No, no, no!* Not another; not my best friend; not Roc.

Bonk! Something whacks the soldier in the helmet, knocking him off his feet. Roc didn't move, so it must've been—

"Tawni!" Adele yells, spotting her behind a pillar. "Run! Get out of here!"

There's a look in Tawni's eyes that tells me she's not going anywhere. As if to prove it, she hefts something over her shoulder and chucks it with two hands, narrowly missing another guard.

That's when all hell breaks loose.

The guard that was nearly hit by what turns out to be an apple-sized metal ball—who knows where Tawni got it— charges toward her. Roc, who seems to be filled with more courage than all of us combined, steps in front of the guard, who's nearly twice his size, and swipes at him with his sword. The guy dodges the blow casually, professionally, and then slashes at Roc's head. He barely ducks under it, his eyes big and wide and scared. He's just realized he's way out of his depth. Tawni continues launching metal balls at anyone wearing red, hitting a few, but mostly missing.

I sprint toward where Roc is now blocking heavy killing blows, trying to use his quickness to keep his opponent on the move. Although Tawni and Roc have eliminated a few of the guards, there are still at least twelve upright and fighting—three of which bar the path to my friend. The clang of metal on metal rings out behind me—Adele's got a fight of her own.

How has everything gotten so out of control? I wonder. The world is falling apart at the seams, and we—a few teenagers— are supposed to stop it? How we ever thought we could succeed, I do not know. But now all that exists is fighting and death and using my last breaths to reduce the size of my father's guard force.

Holding my sword with my left hand, I extract a throwing knife from my belt and snap it at the centermost guard, hitting him in the throat. He falls backward, breathing more blood than air until he dies. I still want to get to my gun, but, strapped to my ankle, it's too far away. Why didn't I holster it higher up? So stupid.

The other two men close from each side, spinning their swords like batons, clearly well-trained in the art of sword fighting. I fake a swing at one, go for the other, who blocks my attempt and counterattacks with a three-cut combination, which I parry while stepping back to avoid a slash from the other guy.

Feeling a presence behind me, I risk a glance back to see Adele cut down one of the four men she's fighting. Considering our disadvantage in numbers, we're doing pretty well. A sliver of hope rises in me, just large enough to delude myself into a vision of victory where dozens of dead guardsmen lie in red piles on the floor; my father shrinks back, cowering in his throne like the coward that he is; me, stabbing him through the chest, my mother's name on my lips—*Jocelyn Nailin*—as I kill my last remaining parent.

When hope rises, that's when things tend to fall apart. A hard lesson.

One of my foes gets inside my sword range, slices my arm, which sends icy, searing, *real* pain through my nerves and nearly makes me drop my sword. I manage to switch my grip to my other hand, however, warding off his next stroke. But then I trip on something—no, no, not *something*; Trevor's dead body—and stumble backward. The guards are on me faster than a starving man on a stale loaf of bread, their sword points under my chin.

Before I die, I have to see her once more. I turn my head and her sword is knocked from her hand, as five—or is it six?—guards surround her. I can't watch this, can't watch her die—kill me first, for God's sake, do it! DO IT! The scream is in my head, but I hear it echo throughout the room as if I really did yell.

Then I realize it's not an echo; it's Roc, yelling "Do it!" and "Kill me!" repeatedly. I follow the sound between the legs of the guards who have me at their mercy. Past them, Roc lies in a similar position to me—on his back, weaponless, blades at his throat—and is screaming his head off, his gaze to the side. I trace the line of his gaze to where Tawni is backed up against a pillar, on the verge of death, just like the rest of us. Roc doesn't want to see her die any more than I do Adele.

I close my eyes, try to picture the good memories of my life: my mother, singing my brother and me a gentle and soothing lullaby before bed; playing tag and hide-and-seek with Roc in the palace gardens, finding him tucked away in the dead center of a thorny rosebush, no clue as to how he got in there; Adele's face, the first time I saw her, the first time I kissed her.

"Enough!" my father screams from only ten feet away. My eyes flash open. "Enough," he repeats. "While admirable, your heroics are fruitless. You're beaten. Accept it. You've had your fun and now it's my turn. Guards! Bind them!"

What? He's not going to kill us, just tie us up? At first the airy bubble of elation swells up in my stomach—my friends not dead; Adele not dead—but then I realize: he wants to destroy our minds before destroying our bodies. Psychological warfare: my father's favorite. The bubble pops and I'm left feeling sick.

Strong arms lift me, roughly twist my arms behind me, shackle my hands together. Around me, my friends are getting similar treatment.

"Relieve them of their weapons," my father orders. A guard on each leg, they start low, removing the knife lashed to my calf, the handgun from my ankle holster, the series of various-sized knives from my belt, the bow and arrows from my back. They already have my sword. I glance over at Adele, who's not making it easy on her guards, squirming and insulting them as they carefully search her. Grinning, one of them grabs her breast.

"Leave her alone!" I shout, which is unnecessary, because Adele kicks the guard in the groin, dropping him to his knees, and then, before the other guards can step in, slams her heel into his face, rocking him back.

"My nose!" he screams, blood gushing between his fingers. "She broke my freakin' nose!"

A rush of pride courses through me. That's my girlfriend.

Adele

"Bravo," President Nailin says, clapping slowly. "Son, you've picked a real firecracker. Too bad she's a filthy moon dweller."

Tristan turns away from me to face his father, says, "You wouldn't know filth if your face was covered in mud."

"What did I say about your temper?" the President says.

The guards work on tying my feet together, determined not to let me break anymore noses. Next time I'll use my head, I think. When I glance over at Roc and Tawni, Roc's already bound and weaponless, feet and hands clapped together with thick rope. The guard who's searching Tawni is as big a pervert as the one I had, his hands still lingering mid-thigh, caressing behind her legs and moving up…

"Knock it off, horn dog," one of the other guards hisses. "She was throwing those cannonballs, she doesn't have any weapons."

The perv guard stands up, smirking, and gives Tawni a quick final pat down, being sure to hit only her curves. I want nothing more than to run to her, kick the sick smile off his face, but my feet are tied now, and I'd only serve to fall on my own face if I tried. Tawni just takes it, her eyes closed, her face expressionless. I hope she's found a happy place to go, somewhere far, far away from here.

Tristan's still trading terse remarks with his father. "You're killing innocent people," Tristan says, trying to reason with the unreasonable. Perhaps somewhere inside he still hopes his father can be rehabilitated.

"I had no choice. They were going to rebel. You know as well as I do that the New City depends on the natural resources the Lesser Realms provide."

"The *Lower* Realms, Father. Not lesser."

"You're a fool, Tristan. You've given up everything for a girl, and a moon dweller, no less. You could have ruled the world!"

"At what cost? The blood of so many is on your hands. You killed Mom? What the hell is wrong with you?" Until this point there's only anger in Tristan's tone, but upon mention of his mother, a hint of profound sadness creeps in.

The President smiles, his teeth bright white under the glare of the spotlight. "You don't know what she did, Son. When you hear it, you'll hate her. You'll know that she had to die."

"I'll never think that," Tristan says. "Anything she did, she did for the right reasons."

"Even if she did it to you?" his father says, his evil smile returning.

Tristan

I'm scared of what my father will tell me about my mom. In my memory, she's perfect, and that's how I want to keep her. Anything he says to tarnish her reputation will only make me hate him more.

271

As we shuffle down the long corridor, our tied-up legs only able to take miniature steps, I wonder what she could have possibly done *to me* that would make me angry at her. All she ever did was love me, care for me, try to give me a good life, provide a buffer from my father. Regardless of what my father says, I vow to forgive her for it, if forgiveness is even necessary.

My thoughts turn to Adele, just a step behind me. These are my last moments with her, for I know my father will kill her or me, or both of us. He'll do it in front of each other, forcing us to watch, destroying one of our minds while he destroys the other's body. But I'll not go down without a fight. They'll have to hold me down with four men, one for each of my limbs, or I'll break through, rip my bonds to shreds, kill everyone in my path. That's what I'm feeling now.

The corridor ends and I realize where we're going: the council room. Although my father holds most of his one on one and smaller meetings in the throne room, he conducts larger meetings with his advisors and vice presidents in the council room.

We enter the room, which is large enough to hold a couple of hundred people on lofted risers, which look down upon a square flat area in the center. Typically my father would walk around in the middle, waving his arms and shouting speeches about the rights of the sun dwellers and new taxes he's planning on imposing. The sun dweller vice presidents would cheer and clap and shout their agreement with his every idea. Now the room is empty and silent, save for us and the sound of our footfalls on the wooden steps descending to the center, which I've always called the pit.

Approaching the pit, my father veers off to the right, takes a seat in the first row. I start to follow, but the guard behind me

272

nudges to continue down. I pause but then obey, wondering what my father has in store for us. Whatever it is, it will be messed up, something only a madman would derive as punishment for disobedience.

When I reach the pit, I look back and up, expecting the rest of my friends to have been ushered down, too, looking forward to one last chance to get close to Adele, to perhaps tell her how I truly feel before it's all over.

I frown when I see how things have been arranged.

My father, still sitting in the first row, is flanked by a guard on each side, followed by Adele and Tawni on opposite sides. Another guard caps things off on each end. The next two rows behind them are filled with more guards. And coming down the steps to meet me in the pit: Roc, his face whiter than I've ever seen it, clutching two swords awkwardly with his bound hands.

It doesn't take a mining engineer to figure out what the plan is.

We have to fight each other. Not like our fun and spirited training fights, but a real fight. And knowing my father it will be to the death.

Adele

I can't watch this. It's too much. If my hands weren't tied behind the chair, my feet clamped tightly together, I'd jump up, give my own life in an attempt to save them. I close my eyes when the President's voice cuts the air beside me.

"Now for tonight's entertainment," he says, almost gleefully. "Son of the President against servant. Friend against friend.

273

Traitor against traitor. However you chop it up, this has real potential for the dramatic."

"I think you mean son of the President against son of the President. Did you forget that Roc is your son, too? No, I won't do it," Tristan says from below. I open my eyes. Based on the fierceness of his eyes, I know his words are a promise.

"We'll see about that, you stupid boy," the President says. "But first, I promised you a story, did I not?"

He stands, a big man with a small mind, ready to deliver the psychological knockout blow before the real fight even begins.

"Your mother…" he says, starting slowly. He pauses, looks at Tristan and then directly at me, his eyes lingering on mine. (It creeps me out if I'm being totally honest.) "…was a bad woman."

"Shut your mouth!" Tristan growls from below. "She's dead at your hands, can't you let her rest in peace?"

The President smiles. "I could…but I won't. Now, another outburst like that from you, and I'll slit your little girlfriend's throat." The cold edge of a steel knife slides along my throat, as one of the guards demonstrates the truth of his threat.

Tristan's face reddens, but he closes his mouth.

"As I was saying, Jocelyn Nailin, my wife—God rest her soul—was a bad woman." He pauses, stares at his son as if daring him to refute his remark, continues. "Do you remember the gift I gave you for your fifteenth birthday, Tristan? The trip we took? Don't say it out loud, for not all in this room are privy to our little secret, although I suspect you've already told your friends."

Tristan only nods. *The earth dwellers.* He's talking about when he took the whole family to the New City.

"A worthy gift, if I do say so myself," Nailin says. "Well, your mother—ah, your mother always was a feisty one—she didn't appreciate me keeping things from the people. As you know, she threw a temper tantrum and I had to put her in her place."

"You abused her," Tristan says through a clamped jaw.

"Abused, punished, call it what you want, but she deserved it. She was meddling in things she didn't understand. Anyway, I thought she had gotten the message to butt out, but as it turns out, her meddling was only just beginning."

He sighs, looks at me again. "You see, she started visiting with one of my top scientists, a genius, a man who always seems to deliver when I need him to create something for me." His eyes are the same color as Tristan's, I realize suddenly, but they look so different, so much darker and full of hate, whereas Tristan's seem to invite me in, almost sparkling with goodness. Strange how two identical sets of eyes can give off such opposite vibes.

He continues: "Your mother, the weasel"—he raises a finger as if to warn Tristan from refuting his insult—"went to *my* scientist, and said *I* needed him to build something for *me*. None of this was true, of course, but he believed her, because why wouldn't he? What wife goes behind her husband's back and lies to his employee?"

Returning his gaze to Tristan, who is standing as still as a statue, his muscles noticeably tensed, he says, "My scientist built what she wanted: a set of microchips, that, when attached to the spinal cord, could communicate with each other and with the brain. What could she want with such devices? It took me a long time to figure it out. But I'm getting ahead of myself. After she got the chips, she disappeared. Do you remember it,

275

son? The day she left us? I thought it was just her throwing another tantrum, not carrying out a treasonous plan against me.

"The next day my scientist came to me, asked me how the microchips were working. Needless to say, I didn't have a clue what he was talking about, and I told him so. He told me everything, about your snaky mother, about what he built for her. I still didn't know what she was planning to do with the microchips, but I knew it couldn't be good, so I sent Rivet after her."

My stomach churns as I remember the grotesque and scarred face of Rivet, the president's killing machine, who I killed after he murdered Cole in cold blood. The thought of him hunting down Tristan's mother makes me ill. Based on the greenness of Tristan's face, I can tell he feels the same way.

And the microchips? Could it be? Could Tristan's mom and her microchips be the link Tristan and I have been missing this whole time?

"I know what you're thinking: how could you? Rivet is crazy—he'd kill her! I gave him strict orders not to harm her, just to bring her back. Well, as it turns out, he couldn't find her and she returned a few days later on her own. It seems she wasn't willing to leave her children even to save herself. She told me she needed a holiday, apologized for leaving without telling me, and said she wouldn't do it again. Can you believe her nerve? Lying to my face like that?

"That's when I made a mistake. I let my anger get the better of me. I killed her on the spot, that filthy, no-good, whore of a wife. I crushed her windpipe like a piece of plastic."

Something snaps in Tristan and he charges the steps, but a guard appears and closes the large metal gate with an ominous clang. Backing up a few steps, Tristan runs at the high wall beneath our seats, springs off his toes, grabs for the ledge at the top, his fingers falling short as he slides down the wall with a dismal groan.

I can't see him anymore, but I can hear him, his anguished, ragged screams of, "I'll kill you!—how could you?—I hate you!" I feel broken inside, seeing him like this, hearing him like this, knowing what he's gone through. Despite being a sun dweller, the son of the President, having everything handed to him since he was born, his life has been every bit as grief-filled as my own, as anyone's in the Lower Realms.

I feel closer to him than I've ever felt.

I want to go to him, but right as I consider how I might be able to break free and jump below, I shiver as the cold steel is once more at my throat. "Silence!" President Nailin bellows. "Or she dies!"

Tristan, still out of sight, stops his yelling, and Roc rushes to him, speaks in soft tones. I can't hear what he says, but a minute later he and Tristan walk back into view. Tristan's longish hair is in his face, disheveled by sorrow-filled fingers. His face isn't moist as I expected it might be; rather, it's cracked, full of lines that I've never seen before, as if each of his father's words were blades, tearing long, bloodless streaks across his forehead, cheeks, and chin. His single dimple is still there, but it's a hole, filled with despair, not a sign of joviality.

The knife slides away from my skin.

"Why'd you kill her? What did she do that was so bad?" he demands.

"Welcome back," the President says. "I was about to tell you when you lost control of yourself. Besides lying to my scientist, she lied to me after I confronted her. She kept on with her lie about taking a vacation. She wouldn't tell me where she really

277

went. I should have tortured her, pushed her farther, threatened you and Killen's lives, *forced* her to admit the truth, but she wouldn't. I guess we're cut from the same mold Tristan—like you just did, I snapped, I lost control. I killed her."

"We're nothing alike," Tristan says. He's back in control of his emotions now. Still angry, yes, but in control. Thinking, trying to gain facts, come up with a plan. "When did you find out the truth?" he asks.

"Oh, now you want to talk? Luckily, I'm in a chatty mood. It wasn't until recently and was quite by accident. When you left, I was furious, wanted to find out where you might be headed, what you might be planning. I was afraid you'd let the bat out of the bag, so to speak. So I had your room searched."

"There's nothing in my room." There's no concern in Tristan's voice, like he believes there was nothing to find.

"There was," his father insists. "You just didn't know it. Before your mother left on her little road trip, she hid something in your room, something she hoped you'd find eventually. But you never found it, never even thought to look for it." He grins. "But I found it, tucked inside your mattress. A brief recounting of her thoughts after seeing the New City, but before leaving the Sun Realm with the microchips. Want to see it?"

Tristan nods slowly.

"Fine. I have no further use for it." He pulls out a thin book, and with a flick of his wrist, flings it over the balcony. Soft-bound, it flutters slightly, its pages flapping, before dropping to the ground beside him. He retrieves it, his hands shaking slightly as he runs them along the cover.

"The pages are numbered—there are only twelve of them. Read page six." His father sits back, his arms folded across his barrel-like chest, as smug as I've ever seen him.

Tristan folds back the cover, his eyes glancing at the writing on the first page, which is probably tempting him to read from the beginning, but then flips a few pages forward. He reads aloud:

"Tristan, I'm so sorry for doing this without your knowledge, but it was the only way I could keep you safe until the time came when you were old enough to stand up to your father. You might be twenty or much older, and I might be gone or dead"—he pauses on the word—"if your father has learned of my actions; but know that I'm with you every step of the way. What I'm about to tell you will be hard to believe, but know that I did it with a pure heart and good intent. It is the truth. Tristan, I implanted a microchip in your back; you have a small scar now."

He looks up at me, his eyes brimming with understanding. "The crescent," I whisper, earning a shift in the President's gaze to me.

Tristan looks down again, finding his place with a finger. "I will now attempt to find the leaders of the Resistance, convince them to implant one of their children with an identical microchip, one that will draw you together eventually, creating a bond that will hopefully save us all. For it is not until you escape the Sun Realm that you will truly understand what the world is like outside of our bubble, how bad it is. It is not enough for you to fight on your own. You must fight alongside the Resistance, even lead them if they will have you."

My heart skips a beat. I can feel the President's eyes on me, but I can only stare at Tristan, who's still reading. I don't hear his words, just feel the intensity as the truth comes out. The confirmation that our bond, our connection, our feelings of energy—at first deep and agonizing pain, and then scalps tingling, spines buzzing—were a fabrication, the result of a microchip on our spines, without which, we'd never have met. Even though part of me already knew it, it still hurts that everything that has mattered to me in the last month has been a fraud. I'm numb with shock and anger and questions, so many questions, most of which I'll probably never get the answers to, and which probably don't matter anyway. Because I'll be dead soon.

Tristan is still reading, and I manage to fight away my thoughts to listen.

"For I know that the fight against your father's evil will last long after my life, long after the Resistance leaders' lives, and therefore, we need someone to keep the fight alive, to combine what you know with the spirit inside those that seek change in this world. I hope you can understand why I did what I did, and forgive me for it."

Tristan stops, closes the book while continuing to stare at it, tucks it in a hidden compartment in his tunic, finally looks up, but not at me.

"You found a way to turn off the microchips?" he asks his father.

"You noticed, did you? What did it feel like, son? Like all the feelings you had for this moon dweller—"

"Her name is Adele."

"Her name doesn't matter! Didn't you realize that she was nothing more than a stupid girl? That your connection with her had suddenly disappeared? I'm surprised you didn't dump her then and come back to where you belong."

To my surprise, Tristan laughs. "Is that what you thought I'd do? I knew you were arrogant, Father, but come on! I never even considered returning to you. And guess what? My love for Adele has nothing to do with some microchip. It never did. *Nothing* has changed."

I hear the end of his speech, but I don't comprehend it. I'm still stuck back on one word. Did he say *love?* My heart is alive and torn, ripped open with the weight of what I've just learned, but buzzing with the excitement of Tristan's profession of love. And if my feelings aren't being pushed and pulled in enough directions already, I realize something else: either my mother or father or both of them were in on everything. Tristan's mother said it in her note. She would try to convince the leaders of the Resistance—my parents—to implant one of their children with the paired microchip. I feel like I've been punched in the gut. I don't know whether to be extremely pissed they would do something like that to me and keep it a secret for so long, or if I should be thanking them for bringing me to Tristan, for whom my feelings are the most mixed up of all.

Love. The word rings through my head, silencing all other thoughts. But do I love him back? Does it matter? The Moon Realm is about to be destroyed and the Star Realm will fall shortly after, and I'm about to watch Tristan face off against his best friend, both of whom I care deeply about.

Tristan's father is apparently also shocked by Tristan's declaration, because two seats down he's fuming, his face a red mess, his hands fisted like clubs at his side. "Then you'll pay the consequence for your choice!" he roars.

"I will not fight Roc," Tristan says calmly.

"Not yet you won't. I have another challenger for you first."

A door opens at the far side of the space that's been turned into an arena. Killen walks through the door.

Tristan

My brother's wearing red body armor and carrying a duel-edged sword, freshly sharpened by the looks of it. He's also wearing a sneer that reminds me so much of my father it's scary. My first thought is to talk to him, but his evil smile washes away any thoughts of trying to change his mind. I'm going to have to fight him—that's all there is to it.

How can I possibly fight after what I've just learned? The confirmation that Adele and I were brought together by something outside of our control, by the actions of my mother, in some crazy, half-chance that we would come together against my father? It all seems so wildly farfetched that it can only be true. What better way to seed a rebellion than to unite the son of the President with the daughter of the Resistance leaders? It's genius, really. And the proof is in the results. We're here, trying to assassinate him, to bring equality and balance to the Tri-Realms. If we'd only succeeded in our mission, it all would've worked to perfection.

Instead, I have to fight my brother.

A guard enters the pit, aims a gun at Roc's head, says, "Drop the swords." It's the first gun I've seen any of the guards using, which is interesting. They could have annihilated us back in the throne room if they'd used guns. Probably another of my father's ideas. He wanted to watch us fight the guards—*for his entertainment.*

Roc obeys, scattering the blades on the floor. The guard escorts him up the steps and sits him in a section separate to Adele and Tawni.

"You want to show you're the strongest Nailin?" my father says. "Kill your brother, or be killed by him. The winner will be my successor."

Turning toward Killen, I say, "Killen, we don't have to—"

Killen rushes at me, his fifteen-year-old body looking more grown up than I remembered. Clearly he's been training. I react quickly, instincts kicking in, as I roll to the side and scoop up both swords, one in each hand. My right hand is sticky with blood from the wound on my arm, but appears to have dried well; there's already a deep, almost black crimson film that's crusted along the gash.

I don't want to fight him, but I also don't want to die yet. Not until I read the rest of my mother's words; not until I can speak to Adele.

I back away, getting a feel for the two swords, letting Killen come to me. Whenever we practiced together growing up, he was always the aggressor, relying on emotion over skill. Things haven't changed.

He lunges at me, slashing his sword with a lightness that shows his improvement. As I block the attack with my left blade, I hear my father clapping heavily, encouraging the guards to shout and cheer. He's enjoying watching his sons try to kill each other.

I flash my right sword at Killen's leg, but he blocks it with a deft defensive maneuver that I've never seen him perform before. When he sweeps a leg at me, I see my opening. I block his kick with a raised leg, catching it on my boot, cut at him sharply with both swords simultaneously. He blocks one with the edge of his blade, but the other one clangs off his body armor with a force that jars my arm and knocks him off balance. I put so much strength into the blow that I nearly cut through the armor.

Killen, wide-eyed and probably realizing that he'd be dead if not for the armor, backs away, staring at the dented metal plate strapped to his side.

"What are you doing, son? Get him!" my father yells. I'm not sure if he's talking to me or Killen (maybe both of us), but Killen looks up, embarrassment pink on his face for just a second. He's still just a little boy trying to please his father. The thought makes me sad and want to drop my sword, but then anger kicks in and he scowls, pushing the body armor up and over his head, letting it drop to the floor behind him.

"It slows me down," he explains. "You don't stand a chance now."

"Don't do this, Killen," I say.

"Scared to die, brother?" he asks, twirling his sword over his head.

I don't answer him, don't want to tell him that I'm scared to kill him. If my mother knew, it would break her heart.

"Time to die, Tristan," he says, charging me.

I step to the side, letting him run by me, blocking his probing swing with my left sword. He pivots and then launches a barrage of blows, side to side, up and down, slash and parry, jab and block. By the end of it we both have a thin sheen of liquid coating our arms and legs and faces.

"I'm just warming up," Killen says.

I'm just biding my time, trying to think of a solution that doesn't involve me killing my brother or him killing me. But there's just no way around it. It seems that in our world, someone always has to die. And it won't be me.

I go on the offensive, distracting him with a left, right, left combination so I can sneak a kick into his chest. It works—I was always better at using my skin-and-bone weapons better than him—and he goes down hard, dropping his sword. Surging forward, I jump on him, lean a knee on his chest, hold him down, the tip of my sword against his breast.

"You're beaten," I say. "Don't make me kill you. Mom wouldn't have wanted this. She wanted us to stand up to Father, to stop him from hurting people."

Breathing hard, Killen says, "I—I can't, Tristan. All I want is for him to respect me, to follow in his footsteps. If I surrender to you he'll always think of me as weak." His face is pale and red at the same time—blotchy. For a second I just see my younger brother, the one I used to play knights and dragons with, who used to sit on my mom's left knee while I sat on the right, who shared a room with me when we were little. And then I blink and he's gone, replaced by a mirror image of my father with one thing on his mind: killing me.

He slips a knife from a hidden scabbard, thrusts it at my face.

Adele

I think it's over, that Tristan will let Killen get up, that maybe they'll hug and make up and join forces against the man who raised them. Yeah, right. That's a happy ending and this isn't a fairytale.

A glint of steel flashes and at first I think Tristan stabbed his brother. But then both brothers strain against each other, exertion in their arms and faces. Tristan still has his right sword hovering directly over Killen's heart, but his other hand, now without a weapon, is holding his brother's wrist, trying to push it away from his face. In Killen's hand: a dagger, sharp enough to kill.

Kill him, I think. *Tristan, you have no choice, you have to kill him. For us. For everyone.*

But still he fights against the will of his brother, tries to push his weapon away. I can feel the spectators—even the guardsmen—collectively holding their breaths as the life-or-death struggle continues. For a moment it appears that Tristan will fight off Killen's knife hand, but then, with a stomach-turning quickness, his brother surges with strength, pushes the knife blade within inches of Tristan's eye. He's about to be half-blinded at the hand of his own brother! I struggle against my bonds, try to rip my hands free, to do something to help. I scream, in anger and fear and frustration as the ropes cut into my wrists, tearing the top layer of skin away until they're raw and tender.

The blade's an inch away, maybe less. One of Tristan's beautiful night blue eyes is about to be torn to shreds.

Suddenly and unexpectedly, Killen's hand falls away, the knife clattering to the floor. Tristan slumps on top of him, his head buried in his brother's neck. *What happened?* I wonder. I'm paralyzed by fear as Tristan's body lies motionless, my mind repeating the same words over and over and over again, until the words mix and swirl around and confuse themselves: *get up, get up, up get, get get, up up, get up, up, up, up.*

He lies still.

Unrequested, a gurgle rises up from my throat, my body's natural reaction to having witnessed what appears to be the death of my boyfriend and his brother. *It can't be*, I deny, trying to will away the inevitable. Not another loss. Not like this.

Tristan moves, just a shudder, as his shoulders begin to quake: he's crying. Sobbing into the neck of his dead brother. Now I know what happened. Tristan listened to the voices in my head, realized the same thing that I did. That he had no choice. Kill or be killed. Killen wasn't going to stop, so he had to plunge his hovering sword into his brother's breast. And yet, upon doing it he's wracked with a profound sadness and sense of loss, perhaps not for the person his brother has become, but the boy his brother used to be. And now he's crying, expressing that sadness in tears that drip onto Killen's skin, mingle with the blood that's surely flowing from the hidden wound in his chest. My eyes well up with tears, but mine are for Tristan, not for his brother.

"Tristan!" the President roars, and I flinch; having been so focused on Tristan and his pain, it was as if everything else fell away.

Tristan stops shaking, his body tense as he slowly turns to face us. Even from a distance, his face glistens with a mixture of sweat and tears. Killen's blood stains his front. I'm glad he's looking at his father and not me, because on his face is only anger, a building rage I've never seen in him before. His dark blue eyes are as black as his father's. "How dare you do this?" he spits out. "He was your son!"

"He was weak," the President says, not a shred of remorse or sadness in his voice. "This was always the way it was supposed to be. You were the strong one, the son to succeed me, to follow in my footsteps. You've just proven your strength. Now I give you one last chance: come back to me, be my son again, take up your role as the future president of the Tri-Realms."

"Or what?" Tristan scoffs.

His father's words are a snarl. "Face the consequences."

"I'll never join you," Tristan says without hesitation.

"Then you and your friends die."

"Then we'll die with honor."

"So be it."

Tristan

The gate opens and Roc is led back into the pit by three guards, who mostly ignore me. One of them unshackles Roc and gives him a sword. The other two carry Killen's body and sword out through a door, closing it behind them, leaving only the blood on the ground and on my shirt as a reminder of what transpired here—of what I did.

I'm numb as I stare at my best friend through blurred vision. When I glance at my father, who stares down with such hatred at me, his last remaining son, the hot rage flares up again, but as soon as my gaze drifts to Adele, it dissipates. I take in her lovely pale skin, her moist, emerald eyes, her forlorn but strong expression. I let the vision linger in my mind long after my eyes move on, back to Roc.

"I won't fight him," I say to my father, still looking at my best friend.

"You don't have to," he says. My eyes dart back to him. He wears a cat-and-mouse expression that screams *I'm better than you!* "But if you don't fight, the moon dweller dies." Once more, a guard pulls Adele's head back by grabbing her hair and slides a knife to her throat. My breath catches in my throat. An impossible choice. Fight Roc, potentially killing him, or refuse to fight and watch the girl I—I—I now know that I love, without a doubt in my mind, die in the most horrific manner. Perhaps there are some that have the moral compass to make such a decision, but alas, I am not such a person. I flounder, breathing raggedly, my mind spinning.

Even to the end, Roc is there for me. He says, "Fight me, Tristan. You have no choice." In his eyes is a plan, perhaps to buy time with a little "safe" swordplay, until an opportunity presents itself. Perhaps something else, I'm not entirely sure.

But it's a sliver of a chance at saving them both, so I grab it. "We'll fight," I say.

"Delicious," my father says. Although I don't look at him, he's licking his lips in my peripheral vision. "But remember, if I so much as get a whiff that you're not really going at each other, that you're holding anything back, she dies anyway."

My heart sinks at his words. Whatever Roc is planning, such a decree surely destroys any chance we have at buying some time. Roc's face, however, doesn't show any concern. In fact, it's quite the opposite: almost shining with peace, his lips closed but slightly curled up in an unexpected smile. *What's he so happy about?* I wonder silently.

"Now fight!" my father commands.

Roc comes at me immediately, not holding back, attacking with a vehemence I rarely even saw in some of our more heated training matches. With precise movements I block his blows easily, noticing his improvement in the few short weeks since we left the Sun Realm. However, even improved, his skills fall well short of my years of training and experience. With each successful defense I spot several holes in his approach, each of which I could use to disarm him. Of course, I ignore such opportunities, because to disarm him would mean the release of the final grains of sand in our already diminishing hourglass. To cover up the fact that I'm holding back, I pretend to stumble, to trip over my own feet, allowing Roc to continue his barrage of fierce and somewhat awkward attacks. *What is he doing?* I still can't get a bead on why Roc seemed so happy before we started fighting and what he could possibly have up his sleeve that will help us in our current situation.

I leap back again, block another powerfully clumsy sword strike, ignore a chance to slip under his arm and kick him, punch him, head butt him, and altogether end the fight. Breathing heavily, we back away for a few seconds, staring at each other. There's a fire in Roc's eyes, but it's not anger or violence toward me, although that's what he's expressing outwardly, it's something else I've never seen in him before. *A plan.*

"Tristan!" my father yells. "You're not trying hard enough. You could have killed your servant eight times already. Don't be so arrogant to think I didn't notice. If the next round is the same, I'll order my guard to slit her throat."

Before this started, I was beaten. My father holds all the stones, and all I have is an ignorant child's hope that perhaps we can get out of this alive. If I don't fight, she dies. If I do fight, Roc dies. Either way, he'll probably kill us all eventually anyway. So why am I fighting my best friend? The answer finally comes to me and I almost bang my head with my fist for being so stupid. *I shouldn't be fighting Roc.* My father is going to win no matter what, but I can at least deny him the pleasure of pulling his puppet strings and making us all dance for him. I have two choices: kill myself or let one of Roc's blows sneak through my defenses to kill me. Maybe it won't save them, but it will at least give them a chance. And I can't let Roc kill me—he'll never forgive himself. So that means falling on my own sword.

A sense of peace washes over me as I know I've made my decision. My lips curl into a slight smile. That's when I realize: Roc felt the same peace, had the same content expression just before we started to fight. He came to the same conclusion, except for himself. To kill himself.

I look at him. He's watching me curiously, but then something changes in his expression. I could never hide anything from him, and I can't now. He knows what I'm thinking.

A flash of concern narrows his eyebrows, and before I know what's happening, he raises his sword—there's a sharp shout from the seats—turns it back on himself—another meaningless shout—and plunges it into his gut.

Adele

Tristan and Roc are just watching each other, perhaps waiting for the other to make a move, when Tawni's voice enters my ears. It sounds different than usual, all sweetness and caring sucked out of it, leaving only a black grit that is still somehow recognizable as her voice. "Stop this or you die," she says.

I turn sharply, hearing one of the guards shout an alarm, but it's too late for anyone to do anything. Tawni's on her feet, which are still shackled together, her arms outstretched, holding a gun. No, not *a* gun. *My* gun. The one my mother gave me,

291

shiny and new and deadly. The one I used to kill my father's murderer, the gun that should be used to kill my father's real murderer: President Nailin. The gun I gave her because I couldn't bear to have it near me. From her wrists dangle the ropes, now unknotted, that once bound her hands together. She's managed to get them undone. But how'd she get the gun off the guard?

I remember: the guard getting frisky with her, groping her instead of properly searching her, not worried about her because she was throwing metal balls—clearly weaponless. Wrong. She bore his roving hands, not fighting back, not crying out, hoping he wouldn't find it. The gun. Tucked safely under her dress in the small of her back, held hidden in the holster I gave her. She could have used it when we were fighting before but didn't, either because she's not used to having a gun at all, or because she was scared of the killing. Either way, I don't blame her. She has it out now and looks ready to use it.

The gun, now aimed at the head of President Nailin, just a few feet away. Too close to miss.

"Stop this or you die," she repeats.

"No, Roc, no!" Tristan yells from below.

I want to turn to see what's happening, but my eyes are transfixed on my nonviolent friend with the gun, a steely determination in her eyes that makes me think she might actually follow through with her death threat. A new Tawni.

"It's already over," the President says, smiling down the barrel of the gun.

Tristan's cries rise up again. "Help me! Someone!" he screams.

I finally turn away from my friend, see the carnage in the arena. What the hell? Did Tristan stab Roc? Distracted by

Tawni's little surprise, I didn't see what happened, but now Roc has a sword in his stomach, and Tristan's kneeling over him, looking up at us, pleading with his torn expression and words. "Please! Someone help me! He's dying!"

My heart beating wildly, I swing back to Tawni. *Do it!* I say with my eyes, not wanting to give her a verbal command for fear that the advance warning will give the President and his guards a chance to make a move.

Tawni's nod is almost imperceptible, more like a twitch; her finger tightens on the trigger; she closes her eyes.

Boom! The gun explodes through my ears and flashes across my vision, but the President was already moving, sensing the attack, diving for the floor. A cry of pain erupts from the seats behind him—one of the guards most likely.

President Nailin rises up, reaches for Tawni, whose eyes are wide, her mouth agape. She bobbles the gun, her fingers turning to jelly, and Nailin manages to swipe at the weapon, knocking it back and between his outstretched legs. It clatters past the guard sitting between us and settles at my feet.

The guard lunges and I know this is it. The moment. The reason my mother sent me on this mission. Because she thought I was the one who could do it.

I sweep my still tied together feet upward, kicking the diving guard in the head. The guy to my right tries to grab me, but I thrust my knees as high up as they'll go, catching him hard under the chin, hearing an awful cracking sound and a roar of anguish. There are yells and screams and voices shouting indecipherable things from behind me and in the pit—Tristan's voice is louder than them all—and from the President, but I block them out, concentrate on one thing: getting my hands free.

As I pull with all my strength, the ropes rip my skin to ribbons, bite my wrists, send searing pain and shock through my whole body in a series of tremors. "Arrrr!" I yell, trying to relieve the agony through my vocal chords. Whoever tied my ropes did a better job than Tawni's because they won't give, won't break, won't untie.

The presence of those who are seeking to stop me is all around, pressing and scrabbling and distorting the air—I have no time to fight at my bonds any longer. Raising my tethered hands high over my back, I strain to get them over my head. I scream again, feeling my joints and muscles and tendons and whatever else is hidden beneath my skin, stretching and contorting and trying to move in such a way that should not be possible. Then I feel it: a massive pop in my left shoulder; splinters of pressure, sharp and brutal, running down my arm; my hands in front of me, still together, but *in front of me!* My left arm dangles unnaturally, but my right is still strong, still ready.

The pain is nothing. My friends are dying, so the pain is nothing.

I grab the gun off the floor, feeling clawed fingers scratching at me from behind, lift it up, whirl to face the man who—by his orders—killed Cole, killed my father, killed Trevor, maimed my sister, who is the object of my mission, of my revenge. Perhaps the fulfillment of my entire purpose for being born into the hell that is the Tri-Realms.

Even now, his face is unrepentant, a grizzled collection of black eyes, stretched and wrinkled skin, and bared teeth. Death and the Devil combined in human form.

"You don't have the guts!" he spits out, his lips gnarled and red.

I don't respond. Words are meaningless now; action is everything.

Death—meet death. I fire, seeing a coin of red appear on his forehead instantaneously, drizzling down his gnarled face in an understated trickle of blood.

He falls back.

Tristan

Roc's dying and I'm pleading to those who will never listen. Something's happening in the stands but I can't understand it through my clouded vision and blubbering lips. A commotion of some sort. Tawni standing up, pointing at my father. A noise, loud, but not as loud as the beat of my heart. My father striking Tawni. A scuffle of some sort. Adele screaming, an awful keening that seems to shatter my heart into a thousand fragments, which roll around in my chest, scratching and tearing me apart from the inside.

Her screaming stops and now she's standing, pointing at my father. Another loud noise and my father falls back, narrowly missing Tawni. *Can someone tell me what's going on? Can someone help me?* I try to yell, but nothing comes out, my voice box rendered useless by some unseen force.

There are more loud bangs from Adele's fingers, which are almost shimmering in the light. A few guards drop to the ground. A gun; she's got a gun. She shot my father. She's shooting his guards. Bending down, she picks up something else: another gun, dropped by one of the dead guards. She shoots again and again until everyone in red has fallen. All dead.

I manage another yell, nothing more than a cry of the pain in my chest.

Roc speaks, his voice weak, just a low rasp. "You'll always be my brother," he says.

His eyes close.

Twenty-Four
Adele

After they all die I finally feel the throb of pain in my shoulder, so strong I nearly pass out. But then I hear Tristan's scream and I will my body to soldier on. I drop into my seat, my hand scrabbling at the nearest dead guard's belt, finding a knife, and although it's difficult with only one hand, cutting my bonds from my hands and feet. Down the aisle Tawni's doing the same with the ropes around her ankles.

We should both be in shock, but perhaps everything we've seen has been so shocking that our bodies don't even know enough to start shutting down. For whatever reason, I'm able to tuck my injured arm across my belly, pick up a gun with my right arm, and move down the aisle, stepping over bodies—over the President's body—and usher Tawni to the steps.

We take them two at a time to the bottom and Tawni pushes through the gate, immediately sprinting across the floor. I try to run, but the pain is too much and I start seeing stars, so I drop back into a more reasonable stride.

When I reach Tristan and Tawni and Roc—poor, poor broken Roc—Tawni's taking charge. Tristan's hysterical. "He's dead. He's dead. My fault. All my fault," he wails, sobbing and choking and gasping.

"Take him," Tawni says to me gently.

I lay down the gun, kneel, put my good arm around Tristan's shoulders, and pull his grief-wracked form into my chest. "Shhh. Let Tawni check him out. She knows what she's doing. Remember? Shhh."

He continues sobbing as Tawni hovers over Roc. Half a sword blade and the hilt are still sticking from his stomach. There's blood around the blade's entrance, but not as much as I'd expect from such a horrific wound. Roc's eyes are closed, like he's only sleeping, his chest doesn't appear to rise and fall, so I expect the worst when Tawni places two fingers on his neck, feeling for a pulse.

I want to join Tristan, cry my eyes out, but I know he needs me to be strong now. Tawni is somehow holding it together, although it's her boyfriend who's lying there, possibly dead. If the roles were reversed and it was Tristan instead of Roc, I'd be a mess, inconsolable. But Tawni just goes about her business, professionally searching for a pulse, her ear near Roc's closed lips, perhaps hoping to feel an exhalation from his nose on her skin.

"He has a pulse, but it's weak," she says. "And he's breathing." Her words should give me some comfort, but when she turns back to me, the look on her face paints a different story. "But he is dying. He needs medical help, right now."

Tristan jerks, his head lifting from my chest, his sobbing ending abruptly. "He's alive?" he says, the last of his tears dripping from his chin.

"Barely. Can you guys carry him?"

There's a light in Tristan's eyes that I thought had gone out for good. "Yes, yes, of course. But shouldn't we remove the sword?"

"No!" Tawni cries. "That's the only thing preventing a significant loss of blood. It might be the only thing keeping him alive."

Strange how the instrument that caused his injuries might now be saving his life.

"Okay. Let's go." Tristan slides his hands under Roc's armpits from behind, props him up.

"Gently. Gently," Tawni says.

I grab his feet with my good arm, leaving the other one hanging limply at my side. "One, two, three," I say and then we lift. He's heavier than I expected, and I almost drop him, but Tawni rushes to help, placing two arms underneath his back.

"Are you okay?" Tristan asks sharply, as if he's only now noticing my injured shoulder.

"I think it's dislocated," I say, "but I can handle it."

Tristan nods, doesn't question my statement. He knows now's not a time to pamper his girlfriend. His friend's life is on the line.

"Where are we going?" Tawni asks.

"The infirmary," Tristan says. "There will still be at least one doctor on call, even during the celebration. You know, for drunks who fall down and get hurt."

"What about the guards?" I ask.

"You killed them all."

I take a short breath when I hear the truth in his tone. "I know I killed these ones, but what about others?"

"We killed a few earlier, and I don't expect there are many others. My father saved them all for the ambush."

I killed all the guards. The thought gives me a gruesome sense of pride mixed with a sick dread at what I've done.

Struggling under the load, we move swiftly through the gate and start up the stairs. I lead, while Tawni and Tristan push from behind. It's like carrying...well, it's like carrying a dead body, to be honest—difficult and cumbersome. I try to push the thought out of my mind.

We reach the top and pass through the exit, using our legs to keep the door from whacking Roc. I move as fast as I can down the hall, the others matching my speed. When we reach an intersection, Tristan says, "Left."

We maneuver around the bend and continue our harried pace. "Here, here," Tristan says. "Through the doors on your right."

I push through the doors back first, twisting my head to look over my shoulder as I enter a stark white room with bright fluorescent lights running along the ceiling.

"Who are you?" a voice says from behind me.

Pushing into the room, Tristan says, "I am Tristan Nailin, son of the now dead president of the Tri-Realms. We have a patient who needs your help."

Without waiting for permission, I lay Roc's feet on a bed on wheels that stands in the center of the room. Tawni and Tristan rotate the rest of him around until he's securely on the mattress. The doctor is gawking at us.

"Tristan? Why yes, of course it's you! Did you say *now dead president?*" the balding, spectacled man says.

"There's no time for any of that," Tristan says. "I order you to save this man's life."

"But he's a servant. Surely you can take him to a regular hospit—"

"Now!" Tristan roars, rising up to his full height.

"Well, of course, I suppose I could make an exception," the doctor says, hurrying to Roc's side. "This does not look good. Not good at all."

"He's still breathing and has a weak pulse," Tawni says helpfully.

"That's good, but they might not last. We need to put him on life support immediately."

"Do it, Doctor," Tristan says. "Whatever it takes."

"Give me space, please," the man says, shooing us to the side like animals or small children.

The doctor goes about his business, wheeling various machines around Roc, fitting a plastic mask over his mouth, strapping something to his chest, just above his heart. The sword continues to protrude from his belly like a piece of grotesque abstract art meant to shock its viewers.

Next the man injects a yellowish fluid in Roc's right arm, and then something pink in the other one. We're all staring, watching things unfold like a play, or live telebox. At some point Tristan grabs my hand, clutching it like it's the only thing keeping him sane, like if I let it go he'll spontaneously combust.

His squeezing gets harder and harder until my hand starts to hurt.

"Tristan," I say, "it's going to be okay."

He looks at me, his eyes misty again. "Is it?" he says. "I'm sorry, that's more than I can hope for right now."

Is it just Roc that's bothering him? Or is it that I—

"Tristan, I'm sorry I killed your father. I know that was the whole point of all of this, but I'll understand if you never forgive me."

Tristan's eyes flick to mine, his anger melting away. "What? No! I'm not angry about that. I would've done it myself if I had the chance. He wasn't my father. Was never really my father, any more than he was Roc's father." There's a sincerity in his deep blue eyes that once again proves how different he is to the ex-president. "I'm just tired. Killen...Roc...Trevor...what my mother did and how she died...it's all too much at one time."

With everything we've just gone through, I'd forgotten about the revelation the President made before he died. It seems so science fiction, so farfetched that it just might be true. "So you believe him?"

"Sometimes the truth hurts the most," he says, glancing at the doctor, who has cut off Roc's shirt, revealing his lean and muscly frame. The body of a servant, a workhorse. "We were ninety percent of the way there on our own. Our matching scars. The instant, almost neurological attraction we had for each other. How it suddenly turned off and the buzzing on our scalps and spine were gone. It all makes sense now."

He's right. In my heart I know that. But a microchip? I'm not sure what I'm more shocked about: that there's a microchip implanted in my spine or that one or both of my parents worked with Tristan's mom to put it there. The only strange thing is…

"How did it turn off all of a sudden?" I wonder aloud. "You know, stop pulling us to each other."

Tawni, who's been watching the doctor treating Roc in silence, suddenly says, "The scientist who created them probably figured out a way to disrupt the signal, maybe cancel them out or something."

Tristan nods. "Sounds about right." He cringes as the doctor paints antiseptic around the point where the sword enters Roc's skin. For some reason it doesn't bother me. The gore, that is. I should be grossed out, ready to spew all over myself, but it just doesn't seem real. I mean, who has a sword sticking out of their gut and requires treatment? Most of them are just taken to the morgue in that situation. Roc's a fighter.

"Did you…?" I say, trying to coax some information from Tristan.

Tristan laughs, which catches me off guard. It's the last thing I expect him to do right now. "Did I what?" he says, still smirking. "Did I stab him?"

I nod, wondering what's so funny.

"No," Tawni answers for him. "He stabbed himself."

The pieces fall together. He wanted to end the fight against his best friend without causing any harm to me or Tawni. My heart swells with love for Roc, for being the kind of person that would willingly give his own life for his friends. "You saw him do it?" I ask Tawni.

She looks away, back to Roc. The doctor is wrapping thick gauze around the sword, mumbling something under his breath. "I sensed it," she says thickly.

Staring at my friend, who's watching the procedure with interest, I say, "What do you mean?"

Finally she looks at me, her eyes welling up with tears for the first time since entering the Sun Realm. It's catching up to her. The fear, the emotional pain, seeing Roc with a sword in his gut, everything. She can be so strong for so long, but eventually everyone needs to let it all out. "I know him, Adele. I know it sounds crazy, but in the short time that we've been talking, I've learned so much about him. Roc is—he's a good person. Genuine, you know? He always talked about how he'd be willing to give his life for Tristan or me or you. It's almost like he's been waiting for an opportunity to be a hero."

"He is a hero," I say, meaning it.

"Damn right," Tristan says.

"From the moment you started fighting," she says, looking past me to Tristan, "I could just sense he was going to do it. No one was watching me—they were all looking at the President, or the action down below, or Adele. I was just a bystander, unimportant. So I worked on my ropes with my hands. The guy who searched me for weapons was more interested in my body than in doing his job. He didn't find the gun you gave me, Adele. And when he tied my wrists he left a lot of slack. I managed to slip the ropes off without anyone seeing. I grabbed the gun and waited for an opportunity." She pauses, blinks away more tears. One slips out and meanders down her cheek. "I was too late," she cries. "Too late to save Roc."

"You did awesome," I say. "You saved the day, Tawni. If you hadn't done what you did, we'd all be dead, Roc included. He's still alive."

We all turn our attention back to the bed at the same time, as if we're just remembering that there's a life and death procedure going on. Slowly, slowly, ever so slowly, the doctor pulls the sword from the wound, applying pressure with the gauze in his other hand. Roc, his eyes still closed, shakes violently as the sword is extracted, but doesn't wake up. "What's happening?" I whisper, a hand on Tristan's shoulder.

Overhearing, the doctor says, "His body's reacting to the trauma. An involuntary spasm, nothing more. He's doing okay, but he's not out of the mines yet."

My hand bumps off the edge of a table and pain surges through my shoulder. "Uhhh," I groan.

"Your shoulder is not okay," Tristan says.

"It's fine," I insist, cradling my dangling arm like a baby. I grit my teeth, try to blink away the pain. "It's not like I have a sword in my stomach."

"I'll fix it right up," Tawni says. "I'll make a sling. But first I have to set it. It's going to hurt like hell though."

I know I'll need treatment at some point, but there are more pressing matters.

"I'm not trying to sound insensitive," I say. "But there's not much we can do here to help Roc. I mean, what do we do next? The President's dead and no one knows yet. The war will continue on until we stop it. People are dying down there. My mom—" My breath hitches.

Tristan takes a deep breath. "I want to stay with Roc."

"But you're the President now."

"What? No. No, I'm not. I don't want to be."

"You are," I press. "Your father's dead. Killen's dead. You're the only Nailin left. Until everything gets sorted out, it's you. You have the power to set things right."

Tristan stares at his feet. "But this is exactly what I never wanted—this kind of power."

I put an arm around him. This is one of the many reasons I fell for Tristan. Yeah, we had microchips pulling each other together, but there was always more to it. He's not like the other sun dwellers who are hungry for power and fame. "That's exactly why you're the right person to have it. Anyway, you can help shape new laws that will spread the power out amongst a broader group with representation from all the Realms."

He looks up and our eyes meet. So soft and so serious at the same time. Another contradiction I love about him. "Go, Tristan. Set things right. End this unnecessary war," I say, clutching my mother's necklace. "We'll look after Roc."

Twenty-Five
Tristan

It's hard for me to leave Roc like that. Although the doctor promises me he'll take good care of him, there's no guarantee he'll be able to save his life. Not that me being there would make a difference one way or the other, but I'd just hate for him to wake up—after stabbing himself to save my life—and me not be there. Some friend I am.

But, on the other hand, Adele is right. Roc would want me to stop the war as soon as possible if I was able to. He wouldn't want me hovering by his bedside while people are dying in the Lower Realms. In the end, it's that thought that convinces me to leave him. I trust Adele to protect Roc and Tawni and herself while I'm away.

As I pass through the familiar halls of the government palace, which has been in my family now for hundreds of years—so long that most people refer to it as the Nailin House—it feels eerie. A good eerie, though, like the place has been cleansed. The air is lighter, the décor brighter, the hallways more open. Nothing has changed except that my father is dead.

Still a few corridors from the grand ballroom, I can already hear the music, growing louder and louder as I approach. People having fun while Roc is dying. Just before turning the corner to the final hall, I catch a glimpse of myself in a large decorative mirror hanging on the wall. *Ugh.* I look like a crazy person: my hair is wild and unkempt like I just woke up or rolled around in the gardens; my face is scarred with the white salt trails of sweat and tears; and my tunic—oh my shirt!—is wet with Killen's blood. Although I'll definitely make an entrance looking like this, I'm not sure I'll get the reaction I'm looking for.

I pause in front of the mirror, remove my shirt, use the clean parts of it to wipe the white off my face and the soaked-through blood from my chest. I open a random door—some meeting room—and toss the soiled and bloody tunic inside; I'm better off going shirtless in this case. Finally, I lick my fingers and maneuver my hair so that my wavy locks fall in such a way that they look both natural and contrived at the same time.

Taking two full breaths, I round the corner. There are two stewards at the end of the hall, in front of a large oak door. When they see me, their eyes widen and they stand up a bit straighter. One of them says, "Master Tristan? But you're supposed to be bedridden. Your father made it very clear you wouldn't be attending the ball tonight." The man is tall and ultra-skinny, with a well-trimmed goatee and a thin mustache.

"I'm perfectly fine—can't you see that?" I return, putting on my best imitation of my father's condescending tone.

"But your tunic!" he exclaims, his face reddening slightly.

"What tunic?" I ask.

"You're—you're not wearing one!"

"It's the Sun Festival. Really, you've got to learn to live a little, Bo," I say, moving between them. "The door please."

Flustered, but not so much that they would ignore a direct command by the son of the President, Bo and his partner each grab one of the double doors and drag it open, sweeping a hand for me to enter. "As you wish, sir. Enjoy the evening."

I smile and enter, waiting for the doors to close behind me before moving further into the room. The music is louder now, but nothing like the pumping base at the first Sun Festival party we attended. Sun dwellers wearing all manner of luxurious attire are dancing and mingling and drinking flutes of wine and nibbling on hors d'oeuvres being carried on silver trays by servants.

I take one step into the room, whistle as loud as I can. "Ladies and gentlemen!" I shout. "May I have your attention, please!"

One by one at first, and then in groups, the people stop moving and a hush falls over the room. The music stops. All eyes are on me, but I feel no fear. My father is dead, his guards dead. As Adele said, I'm the only Nailin left.

"I have an announcement to make!" I say, half-aware of a group of deeply tanned young girls who are giggling and pointing at my bare chest. "My father, the President of the Tri-

Realms, and my brother, Killen, were both killed in an unfortunate accident."

Although things were relatively quiet when I first made my entrance, now it's like all sound has been sucked from the room. There's not as much as the shuffle of someone's feet, the clinking of a glass, or a whispered remark. Even the giggling girls have stopped giggling, their jaws dropping open in a similar fashion to the rest of the partygoers.

A man steps forward, one of my father's generals, not on the front lines with his men, but attending the party of the year. Some leader. "What do you mean *killed?*"

The question is so dumb and yet I know why he would ask it. To these people the President is invincible, almost immortal, a symbol of solidarity and the way of life that they love. And so I answer: "My father is dead," I repeat. "And my brother. A new weapon was being demonstrated for them and the guards, something went wrong, and they were all killed. One of the housemaids called me down from my room as soon as it happened." The truth may come out later, but for now I have a war to stop. And if I have to tell a little white lie to buy these people's cooperation, I'll do it.

It works. "My God," the general says. "But that means that you're the—the—"

"President of the Tri-Realms," I finish for him. "Still President Nailin, just in a different size and shape. And younger, too," I add. I feel strange just saying it, like it's a joke, which it sort of is, in a way.

The silence drops to the ground, shattering like a broken glass into a million pieces that burst into a plethora of sounds: People yelling, "Long live President Nailin"; girls screaming,

"Marry me, Tristan!"; the dull buzz of conversation as people weigh in on what this all means for the Tri-Realms.

It's distracting and I don't have time for it. "Silence!" I roar, doing my best to sound and look strong and in control. "I need to see the generals in private. Now," I add to convey the urgency of the request.

With a shrug, the general waves a hand indicating that the other generals in the room should follow. I push through the doors, past the stewards—who scramble to hold them for me—and down the hall, opening the first meeting room door I come to that's not the one I chucked my bloody tunic into. The generals—all men, of course; my father wouldn't dream of having a woman as a war leader—come in after me.

"Take a seat, gentlemen," I say, wishing I could address them as *scoundrels*, which seems more fitting.

"Is he really dead?" one of them says, a largish man with a thick, gray beard. All of them are wearing gray or black dress tunics, complete with bow ties and shiny shoes. Ready for a night of frivolity.

"Yes," I say. "But there will be time for mourning him later. We have urgent matters to attend to. The war."

"Of course. You'd like an update?" another general says, pushing his blue-plated glasses higher on his nose.

"Make it quick," I say.

"In short—we're killing them," the man says, pride lighting up his face.

"Well, stop," I say.

The man raises his eyebrows. "Stop, sir?"

"Yes. Stop. A simple word, meaning to discontinue, end, or otherwise cease one's current behavior. Stop the war. Stop the killing. Call a temporary truce until I can meet with the moon and star dweller leaders."

"Meet with them, sir?" I swear my father's generals are as dumb as rocks. Stop, meet: these are not hard words to understand.

I sigh. "I want to meet with them, discuss how to end the war peacefully."

"But we're winning, sir."

"I don't care if we're winning!" I scream, letting all the emotion of the last few hours come out through my mouth. "Give the order to stop. Now!" I hand him the comm set in the center of the table. "Start the process. And if I hear about anyone killing any moon or star dwellers after the order is given, they'll be put to death. Is that clear enough for you, general?"

The general, white-eyed and paler than usual, takes the comm set and presses a button.

Twenty-Six
Adele

It will take more than one dead president and a ceasefire to make things better for everyone. Surely Tristan's claim to the presidency will be challenged once they realize that it was no accident that killed the President. A full investigation is already underway.

I sit in a chair with my arm in a sling, Tristan beside me reading his mom's book. Tawni sits abreast of Roc, who continues to lie sleeping in the white hospital bed, his stomach heavily bandaged. The doctor said the procedure went well, that he checked all his vital organs and that "Quite frankly, he got lucky. Everything appears to be okay in there." So he sewed him up, pumped him full of painkillers, and told us Roc will wake up when his body is good and ready.

Tawni hasn't left his side since the doctor gave her the okay to move in beside him. For two days she's sat by him, sleeping with her head next to his. She's holding his hand, rubbing his thumb gently with hers. She's singing something so softly that I can't make out the words or the tune.

Yesterday we cremated Trevor. I was trying to be strong for him, like he was till the very end, but when Tristan spoke some of the finest words I'd ever heard about someone, I broke down, my face turning from stolid to a wet mess in a heartbeat. I thought about all he had been through in his life, how happenstance and my mother's kind heart had brought him into my life, how he had saved me from the barrel of Brody's gun, how he had saved Tristan. Even after the tears on my face had long dried up, my heart has continued to weep every second. I'll truly miss him.

Although Tristan and I, like Tawni, wanted to stay by Roc's side, we had other matters to attend to. Tristan checked in on the status of the ceasefire every fifteen minutes, ensuring it was being carried out with precision and without fail. He also identified a few of the servants that he knew were loyal to Roc and who would most likely be able to keep a secret. Together we worked with them to dispose of the guards' bodies, dumping them in a giant furnace where no investigation would ever uncover the truth of how they met their sudden and untimely demise. We scrubbed the blood clean from the floors of the throne and council rooms. When we finished it was as if nothing had happened in either place, which was a strange thing to behold. I feel like half my life has been spent in those two rooms. If you base it off the intensity of emotions, I *have* spent half my life in the Sun Realm.

We left Tristan's father's body for last, because we couldn't burn it. The generals and advisors will want to see a body, will want to hold a ceremony, so we asked a few of the servants to clean him up, dress him in fresh clothes. It sickens me to think he gets special treatment even in death, but it's an evil required to maintain the ruse that his death was no more than an unfortunate accident.

As I continue to watch Roc's steady and beautiful breathing, I begin playing with an idea in my head for a few minutes, considering how best to ask Tristan. Perhaps I should just tell him what I want, rather than asking permission. He may be the President now, but I've always had a problem with authority.

Tristan

I'm fascinated by the book my father gave me—my mom's book. It's like she's still alive in the pages, in the words, because they're all new to me. I'm vaguely aware of Adele, Tawni, and Roc as I read each page twice, sometimes pausing to read a single sentence three or four times. The words are precious to me and I want to make them last.

I flip to what is unfortunately the last page, take a deep breath, feel a strange sense of loss, like I'm losing my mother all over again, and then start reading, hearing her voice in my head as I memorize each word:

I made it back from the Moon Realm, Tristan. I did it. Convinced a woman, a Resistance leader to implant her daughter with the matching microchip. She's not just any girl, son. She's special, like you, a real fighter. While I talked to her mother we watched her out back with her father, another Resistance leader. He was teaching her to fight, except she didn't need any teaching. It was as if she'd been fighting for years, which, her mother assured me, she had been. Her name is Adele Rose.

Although it's a longshot, I hope together you will be a force that even your father would never expect.

Tristan, if you've made it this far, then I hope to God that you've won, that you've found Adele Rose, that together you've made a difference for yourselves and for the Tri-Realms. Although I know the actions I took were drastic, radical even, in my heart I know I did the right thing for you and your brother. Take care of Killen. His heart isn't as pure as yours, and your father gains a greater hold on him each and every day, but I know there's goodness in him—you just need to show him the way.

I'm sorry I couldn't talk to you more openly and honestly about what I was planning, but in case anything went wrong I didn't want your father to think you were involved. I'm sorry for the microchip, Tristan. It's already in your back. I slipped you some sleeping medicine and had your father's scientist implant it a few days ago. I hope I'm not making a terrible mistake, but drawing you to the Resistance seems like the best backup plan in case your father gets to me before I can tell the world about the New City.

Stay strong, my son. Do what you can to unite the Tri-Realms and give the people the opportunity to go above, if that's what they wish. Know that I'm always with you and that I always love you. –Your Mom.

I close the book, wipe a tear from my eye. I can't read this page a second time. Not yet. There are too many emotions on that page. My brother. I never even had a chance to try to convince him that he was headed down the wrong path. And now he's dead. I've failed my mother with him already.

316

I've already forgiven my mother for the microchip. After all, it led me to Adele, who I love deeply, whether it started by natural attraction or neurological manipulation.

As far as uniting the Tri-Realms and telling the people about the New City, that's something I will work hard to do, although I know it will be a long, hard road.

Out of the corner of my eye, I notice Adele watching me. "Are you okay?" I ask.

"I'd like to go above," she says.

Twenty-Seven
Adele

The last few days have been a whirlwind of activity and emotions. First I explained to Tristan why it was so important for him and me to go above before telling the rest of the Tri-Realms what was up there. This was going to be major news—unprecedented really—and there would be lots of questions. We needed to know the full story so we'd be in a position to answer as many of those questions as possible. We also needed to get an idea of the political climate: the population of the New City, the interest in taking on additional citizens, the complexity of building more cities. There are so many details we need to think about before we tell the underground dwellers what they've potentially been missing out on. Knowing what we know, it's our duty to be prepared.

Tristan agreed, which was good, because I really didn't want to have to fight him on it.

The second day Roc woke up. When he did, he was very confused, and kept saying things like, "All my best friends are in heaven?" or "Are you sure I'm not still dreaming?" Even unable to sit up he was able to make us laugh. And he grinned like a banshee when Tawni laid the biggest, longest kiss on him I've ever seen.

Even in Roc's bedridden condition, he was still full of his usual Roc-ish wisdom and advice when we told him about our planned journey above. "The people will care about the small things," he said, barely able to lift his head off his pillow. "Remember everything, or take copious notes if you can't. From the colors, to the sounds, to the smells, to where people go to the bathroom, to how they dress, to the taste of the air— they'll care about *everything*."

"Thank you, Roc," I said, "for the advice, and, well, for everything." I squeezed his hand and blinked away the tears.

His brown eyes were bright with understanding but dry. "Tristan might not be as cool as me, but he's still my brother. And you'll always be my adopted sister. And Tawni—you all know how I feel about her. I'd do anything for you guys." I turned away before my emotions painted my face. After all the death, the violence, and nearly taking his own life, he was still good old Roc, the truest friend in the world.

It was a good day. There were tears, there were hugs, there were laughs.

The third day Tristan addressed the people of the Tri-Realms via video message. He didn't want to do it live—not just yet—preferring to write a script and then read it. It was broadcast to every Realm on their teleboxes. He confirmed the reports that his father and brother were dead and that everything was under control with him at the helm. He accepted the automatic nomination to the presidency that he's entitled to as eldest son of the deceased president. Finally, he assured the Lower Realms that the ceasefire would continue indefinitely until a series of meetings could be held amongst Sun, Moon, and Star Realm leaders. The purpose of the meetings would be to determine what was best for all citizens of the Tri-Realms in terms of taxes, living conditions, et cetera.

Then he spent an entire day on the phone—bless his heart—trying to track down information on my mother. I watched him the entire time and when I finally saw him smile and his eyes light up, I hugged him as he confirmed the news: *She is alive!* He set up a video conference with her right away, and I was able to see and talk to her and Elsey again. We swapped each of our own crazy stories from the last few days, cried tears of joy, and discussed what was happening in each of the Realms we were in. Toward the end I told them what Tristan told us above the earth's surface. My mom just nodded like she wasn't surprised, told me she'd suspected something like that was happening, and told me to be careful when I went above, which I told her we were planning.

I said I knew about the microchip but didn't slam her with questions. She said she was sorry and that was enough for me. Ending the call was the most difficult thing I've ever had to do.

The fourth day we prepared for our trip above, by gaining access to his father's most confidential files. We read everything we could about the New City. Most of it was disturbing. You see, although Tristan's father had given him a tour of the New

City, had bragged about it, had told him all kinds of amazing things, he hadn't told him the whole truth.

He'd made it sound like he wielded control over the New City, that he ruled above and below the earth, when in fact, he didn't. The memos and bulletins we read in his files painted a very different picture. Although he still had complete power over the Tri-Realms, the New City was governed by its own president, a man named Borg Lecter. Not long after the New City was built, the people had rebelled against Nailin's control and unwillingness to live aboveground. So they selected their own leader and started running things the way they wanted. However, they continued to trade with President Nailin— swapping solar energy for gemstones and iron ore—and allowed him to come up to visit whenever he wished, under strict supervision, of course. In a memo, President Nailin himself admitted to having very little interest in the affairs of the earth dwellers, and, in fact, preferred to maintain the status quo belowground. Clearly he knew that if he told the people of the Tri-Realms about the earth dwellers, it would ruin everything he'd worked so hard—off the sweat and blood of the moon and star dwellers—to build.

In other words, on Earth Tristan has no power, which changed everything when it came to our approach to going above. Initially we had planned to just go up the same tube that his father had once taken him, through the quarantine and cleansing, and into the city. Now that sounds like a huge risk. Who knows how President Lecter will receive the son of the President, who is now *the* President, a potential rival to him. And if he starts asking questions, he might not like the answers. Like what if he learns of Tristan's decision to tell the citizens of the Tri-Realms about the New City? That may not go over so well.

So Tristan spoke to his father's secret engineers, the ones who control access to aboveground, and learned of an alternative entrance, one that his father built in the event that he wanted to attempt to seize control of the New City once more, or if Borg Lecter ever tried to deny him entrance or access to the abundant flow of energy provided by the sun.

So now, on the fifth day since fulfilling our mission, that's where we're headed, to the alternative entrance. We're in a car, being sped along the sun dweller streets by his driver, passing the typical sun dweller sights that I'm still not at all used to, like flourishing clothing stores and packed restaurants. The artificial sun is high in the sky and providing yet another perfect day in paradise.

As I take in the sights, I think about Tawni and Roc, who we've had to leave behind. Appropriately, Tristan ordered all his vice presidents to report directly to Roc and Tawni, who have his full authority while he's gone on a "short business trip." Roc is on the mend, but while his body's still a long way from his usual, athletic self, his mind is as sharp and good as always, and of course Tawni is there, too. She's proven she's come a long way from the tall, skinny girl who was around for moral support and the occasional hug. She saved us all.

We reach the outskirts of the city, drive along the edge of the cavern wall for about fifteen minutes, and then stop randomly in what appears to be the middle of nowhere. The driver reaches up and presses a button on a small controller attached to the roof. Gears churn and cycle to my right, where the cavern wall opens up like a giant door. The transition from the wall to the door is so seamless, so well hidden, that I barely notice it.

We pull into the hidden tunnel, where we are immediately flanked by two men in dark gray lab tunics, who promptly open our doors. "Welcome," one of them says to Tristan. He nods. "Are you sure you want to do this?" the guy asks.

"You have your orders," Tristan says.

The man escorts us to a tube much like the one Tristan described when he first told us about the earth dwellers. The tube is thick glass and extends straight up and into the rocky roof fifty feet above. At the base is a pod with an ovular opening on one side.

Before we get in, the man says, "On your orders, we'll keep the transport pod aboveground, so when you're ready to return to the Sun Realm it will be waiting for you. All you have to do is press the button inside and we'll have someone standing by twenty-four hours a day to get you back."

"Thank you," Tristan says, holding my hand as we step in. The inside of the tube isn't that different than that of a train car, except there are no seats. The doors close.

Neither of us speak as the pod starts to rise. The engineers grow smaller and smaller and then disappear entirely as we enter the vertical tunnel. Everything is black now except for the inside of the pod, which glows softly, powered by some unknown source.

I have so many questions to ask him about aboveground, about the earth dwellers, but I know what his response will be if I ask him—"Just wait and see"—so I don't speak. I don't really have anything else to say as my complete focus is on what I'm about to experience.

As he warned, the trip takes about thirty minutes, during which time we just sit in silence, holding hands, gently rubbing our fingers together, just like the first night we spent together, after Cole died. It seems like ten lifetimes ago. In fact, I feel like it happened to a different person—not me.

Eventually, the pod slows and then creeps to a stop. The doors open, casting an eerie glow into the dark space beyond. Tristan grins and steps out, pulling me behind him. As we learned from the engineers when we were planning our trip, this pod concludes in a cave a few miles south of the New City, well out of range of their city watchmen.

Although we know it's daytime, the cave is pitch-black so Tristan flicks on a flashlight. The cave appears to be natural, but clearly someone—Tristan's father's engineers most likely— has leveled it out and excavated an easily travelable tunnel to the outside. As we head down the path, I feel as much at home as if I was back in subchapter 14. Tunnels and caves are as normal as it gets for me.

But then I see it: a light. A circle of white-yellow, as bright as I've ever seen, like a halo, streaming into the end of the tunnel.

"Is that it?" I whisper, afraid that if I raise my voice I'll shatter the light.

Tristan nods, grinning. "That's it. A ray of sun, brighter than a thousand of our artificial suns combined."

We run now, together, still holding hands, whooping and hollering and carrying on like a couple of school kids. As we approach the end, the light is so fierce I have to shield my eyes with my hand. "It's beautiful," I murmur. "But how do you bear to go under it?"

Tristan laughs. "It'll take some getting used to. Your eyes have never seen this kind of light. Here—I brought these. He hands me a pair of dark sunglasses and a floppy hat.

Grinning, I slip on the dark glasses and don the hat. "You ready?" Tristan asks.

"Ready," I say, my smile growing bigger than I thought possible, my heart doing leaps and spins, my skin tingling with anticipation. My life is about to be changed forever.

We step into the light, which, despite the sunglasses and hat, blinds me, forcing me to close my eyes. Still blind, I let Tristan pull me forward a few more steps, feeling more and more warmth on my skin with each pace forward. It's a beautiful warmth, full of tingles and heat and *life*. I desperately want to open my eyes, to see the sky, to see the clouds, but I know my eyes aren't ready yet; they're still acclimating themselves to this new world.

We stand in the sun for a few minutes, just soaking it up. "Want to try opening your eyes?" Tristan asks.

Yes, I nod hungrily. I start with a squint, but am forced to shut my eyes tight again as the sunlight tears through my retinas. Every thirty seconds I try again, each time trying to open them wider and wider before clamping them shut. By the tenth or eleventh try I can keep them open for a few seconds, each time getting a peek at the world around me. First the red of the sky, so alien and bloody and big—bigger than anything I've seen in my entire life. Then a scattering of clouds, thin and hazy and yellow-gray and floating—actually moving!—across the sky. But none of it is how my grandma described it to me when she passed a story told by her grandmother to her mother and then to her, down to me. The sky should be blue, rich and majestic and awe-inspiring. The red reminds me so much of death. And the clouds! According to my grandmother, they should be white and fluffy, "like the beds of angels," but instead they're like fiery wraiths, scattering blades of sun like instruments of death across the barren landscape.

Next, something dark with wings loops across the sky. "A bat!" I scream. "They have bats!"

Tristan chuckles. "They do have bats but they're in the caves and only come out at night. That's a bird. A hawk I think they call them."

"A bird," I murmur, growing bolder as I keep my eyes open for good this time. I scan the area around me, trying to commit every detail to memory.

"I'm happy to be here with you, to share this moment," Tristan says, cocking his head toward me.

I let go of his hand, curl both my arms around his back, interlace my fingers just above his waist. Look up into his navy-blue eyes, which glisten with emotion under the brightness of the real sun. We ignore the beauty around us and just look at each other for half a minute, until Tristan finally laughs.

"What are you thinking?" he asks.

"I—I..." I can't get the words out, not because I don't want to say them, but because I'm feeling *so much* that I almost can't breathe.

Tristan cuts off my awkward stuttering with a kiss that takes any remaining breath I have completely out of me, swells my heart as big as a balloon, brings back the neurologically manufactured tingles and buzzing that we thought we'd lost.

When he pulls away I can breathe again, and the words that seemed so difficult to say a moment ago, feel so effortless now. "I lo—"

"I know," he says, cutting me off. His smile his bigger and more beautiful than ever before.

I laugh, swatting him playfully on the arm.

That's when someone clears their throat off to the side. We both jump slightly, and turn to see who has managed to sneak up on us. Instinctively I draw my sword, which hangs from my belt—a precaution we both agreed was necessary.

Three young women stand before us, deeply tanned, short-haired and wearing only loose rags to cover their chests and torsos. They are all beautiful in an exotic sort of way, but my eyes are drawn to the one in the middle, a tall, muscled girl with intensely attractive chestnut brown eyes. Her cheeks are high and tight and complement her delicate chin. Her features would rival that of any sun dweller model I've seen on the cover of magazines.

She speaks, her voice firm and full of authority. "In the name of the sun goddess, tell me who you are," says the first earth dweller I've ever met.

Keep reading for a special bonus short story about what was happening to the moon dwellers while Adele and Tristan were on their mission, and for a sneak peak at the first book in the Country Saga (a Dwellers sister series), *Fire Country*, coming in February 2013!

Acknowledgements

It's strange writing acknowledgments for a single book when those whom I'm indebted to have helped me with far more than just the pages of this novel. First and foremost are my readers, who have taken a chance on one or more of my books over the last whirlwind year, spending your hard earned dollars on an unknown author, and giving me the chance to make my dreams come true, as I've embarked on writing as a full-time career. Without you, I'd still be sitting in a cubicle, dozens of stories still stuck in my head, waiting to be told. From the bottom of my heart, thank you.

To my editor, Christine LePorte, we started this journey together with *The Moon Dwellers*, and now this is our third book together! Your wisdom and dedication to maintaining the quality of the Dwellers Saga is truly admirable. I can't wait to see how the next three books we create together turn out!

A super, special (dare I say ginormous) thanks to my creative and dedicated marketing team at shareAread, particularly Nicole Passante and Karla Calzada, who have helped to get a ball rolling down a hill that won't stop for many years to come. I'm forever in your debt.

A humble thanks to my magnificent (and honest) beta team who gently pushed *The Sun Dwellers* in the right direction, and very wisely told me to get Anna's story out of the novel and into a short story! So thank you, Laurie Love, Alexandria Theodosopoulos, Karla Calzada, Christie Rich, Kayleigh-Marie Gore, Nicole Passante, Kerri Hughes, Terri Thomas, Lolita Verroen, Zuleeza Ahmad, and Kaitlin Metz. And as always, as a special thanks to the boss of the beta readers, my beautiful wife, Adele, who I must agree all edits with. I'm so lucky to have you in my life—I wouldn't be doing any of this if it wasn't for you.

To my unbelievably supportive friends in my Goodreads Fan Group, I can never thank you enough for what you've done (and continue to do) for me. To have the group grow to such an incredible size in less than 6 months is simply mind-boggling.

And last but not least, I just want to say that the cover is once again perfect for the book, which I could never achieve on my own. So thanks to Tony Wilson at Winkipop Designs; you are the finest artist-ninja-surfer I know. I can't wait to see the cover for the final Dwellers book, *The Earth Dwellers*.

Discover other books by David Estes available through the author's official website:

http://davidestes100.blogspot.com or through select online retailers including Amazon.

<u>Young-Adult Books by David Estes</u>

The Dwellers Saga:
Book One—The Moon Dwellers
Book Two—The Star Dwellers
Book Three—The Sun Dwellers
Book Four—The Earth Dwellers (Coming Nov. 2013!)

The Country Saga (A Dwellers Sister Series):
Book One—Fire Country (Coming March 1, 2013!)

The Evolution Trilogy:
Book One—Angel Evolution
Book Two—Demon Evolution
Book Three—Archangel Evolution

<u>Children's Books by David Estes</u>

The Nikki Powergloves Adventures:
Nikki Powergloves- A Hero is Born
Nikki Powergloves and the Power Council
Nikki Powergloves and the Power Trappers
Nikki Powergloves and the Great Adventure
Nikki Powergloves vs. the Power Outlaws (Coming in 2013!)

Connect with David Estes Online

Facebook:
http://www.facebook.com/pages/David-Estes/130852990343920

Author's blog:
http://davidestesbooks.blogspot.com

Smashwords:
http://www.smashwords.com/profile/view/davidestes100

Goodreads author page:
http://www.goodreads.com/davidestesbooks

Twitter:
https://twitter.com/#!/davidestesbooks

About the Author

After growing up in Pittsburgh, Pennsylvania, David Estes moved to Sydney, Australia, where he met his wife, Adele. Now they travel the world writing and reading and taking photographs.

ANNA'S STORY
A DWELLERS SHORT STORY

Chapter One
The Moon Realm

The reports are coming so fast that General Rose is not even reading them anymore:

Sun dwellers troops were spotted in the tunnels around subchapter 9...

A platoon of red-uniformed men was seen just outside of subchapter 32...

The shot fired appears to have been a warning shot, but subchapter 14 citizens have been warned to stay indoors, as far underground as possible...

She stacks the unread reports in a neat pile on the corner of her stone desk, closes her eyes, wonders whether she's made a horrible mistake in sending her daughter on such a low-odds mission. *You had no choice*, she reminds herself. Everything is as it was meant to be, as it was planned by two plotting and scheming mothers two years earlier.

She'd never heard from the First Lady after that day. Then came the reports from the Sun Realm that President Nailin's wife had disappeared mysteriously. Although she was glad the hooded woman had not returned to her abusive husband, she was somewhat surprised that she'd left her two sons behind, in the care of a madman. For a moment she wonders where the First Lady is now.

A knock on her door snaps her out of her thoughts. "Come in," Anna says firmly.

General Ross enters, his typically stolid face grim. His dark skin is like a shadow in the dim lighting. "Have you seen the latest reports?"

"I skimmed them," she admits, waving at the pile on her desk. "But that's all it took to get the picture. We're screwed."

"I'd consider tweaking that speech before you address your soldiers," he says, his flat face hiding the joke.

She smiles, despite herself. Ever since the star dwellers generals were released from the President's threat on the lives of their families they were growing on her. General Ross in particular.

"All we have to do is hold them off long enough for your daughter to come through for us. Without their leader, they'll retreat. There'll be chaos. We'll be able to take advantage of it."

She nods. "I know. Adele will come through. They all will." But there may not be a Moon Realm left to fight for when they do.

Anna leaves that part out.

Chapter Two

The eve of the Sun Festival brings dark thoughts for her. Earlier, President Nailin made an announcement that the 500-year celebration would "go forward as planned, war or no war!" Anna Rose suspected this might happen, but instructed the other generals not to mention it to the mission team, to her daughter, choosing only to inform Trevor. She wonders now if that was a mistake.

Her theory: better not to complicate things. For all she knew, the Festival would be cancelled and it would have no bearing on the mission, and even if it weren't cancelled, it might benefit them by way of a distraction. As they agreed, Trevor will tell them all of that. It's the same thing she would have told them beforehand.

But she could have just told them, so they were fully prepared.

Better not to worry them.

Should've told them.

Don't complicate things.

Either way, she reminds herself, you can't change things now. You have to trust they'll adapt on the fly. They will.

Another distant *Boom!* shakes her bed, where she lies not to sleep, but to think. Despite the barricades and tripwire, it took less than an hour for the sun dweller army to infiltrate subchapter 1 of the Moon Realm, allowing them to wheel in their launchers and begin the assault. The bombing's been nonstop for more than two hours.

There will be no sleep tonight.

Not for the Resistance, not for the moon dweller troops, not for the thousands of elderly, children, and disabled innocents sitting huddled together, their knees to their chests, in the cellars and basements and safe houses strewn haphazardly across the city—and certainly not for General Rose.

She closes her eyes and says a silent prayer, for the Moon Realm and for Adele.

Chapter Three

The bombing stops at two in the morning. The silence is loud and thick and rings in General Rose's ears. She waits ten minutes to confirm that it's not just a normal lull before another round. The rough whispers of hundreds of soldiers paint through the stale bunker air like an artist's brush. The messages are obvious: eagerness, worry, determination, fear.

"What do you think it means?" the young woman beside her asks.

Anna looks at her curiously. Maia. Far too young to be a member of the Resistance Council, and yet she is, nominated and voted in shortly after Anna and her husband were abducted. There's no fear in her dark eyes, only curiosity. Something about her is as strong as steel.

"They wouldn't stop unless they had other plans," Anna says.

"You think they're coming on foot?" Maia asks.

"I don't want to speculate," she says, picking up the phone that's bolted to the brown bunker wall. "General Suzuki? What's the status in subchapter twenty-four?"

The answer crackles through her headset: *The bombing has stopped.*

"Do we have eyes on the borders?" she asks.

It's too soon.

"Okay. I'll call you if I have anything."

Slipping the phone back into place, she says, "The bombing has stopped everywhere. We need a visual on the borders."

"I'll go," Maia says without hesitation.

"No," Anna says. "It's my responsibility."

"But you're the general."

"Exactly. Stay here."

"I'm coming with you," Maia says, her voice firm.

Anna considers pulling rank, but then settles for the compromise. "Okay. Let's go. Sanderson—we're going above to check things out. You're in charge."

As they make their way to the thick iron door that separates the bunker from the outside subchapter, Anna studies Maia with interest. Her gait is confident, a mirror image of her expression. Despite her mere twenty-five years of age, Anna knows this woman is experienced beyond her years, either by choice or by fate.

Two burly guards unlock the barrier and pull it open before them, exposing a short tunnel that leads to a flight of stairs that ascend to the surface. A heavy dust-filled mist hangs in the air, swirling eerily before the soft lantern glow. Covering her mouth and nose with her tunic neckline, Anna moves forward quickly, Maia a step behind. The dust haze gets deeper as they climb the steps, and the smell of gunpowder and molten lead remind Anna of the Uprising.

They reach the surface, where the fog is settling on the debris from the bombing, coating the world in a thin layer of gray powder. Anna gasps as she surveys the extent of the damage.

"My God," she says.

"They've destroyed it all," Maia says.

Anna nods because she's right. The subchapter, once beautiful in its elegant design, with symmetrical city blocks and narrow canals, is in shambles, its buildings toppled, its waterways filled to the brim with chunks of large stone blocks. The Dome, the large half-sphere at the center of the city, is ripped in half, mangled beyond recognition, the subchapter's symbol of solidity and order reduced to ash and debris. And the strange thing: they can see it all from where they're standing.

"The lights are back on," Anna realizes, gazing at the cavern roof, where the rectangular panel lights are shining brighter than she's ever seen them.

"And they're brighter," Maia says, reading her mind.

"This can mean only one thing," Anna says, dread filling her. "The sun dwellers are coming."

At that moment, a horn blares, drawing Anna's attention to the eastern corner of the city, where an inter-Realm tunnel leads to the Sun Realm.

Hundreds of red-clad sun dweller soldiers pour from the maw of the tunnel, letting loose a thunderous war cry, climbing over half-crushed stone blocks and cracked gray columns.

"Move!" Anna shouts, just as a flash of flame erupts in the distance. Her words are unnecessary, as Maia is already on the run, seeking shelter behind one of the few upright stone walls.

BOOM!

An eruption of rock and fire and pain—from the splinters of stone shrapnel on her face and arms—announces the arrival of incendiaries preceding the ground troops. Covering her head with her hands, Anna races after Maia, diving for cover just as another blast shatters the abnormally bright night.

"We've got to get back to the bunker...warn the others," Anna says, breathing heavily.

"I'll go," Maia says, moving out from the wall before Anna has a chance to argue. She begins to pursue the young warrior, but is stopped when another bomb explodes, throwing Maia back and into her arms, knocking them both flat on the ground. Her ribs are on fire and her lungs full of dirt, but she manages to wheeze, "Maia—are you okay?"

"I'm fine," the girl says, rolling off of her. "You?"

"I'll survive."

"We've got a problem, General," Maia says, looking back toward the bunker. Following her gaze, she watches as a massive stone block settles over the mouth of the entrance.

"Dammit," Anna says. "We'll have to get to the other entrance."

"Follow me," Maia says, once more surprising Anna with her courage and strength. Moving out from the cover once more, Anna chases Maia across the broken terrain, staying low to avoid detection by the enemy. The war cries have stopped, but she knows they're still coming, and it's only a matter of time before the sun dweller soldiers manage to navigate the maze of fallen buildings and clogged canals.

As Maia hurdles a low wall, there's another explosion, this time just to her right, and she's thrown harshly to the side, tumbling down a small rise and into the blackness of a cellar. Just before she disappears, she cries out.

Her head on a swivel, Anna climbs over the wall and creeps down the hill toward the opening, hissing, "Maia!"

No response.

Thumbing her flashlight back on, she steps through the opening, descends a dozen stone steps, and flashes the light on Maia, who's against the wall grimacing, clutching her ankle and breathing sharply through her teeth.

"Did you hit your head?" Anna asks.

"No. My ankle. I sprained it," Maia says.

"It's too hot out there at the moment," Anna says. "I don't think I can carry you to safety without getting us both killed. I'll go get help."

Maia nods, her eyes a steel-gray. "I'll be here," she says, forcing a laugh through her locked teeth.

Turning, Anna moves to climb from the cellar when the ground shakes from another blast.

CRACK!

A terrible sound of destruction rends the night. A huge stone block looms over the cellar entrance, rocking slightly, as if trying to decide which way to fall.

CRASH!

It topples, blocking the exit and thrusting the cellar into complete darkness, save for the thin beam of Anna's flashlight.

Her heart sinks as she realizes: the cellar is now their tomb.

Chapter Four

The first ten minutes were the worst. Breathing in plumes of dust-ridden air from the explosion, coughing and coughing, but never managing to expel the choking fumes; hearing the deafening blasts of bombs going off all around them, the ground shaking, the roof threatening to cave in; wondering when the first sun dweller soldiers would arrive, whether they would break through the barricaded cellar opening, hot metal death flying from their automatic weapons: it was ten minutes of expectation. Expectation of pain—expectation of death.

General Rose huddles next to Maia, not embarrassed by the physical contact between leader and warrior, desperately needing the comfort of having a friend nearby.

I'm going to die without seeing either of my daughters again, Anna thinks to herself pitifully. Her husband's face pops into her mind, giving her strength.

No! I will not go quietly into the night. This fight I've fought for so many years will not be lost, not while I'm still breathing, while my heart's still beating, while blood continues to pump through my veins.

"We're going to be okay," Anna whispers.

"I know we will," Maia replies.

For a few minutes they continue to wait for something to happen, but the bombing stops, leaving the only sound their haggard wheezing. But even that is silenced eventually, as the dust settles in a layer of gray powder on the ground. The air is breathable once more, and both women take the opportunity to cleanse their lungs with the fresh oxygen.

"I've always really admired you," Maia says.

Anna's eyes jerk to the young woman's. It's not what she expected her to say. Not with an injured ankle in a caved-in cellar in the middle of a warzone. "Really? Why?"

"Because you're strong and courageous. You put the lives of others above your own. My mother said you would be the one to change things."

Anna laughs uneasily. "It doesn't appear that way, does it?"

"It's not over yet."

Once more, Anna's taken aback by the strength of the girl who's barely half her age. "Where'd you come from?" she asks, finally letting her curiosity get the better of her.

"Death," Maia says, her voice a whisper in the dark.

"Tell me," Anna says.

"My father was a revolutionary, like you and your husband. My mother stayed home with us, a somber woman, always expecting my father not to come home one day."

"Who was your father?"

"James Berg. He was in the Resistance for two years before the Uprising." There's a hint of pride in Maia's voice.

Anna nods. "Yes, James, of course. I didn't know him that well, but I remember his passion for the cause. He was always going on about how wonderful the world would be once we put it right."

Maia laughs. "He said similar things at home. He was the opposite of my mother, always seeing good in people and in the future, whereas my mother only saw our situation worsening. In the end, she was right, I guess."

"Your father was killed during the Uprising." A statement Anna knows to be true. She remembers the names of every individual who lost their lives in 475 PM. To her, remembering the dead is every bit as important as respecting the living.

Maia takes a breath. "It was a normal day for us. The Uprising was something happening far away, never getting close to our subchapter. Father sent us messages on an almost daily basis, reassuring us that he was alive and well and that the Resistance would win in the end, that good would conquer evil. He loved using language like that, righteous and grand." Maia clears her throat, swallows, continues: "No message came that day, but that didn't worry me, as some days there was no mail at all. We knew there would be a message the next day. We were just sitting down to dinner when a knock came at the door, which was also not unusual. Neighbors, clients of my mother's—she knitted thick tunics especially made for miners—our friends: we frequently had people stopping by the house.

"And yet I'll never forget the look on my mom's face: utter fear. I'd never seen her face so white—ghostly is the only way I can describe it—her eyes like the eyes of a stranger. It made me shiver when I saw her, and just like her, I knew. There was no friend at the door. No neighbor. No client. Only death."

"The Resistance came to give you the news?" Anna asks.

Maia nods. "Sort of. All they said was, 'I'm sorry,' and then, 'Turn on the news.' We did, of course, and we learned that the Uprising had been snuffed out by the Sun Realm in one foul swoop."

"'The Massacre' they coined it. A name given by the President himself."

"Yes. My father died in the Massacre."

Wait. Something doesn't make sense. "How old are you?" Anna asks.

"Twenty-nine," Maia says.

Twenty-nine! Anna's estimation of the girl's age was off by half a decade. "You were four years old," Anna murmurs.

"Yes. At that age I still thought my father was invincible. I didn't understand. Yes, I know, Daddy's dead, but when is he coming home? My mother didn't know how to respond to my questions, which were relentless. Yes, you said yesterday that Daddy's not coming home, but this is a different day. Today he's coming home, right? I remember hearing her crying at night and going in her room, asking her *What's wrong?* A couple of years passed and I grew up, finally gaining an understanding of death and what it meant for our family. Daddy was never coming home, because he wasn't in the Tri-Realms anymore, was somewhere else where we couldn't see him."

"You're religious?"

"Not really, but we always talked about how Daddy was in a better place, how he was still watching us. I loved talking about him, but I think it was hard for my mother."

"What happened next?" Anna asks, intrigued by the story.

"I got older. When I turned twelve my mother changed. She started disappearing at night, while I was sleeping. I never questioned her about it, but one night, I decided to follow her. She didn't go far—just down the street.

"She approached a house, said something through a stone door on the side, and the door opened. I stayed in the shadows, watching the door for a few minutes, as a dozen other women did the same thing. When ten minutes passed without anyone else appearing, I moved in."

A smile forms on Anna's face, to which Maia raises an eyebrow. "Go on," Anna encourages.

"I tried the door, but it wouldn't budge. As a kid I always liked climbing things, so I wasn't scared at all about clambering up the high stone wall surrounding the property. The top of the wall was rounded, so I had to balance very carefully as I crept along to the back of the house. Before I was halfway, I heard sounds: women talking, occasional grunts and groans, a thud or two.

"When I cleared the edge of the house and my line of sight was no longer obscured, I was shocked at the sight before me. There were four or five lines of women—perhaps thirty in all—dressed in black battle fatigues, like the ones I'd seen Father wear. Perfectly synchronized, they were punching and kicking and swinging staffs, mimicking the movements of a woman dressed in white battle gear, who was leading them."

Anna's smile widens. She nods vehemently. "The Women for Liberty Movement," she says. "Or WLM."

"Yes," Maia says. "Although I didn't know that at the time. And you know what? The woman in white was you."

Chapter Five

"Really? It was me?" Anna says, somewhat surprised.

"Yes," Maia says. "It was the first of three times I saw you. I followed my mother at night several times after that. She always went to the same house, and the same thing always happened. The training was different each time, and I found myself practicing the movements around the house when my mother wasn't watching.

"There were different instructors most nights, but you never came back. I suspect you were travelling around, conducting similar training all over the Moon Realm." Maia stops, looks to Anna for confirmation.

"That's correct. I loved those times, for as dark as they were, we were a part of something important, something special. A group of women with one goal: to restore liberty and equality to the Tri-Realms." Anna puts her arms behind her head and stares at the ceiling, lost in thought. Those days seem so long ago to her. A lifetime ago.

"I joined the WLM," Maia says, and Anna's gaze jerks back to her.

"When?"

"That same year."

"That's not possible. Sixteen years old was the age requirement. You said you were twelve."

Maia grins and then twitches. Rubbing her ankle, she adjusts her position. Anna moves the flashlight so she can better see Maia's face, which is streaked with sweat and moistened dust. Everything about the twenty-nine-year-old's story interests her.

"That *was* the requirement. Primarily because of concerns that younger children might blab about things. Secrecy was of the utmost importance."

"Right. We'd had problems with spies in the past. The Uprising was stopped so quickly because of them, did you know that?" Anna asks, raising her eyebrows.

"No. What happened?"

"The Resistance had everything planned. Strategic stealth attacks on key sun dweller facilities, like generators and weapons manufacturing; mass infiltration of the Sun Realm through shipping tunnels; scrambling of communications through targeted electro-magnetic attacks. But the plan never even got off the ground. There were hordes of sun dweller soldiers at each key location. It was like President Nailin had copies of all of our coded communications with a key to crack the code. It wasn't even a fight. Many of us were killed, although some, like me and my husband, managed to escape. The only way we could've been defeated so badly is if there was a traitor near the top feeding information to the sun dwellers."

"Which is why you were so careful to maintain the secrecy of the WLM," Maia notes.

"Exactly. Which is why a twelve-year-old wouldn't be permitted to attend our meetings, or even know about us, except by sneaking around in the shadows and climbing stone walls," Anna adds, chuckling slightly.

"What can I say? I was a curious little girl. But I also joined the WLM that year."

"How?"

"Well, I continued my *sneaking* and *climbing*," Maia says, one side of her lip curled up. "And then one night I got too complacent. I was hugging the wall, watching the women train, so tired I could barely keep my eyes open. And then I couldn't anymore. My eyes closed for just a second, or maybe it was longer—I have no idea—when my eyes snapped open and I was falling, tumbling from the wall. I scraped at the stone, splitting a few of my nails open as I tried to hang on, but I'd already gathered too much momentum. When I thudded onto the hard rock patio, all eyes turned toward me. I was wheezing, trying to get my breath back, dazed and afraid and bruised."

"I'm sure your mother was thrilled to see you," Anna says sarcastically.

Maia laughs. "I wouldn't quite describe it that way. Furious is more like it. I'd never seen her that angry. My mother had never laid a hand on me growing up, but this time, despite the fact that I was injured and gasping for breath, she grabbed me by the ear, hauled me to my feet, and marched me out of there.

"My knee was throbbing and I could barely put any pressure on it, but my mom had me by the collar of my sleeping tunic, practically lifting me off the ground. Once home, she sat me down, refusing to look or talk to me, and dressed my wounds, applying expensive ointment for faster healing. I just watched her, confused at her behavior. Was she mad, or wasn't she?

"When she finished, she pulled up a chair, sitting across from me. It was the middle of the night, mind you, but I don't think sleep was on either of our minds. Finally, she looked at me, her blue eyes darker than usual, her face still moist from the training session and dragging me home. 'You can *never* speak of what you saw tonight, is that clear?' she said. I nodded sheepishly. I wouldn't have told anyone anyway, but promising my mom guaranteed it. It wasn't in my nature to break a promise, still isn't."

From the little Anna knew about Maia, she believes her. The courage she had seen her display, her solidarity, her calm demeanor: everything pointed to Maia being a woman of character and honor, worthy of trust. "A wonderful story," Anna says, "but you still haven't said how you managed to join the WLM. So far, I'd say it's a long shot, but I must say, I'm rooting for you."

Grinning, Maia says, "Thanks. I almost forgot. It wasn't until I saw you the second time that I even knew I wanted to join."

Chapter Six

The trampling thunder of boots on rock hushes them both into silence. There's no fear on either of their faces, just a cautiousness that's born of courage under fire. The soldiers pass by directly overhead, and then across the mouth of the barricaded cellar opening, casting wraithlike shadows across the thin beams of light that sneak through cracks in the large stone that bars the entrance.

Heavy voices shatter the night, yelling commands and warning of threats. Shots ring out and anguished cries cause Anna to visibly wince. At least one moon dweller has been killed, probably several. More gunfire. More shouting and screams of pain. More death.

Anna's fists clench at her sides, one around the handle of her gun, and the other around a sharp rock that cuts into her skin, providing her a small measure of comfort.

"I want to be out there, too," Maia whispers, glancing at Anna's angry hands.

Discarding the rock, Anna shines her flashlight around the cellar once more, hoping one of the four walls has disappeared, revealing a hidden passageway. Thick gray rock stares back at her, its arms crossed.

"We could make some noise," Anna suggests, knowing full well it would be suicide.

"We could," Maia agrees, but neither of them raises their voice above a whisper.

Another flurry of explosions cut through the quiet, someone shouts "Move!" and then the clop of dozens of footsteps fades away, into the distance.

"Where were we?" Anna says, her heart still beating too fast. She's anxious to distract Maia from what's happening outside. She could use a distraction, too.

"Joining the WLM," Maia says, eyeing the stripes of light from the door, once more unbroken.

"Ah, yes. Please continue."

"Well, like I was saying, I didn't really even think about joining the WLM until I saw you for the second time. My mother, under the permission of WLM leadership, was able to explain the bare minimum about the WLM. She didn't need to say it, but she told me I couldn't join because I was too young. I asked if I could watch the training sometimes, and she and the WLM agreed, although first I had to take a solemn oath of secrecy, which I did."

"I wrote the oath," Anna murmurs, staring at the ceiling once more.

"I didn't know that," Maia says. "I watched the women train several times, enjoying the way they moved, all graceful and coordinated. It was almost like dancing. Soon they began fighting each other, and I remember having to clean up my mother's bloodied noses and other nicks and cuts on many occasions. She was getting stronger all the time, more capable, one of the better fighters in the group. I was proud of her.

"I still practiced the movements, but now I didn't have to hide it from my mother. She didn't encourage me exactly, but she didn't try to stop me either. Soon I knew them by heart, and even began joining in at training, although they wouldn't permit me to stand in line with the other women. But even tucked in the corner I felt like a part of the group."

"But you weren't—not really," Anna says.

"No, I wasn't. But then my mother told me she had to go away for a few days, and that a neighbor would be looking after me. When I asked her where she was going, she admitted that it was a WLM conference. I begged her to let me come with her, and to my surprise, she agreed. Of course, she cleared it with the WLM first, who had apparently grown quite fond of having me around.

"It was the first time I'd left our subchapter. The train was like a ride, the gray walls whipping by, people hanging onto poles and tucked in rows of small seats. I loved every second of it.

"When we arrived I was shocked at how many women were there. Thousands. The conference was being held under the guise of an annual sewing and homemaking seminar, but it was by invitation only, so only those in the WLM could attend. We sat in a big auditorium with a stage. It was the biggest place I'd ever seen, and I later learned that it was called the Dome."

Images of the crumbling Dome fill Anna's head, side by side with her memories from the day of the WLM conference. Oh how things change, and not always for the better. "I have many fond memories of that day," Anna says wistfully. "Thousands of strong women—fighters—willing to take up a dangerous cause. They did it for their husbands, for their children, for those who had already fought and died. Each and every one of them was a true hero."

"I felt the same way at the conference that day," Maia says. "Beautiful speeches by beautiful women. I felt a soaring in my heart like I'd never felt before. But it wasn't until you spoke that I knew what I wanted."

"My 'Now Is the Time' speech," Anna says, hearing her own words spoken through her head. "It was definitely one of my best."

"It was perfect," Maia says, almost reverently. "You found a way to pour your soul into words and ideas like I'd never heard before. When we returned home, I pleaded with my mom every day to join the WLM, sometimes asking her twenty times a day, until it almost became part of our routine. Wake up. Ask 'Can I join?' Mother says 'No.' Eat breakfast. 'Can I join?' 'No.' And so on and so on all day, every day. I learned a lot about my mother's patience during that time. If I were her, I might have slapped me."

"She sounds like a special woman." Anna can't help but to think of her own mother, Adele's and Elsey's grandmother. Another special woman, patient and kind and tougher than anyone ever really knew.

"She was," Maia says, pursing her lips.

"She passed?" Anna asks.

"Nine years ago. During a special mission for the WLM."

"She was in the special mission's corp?"

"Yes. She was recruited six years after I joined the WLM, when I was eighteen. She carried out a number of successful missions, but they were dangerous and it was just a matter of time before bad luck caught up with her."

"I'm so sorry," Anna says.

"She died doing what she believed in—for that I'm thankful. We had eight wonderful years together in the WLM. The bond we had during those years was unbreakable."

"So how did you manage to convince her to let you join when you were only twelve?" Anna asks, still curious as to the beginning of Maia's evolution from a young, helpless young girl to the strong woman she is today.

"I didn't," Maia says, chuckling. "I ambushed her one night at training. There was a break while they set up for hand-to-hand combat. I walked right up to the trainer and asked to join. The look on my mother's face was priceless, I'll never forget it, a mixture of wide-eyed shock and unexpected pride. My petition went to WLM leadership and I was allowed in, the only one under sixteen. 'A special case' they called it."

"I'm surprised I don't remember it," Anna says, straining to recollect from seventeen years earlier.

"Your name was on the approval form," Maia says, winking, "although I suspect it was a forgery by one of your assistants."

Anna laughs, remembering how much she hated paperwork. "You're probably right. I almost never signed anything, at least not when I could help it." Her laugh is cut off when the stone at the entrance begins to move.

Chapter Seven

A beam of light cuts through the darkness and into Anna's eyes, blinding her.

"Move!" Maia hisses, clambering to her feet, dragging Anna after her. Together they move out of the light, against the side wall, as a giant metal claw rolls the stone away, unblocking the entrance to the cellar.

Only the sun dwellers would have technology like that.

This is it.

The last stand. Take out as many of the sun dwellers as possible to make it easier on the others.

Ever so slowly, Anna slips her gun from its holster. Beside her, hobbling on one leg, Maia does the same. Two women, connected by time and circumstance, brought together with a chance to do this one thing for the cause. Two women, capable and strong and ready.

For what?

To die for what they believe in. To die for those they love. To die for good.

But only if someone kills them.

A shadow cuts into the beam of light; footsteps cut into the night. "Anyone down there?" a voice yells out, gruff and no-nonsense.

Anna takes a silent breath, waits.

"I think it's empty. Give me a sec to check it out," the grizzly voice says.

As slow footsteps descend the steps, Anna analyzes the situation. Sun dwellers. Opening bunkers and cellars and hideaways. Looking for survivors to kill or capture. Kill any soldiers or civilians who don't cooperate. Capture all the others. Anna and Maia: definitely on the kill list.

Only one choice: kill or be killed.

Anna sees him now, illuminated by the light, stopped halfway down the staircase. Tall—at least six foot—built sturdy like a tank, wearing a sharp red uniform, unmarked by the nearly uncontested romp through the subchapter.

He peers through the gloom on the opposite side, slides through the lighted area in the middle, and then scans the other side, his eyes passing directly over where Anna can see him, but he can't see her. Her heart is in her throat, her finger on the trigger, just a twitch away from ending the man's life. She hesitates, knowing full well that a gunshot will bring a swarm of sun dwellers into the hole. Their only real hope is if he leaves.

He scans back the other way, and then turns, taking one step up. Anna slowly lets out the breath she's been holding as he takes another step away, a miracle step. A third step washes all the fear away, until he turns, his eyes locking on something.

Anna follows his gaze to where it rests on the ground in the middle of the lighted area, curious as to what has made him pause. It's exactly where they were previously sitting against the wall.

That's when she's notices how dirty the cellar floor was from the explosions and cave-in, a thin layer of dust covering everything.

Everything except where they were sitting, where the outline of two bodies, four legs, and the scrape of their feet as they made their hasty escape, is stark and visible—unmistakable.

He takes a step back into the cellar.

Chapter Eight

Anna's body is way ahead of her brain. While her mind is still trying to wrap itself around the danger that confronts her, her legs are moving and her fingers are tightening on the butt of her gun.

The soldier reaches the bottom step, his footsteps slow and cautious. But not cautious enough.

She strikes from the shadows to the side, using her weapon like a club, slamming it into the back of his head, where she knows it will have the greatest and fastest effect. As planned, he's unconscious before he even has time to cry out, his body slumping like a sack of potatoes. Although her arms dart out to catch him, she's not fast enough and he crumples to the stone, his weapons belt rattling off the bare rock, sounding ominously like the bones of a skeleton rattling in its coffin.

From above, she hears, "Quincey! You comin' back up or what?"

She has no time to lose—a second could mean the difference of life or death, seeing her daughters again or not.

Grabbing the red-clad soldier by his boots at the ankles, she starts to drag him from the light, wishing he wasn't so well fed. Then she feels Maia beside her, pulling at his arms, helping her get the job done twice as fast.

Back in the shadows, she tries to catch her breath as she reassesses the situation. First off, she was lucky that the wound didn't bleed too much—no trail of blood will lead the other soldiers to where they're hiding in the dark. The second thing of importance is that she still doesn't hear voices above them, which might mean there isn't a full platoon of sun dwellers ready to charge down and overwhelm them. Which might mean they've spread themselves so thinly to search the rubble for survivors hiding in cellars and bomb shelters that there are only a few soldiers in each place.

"Quincey?" the voice yells again from above. It's the same voice. Perhaps they got really lucky. Perhaps the soldiers are working in *pairs*, which, of course, would mean they now had the advantage in numbers.

"He's probably messing with us," another voice says, this one deeper. "He's always been a prankster."

"If he is, I'll kill him myself," a third, much raspier voice says. "This isn't the time for pranks or messing around."

Three distinct voices change the odds completely.

"What do we do?" Maia says, her lips practically touching Anna's ear in the dark.

"Follow my lead," Anna says, unclasping something black and egg-shaped from the fallen soldier's belt.

Chapter Nine

Before the soldiers are even halfway down the staircase, Anna pulls the pin—one, one thousand, two, one thousand—and throws the grenade, silently praying her aim is true. She doesn't, however, give herself the advantage of watching its flight; instead, she pushes Maia to the side, throwing her own body over the young girl's and her arms over her own head.

There's the distinct clink of metal on stone, but she doesn't know if she's hit the far wall, like she intended, or if she inadvertently caught the edge of the stairs, rebounding the handheld explosive device back toward her.

The chatter of automatic gunfire explodes somewhere, bullets zinging and ricocheting off hard rock, distant enough to be safe. And then:

Boom!

The grenade's explosion is deafening, and although Anna is very much aware that she's still alive—and therefore, the distance she threw the grenade sufficient—sharp bits of shattered rock sting her as they rain down upon her arms and back, piercing her skin.

Someone cries out in the night—maybe more than one somebody.

Anna waits a moment longer, to be sure she won't get a jagged splinter of rock in the eye, and then springs to her feet, simultaneously pulling Maia by the crook of her elbow up, too, hoping the young warrior's ankle will hold up under the frantic pace they'll have to assume.

Peering through the yellowish haze and dust particles, Anna sees only red. A body to her left, red-suited and limp: the red from his uniform seems to have liquefied, spreading around him on the stone like a dark pool, making it hard to distinguish where he ends and the pool begins. To her right, there's a nameless soldier, black and red and dead. The third soldier is straight ahead, still alive, clutching the edge of the half-destroyed staircase, as if holding onto it is the only thing he has left—which is probably true. He's holding on with only one arm, not by choice but out of necessity, as his other arm is lying separately on the ground, between the other two fallen sun dwellers.

Anna knows it was her work that caused this. She's not proud of this irrefutable fact, but she's also not ashamed. She did what she had to do. For herself, for Maia, for her family, for the people. *I won't die here. Not now.* Although she knows her strong and confident promise is not a predictor of the future— nor has she ever felt one speck of clairvoyance inside her—it gives her comfort to know she's still fighting.

She steps over the arm, takes aim, and puts a bullet into the back of the guy's—who's still clutching the steps like a lifeline—head.

It's not anger or revenge or even her survival instincts that prompts her actions—no, that's not it at all. She does it to end his suffering.

Chapter Ten

Three dead, one unconscious. It could have been worse. It could have been them.

Although Anna was initially concerned about Maia—her face was ghost-pale and her fingers trembling as she helped tie up the unconscious guy—she seems okay as she ascends the steps at Anna's side. Even so, better to check.

"You okay?" Anna says.

"My ankle's feeling a bit better, I should be fine," Maia says, glancing down.

"I don't mean your ankle."

Maia looks up, makes eye contact for a second, but then returns her gaze to her feet. "Oh."

"Look, I know that was...*violent* back—"

"I've seen plenty of violence in my life," Maia interjects. "It isn't that. You did what you had to do. It's just..."

Anna stops near the top of the steps, watching the entrance to the cellar carefully for any more unwanted visitors. "It's just what, Maia?"

"I froze," Maia says. "I couldn't have done what you did. I was scared and I just froze up. I thought I was ready for this, but I'm not. What you did, it was incredible."

"Violence is never incredible," Anna says, cocking her head to the side when a shot from a rifle cracks in the distance. "But it's sometimes necessary. No one's ever ready for it when it comes."

"Then how do you act when the time comes?" Maia's question is a simple one, but something tells Anna the answer is vital to the girl's chances of getting through the next few hours alive.

"Everyone's different, but what I do is think of all the people who are counting on me to come through for them, the people I want to see again, and I do everything for them. When I threw that grenade I was thinking of how brave Adele is, going to the Sun Realm. When I attacked that guy, Elsey was in my head, how if I didn't knock him out I might never see her sweet face again." In any other circumstance, tears might fill Anna's eyes, but at this time, in this place, Anna's eyes are dry, so dry they sting a little. She knows that tears are a luxury she can't afford during war.

"But…I don't have anyone," Maia says.

"You have me," Anna says. "Never forget that."

She climbs the last two steps, gun drawn, her finger tight on the trigger. Adele and Elsey, and now Maia, swim through her thoughts as she prepares for war.

Chapter Eleven

Each footstep coincides with the slam of her heart against the inside of her chest.

Being outside the cellar again feels strange. She was so certain its four walls were the last she'd ever see, but now, by a stroke of luck or pure will—or fate perhaps—she has a second chance to make her daughters proud.

To her left she spots a threesome of hunting sun dweller soldiers; in their crimson uniforms they look like three smudges of blood on a backdrop of smoky gray. She ducks behind a crumbled wall before they turn her way. Beside her, Maia says, "They're everywhere. How will we get past them all?"

"We will," Anna says, fierce determination pulsing through her like an electric charge. "They're spread out and they don't expect much resistance." *And little do they know: there's a few thousand moon dweller soldiers trapped underground, if we can just get them out…*

She skates along the wall, the barrel of her gun seeing everything her eyes do, her head on a swivel, her anger rising with each piece of rubble she steps over. Any fear she felt upon ascending from the hell of the cellar is gone, wiped clean inadvertently by the bloody rags of a warring and oppressive government.

Leaving the cover of the wall, she cuts between a pair of crumbling houses, darts across what used to be a residential street, and slips behind another house; this one is still standing, save for its roof, which looks as if it's been pummeled a dozen times by a wrecking ball. She hears voices nearby.

After glancing at Maia, who seems calmer since leaving the cellar, she heads toward the sound, hopping a wall and galloping across another rubble-strewn backyard. At the next wall she pauses, and then, upon hearing voices, motions toward the other side of the wall: *soldiers beyond*, her finger says.

She creeps along the wall, moving in between two houses, then hops the wall, immediately flattening herself on the stone sidewalk next to the neighboring house. Maia land softly behind her. The sounds are close—just behind the house.

They tiptoe along the house, until they're close enough to make out what the voices are saying.

"On your knees!" a deep voice bellows.

"This is our house. You have no right to do this!" a man says.

"Please, Bear, do what they say," a woman pleads.

"You should listen to your wife," the deep voice—a sun dweller soldier most likely—advises.

"Marley, these people, they think they can push us around because we let them. Well, no more. I won't get on my knees. I won't!"

Thud! A groan of pain. A woman's scream. "No, no, no! Leave him alone!" Thud, thud, thud, thud! "Stop it! Stop kicking him!"

The sun dweller soldiers are distracted by the beating they're giving some poor moon dweller. Anna sneaks a peek, sees four red coats, three of which are relentlessly kicking someone on the ground. Big: not the soldiers, the guy getting kicked. Probably why his wife called him Bear—a nickname, most likely.

The fourth soldier stands nearby, supervising. The commanding officer. He's smiling. Someone needs to change that.

Anna motions to Maia to split up, to circle around to the left while she goes right. Maia's eyes are wide, but Anna notices that the steeliness has returned. Good timing.

Seeing Maia nod in understanding, she darts out from cover, veers to the right—the distraction. Before anyone sees her, she's upon the first kicking soldier, pistol whipping him in the back of his head with her gun. The next red-clad bully is too busy stomping on the helpless innocent to notice his buddy's fall. The CO, however, does notice and starts to say something, "Watch ou—" but is cut off when Maia sticks the cold steel of her gun to his temple. "Don't move," she says.

Anna, still moving, kicks high and hard, catching the second soldier in the neck, rocking him to the side and into soldier number three, who is turning, finally realizing something is happening. They go down in a tangled pile, the blood from a wicked gash on soldier two's forehead streaming down his nose, lips, and neck, mixing with the red of his uniform. He's clutching his head, his face pale, his mouth contorted in a silent groan of agony.

She levels her gun at his head.

"Who are you?" the CO asks, Maia's gun still tight against his head.

"We'll be asking the questions here," Anna says, keeping one eye on the CO and another on her pile of soldiers. "First one: do you want to die?"

"No, of course not," the CO grunts. "But in about two seconds, when I'm supposed to check in and I don't, there will be dozens of soldiers swarming this place, so I suggest you—"

BOOM! The bullet rips into the CO's thigh, just above the knee. He cries out in pain, topples over, clutches his leg.

Maia stares at Anna, her gun limp at her side. "You—you shot him," she says.

"He was lying to me," Anna says, her voice sounding strange and guttural even to her own ears. "I—I had to show him who's in charge here." The red-hot anger she felt a moment earlier is ebbing, being replaced by a degree of remorse, something she always feels after inflicting pain on another, even an enemy; it's something she can't afford right now. Action is the only remedy.

She thrusts a foot at already-injured soldier two, who tries to block it by throwing his hands over his head. Instead of going high, she stomps on his stomach, earning another groan and the move of his arms from his head to his gut. Lashing out again, this time at his head, she feels the satisfying—and somewhat sickening—thud of her boot off his skull. His head snaps back, cracks into the jaw of soldier number three, who lets out a bloodcurdling howl, and then lolls to the side, his eyes rolling back into their sockets.

Soldier three is clutching his mouth, blood pouring out from between his fingers, his face all scrunched up. "War is hell," Anna says, bringing her gun down on the crown of his head. He slumps over, unconscious.

Turning to face Maia, her body hot with violence, she says, "Knock him out."

Maia looks at the CO, back to Anna, says, "Can't we just tie him up, gag him?"

"He'll get loose and then he'll try to kill us. We don't have time for prisoners, and I don't believe in killing defenseless soldiers, even ones like these."

The CO rolls over in the fetal position, his face a shattered mess of pain, his pant leg a darker red than the rest of his uniform. "You already shot me," he spits out. "Just finish the job."

"I'm not letting you off that easy," Anna says. "You'll pay for your crimes before a war tribunal. Maia?"

Maia takes a deep breath, closes her eyes for just a moment, and then swings her gun like a hammer, whacking the CO sharply across the temple. His writhing stops, his body still with unnatural sleep.

Letting out a deep breath, Maia looks at Anna. "That was horrible," she says.

"Violence always is," Anna says.

"You made it look so easy, almost like you enjoyed it."

Anna cringes. That's the problem. She was so full of anger at these horrible men that she did sort of enjoy it. She knows she's flirting with a dangerous line between fighting against evil and joining them. It's a line she has vowed never to cross.

"She did it for us." Anna and Maia both jerk to the side, spot the woman, the man's wife, on her knees, her hands clasped together as if in prayer. "Thank you," she says. "Thank you so much."

Her husband stirs, sits up, rubs his head as if clearing his mind from a bad dream. He truly is a giant, with rock-like fists, a chest the size of a beer barrel, and a head twice the circumference of most adult humans. His lip is swollen and fat, one of his eyes bloodshot, painted with black and blue beneath it. But he's smiling. Smiling at his wife, who's smiling back at him.

"Oh, Barry!" she cries, clambering to her feet and launching herself at him. She lands on him so hard that, if not for their significant size difference, she might have flattened him.

Maia watches the heartfelt reunion with moist eyes, while Anna watches Maia. She's so young, full of courage, unmarked by the horrors of life. She silently hopes the war will be over quickly and in their favor, so the innocence and naivety of this girl can persevere for years to come.

She thinks of Adele again, in the belly of the beast, having already endured so much emotional and physical pain, forced to endure more. She hopes her youth hasn't passed her by these last seven months, when everything changed.

Chapter Twelve

She leaves the rescued moon dweller couple in what she hopes is a safe place—a hidden bomb shelter beneath the floorboards of a shed. It's a neighbor's, who had invited Bear and his wife to stay there with them, but they opted instead to remain in their own cellar. A bad choice. But now the kind neighbor welcomes them with open arms and a warm drink, as Anna and Maia seal the trapdoor behind them.

"I'm so glad we got there when we did," Maia says. "That was amazing seeing their eyes light up when they hugged each other."

Anna tries to smile, but only manages a thin line. It was a fulfilling rescue, yes, but only a small victory against an enemy set on digging out the city's residents. With the army barricaded underground, there's no one to oppose them.

"We have to get to the base," Anna says.

"It's not far," Maia says.

"The way this place is swarming with cockroaches, it's far enough."

"We'll make it." Now who's the optimist?

Anna really smiles this time, not hugely, but sincerely. A little shot of hope is just what she needs. "You're right. We'll make it."

They exit the shed, running low to the ground, keeping their heads below walls and crumbling houses. Less than two blocks away is the old church with the underground caverns, where the temporary army base was set up. The once-high steeple no longer stands tall and beckoning. Now fallen, it is but a reminder of what the church used to stand for. From behind a wall, Anna can see that the main church structure—in which stands the primary entrance to the underground tunnels—has imploded upon itself, and now looks more like a raw granite stockyard than a place of worship.

The secondary, hidden entrance to the tunnels was, of course, the one from which Anna and Maia exited, and was destroyed just as they escaped its bounds. She knows her stalwart men and women soldiers will try to dig their way out, perhaps even use small explosives to blast through the blockades, but it will take time. Perhaps if they remove some of the larger blocks from the other end, it will give them a chance to break free. Then the battle will truly begin.

Anna clings to this faint and distant torch of hope as she hops the wall, sprints across a back patio, and ducks behind the next wall. Using this method, the women erase one block from the distance between them and the church. One block to go.

Voices shout through the thick and dusty air, but she's unable to ascertain their direction or distance. When they fade and don't return, she leads Maia across the next block, sticking to the shadows and narrow side and rear laneways. Every once and a while she stops to listen for the enemy, tilting her ears in each direction like an animal.

In this manner, they reach the church unseen. Ducking behind a boulder the size of a truck, she surveys the destruction zone.

"Which entrance should we try?" Maia asks.

Given the entire topside of the church collapsed on the primary entrance, the amount of heavy rock and cement is an impenetrable fortress, one made dangerous by shifting rubble and unexpected pockets of empty air. It could take days to dig them out that way.

"Secondary entrance. We'll be more exposed, but there's much less blockage."

Maia nods. "That's what I was thinking."

"I'll go out first," Anna says. "Just in case someone's watching the area." She starts to move out, but Maia puts a hand on her shoulder, stopping her.

"We're doing this together."

Anna sighs, half-concerned, half-relieved. "I thought you might say that."

Chapter Thirteen

The women steal out into the open, their eyes flicking rapidly in every direction. They reach the entrance to the bunker, where the original chunk of stone that blocked their return to the base has been joined by two dozen other smaller hunks of stone shrapnel. Through small gaps in the blocks, Anna determines that half the tunnel has caved in beyond the exterior blockage. Through the muddle of brown and gray rocks, a muffled sound arises: *thunk, thunk, thunk.*

"They're there," she says excitedly. "They're trying to break through." A rush of hope flows into her, giving her just the spark of energy she needs. "C'mon, let's do our part from this side. Start with the small pieces, work our way up to the big ones."

For a half hour they struggle and strain against the weight of the "small pieces," which are anywhere from twenty to eighty pounds, some so heavy it takes both of them just to roll them off the pile. Every second Anna expects to hear the chatter of sun dweller gunfire, but it never comes. Removing the next to last of the small stones, she wipes a dirty hand across her dirty forehead, trying to keep the sweat out of her eyes. Maia's face is equally filthy. "There," she says, prying off the final manageable chunk and watching it crash from the pile.

Breathing heavily, Anna says, "Now for the big ones. We'll need to find something to use as a lever."

Together they search for something—anything—that might give them a chance at success. Anna leads them onto the pile that was once a church, moving slowly to avoid alerting any spying eyes to their presence. Atop the pile, Anna scans the surrounding area, immediately spotting three sets of red uniforms blotted against the drab landscape. The arrogance and stupidity of the sun dwellers as evidenced by their uniforms, she thinks.

"Stay down," she warns Maia. Together they flatten themselves against the pile until each of the groups move out of sight.

They take turns searching for a lever while the other one keeps watch. Anna's taking her second turn searching when she sees it. A long, metal pole, decorated with an exquisite brass handle at one end, with beautiful ornamental designs of the Sun, Moon, and Star Realm insignias painted on the side. At the other end is a cap with a bronze cross. The pole was likely used for some ancient ritual involving the salvation of those attending the church. Now it will be used for a similar purpose, she thinks, only this time it will involve the salvation of all of us.

She pulls it from under a boulder, cringing as the steel shrieks along the sharp edge of the stone. "Take this," she says, feeding the handled end to Maia.

"This is perfect," Maia says, taking it. With Anna holding the cross-end and Maia the handle, they climb down the pile, returning to the secondary bunker entrance.

They test out the lever on several medium-sized rocks, jamming the cross-end beneath them and using their collective strength to force the loads up and off the pile. With each small victory, Anna's energy wanes and the steel rod bends more and more. After the sixth rock is removed, she says, "We need to try to remove that big one before us or the pole breaks."

In agreement, Maia shoves the cross under the largest block of all, the one that originally trapped them on the outside. Taking their positions, Anna on the outside, Maia on the inside, they lean on the steel cylinder, trying to force their entire weight down on the end of the lever.

Nothing.

Gritting her teeth, Anna continues pushing, determined not to let a hunk of rock get the better of her. Finally, it starts to give way, but then—

CRACK! She cries out as the rod gives way beneath her, catapulting her headfirst. She crashes on her shoulder and neck, pain lancing through her back and into her legs. Something falls on her, and she gasps as the air leaves her chest.

"Oomf!" Maia grunts, coming to rest on top of her. "General! Are you okay?" she asks, rolling to the side.

For a minute Anna can't breathe as she bites at the air, fruitlessly trying to capture it. Then finally: whoosh! She gets a full breath down her throat and her lungs inflate. Panting, she says, "I'm okay, you just knocked the wind out of me, and—"

She cringes as she tries to stand, feeling pain roar through her body.

"General, let me help you," Maia says, grabbing her under the arms. "What hurts?"

Anna thinks for a second, blinking away stars and tears. "Everything at the moment," she says, wishing it was a joke.

"Okay. You rest, I'll try again."

"Forget about it. I might be older than you, but I'm just as tough. Give me a sec. I'll help."

While Anna prepares herself for a whole new world of pain, Maia retrieves the pole. "The cross snapped off, that's what caused the problem," Maia explains, showing Anna the mangled end of the rod.

"Good. Then it shouldn't happen again." That's when she hears it: a shudder of the earth, a slight tremor caused by something below the surface.

"It's them!" Maia says elatedly. "They're trying to blast their way out."

Anna cranes her neck and hears voices now, still muffled but closer than the sound of the pickaxes she heard earlier. "Let's help them out," she says, arching her sore back to stretch it out, feeling her muscles groan in protest.

Maia plunges the naked tip of the rod back under the massive tombstone block, and then reassumes her position on the inside of the lever. Anna joins her, says, "One, two, three," and then they jump up, using gravity and body weight and raw strength to shove the metal downwards. Plumes of pain roll up through her back and neck, causing a spontaneous headache that throbs in the back of her skull. Her arms ache from the last hour of exertion and stress and killing. But still she presses on. As before, nothing happens at first. Thirty seconds pass and she feels her veins popping out as she holds her breath, trying to push a little harder.

It happens.

The block starts to move, and this time it's not in preparation to snap the end of the rod off; rather, it moves up under the pressure driven from the back end of the lever all the way to the front. It's just a slight bob upward, but the movement is enough to allow Maia to shove the pole further under, giving them even greater leverage. Anna keeps pushing, pushing, pushing, harder than she ever has except maybe during childbirth.

An inch of movement turns into half a foot and then a foot—and then the block is teetering on its edge, pushed from behind by the lever and pulled from the front by gravity. With a final shove, Anna and Maia break the tie, sending the block tumbling from the entrance, down a small incline, where it lands with a satisfying and dangerous *Thud!*

Anna's smile is reflected on Maia's face, neither of them needing words to express their shared sense of accomplishment and hope.

As they stare down at their fallen foe, there's a rush of feet as dozens of sun dweller soldiers pour from behind houses and buildings, a flooding river of red.

Anna closes her eyes and prepares to draw her weapon; she won't be taken alive.

Her last regret: that Maia will probably die along with her.

Chapter Fourteen

From behind the stone block, they fire their weapons again and again, dropping a dozen sun dwellers before the *click click click* of their weapons informs them that they're out of ammo, out of luck, and out of time.

Looking at Maia, Anna says, "You've done good, kid. I'm proud of you."

Maia looks back at her, her eyes filled with tears of sadness and maybe a hint of pride. She says, "It was an honor to serve with you, general."

Anna nods and then does the only thing that might keep them alive. She tosses her gun out, yells, "We surrender!"

Slowly, she raises her hands above her head, expecting her fingers to be blown off at any second. No one shoots, so she stands up, seeing only red and black. At least thirty red-uniformed soldiers move in on her, their black guns trained on her head and chest. "There's one other with me," Anna says, so as to not surprise them when they see Maia.

Maia rises up slowly, follows Anna out into the open, leaving her spent gun behind the rock.

Surrounded, Anna gazes at the faces around her. Angry, bloodthirsty, scowling. Not friends. A man steps forward, his uniform decorated with several ribbons and silver medals. An important man. The leader of these men. He says, "By order of President Nailin of the Tri-Realms, we are authorized to put you to death for resisting the laws and statutes of the government. Do you have anything to say for yourselves?"

Anna's not listening anymore. She's remembering her daughters on a day long ago, their identical jet-black hair swirling around their backs as they run through the house, full of energy and imagination as they play some made up game that she never really understood. Their expressions of pure childish delight on their faces mask the truth of their situation. They have no money. They have no food. They'll be lucky to last the year. And yet Adele and Elsey find joy in each other.

One foot in the past and one in the middle of a war, Anna smiles, content with the life she's lived, sad that she'll never see her daughters again, but proud of who they are, what they've accomplished. She hopes Adele will forgive her for implanting the microchip, that she'll understand why she did it, that she'll realize what she was hoping to accomplish. She closes her eyes and her husband's face appears as she prepares to meet him on the other side.

"Nothing to say? Good. That makes things quicker. Shoot them," the man says.

Feet scuffle nearby as her executioners step into position. She waits for the *bang!* and the burn of hot metal in her body, but instead there's a crackle of static and then a voice.

"Ceasefire!" the voice says. "Under order of President Nailin, ceasefire!"

Anna opens her eyes.

THE END

~*~

A SNEAK PEEK
FIRE COUNTRY
BOOK 1 OF THE COUNTRY SAGA
Available anywhere e-books are sold March 1, 2013!

Chapter One

When I'm sixteen and reach the midpoint of my life I will have my first child. Not because I want to, or because I made a silly decision with a strapping young boy after sneaking a few sips of my father's fire juice, but because I must. It is the law of my people; a law that has kept us alive and thriving for many years. A law I fear.

I learned all about the ways of the world when I turned seven: the bleeding time, what I would have to do with a man when I turned sixteen, and how the baby—my baby—would grow inside me for nine months. Even though it all seemed like a hundred years distant at the time, I cried for two days. Now that it's less than a year away, I'm too scared to cry.

Veeva told me all about the pain. She's seventeen, and her baby's five months old and "uglier than one of the hairy ol' warts on the Medicine Man's feet." Or at least that's how she describes Polk. Me, I think he's sort of cute, in a scrunched up, fat-cheeked kind of way. Well, anyway, she said to me, "Siena, you never felt pain so *burnin'* fierce. I screamed and screamed…and then screamed some more. And then this ugly *tug* of a baby comes out all red-faced and oozy. And now I'm stuck with it." I didn't remind her Polk's a *him* not an *it*.

I already knew about her screaming. Everyone in the village knew about Veeva's screaming. She sounded like a three ton tug stuck in a bog hole. Veeva's always cursing, too, throwing around words like *burnin'* and *searin'* and *blaze*—words that would draw my father's hand across my face like lightning if I ever let them slip out of my mouth—like they're nothing more than common language.

In any case, everything she tells me about turning sixteen just makes me wish I didn't have to get older, could stay fifteen for the next seventeen or so years, until the Fire takes me.

It's not fair, really, the boys get to wait until they're eighteen before their names get put in the Call. I would kill for an extra two years of no baby.

Veeva told me something else, too, something they didn't teach us when I was seven. She told me the only good part of it all was when she got to lie with her Call, a guy named Grunt, who everyone thinks is a bit of a shanker. I've personally never seen him do a lick of work, and he's always coming up with some excuse or another to avoid the tug hunts. Well, Veeva told me that he makes up for all of that in the tent. Most of what she told me made my stomach curl, but she swore on the sun goddess that it was the best day of her life. To her, shanky old Grunt is a real stallion.

But even if there was something good about turning sixteen, there's still no guy in the village that I'd want to be my Call. I mean, most of them are so old and crusty, well on their ways to thirty, and even the youngest eligible men—the eighteen-year-olds—include guys like Grunt, who will also be eligible for my Call because Veeva has to wait another two years before she can get preggers again. No matter how much of a stallion Veeva claims Grunt is, I don't want to get close enough to him to even smell his fire juice reekin' breath, much less lie with him in a tent.

"Siena!" a voice whispers in my ear.

I flinch, startled to hear my name, snapping away from my thoughts like a dung beetle scurrying from a scorpion. Laughter crowds around me and I cringe. Not again. My daydreaming's likely cost me another day on Shovel Duty, which we like to call Blaze Craze when our parents aren't listening.

"Youngling Siena," Teacher Mas says, "I asked you a question. Will you please grace us with an answer?" One of the only good things about turning sixteen will be not being called "Youngling" anymore.

I feel twenty sets of eyes on me, and suddenly a speck of durt on my tugskin shoes catches my attention. "Can you please repeat the question, Teacher?" I mumble to my feet, trying to sound as respectful as possible.

"Repeating the question will result in Shovel Duty, Siena, which will bring your total to four days, I believe."

I stare at my feet, lips closed. I wonder if Teacher *not* repeating the question is an option, but I'm smart enough not to ask.

"The question I asked you was: What is the average life expectancy for a male in fire country?"

Stupid, stupid, stupid. It's a question that any four-year-old Totter with half a brain could answer. It's blaze that's been shoveled into all our heads for the last eleven years. "Thirty years old," I say, finally looking up. I keep my eyes trained forward, on Teacher Mas, ignoring the stares and the whispers from the other Younglings.

Teacher's black hair is twisted into two braids, one on either side, hanging in front of his ears. His eyes are dark and slitted and although I can't tell whether he's looking at me, I know he is. "And females?" he asks.

"Thirty two," I answer without hesitation. I take a deep breath and hold it, still feeling the stares and smirks on me, hoping Teacher will move on to someone else. The fierceness of the fiery noonday sun presses down on my forehead so hard it squeezes sweat out of my pores and into my eyes. It's days like this I wish the Learning house had a roof, and not just three wobbly walls made from the logs of some tree the Greynotes, the elders of our village, bartered from the Icers. I blink rapidly, flinching when the perspiration burns my retinas like acid. Someone laughs but I don't know who.

Teacher speaks. "I ask you this not to test your knowledge, for clearly every Youngling in fire country knows this, but to ensure your understanding as to our ways, our traditions, our *laws*." Thankfully the heads turn back to Teacher and I can let out the breath I've been holding.

"Nice one, Sie," Circ hisses from beside me.

I glance toward him, eyes narrowed. "You could have helped me out," I whisper back.

His deeply tanned face, darker-than-dark brown eyes, and bronzed lips are full of amusement. I hear what the other Younglings say about him: he's the smokiest guy in the whole village. "I tried to, dreamer. It took me four tries to get your attention."

Teacher Mas drones on. "Living in a world where each breath we take slowly kills us, where the glass people kill us with their chariots of fire, where the Killers crave our blood, our flesh, where our enemies in ice country and water country close in around us, requires discipline, order, commitment. Each of you took a pledge when you turned twelve to uphold this order, to obey the laws of our people. The laws of fire country."

Ugh—I've heard this all before, so many times that if I hear one more mention of the laws of fire country, I think I might scream. Nothing against them or anything, considering they were created to help us all survive, but between my father and the Teachers, I've just had enough of it.

Watching Teacher, I risk another whisper to Circ. "You could have told me what question he asked."

"Teacher would have heard—and then we'd both be on Blaze Craze."

He's right, not that I'll admit it. Teacher doesn't miss much. At least not with me. In the last month alone, I've been caught daydreaming four times. Wait till my father finds out.

"The Wild Ones steal more and more of our precious daughters with each new season." Teacher's words catch my attention. *The Wild Ones.* I've never heard Teacher talk about them before. In fact, I've never heard anyone talk about them, except for us Younglings, with our rumors and gossip—not openly anyway. My head spins as I grapple with his words and my thoughts. The Wild Ones. My sister. The Wild Ones. Kendra. Wild. Sis.

"It is obvious I have captured the attention of many of you Younglings," Teacher continues. "It's good to know I can still do that after all these years." He laughs softly to himself. "Surely you have all heard rumors of the Wild Ones, descending on our village during the Call, snatching our new Bearers from our huts, our tents, and our campfires." He pauses, looks around, his eyes lingering on mine. "Well, I'm here today to confirm that some of the rumors are true."

I knew it, I think. My sister didn't run away like everyone said. She was taken, against her will, to join the group of feral women who are wreaking havoc across fire country. *The Wild Ones do exist.*

"We have to do something," I accidentally say out loud, my thoughts spilling from my lips like intestines from a gutted tug's stomach.

Once more, the room turns toward me, and I find myself investigating an odd-shaped rock on the dusty ground. Hawk, a thick-headed guy with more muscles than brains, says, "What are you gonna do, Scrawny? You can't even carry a full wash bucket." My cheeks burn as I continue to study the rock, which sort of looks like a fist. In my peripheral vision, I see Circ give him a death stare.

"Watch it, Hawk," Teacher says, "or you'll earn your own shovel. In fact, Siena's right." I'm so shocked by his words that I forget about the rock and look up.

"I am?" I say, sinking further into the pit of stupidity I've been digging all morning.

"Don't sound so surprised, Siena. We all have a part to play in turning this around. We must be vigilant, must not allow ourselves even a speck of doubt that maintaining the traditions of our fathers is not the best thing for us."

"I think the Wilds sound pretty smoky," Hawk says from the back. There are a few giggles from some of the more shilty girls, and two of Hawk's mates slap him on the back like he's just made the joke of the year.

"What do we do, Teacher?" Farla, a soft-spoken girl, asks earnestly.

Teacher nods. "Now you're asking the right questions. Two things: First, if you hear anything—anything at all—about the Wild Ones, tell your fathers; and second—"

"What about our mothers?" someone asks, interrupting.

"Excuse me?" Teacher Mas says, peering over the tops of the cross-legged Younglings to find the asker of the question.

"The mothers? You said to tell our *fathers* if we hear anything about the Wilds. Shouldn't we tell our *mothers*, too?"

I look around to find who spoke. Lara. I should've known. She's always stirring the kettle, both during Learning and Social time, with her radical ideas. She's always saying crazy things about what girls should be allowed to do, like hunt and play feetball. My father has always said she's one to watch, whatever that means. I, for one, kind of like her. At least she's never made fun of me like most of t'others.

Her black hair is short, like a boy's, buzzed almost to the scalp. Appalling. How she obtained her father's permission for such a haircut is beyond me. But at least she's not a shilt, like so many of the other girls who sneak behind the border tents and swap spit with whichever Youngling they think is the smokiest. I've always admired Lara's blaze-on-me-and-I'll-blaze-on-you attitude, although I'd never admit it for fear of my father finding out. He'd break out his favorite leather snapper for sure, the one that left the scars on my back when I was thirteen and thought skipping Learning to watch the hunters sounded like a good idea.

"Tell your fathers first, and they can tell your mothers," Teacher says quickly. "Where was I? Oh yes, the second thing you can do. If the Wilds, I mean the Wild Ones, approach you, try to convince you to leave, whisper their lies in your ear, resist them. Close your ears to them and run away, screaming your head off. That's the best thing you can do."

Pondering Teacher's words, I look up at the sky, so big and red and monster-like, full of yellow-gray clouds that are its claws, creeping down the horizon in streaks, practically touching the desert floor. And a single eye, blazing with fire—the eye of the sun goddess. It's no wonder they call this place fire country.

Chapter Two

"Why would the Wilds whisper lies in my ear if they're going to kidnap me anyway?" I ask Circ the first chance I get after Teacher dismisses us from Learning. My voice sounds funny because I've pinched my nose shut with my finger and thumb.

Circ laughs at my voice, and then says, "They're not going to kidnap you, Sie." I snort, because his voice sounds even funnier with his nostrils clamped tight. My fingers come off my nose for a second and I get a whiff of the blaze pit that sits a stone's throw to the side. Screwing up my face, I pinch harder, until it hurts. A little pain is better than the smell.

"I don't mean *me* me. I just mean hypothetically speaking. If the Wilds were to try to kidnap me"—I look at Circ, trying not to laugh at the sight of his squashed nose—"or any other Youngling girl, why wouldn't they just grab her from behind, put a hand over her mouth, and carry her away in a burlap sack?"

"Maybe they're all out of burlap?" Circ says, cracking up and losing the grip on his nose. He sticks out his tongue as the foul odor sneaks up his nostrils. The tips of his moccasin-covered feet are touching mine as we sit cross-legged across from each other. We've always sat this way since we were just Totters.

"C'mon," I say, clutching my stomach, "I'm being serious." The only problem: it's hard to be serious when I can't stop laughing.

"I don't know, Sie, maybe it's easier if they can convince you to come with them, rather than having to haul your tiny butt away with you kicking and screaming."

It's a good point, but still...

"Something just doesn't smell right," I say, and we both crack up, but then just as quickly fall over gagging from the thick, putrid latrine air.

"Let's get this over with, then we can talk," Circ says, covering his mouth and nose with a hand.

I smile behind my own hand. "Thanks for helping me with Blaze Craze," I say.

"Just promise me you'll stop daydreaming in class." He plucks his shoes off with his spare hand, one at a time, and then pulls his thin white shirt over his head. I've seen him shirtless a thousand times, from Totter to Midder to Youngling, but this time I force myself to look closer, because of what all the other Youngling girls are saying about him. *Circ is so smoky. What I wouldn't give for five minutes with Circ behind the border tents. You're close with Circ, aren't you, Siena? Could you give him a message for me?* Of course I say I will, but I never do. If they don't have the guts to say whatever they want to right to his face, then they're not good enough for him. Plus, the thought of Circ behind the border tents with some shilty Youngling makes me a bit queasy.

383

Anyway, I try to see Circ from their perspective, just this one time. To call his skin sun-kissed would be the understatement of the year, like calling a tug "Sort of big," or a Killer "Kind of dangerous." It's like the sun is infused in the very pigment of his skin, leaving him golden brown and radiant. He's strong, too. Almost as strong as iron, his stomach flat and hard, his chest and arms cut like stone. But he's always been this way, hasn't he? Still staring at his torso, present day Circ fades from my vision and is replaced with images of him growing up. Circ as a Totter, five-years-old, small and bit pudgy in his stomach, arms and face; Circ turning eight and becoming a Midder, less chubby but still awkward-looking, with too-long arms and legs; Circ at twelve, a full-fledged Youngling, much taller and skinnier than a tent pole, not a bulge of muscle anywhere on him.

The images fade and Circ stares at me. "What?" he says.

"Uh, nothing," I say, shaking my head and wondering when Circ became so smoky. It's like with every passing year he became more and more capable, while I stayed just as useless as ever. He's good at everything, from hunting to feetball to Learning. And all I'm good at is daydreaming and getting in trouble. He's smoky, and as my nickname suggests, I'm scrawny.

"You were daydreaming again, weren't you?" His words are accusing but his tone and expression is as light as the brambleweeds that tumble and bounce across the desert.

"You caught me," I mumble through my hand.

I see his grin creep around the edges of his fingers. He stands up and offers a hand. "Care to shovel some blaze with me, my lady?"

Despite my self-pitying thoughts, he manages to cheer me up, and I take his hand, laughing. He pulls me up, hands me a shovel. While I carry my shovel, Circ wheels a pushbarrow, and we follow our noses toward the stench, which becomes more and more unbearable with each step. You've done this before, I remind myself. You just have to get used to the smell again.

If the smell is bad, the heat is unbearable. Although the heart of the summer is four months distant, you couldn't tell it by the weather. The air is as thick as 'zard soup, full of so much moisture that your skin bleeds sweat the moment you step from the shade, as if you've just taken a dip in the watering hole. All around us is flat, sandy desert, which radiates the heat like the embers of a dying cook fire. With summer nipping at our heels and winter approaching, almost everything is dead, the long strands of desert wildgrass having been burned away months earlier. A few lonely pricklers continue to thwart death, turned brown in the sun, but rising stalwart from the desert; we call them the plant of the gods for a reason, bearing milk even in the harshest conditions. Without them, my people might not survive the winter.

We reach the edge of the blaze pit and look down. It's a real mess, as if no one's been here to shovel it for weeks, maybe even months. It's going to be a long afternoon.

"Maybe we can just cover it with durt," I say hopefully.

Circ gives me a look. "Don't be such a shanker—you know it's not full yet."

"I'm not a shanker!" I protest.

"Well, you sure sound like one," Circ says, grinning. Now I know he's just trying to get me all riled up.

Determined to prove him wrong, I roll up my dress and tie it off at the side, and then clamber down the side of the pit, feeling the blaze squish under the tread of my bare feet. Gross. Some even slips between my toes. The smell is all around me now, a brownish haze rising up as the collective crap of our entire village cooks under the watchful eye of the hot afternoon sun. Not a pleasant sight.

Gritting my teeth, I start shoveling. The goal is to even it out, move the blaze that's around the edges to the center. You see, people come and dump their family's blaze into this pit, but they're sure as scorch not gonna to wade down into the muck and unload it in a good spot; no, they're gonna just run up to the pit as fast as they can, dump their dung around the edges and then take off lickety-split. That causes a problem: the blaze keeps on piling up around the edge, usually the edge of the pit closest to the border tents, until the pit is overflowing despite not being even close to full. Then a lucky shanker like me—not that I'm the least bit shanky—gets punished, and has to use a shovel and old-fashioned sweat and grit to move the blaze around. Or if the pit is full, you get to cover it with durt so people can start using the next one. That's what I was hoping for earlier.

Anyway, I get right into it, heaping the scoop of my shovel full of stinky muck and tossing it as far toward the center as I can get it. Some of it splatters my clothes, but that's inevitable, so I don't give it another thought. Clothes can be cleaned, but the job's not gonna get done without us doing it.

A moment later Circ's beside me, and within two scoops, his bare chest is glistening with a thin sheen of sweat that reflects the light into my eyes like thousands of sparkling diamonds. Every once in a while, one of us gags, our throats instinctively closing up to prevent any more of the blaze haze from penetrating our lungs. Can a person die of excessive blaze fume inhalation? With three more Shovel Duty afternoons to come, I'm certainly gonna put that question to the test.

Scoop, shovel, gag, repeat.

It goes on like that for an hour, neither of us talking, not because we don't want to, but because we can't without choking. At some point I become immune to the smell, but I know it's still there, like an invisible force lying in wait for its next victim. My supposedly nonexistent muscles are all twisted up, as if a hand is inside my skin, grabbing and squeezing and pounding away. Each shovelful gets smaller and smaller, until there's almost no point in scooping so I stop, try to jab the shovel in the blaze so it stands upright, but I don't do it hard enough and it just falls over.

Circ stops, too, and looks at me, a smile playing on his lips. "You look like blaze," he says, full on laughing now. I *feel* like blaze, too, but I won't say that.

Instead, I get ready to tell him the same thing, but then I notice: although his legs are spattered and dotted with brown gunk, from the knees up he's spotless; he's dripping beads of sweat like the spring rains have come early, but he doesn't look tired; his tanned arms and chest are machine-like in their perfection. He doesn't look like blaze at all, so I can't say it, not without lying, and I won't lie to Circ.

"Sorry, I didn't mean—I was just joking around," Circ says.

My eyes flick to his. How does he know what I'm feeling? Does he know what I see as I look at him, that I see him as perfect? I realize I'm frowning.

"No biggie," I say, my lips fighting their way against gravity and exhaustion into a pathetic smile. "I was joking, too."

Circ studies my face for a moment, as if not convinced, but I look away, scan the pit, try to determine our progress. "Ain't much in it," I say.

I feel Circ's stare leave me, like it's a physical thing touching my cheeks. "We did more than you think. Another hour and we should be nearly there," Circ says.

Another hour. Ugh. Maybe I am a shanker—another hour might kill me. I think I make a face because Circ says, "Don't worry, we'll do it together. Let's rest for a minute and then we'll start again."

Rest: I like the sound of that. There's nowhere to sit in the pit, unless you want to sit in a big ol' pile of blaze, so we climb back out, slipping and sliding on the slope. Once I almost fall, but Circ grabs me by the arm and keeps me upright. My head's down when we near the top and I hear a voice say, "Having fun yet, Scrawny?"

I look up to see three Younglings staring down at me. Hawk's in the middle.

Stopping, I let Circ pull up alongside me. Caught by surprise, I'm tongue-tied, unable to find the right words to send these punks packin'. Circ, on the other hand, he always seems ready for anything. "Get the scorch out of here, Hawk. We're working."

"Mmm, shoveling blaze. And from the looks of it doing a pretty piss-poor job of it." One of his mates, a guy they call Drag, coughs out a laugh.

"Like you'd know anything about it," Circ says, taking a step forward.

"You're right. I don't know a searin' thing about blaze, other than it comes out from between my cheeks about a day after I eat a load of tug meat. And then you get to shovel it."

He laughs. "But the only thing I don't understand, is why you're here, Circes. Wasn't the punishment for Scrawny?" There's a gleam in Hawk's eyes that makes me shiver, despite the oppressive midafternoon heat.

"I don't abandon my friends," Circ says calmly, although I see his fingers curl into fists. "And don't call her that name." Another step forward, just one away from the lip. Hawk's friends take a step back, but Hawk doesn't move.

"But that's what she is, right? I mean, look at her. She's skinny, not an ounce of muscle on her—"

"Watch it." Circ's voice is a growl.

"—she's got legs that are wobblier than a newborn tug's—"

"Shut it!"

"—and her chest is flatter than the Cotee Plains."

Circ moves so fast I almost slip again just watching him. I don't even see the step or two he takes before he's on top of Hawk, pounding away with both fists. Hawk's doing his best to block the blows, but he's making a strange high-pitched noise that tells me plenty of Circ's punches are getting through. Drag and the other guy, Looper, seem so stunned at first that they just stand there, but then finally get their act together and jump on top of Circ, each grabbing one of his arms from behind, pulling him away from Hawk.

Circ struggles, but they've got him so tight he can't get his arms free. I'm frozen, as if the coldness of ice country has suddenly descended on from the mountains, gluing my feet to the sludge beneath me.

Hawk stands up.

They're going to hurt him—

Hawk steps forward, wipes a string of blood from his nose, his mouth a snarl.

—all because of me—

The first punch is below the belt and Circ groans, doubles over, unable to protect himself.

—I have to do something.

My feet finally move, come unstuck, as if someone else is controlling them. I'm not Scrawny anymore, not a Runt, not Weak, not any of the other names that I've been called my entire life. I'm Siena the brave, and Circ is my friend, and he needs me.

Hawk sees me coming and moves to cut me off, but he's too slow. My muscles ache from the shoveling, but I block it out, block everything out, except for getting to the guys holding Circ's arms; if I can just unloose one of them…

I trip. Maybe on the lip of the blaze pit, maybe on a random rock I don't notice, maybe on my own feet for all I know—it certainly wouldn't be the first time—but regardless, I start tumbling headfirst, out of control, my arms and legs flailing and flopping like an injured bird as I try to regain my balance.

I don't.

I crash into the back of Looper, who feels more like a boulder than a Youngling boy, my nose crunching off his iron-like elbow, which fires backwards, knocking me off my feet. I'm in a pile on the dust, covered in blaze and durt and a bit of warm blood that trickles from my nose and onto my lips and from the scrape that I feel on my knee.

"Stupid, Runt," Hawk says, looming over me, his shadow providing a much needed reprieve from the relentless sun. "You two aren't even worth the blaze you've been shoveling."

He kicks me once in the stomach and I groan, clutch my ribs, which feel like they're cracked in at least two places.

With my cheek against the dust, I see Circ struggling against the boys, bucking and twisting, but they're strong, too, and they have the advantage in numbers and energy. Hawk laughs and saunters back over to Circ. "Don't worry, I won't hurt your girlfriend anymore. She practically knocked herself out anyway." Violence spreads across his face once more and he slams his fist into Circ's stomach twice and then, winding up, whips a wild haymaker that glances off Circ's jaw with a vicious thud. Drag and Looper throw him to the ground, where he slumps, unmoving.

All I can think is:

My fault.

Chapter Three

Winter is approaching, and with it, the dust storms. Already I can feel a change in the wind, as if it's grown arms and legs and a face with a mouth that howls and cries as it approaches. Every few minutes it reaches its boiling point and sweeps a cloud of dust into the air and into my face. I close my eyes, cover my face with my hands, wait for the tiny pricks of sand to cease. Then I soldier on toward the village watering hole.

It's getting late, the sun having sunk deep on the horizon, where the thickest yellow clouds swirl like a toxic soup, turning the sky darker and darker brown with each passing moment. Soon the sun goddess's eye will wink shut completely as she passes into sleep.

I'm glad it's getting late for two reasons: if I run into anyone, it will be harder for them to see my blaze-, durt-, and blood-covered skin; and it's less likely anyone will still be at the watering hole. Circ went to his family tent to get cleaned up, but I'm too scared to face my father looking like this. I didn't tell Circ I wasn't going home right away, and he didn't ask, which I'm glad about, because he probably would have wanted to come with me, which I really can't handle right now.

I'm still muddling through everything that happened. Circ apologized about a thousand times on the way back toward the village, until I finally told him to "Shut it!" He has nothing to apologize about—it's me who messed everything up.

When I reach the watering hole no one's here.

I sit on the edge and look at the murky brown face in the water. I'm just plain old Scrawny again. I've been called it a thousand times, probably more times than Siena, so why shouldn't it be my name? Add it to the number of times I've been called Runt, Stickgirl, and Skeleton, and you'll have a number greater than the total people in the entire village.

Rippling Scrawny looks back at me, Real Scrawny. Her long, black hair is stringy with sweat and durt. Her thin face is dark brown from the sun but featureless, muddled, with chestnut eyes that almost disappear beside her skin. The dress she wears is frayed and torn, soiled from a day spent shoveling crap and scrabbling in the dust. Her bone-thin arms are like the weakest, topmost branches of the trees she's seen on the edge of ice country, good for nothing but swaying in the wind. And...

—she's got legs that are wobblier than a newborn tug's—
—and her chest is flatter than the Cotee Plains.

I close my eyes, hating Hawk's words because they're true.

When my bleeding time first arrived I was scared, but also excited. Bleeding meant becoming a woman, finally finding my place in the world. But it never really materialized. I didn't become a woman, just stayed a scrawny girl, the bumps on my chest no more than mosquito bites, my hips remaining as flat and straight as an arrow. The only thing that identifies me as a girl is my long hair. My reflection shatters when the tears drip off my chin.

"It doesn't have to be like this," a voice says from behind, startling me. I go to turn but then remember my tear-streaked face. Cupping a hand in the water, I splash a bit onto my cheeks and then turn around, rivulets of tear-hiding water streaming down my cheeks, neck, and beneath my dress.

Lara. With her scalp-short haircut, she looks more like a boy than ever in the darkening evening air. Even more like a boy than me—but at least she looks like a *strong* boy, her arms tanned and toned, her jaw sticking out a little. Solid—that's the word for her.

"Like what?" I say, remembering what she said.

"Crying because you don't think you're pretty, shoveling other people's blaze, being forced to *breed* when you turn sixteen. The Call. All of it can be avoided."

"I wasn't crying," I say. "And it's not breeding." She makes it sound like we're animals, hunks of meat. Look at me—do I look like meat?

She offers a wry smile, her lips barely parted. "Mm-huh. They pick a guy, they pick a girl, stick you together, and nine months later out pops a kid. Sounds like breeding to me."

My throat feels dry. I haven't had a drink in hours. "Whatever, Lara. Look, thanks for coming by to try to..." Cheer me up? Be my friend? Scare me? "...do whatever it is

393

you're doing, but I really need to get cleaned up and get home."
I try to stand, but my legs really are as wobbly as a tug's, and I
put a hand down to steady myself, settling for a crouch.

Lara raises an eyebrow, as if I've said something
unexpected. "Just let me know if you want to hear more," she
says, and then whirls around and stalks off toward the village.

I watch her go. Weird. I'm not sure what that was all
about, but at least it stopped my steep dive into a pit filled with
stuff far worse than blaze. Self-pity.

When I turn back to the watering hole, its face is glassy
again, and there I am.

I swipe a hand through the water so I don't have to look at
myself.

~~~

My skin is clean again, free of blood and durt and worse things.
The water even seemed to wash away the self-pity, at least
temporarily. I almost feel refreshed.

My dress, however, is a different story. No matter how
hard I scrubbed, I couldn't get all the stains out, and now it
looks even worse because it's sopping wet, dragging along
below me like a wet blanket.

The moon goddess is out tonight, her eye bright orange in
the dark, cloudless sky. Her godlings are scattered all around
her, filling the firmament with twinkling red, orange, and yellow
lights. I find myself wishing I were one of them.

The watering hole is a short walk to the village, but tonight
I wish it was longer. I dread facing my father.

My father ain't Head Greynote, but he's searin' close. At
thirty two years old, he's already beaten his average life

expectancy, and if it wasn't for Greynote Shiva, who's thirty five, he'd be at the top. Most men die within one year of turning thirty. Shiva hasn't come out of his tent in a few weeks, and rumor has it he's got a bad case of the Fire, and he'll be dead within the month. My father will take his place.

I pass the first of the border tents, which are inhabited by the village watchmen and their families. The guard ignores me, continues to scan the area beyond the village, his bow tightly strung and in his hand. The attack from three months ago has left everyone tense.

As I zigzag my way through the tightly packed tents, I see all the usual nighttime village activities: a woman hanging wet clothes from a line; Totters playing tag, squealing with delight, their mother scolding them for making too much noise, one hand on her hip and the other holding a wooden spoon; a big family praying to the sun goddess before eating dinner— probably 'zard stew or fried pricklers—this one a man with his three partners and nine children. A Full Family. A rare thing to see these days.

Most of the tents are boxy and upright, a standard collection of ten wooden poles of varying lengths based on size of family, knotted tightly together with cords at each corner. Four of the poles are dug into three foot deep holes and form the tent corners, rising up to meet the side and cross beams which run along the upper sides of the tent, as well as through the middle of the ceiling, forming an X, and helping to support the heavy tugskins, which are knitted together and provide the tent covering.

However, some of the tents are half-collapsed, their support poles cracked, bent, or rotted. Anything from strong winds to wild animals to age and decay could have caused the damage, but the families that live in these tents are forced to make due, as they won't be allotted any further wood unless the sun goddess grants a miracle and trees start growing in the desert, or the contract with the Icers can be renegotiated with more favorable terms.

We used to live in one of those broken down tents.

But now, because my father's a top ten Greynote, we get to live in a sturdy wooden hut.

I reach the end of the eastern tent fields and cut across the eye of the village, which is the quickest path to the west side, where the families of the oldest Greynotes live. I'm not sure why I'm in such a hurry all of a sudden—I think because being alone in the night scares me.

As it has for every night I can remember in my life, a large fire roars in the village center, casting a reddish-orange halo of flickering light in every direction. Men sit on stone benches drinking fire juice and telling boisterous stories and jokes that end with raucous laughter from their mates. There are no women in sight.

A group of Youngling boys sit with the men and try to act grown up by being every bit as loud as their fathers. They even sip out of leather flasks, which are likely filled with cactus milk or perhaps milk from their own mother's teats.

I hurry by, giving the fire a wide berth, keeping my head down so as to not draw any attention to myself. Considering I look like a drowned rat, that's easier said than done. When I do glance over at the fire to confirm I'm in the clear, one of the Younglings stands up, stares at me. *No*, I think. It's Hawk. Here we go again.

Forcing one foot in front of the other, I keep moving swiftly, not running, not walking, but preparing myself to run like scorch if necessary. But Hawk doesn't move, just watches me, his eyes following me across the village, his lips curled into a smile. He points, says something to his buddies, and they all laugh. I let out a long exhalation when I pass out of their sight and between two of the Greynote huts.

Away from the glow of the fire, it's dark, and I stop in the shadows, panting, trying to force the thud, thud, thudding in my chest to slow down. I lean against the side of one of the sturdy huts, suddenly feeling the need for something to support me. For a few minutes, I just breathe, in and out, in and out, a simple act that my body normally performs automatically, without me even thinking about it, but which now seems so difficult, as if it requires every bit of my energy to make the oxygen fill, and then exit, my lungs.

Eventually, however, my heartbeat does slow, my breathing does return to normal, and I'm able to move on. My only concern now is what my father will say when he sees me. Or more accurately, *what* he will do to me.

Fire Country by David Estes, coming March 1, 2013!

Printed in Great Britain
by Amazon